DEVIL AND THE DEEP

A DEEP SIX NOVEL

JULIE ANN WALKER

sourcebooks
casablanca

Published by Sourcebooks Casablanca, an imprint of Sourcebooks, Inc.
P.O. Box 4410, Naperville, Illinois 60567-4410
(630) 961-3900
Fax: (630) 961-2168
www.sourcebooks.com

Printed and bound in Canada.
MBP 10 9 8 7 6 5 4 3 2 1

To my parents, Ian and Yvonne…

From Robin Cook to Louis L'Amour, Nora Roberts to Stephen King, our bookshelves were always spilling over with scintillating fiction that allowed me to take journeys of the heart and go on adventures of the mind. That has shaped my life in the absolute best way. Thank you both for being readers and instilling the love of reading in me. This one's for you!

The sea, once it casts its spell, holds one in its net of wonder forever.

—Jacques Cousteau

Prologue

June 9, 1624...

BLOOD!

The silent cry rang inside his head as sweat slipped down the groove of his spine like a snake oozing along a vine. His cracked rib protested every laboring breath against air thick with humidity and the sickly sweet aroma of fallen vegetation that rotted in the baking sun. And his heart...

His heart screamed for the blood of his enemies.

Bartolome Vargas, King Philip of Spain's most decorated sea captain, instinctively reached for the short sword he kept in a scabbard on his belt, malice swimming through his veins like a living creature. But his searching fingers found no blade, just dry, cracking leather. Two weeks ago, his trusty cutlass had been swallowed by the same ravenous seas that had gulped down his beloved galleon.

Just as well.

If he attacked the trio of Englishmen who had rowed to shore, he would reveal himself and the remaining thirty-five members of his crew. Reveal that this small, deserted island held the secrets to what had become of the mighty Santa Cristina *and the vast treasure she carried in her big belly.*

Crouching just inside the tree line of silver palm,

pitch apple, and mangrove, Bartolome took his eyes off the intruders and turned his attention to their ship. The brigantine jauntily flew the Union Jack and bobbed just beyond the reef that had protected this island from the worst ravages of the storm. Her sails were furled, her twin masts speared into the cloudless sky, and unbeknownst to the scurvy English bastards who crewed her, she was anchored a short distance from the sunken remains of the Santa Cristina.

The proximity made Bartolome's skin crawl, so much so that he glanced down to assure himself he had not been overrun by sand fleas. Then, the tree the Englishmen had come ashore to cut down as a replacement for their cracked yardarm succumbed to their saws, the trunk letting out a painful squeal, and Bartolome quickly returned his attention to the scene at the edge of the beach. The tall, straight mangrove had withstood the ravages of the storm, but it could not withstand the brutal will of man. It tumbled onto the sand, its leaves scattering and rolling, pushed by the hot wind like flotsam and jetsam.

"Bloody hell," one of the men cursed, wiping a hand over his sweating brow. "I got t' take me a terrible piss, but when I do I feels like me cock is ablaze."

"Ha!" another barked, his laugh like a blunderbuss, loud and obscene. "I told ye t' stay away from that redheaded harlot in Tortola. She be riddled with disease."

The first man grinned and shook his head, lifting his hands as if to say the lady's pleasures outweighed the price he now paid for having sampled them. Then he walked toward the tree line, straight for Bartolome's hiding place.

A leaf rustled behind Bartolome, and he slowly turned his head, giving his chin a subtle shake when Rosario, his midshipman, prepared to step from behind the bush that concealed him. Steady, *Bartolome told Rosario with only his eyes. He swung his gaze around the dense undergrowth of the forest, catching the attention of as many of his remaining crewmen as he could spot amidst the verdant foliage. Upon each, he bestowed the same look:* Hold steady, man.

Then he returned his scrutiny to his approaching enemy. Despite the heat, goose bumps peppered his flesh when the Englishman stopped beside a tree that was a gangplank's span from the one Bartolome hid behind.

Close. Too bloody close.

Fear left a metallic taste on Bartolome's tongue. Sweat dripped from his brow into his eyes, burning, but he dared not brush it away. He dared not move. He dared not breathe.

The bilge-sucking Englishman supported himself against the trunk with one hand, using the other to pull low his drawers and find his prick. "When I be on lookout duty, I spied me seven more privateers huntin' these waters for that bloody Spanish galleon!" *he called over his shoulder to his fellow crewmen who were busy sawing the limbs from the felled tree.*

Bartolome had always thought English a distasteful language. So harsh. So hacking. But one word was worse than the rest.

Privateers.

It was a fancy term for pirates. Bloodthirsty, treasure-hungry savages who hid their thievery and murder behind their letters of marque, documents bestowed by their government giving them the legal authority to attack enemy ships, press the foreign sailors into service, and loot whatever booty they could find.

And they are hunting for us.

"She be deep in Davy Jones's locker!" the man continued, grunting as he jiggled the last drop of putrid piss from his diseased member. "Else she be found by now! We should head toward New Granada! I heard tell there be easy targets there!"

"Ye want t' be the one t' tell the captain that, ye daft bugger?" the one with the blunderbuss laugh called back, shaking his head.

The Englishman muttered something under his breath before turning to rejoin his mates on the edge of the beach. When he had gone some distance, Bartolome let out a slow, ragged breath and watched the three men finish cleaning the branches off the tree before dragging it across the sand toward their skiff. The whole time his mind raced through the pitiful options left to him.

He had hoped King Philip would send ships from Havana to search for the Santa Cristina *and her missing crew. Every day of the past two weeks he had scanned the oceans through the magnifying lens of his spyglass, yearning to see a ship flying the Spanish flag. But none had appeared. Now he knew why.*

English pirates are swarming the seas like locusts.

The thought of what Spain's enemies could do with the great ship's treasure had Bartolome's empty stomach swirling as if he had sucked down bad grog. Then he felt Rosario at his side. The midshipman hitched his chin toward the English sailors rowing across the lagoon. "What did they say, Captain?" Rosario asked.

When Bartolome told him, Rosario's eyes rounded. "'Tis still possible for rescue," he insisted. "We just have to remain patient, remain hidden."

"I know."

"But very soon the summer storms will be upon us. The winds will ravage this island and the seas around it, spreading the treasure and making salvage futile."

"I know that too." A pit of dread took root in Bartolome's belly.

Rosario placed a hand on his forearm. "Then what are we to do, Captain?"

Bartolome swallowed, the task before him daunting. But if twenty years at sea had taught him anything, it was that all things were possible through determination, hard work, and the help of God. "We find a way to raise the treasure ourselves," he said, his jaw stony with resolve. "And then we bury it."

Chapter 1

Present day
4:12 p.m. ...

BRANDO "BRAN" PALLIDINO BLINKED AND REREAD THE email in his inbox for the third time.

> Hi, Bran!
>
> This Thursday night I'm chaperoning those three scholarship recipients I told you about on a camping and snorkeling trip to the Dry Tortugas. The park is pretty close to Wayfarer Island, right? Any chance you could sail over? The students would love to hear about your search for the *Santa Cristina*. And I'd love to see you!
>
> Maddy

Thanks to the hellacious storm that had blown through the Straits of Florida over the weekend and knocked the satellite dish off the roof of the rickety two-story island house, this was the first time Bran had been able to check his email in nearly five days. Which meant Thursday was today. And Maddy Powers, the woman he'd met three months ago on a mission he should have never been on, the same woman who since then had filled his thoughts during the day and his dreams at night, was a mere fifteen nautical miles away.

So close…

The memory of the kiss he'd stolen right before he hopped overboard from her father's yacht blazed through his brain. Soft lips. Sweet breath. An eager tongue that stroked his until—

Oh, eh! Was that his heart beating a rhythm to do a Macy's Thanksgiving Day Parade proud? Were those his ears buzzing? Was the idiot in his pants swelling with the memory? To his dismay, the answer was *yes* to all questions.

Funny how he could remain cool as the proverbial cucumber when he was forced to assemble an M4 in the dark under heavy fire. But put him within spitting distance of one miniscule, sassy-mouthed Texas-tornado-of-a-blond and he turned into a total chump.

Madison "Maddy" Powers…

Even her name was enough to have butterflies fluttering drunkenly inside his stomach.

Reaching for the glass of water near his hand, he took two big gulps, hoping to drown the mothersuckers. Then he cocked his head, listening, when the slamming of the screen door was followed by the echo of voices and the *clickety-clack* of scrabbling dog claws.

"Everyone has catnip. That certain something that drives them wild. That one specific thing they just can't get enough of." Alexandra "Alex" Merriweather's words drifted into the kitchen from the living room.

"Are you still talking?" Mason McCarthy's

voice sounded like a bass drum following Alex's squeaky soprano.

"Mine is *Sex and the City*," Alex admitted, ignoring Mason's question. "My field of study requires that my nose be buried in books all day long. So when I relax I want mindless, wanton entertainment. I want Sarah Jessica Parker and her gal pals. I want boobs and booze and boinking."

Boinking?

Despite the drunken—and now sodden—butterflies in his stomach, Bran felt a grin tugging at his lips. Alex had only been part of their crew for ten short weeks, but she'd wiggled her way beneath their skins. *Kinda like a damned chigger*. In no time, they'd grown to love her like a kid sister.

"I have the first season downloaded onto a thumb drive," she continued. "If Bran didn't get the satellite dish working, what do you say to watching a *Sex and the City* marathon with me?"

"No," Mason replied, never one to use ten words when one worked just fine.

"Why not?" There was definite pique in Alex's tone.

"Because I have robust mental health and I don't want that to fuckin' change." Mason was a Southside Boston boy, so his speech—when he actually spoke— tended to be liberally sprinkled with f-bombs.

"Oh, ha-ha. Very funny," Alex said just as Mason appeared in the doorway.

Mason wasn't a tall man, topping out at only 5′11″. But what he lacked vertically, he made up for horizontally. With hulking shoulders and massive arms, he looked less like the SEAL he was—they might have officially snapped their final salutes to the Navy, but once a SEAL, always a SEAL—and more like he should be guarding the gates of hell. Slobbering and panting noisily near his feet was Meat, the English bulldog that followed Mason around like a fat, furry, excessively *wrinkly* shadow.

Bran wasn't sure why, but he slammed the lid of the laptop and felt color rise in his cheeks. Mason glanced at the computer, then at Bran, lifting a brow. To Bran's relief, Mason said nothing.

He couldn't say the same for Alex. Standing next to Mason, she looked diminutive—diminutive and about twelve years old, thanks to her riotous mop of curly red hair and the sprinkling of freckles across the bridge of her nose. The first words out of her mouth were, "I take it you got the satellite dish up and running." The *next* words out of her mouth were, "So, are you catching up on your daily dose of porn or what?"

Daily dose of… Bran choked.

"No judgment here." Alex held up her hands. "Just…" She glanced around the kitchen, wrinkling her nose. "Not where we eat, okay?"

Bran shook his head and gave her a long-suffering look. "It wasn't porn."

Alex's expression telegraphed her disbelief. "What else would make you slam the lid on that thing like you were trying to keep a barrel full of snakes from popping out of the screen?" Her green eyes flashed behind the lenses of her tortoiseshell glasses.

Uh-oh. Bran knew that look. He didn't like it one bit. "Don't do it," he warned.

"Do what?" She blinked innocently.

"Whatever it is you're contemplating that's likely to piss me off."

"Oh." Alex nodded sagely. Then, proving she wasn't the least bit scared of him—and that she had the reflexes of a ninja—she snatched the laptop from him, dancing out of his reach when he tried to lunge over the kitchen table to retrieve it.

"Ah, ah, ah!" She cackled like she was auditioning for the part of Cruella de Vil while turning her back on him and holding the laptop away.

"*Fungule*, Alex!" he cursed. The New Jersey Italian boy came out in him when he got worked up.

"You know the rules." She tsked. "We have to share."

Wayfarer Island was a remote spot of land between Cuba and Key West. It was officially owned by the U.S. government, but for the last century or so it had been leased to LT's family—LT being Bran and Mason's former commanding officer, the one who had invited them to join him on his hunt for the legendary ghost galleon when they bugged out of the Navy.

To recap, for months now Bran had lived on this island with endless sun, cerulean waters, and a cooling breeze that rustled through the palm trees and a person's hair. Sounded pretty good, right? In fact, what could be better?

Well, Bran could list a few things that were better. *For starters, how about some damned cellular service?* Unfortunately, that was a pipe dream since they were hell and gone from the nearest cell tower. They had to rely on their marine radios and one lonely satellite phone to communicate with the outside world by any means other than the laptop.

So, how about some damned electricity? Okay, to be fair they *had* electricity. But the solar panels attached to the roof of the rambling house supplied just enough juice to keep the refrigerator, the Wi-Fi, and a few other items working. Which was why they all *shared* a laptop, taking turns watching movies or sports, or emailing friends and family back on the mainland.

"I'm dying to see what you were looking at that made you blush to the roots of your hair," Alex said, plopping into the ladder-back chair across from Bran. She shoved her glasses up on her pert nose and grabbed the silver tin of biscotti next to the salt and pepper shakers. Prying open the lid, she took out a biscuit and bit off half, talking with her mouth full. "If not porn, then what? Ooooh, the mystery! It must be solved!"

A crumb of biscotti flew from her mouth to land on the table. She absently brushed it onto the floor where Meat was waiting to lap it up like it was manna from heaven.

Alex was a historian by education, a translator of centuries-old scripts by training, and a savant when it came to inane trivia, which she tended to offer up without encouragement and much to the annoyance of everyone around her. Three months ago, Bran, LT, Mason, and the other three guys from their SEAL Team—now the owners of the Deep Six Salvage Company—had hired her to translate the historical documents housed in the Spanish Archives that pertained to the hurricane of 1624. They'd hoped she could give them a leg up on their hunt for the *Santa Cristina*.

Two weeks later, Alex had surprised them by insisting that the *ringed island* written about in the old documents was, in fact, *not* the Marquesas Keys, where treasure hunters—including LT's father—had always assumed the grand ol' ship went down, but their own Wayfarer Island. Then she'd surprised them *further* by requesting to come onboard the venture. Not to share in the treasure once they found it, but because she wanted to base her doctoral dissertation on the search for and excavation of the famed shipwreck.

At the time, Bran had thought it was a win-win situation. For room and board—*which, let's admit, isn't much on Wayfarer Island*—they got their very own on-site historian and translator, and *she* got a story that was sure to get the letters *P*, *H*, and *D* printed right after her name for the rest of her life. But now, as Alex took another huge bite of biscotti and lifted the lid on the laptop to read the email glowing there, Bran seriously considered changing his opinion on that whole win-win thing. *Another* thing about Alex: She was nosy by nature. She made sure to get her fingers in every pie that was ever cooked up on the island.

"I'm sorry." He frowned. "Have you never heard of the word *privacy*?"

"Thursday is today," Alex said, ignoring his question and pointing at the laptop's screen.

"No shit, Sherlock," was his totally mature reply. He felt color rising in his cheeks again. *Damnit*.

"Sooooo…" Alex dragged out the word, wiggling her eyebrows. "You planning to go see her or what?"

Bran opened his mouth to respond with *Or what*. His relationship with Maddy was perfect in that it wasn't really a "relationship" at all. Sure, they exchanged emails every day—sometimes more than a dozen. Sure, they had the occasional three-hour satellite phone conversation. But the nature of the Internet and the distance between them created and maintained an inherent casualness. A natural informality. *Which is exactly how I like it*. He was thwarted from responding, however, when Mason asked, "See who?"

"Madison Powers." Alex singsonged the name, making Bran grit his teeth. "Apparently, she's camping on the Dry Tortugas tonight with three scholarship recipients."

"Mmmph," Mason muttered, walking over to scoop kibble out of the bag they kept beneath the farmhouse-style sink.

Woof! Woof! Meat barked in canine fervor, his claws scrabbling on the floor as he raced over to Mason, his nub of a tail swinging back and forth. The only thing Meat loved more than Mason was food. Any food. All food. Even some shit that wasn't food.

Cock-a-doodle-doo! L'il Bastard, the rooster that had stowed away on their sailboat on a return trip from Key West, happily answered from his perch outside on the wraparound porch railing. His crowing carried inside on the sweet, salty breeze blowing through the open windows.

And that was how it'd been from the beginning. Meat barked and L'il Bastard answered with a raucous crow. Or vice versa. Which made for some really early, incredibly *noisy* mornings on the island.

"Mmmph." Alex parroted Mason's grunt. "You use that so often I wonder if I shouldn't petition Webster to add it to the dictionary."

After filling Meat's bowl, Mason leaned back against the sink. By way of an answer, he crossed his arms.

Alex rolled her eyes and shook her head as if she'd never met a more exasperating man. When Bran said they'd grown to love Alex like a kid sister, he'd forgotten to mention *with the exception of Mason*. Alex and the big guy seemed to have taken an instant dislike of each other. And the only thing Bran could figure was that it was because Mason rarely spoke and Alex rarely shut up. A case of verbal oil meeting nonverbal water.

"So?" Alex asked, turning back to Bran.

"So what?" He scowled at her, picturing all the ways he could strangle her where she sat. Twelve…maybe thirteen. After that, his imagination failed him.

"Are. You. Going. To. *See*. Her?"

"*No*." He hoped the one word, spoken with finality, would put a period on the end of the conversation.

He should have known better.

"But you *like* her, don't you?" There was a line between Alex's eyebrows. "I mean, there was that time one of her emails came in while I was using the laptop. I thought you were going to tear my arms off if I didn't hand over the machine."

"That's not exactly how I remember it happening," he muttered. Then, because he knew she would continue to press him, he added, "And I *do* like her. But that doesn't mean I wanna drag my ass all the way to the Dry Tortugas to entertain a trio of teenagers."

Alex narrowed her eyes. And there was *another* look he didn't like. He firmed his jaw and prepared himself to patiently withstand whatever bit of irritation was about to come out of her mouth. He didn't have long to wait.

"I call bullshit," she said. "My woman's intuition tells me there's more holding you back."

Of course there is. It was the same thing that had held him back since…well…forever. But talk of the asshole who'd supplied Bran's Y chromosome and left him with a terrible legacy was strictly off-limits.

Bran glanced at Mason. The look they exchanged spoke a thousand words. And since Alex was nothing if not observant, she pursed her lips. "Why do I get the feeling I'm missing something here?"

"Can we change the subject?" Bran asked, but really it was more of a demand. "I think I might be breaking out in a rash."

The look Alex leveled at him said she suspected he had the emotional maturity of a kumquat. "What is it with you men that you can't talk about your feelings if—" The slam of the screen door stopped Alex mid-sentence.

Good. Bran wasn't kidding about that rash. Talk of Maddy—or more precisely, talk of his *feelings* for Maddy and why he could never allow them to blossom and grow—made his skin crawl.

"Where the hell is everyone?" LT's deep voice blasted from the front of the house.

Since LT's craggy old seaman of an uncle, John, and the other three members of Deep Six Salvage had sailed their new salvage ship to Key Largo so a renowned mechanic could retrofit some specialty items onto the vessel, Bran assumed by *everyone* LT meant the three of them.

"In here!" he called.

Alex shot him a *to be continued* look.

He answered her with a false smile that said, *Not on your life*, then sobered when LT and LT's fiancée, former CIA agent Olivia Mortier, traipsed into the kitchen. They were both in swimsuits, hair drenched, bare feet leaving puddles on the worn wood floorboards. Their expressions fell into a category one might call Quintessential Kid in the Candy Store.

"Would you two stop being so damned happy all the time?" Bran harrumphed, exaggerating a headshake. "It's sickening."

Even though Mason muttered an agreement, neither of them meant it. Bran, Mason, and the rest of their teammates were overjoyed that their former CO had met his match and fallen head over heels in L.O.V.E. If any of them deserved happiness, it was LT.

"So we were out spearfishing off the reef," Olivia said, ignoring them. Bran cocked his head at her twinkling eyes and rosy cheeks. His sixth sense told him something was up.

"When I saw somethin' that at first just looked like another piece of coral," LT added, his Louisiana drawl peeking through even though he'd spent most of his formative years in the Keys.

"But it wasn't coral," Olivia said, nearly vibrating. Bran imagined he could actually *see* those wavy cartoon lines rippling through the air around her body.

"No sir." LT shook his head. "It surely wasn't."

"When we broke off the crustaceans, you'll never guess what we found," Olivia said.

"Not in a million years," LT added.

"Not in a *bazillion* years!" Olivia crowed.

"For chrissakes! What *was* it?" Alex demanded.

"The hilt of a cutlass!" LT boasted, whipping the artifact from where he'd hidden it behind his back.

For a couple of seconds no one moved, no one dared breathe. Then it was like someone had pressed an ejector button. Bran, Mason, and Alex all scrambled to get a look at the relic balanced in the center of LT's open palm. The thing was black with corrosion, but its shape and markings were unmistakable.

"Stop shoving, you big lummox!" Alex complained when Mason jostled her. The first two words held just a hint of a lisp, which Bran had noticed grew more prevalent when Alex became agitated.

"Mmmph," Mason said, bending forward to inspect the hilt.

"Mmmph," Alex parroted again, rolling her eyes.

"Cut the shit, you two," LT said. "And while you're at it, Mason, fire up a kerosene lantern. I want to get some good light on this thing. Alex, you run upstairs and grab the translation of the *Santa Cristina*'s manifest. Let's see if I'm lucky or just good."

Despite the excitement of the find, Bran felt his eyes pulled over to the laptop as if by some invisible force.

Maddy Powers…

Well, at least now he had a valid excuse to forgo a sail to the Dry Tortugas.

More like an excuse to be a lousy, no good fraidycat, an annoying voice whispered. To which he promptly replied *Oh, go suck a bag of dicks, why doncha?*

Chapter 2

"HI!" MADDY WAVED TO THE PARK RANGER WAITING TO greet her as she trudged up the steep beach of Garden Key, the main land mass among the batch of remote islets in the middle of the Gulf of Mexico that made up Dry Tortugas National Park. *Tortuga* meant "tortoise," a name given to the islands by Ponce de Leon in the fifteen hundreds. A couple of centuries later, the U.S. tried to make Garden Key useful by building a fort there, but faulty engineering, illness, and the Civil War thwarted that effort, and the structure was abandoned before its completion.

Garden Key was the only place in the Dry Tortugas that was inhabited. If you considered the lonely park ranger who lived in the little cottage on the edge of the beach an "inhabitant." From what Maddy had read, the park rangers assigned to the island only did three-month stints to ensure the isolation and loneliness didn't get to them.

All work and no play makes Jack a dull boy.

Brrr. The things one learned from the movies.

"Hello!" the ranger called, ripping Maddy's mind away from the scene in *The Shining*. "Welcome to beautiful Garden Key and the Dry Tortugas!"

As Maddy extended her hand to the young park ranger—the operative word here was *young*; if the ranger was much more than twenty years old, she'd eat her snorkel gear for dinner—she let her eyes roam over the facade of the unfinished garrison known as Fort Jefferson. Its red bricks stood out in harsh contrast to the aqua waters surrounding it, and the little light-house, painted black and perched atop one corner of the hexagonal curtain wall, brought to mind an old sentry, battered by the wind and rain but still standing tall. She couldn't wait to give the scholarship girls a grand tour tomorrow after breakfast. She'd studied up and knew all the good stories sure to inspire awe in the imaginations of her charges. But for now...

"I'm Maddy Powers," she said, giving the ranger's hand a firm shake before turning to watch the three teen-agers trudge toward her, carrying the sleeping bags and pup tents the pilot of the floatplane had passed to them from the aircraft's small cargo hold. "Looks like we'll be your company for the night."

"Glad to have you, ma'am." The ranger nodded, grin-ning and flashing a killer set of dimples.

Maddy faked an exaggerated wince. "Oh, please call me Maddy. I've been travelin' with seventeen-year-olds all day, so I already feel older than dirt."

The young man made a face, and the tips of his ears lit up like the Fourth of July. *Lordy, would you look at that?* "I'm s-sorry," he stammered. "I meant no disre-spect, ma'am, and I can promise you th-that..."

He trailed off when he realized he'd "ma'am-ed" her again, which might have something to do with the stink eye she pinned on him. He suddenly found the sand at his feet immensely interesting and starting digging for some mysterious object with the toe of his hiking boot.

Maddy chuckled and resisted the urge to brush his hair out of his eyes and tell him he should give up trying to grow that scraggly excuse for a beard. Instead she nudged him with her elbow—Maddy met a lot of strangers but her natural amiability meant they rarely stayed that way for long. "No, *I'm* sorry. I have four older brothers, so takin' folks with dangly bits to task is pretty much all in a day's work for me. And then when I'm forced to get up before the butt crack of dawn— that's four a.m., in case you were wonderin'—and pick up teenage girls who conspired to create an evil *morning person*"—she made quote marks with her fingers— "trifecta, I tend be even *more* persnickety."

Her momma told her she had a gift for gab, and when she paired it with her friendly smile—like she was doing now—she was pretty good at putting folks at ease. Then again, it wasn't ease she saw on the young ranger's face when he blinked at her.

Are those some of his IQ points I see floatin' out of his ears?

Uh-oh. She was pretty sure they were. And the look on the man's face was one she knew well. It was the same one her big, dumb brothers donned anytime a woman with cleavage and fluffy Texas hair walked by. In a word: love-struck.

Or is it two words when there's a hyphen in the middle?

Whatever. Either way she was caught off guard and—

"Oooh," Louisa Sanchez said as she made her way to Maddy and the ranger. "I think Señorita Maddy has an admirer. Would you look at him blush!"

"Louisa," Maddy scolded. "Mind your manners or our host here, Ranger…" She glanced at the green lettering stitched above the park ranger's breast pocket. "Your name is Rick? So, like, Ranger Rick? Ha! Where are Scarlett Fox and Boomer Badger?"

"Who?" Ranger Rick blinked and cocked his head, the joke having landed as softly as a cow falling off a catwalk.

"Oh." Maddy shook her head. "Um…you know, of the children's magazine? Ranger Rick the raccoon?"

"Who?" Rick asked a second time, the tips of his ears turning red again.

"Um…" She trailed off, now feeling older than dirt *and* foolish. Luckily, the sound of the floatplane's engines *whirred* to life and saved her from having to finish.

The smell of aviation fuel mixed with the sweeter scents of sunscreen and sun-baked sand, and Maddy waved to the pilot as he carefully backed the aircraft away from the sand and into the water. She shaded her eyes against the setting sun and watched the plane's pontoons glide over the tops of the gentle waves for a few dozen yards before its wings caught the breeze, lifting the aircraft into a sky that was a happy kaleidoscope of pinks and oranges and reds.

Nothin' quite like a sunset in the Keys, she thought, listening to the buzzing rotors compete with the screaming seagulls who swooped and dove and looked for their last meal before calling it a night. She turned to Rick. "So where should we set up camp?"

"You're the only ones registered to overnight on the island," he said. "Feel free to take your pick."

"Ohhhh." Maddy turned to the teenagers and wiggled her eyebrows. In good weather, Garden Key received frequent visitors via the daily fast ferry or, like Maddy and the girls, via a chartered floatplane. Most people stayed for a few hours, exploring the fort and snorkeling around the old pilings, before returning to Key West. But a few camping licenses were issued for those tourists who wanted to experience a night in the middle of nowhere. Luckily for Maddy and the girls, they seemed to be the only ones brave enough to attempt it this night. "Go find us the primo spot. I'll be there in a bit and we'll make some s'mores."

"Yo, I get it, Miss Maddy." Donna DeMarco gave her an exaggerated wink. "You want the cute park ranger all to yourself."

"Please." Maddy rolled her eyes and shooed the girls up the beach. "I'm old enough to be his…" Not mother. "Older sister," she finished lamely, and the girls snorted with laughter.

One thing Maddy had learned in her short time with the teens: Nothing got by them. They were all smart as whips.

Well, duh. Scholarship recipients, remember?

Right. When she'd approached her father—the owner of Powers Petroleum, the largest oil company in the United States—about starting a scholarship fund to support Houston-area girls who expressed an interest in pursuing a degree in petroleum engineering or petroleum geology, she hadn't expected to be inundated with two hundred essays. And even though all of the applicants were deserving in some way, the three she had finally selected had really stood out on paper. When she met them, they stood out in person too.

There was Louisa Sanchez, black-eyed and dark-skinned. She was from what many would call the "bad" part of Maddy's home city, born to parents who had emigrated from Mexico in the hope their daughter might grab hold of the American Dream with both hands and live it to its fullest.

Sally Mae Winchester was a bird-like blond girl from a tiny, rural community outside the city. Shy and timid, she had a Southern drawl thicker than Maddy's. But underneath Sally Mae's demure exterior were a keen mind and a desperate desire to make something of herself.

And then there was Donna DeMarco with her long, dark hair and too-wise-for-her-age eyes. Donna was a recent transplant to Houston and liked to portray herself as a tough Jersey girl. But that was just a ruse to hide her heart of solid gold. Donna's mother had died when she was a baby, and the only way her father managed to keep food on their table was working as a truck driver. The problem was that he had debilitating rheumatoid arthritis. So Donna's dream was to one day make enough money to support her "old man," as she called him, so he wouldn't have to suffer the agony of keeping his fingers wrapped around a steering wheel.

Maddy smiled at their slender backs as they giggled and teased each other while making their way up the small, narrow beach in search of the perfect campsite. Whether it was fund-raising parties or research grants, Maddy was always proud of the work she did for the charitable side of her father's business. But she felt a particular fondness for the scholarship fund and these three girls.

She was still smiling when she turned back to discover the young ranger staring at her, once again wearing that look. *The* look. She wondered if she should suggest he make a trip to the nearest optometrist for a vision test.

I mean, come on. She *didn't* have cleavage—at least not much to speak of. And she certainly didn't have big, fluffy Texas hair. In fact, she hardly had *any* hair, thanks to her impetuous nature and her ready-for-anything stylist. She'd told Eduardo she wanted "the Michelle Williams look," but she was pretty sure he'd saddled her with a Justin Bieber 'do, circa 2009, instead. That belief was only compounded when her brothers started calling her a Belieber.

Not that she was an ogre or anything. Her youngest brother assured her she was still "passable." *Gee, thanks*. And she'd had her fair share of male admirers who called her "cute." But the fact remained that she'd never been the kind of gal to inspire insta-love or even insta-lust, so what the heck was wrong with Ranger Rick that he—

Now, hang on a cotton-pickin' minute here! Don't sell yourself short, sister. Did you forget about Bran Pallidino?

And the answer to that question wasn't just *no*, but H. E. to the double L *hell no*, she hadn't forgotten him. Forgetting him would be impossible. For one thing, and to quote her dear paternal grandmother, he was *handsome as a hatchet*. With his wavy, mink-colored hair, flashing brown eyes, and pirate smile, Bran Pallidino could beat any of Hollywood's hunks for the top spot on *People* magazine's Sexiest Man Alive list.

For another thing, he had saved her from the crazed terrorist who had hijacked her father's yacht. *Yessiree, Bob. So* that *happened*.

And lastly, in the months following the hijacking,

he'd helped her deal with the onset of delayed shock, nightmares, and what some might diagnose as a mild case of PTSD. Through hundreds of emails and the occasional satellite phone call, he'd been her sounding board, her sympathetic ear, her support and her light when the memories threatened to get too heavy and dark.

Yep. Bran Pallidino was many things. Brave. Funny. Sometimes taciturn. But one thing he was *not* was forgettable.

He is also not here…

She'd tried not to let the emptiness of her email account—the glaring, insolent, *taunting* emptiness of her email account—get to her. She'd tried telling herself he hadn't responded because he was too busy hunting for the mighty *Santa Cristina*. But now that she was here, so close to Wayfarer Island, so close to *him*, she couldn't help but wonder if the reason he hadn't answered her invitation was because she'd read too much into their little online exchanges.

Perhaps what she'd thought was a solid friendship—and what she'd hoped was a burgeoning romantic relationship—was, in fact, neither. Perhaps he'd simply helped her through a difficult time because he was Bran, heroic and gallant and unable to countenance the thought of a damsel in distress.

Ugh. And here she'd planned this whole trip just to get close to him. Just to see him again.

Oh, sure. She'd tried to convince herself she'd done it because the girls deserved something special to celebrate their scholarships. But even her father had seen through her ploy. When she'd told him about the trip, he'd rubbed his big, bushy Magnum PI mustache and said with a considering frown, "Is this really for the girls? Or are you doin' this so you have an excuse to go see that treasure-huntin' man your momma tells me you been emailin'?"

Busted. I should have my philanthropist's license revoked.

"I know who your father is," Rick said, seeming to read her thoughts. "I saw him on TV once. Some news special or something. He was talking about how he'd gone from roughneck to oil tycoon by relying on spit, grit, and a get'r'done attitude." Rick's lips twitched.

"It was *60 Minutes*." Maddy shook her head with affection. It'd only taken her father ten minutes to have Morley Safer eating out of the palm of his hand. "And that's not an act. My daddy still wears Wranglers with Skoal rings worn through the back pockets and his favorite sweat-stained Stetson to work every day. I guess you can take the man out of the oil fields, but you can't take the oil fields out of the man." *And I wouldn't have him any other way.* She didn't have to say that last part aloud; it was obvious in her tone.

Still shielding her eyes against the last glowing rays of the sun, she watched the floatplane disappear over the horizon. And that's when she felt it. The remoteness. The...*aloneness*. There was nothing around them but miles of waves that glinted silver in the dying light. No sounds except for the chatter of the girls and the waves lapping against the sand. The isolation was profound. Absolute. Scary and exciting and exhilarating all at once.

Okay, so Bran or no Bran, she was going to make this experience a great one. For the girls. For herself.

Because they deserved a vacation. An adventure. And, by God, after what she'd gone through three months ago, so did she.

And maybe you can use this time unplugged from all your gadgets and away from your empty email account to reassess your feelings for one former Navy SEAL turned treasure hunter, her conscience whispered.

Sure. Okay. That's totally what she'd do, and—

"Were you expecting company?" Rick asked.

"Why? What's…"

She didn't finish her question. When she turned in the direction the ranger was looking, she spotted a small deep-sea fishing vessel slowly sailing toward the island.

Her heart leapt. Actually *leapt*. If it weren't for her rib cage, she was pretty sure the thing would have burst from her chest *Alien*-style. One word, one *name*, seemed to whisper on the wind. *Bran*.

So much for reassessing her feelings…

———

6:23 p.m. …

"They're on the island. My guys are in position, advancing slowly and waiting on your signal to go in strong," Tony Scott told Gene Powers.

Sitting on the sofa beside Gene on the small sixty-foot motor yacht they'd rented under a false name with false identification, Tony watched the older man try to swallow the lump in his throat. And not for the first time, he wondered if Gene had the stomach to go through with their plan.

Just keep your shit together a little while longer, he thought, impatience gnawing on his backbone like a junkyard dog.

"Once we cross this line, there's no goin' back." There was a tremor in Gene's voice. It matched the one in the man's hands as he absently picked at the stitching on the edge of the blue pillow tossed into the corner of the molded seating area at the back of the vessel.

Tony had always respected Gene for his courage and sense of adventure when it came to business—and to living life, for that matter—but the old fart was proving to lack the intestinal fortitude to get down and dirty when the occasion called for it. And this occasion definitely called for it.

Which is where I come in.

"I know there's no going back." He reached out to squeeze Gene's wiry shoulder. "I'm ready. Are you?"

"*No*," Gene spat. "I can't help but think there's got to be another way."

Tony bit the inside of his cheek, girding himself to have the same argument they'd been having for the last week. As patiently as he could, he said, "Gene, we've been through this a million times. No venture capitalist will touch us. We've exhausted all our reserves and the reserves of our investors. We need cash."

"Maybe I could ask him again," Gene said, something close to desperation in his eyes. They both knew to which *him* Gene was referring.

"He's already told you no three times," Tony reminded him. "He thinks it's a bad investment. He's grown risk averse over the years. Too risk averse. And he's pushed you to this."

"No." Gene shook his head. "It wasn't him. It was OPEC. Goddamned OPEC!" Gene cursed, taking off his Stetson to run a hand through his gray hair. His droopy handlebar mustache quivered when he glanced out at the open ocean, hoping to see a way out. But Tony knew that nothing but endless, undulating waves surrounded the vessel. Certainly no other solution to their problem.

If they wanted to save the oil business, this was it. A Hail Mary pass in the final minutes.

"Goddamn OPEC," Gene said again, pounding his fist on the arm of the molded fiberglass sofa before replacing his cowboy hat. The Organization of Petroleum Exporting Countries—made up of the twelve most oil-rich and least American-friendly nations—was a cartel that kept a stranglehold on the world through its control of the majority of the earth's crude oil reserves. And right now it had a stranglehold on their company. "I don't know why we didn't bomb the shit out of all of them when they first incorporated sixty-five years ago."

"We didn't 'bomb the shit out of all of them' because leveling entire nations just to make sure they couldn't profit from their own natural resources would've been frowned upon by…well…pretty much everyone," Tony explained, noticing the time on his gold GMT-Master Rolex and getting increasingly antsy as the seconds ticked by.

"Well, now they're tryin' to stop *us* from controllin' and profitin' from *our* natural resources," Gene snarled. "How's that fair?" Before Tony could respond, Gene answered his own question. "I'll tell you how. Plain and simple, it *ain't*."

"That's why we have to see this through," Tony said. "If we do this, we'll have enough cash to get a couple of the new ventures up and running. Once they are, they'll fund the rest. And then when everything is online and we're pumping out hundreds of thousands of barrels of crude a day, the United States will be safer than it's ever been. And that'll be thanks to us. You and me, Gene. Just imagine it."

The only reason Gene had finally agreed to this scheme was because Tony had couched his arguments in a bunch of flag-waving hoopla. It had worked like a charm then. It worked liked a charm now.

"You swear to me no one will get hurt," Gene demanded. His bottom lip, visible beneath his ridiculous mustache, quivered.

Oh, for God's sake. If the man started crying, Tony would be hard-pressed not to slap his face.

"My guys' plan is sound and every scenario has been accounted for."

"Your guys." Gene shook his head, sounding so much like Foghorn Leghorn that Tony was surprised he didn't start his next sentence with *I say, I say.* "You keep callin' them that. Where did you find them anyway?"

"You'd be amazed at how many ex–armed forces types are willing to sell their services for the right price."

Gene grimaced.

Poor Gene. Always thinking the best of people. It was genetic. Everyone in the Powers family suffered from the same affliction.

"Come on, Gene." Tony sighed. "It's just three girls, one woman, and a wet-behind-the-ears park ranger. It'll be a breeze."

"A breeze, huh?" Gene smoothed his mustache and wet his lips with his tongue. "Then tell me again why there are guns involved."

Tony smiled, but the expression held no humor. "Surely, since you're a born-and-bred Texan, I don't need to explain that to you." When Gene scowled his impatience, Tony elaborated. "Shock and awe, my man. Shock and awe. Besides, we need to make this thing look legit if we want him to pony up the cash and do it quickly."

"Shock and awe better be *all* it'll be." Gene pressed a hand to his chest as if his heart was hurting. That's all Tony needed, for the waffling old cuss to have a heart attack. *Although, on second thought…* If Gene keeled over with a coronary, Tony would be left at the helm. Which would make things *so* much easier.

"If anything happens to Maddy," Gene said, shaking his head, "I'll never—"

"Nothing is going to happen to her," Tony assured him. When Gene searched his eyes, he made sure his expression reflected one-hundred-percent sincerity.

Gene turned to stare out at the ocean again, a muscle ticking in his jaw. Tony simply sat and waited. Gene had donned his decision-making face, and Tony knew better than to intrude. Finally, Gene blew out a breath. "Okay. Let's do this."

Tony flashed Gene a reassuring wink before lifting the satellite phone in his hand and barking two words: "Go time."

Chapter 3

6:35 p.m. ...

"I DON'T THINK I'M *ALWAYS* RIGHT," MASON SAID. "I JUST think I'm hyper-fuckin'-competent, which leads to a higher-than-usual occurrence of being right."

"Well, I guess you really put me in my place, didn't you, Mr. Muscles McSmartypants?" Alex countered. "But I'm telling you, I heard somewhere that—"

"And here comes the useless trivia." Mason's exasperation was evident to Bran, even though he was high above the deck of the catamaran in the captain's chair, busy keeping the mainsail full of the warm wind blowing across Hawk Channel and trying to read the fast currents doing their best to pull the sailboat off course.

"Just so we're clear," Alex huffed, crossing her arms and glaring at Mason, "I think I like you better when you aren't speaking."

Bran frowned down at the two of them. They'd been trading insults since he weighed anchor and set sail for the Dry Tortugas. It was amazing how two people could take such extreme delight in rubbing each other the wrong way.

Amazing and annoying. *Definitely* annoying.

"Remind me again why you two are here?" he called to them. Then, on second thought... "Remind me again why *I'm* here?" There had to be a reason. Although, for the life of him, he couldn't remember what it was.

Alex turned and shaded her eyes against the glare of the running lights he'd clicked on after the sun sank slow and lazy into the sea to the west. The moment it had touched the water, however, it was as if something hungry was waiting for it there, sucking it down quickly and leaving nothing but a reddish-orange smear in its place. Stars were breaking through the darkening sky overhead, and the blue waters had turned a silvery gray in the deepening dusk.

Bran loved being at sea. Out here he was so free and... removed. Out here he could forget who he really was.

"You're here because your pride wouldn't let you back down when LT started making *bok-bok* noises at you after I told him about Madison Powers's invitation," Alex called to him, a grin kicking up the corners of her mouth.

Roger that. Now he remembered. His best friend *had* always known how to goad him into doing things he didn't want to do. *The rat bastard.*

"I'm here because I've never been to the Dry Tortugas and the historian in me considered that a crying shame," Alex continued. "Plus, there's nothing any of us can do to prepare for the search dives tomorrow. And if I stayed around Wayfarer Island, I wouldn't get any sleep. I'm too amped up."

Amped up. Because after carefully cleaning the hilt of the cutlass, they'd discovered markings that fit the description of a short sword belonging to none other than the great Captain Bartolome Vargas himself. Which meant Alex's theory about the *Santa Cristina* having gone down in the waters around Wayfarer Island might actually prove correct.

Bran should've been vibrating with excitement too. But no matter how hard he tried, he couldn't get more than half his mind to focus on the amazing find. The other half remained stubbornly obsessed with the distance that separated Wayfarer Island and the Dry Tortugas. With the distance between him and the wonderful, wise-cracking, completely *off-limits* Maddy Powers.

So close.

And getting closer by the minute.

He lifted a set of field glasses to his eyes. Through the magnified lenses, he could just make out the few spot-lights on the seawall that separated the moat and Fort Jefferson from the gulf waters surrounding Garden Key. Now that the sun had set, a soft yellow glow flashed from the little lighthouse built atop the edge of the fort's curtain wall, illuminating the white hull of what appeared to be a deep-sea fishing vessel that was in the process of anchoring itself a few dozen yards from the little beach that ran along one side of the islet.

So damned close. And he hadn't the first clue what he was going to say to her once they were actually face-to-face.

Long time, no see was too flippant and trite consider-ing the hell they'd been through together and all they'd since shared. *Sorry I didn't respond to your email; the satellite dish went down* while technically correct still sounded like a big, fat excuse. So that left…what? The truth? *I didn't wanna come 'cause you scare the shit outta me. You make me want things I shouldn't want and contemplate things I shouldn't contemplate.*

Like *that* was going to happen.

And damnit, now those ridiculous butterflies were back. He reached for the bottle of Gatorade in the cup holder near his elbow, determined to drown the fluttery little suckers. *Again*. But before he could lift the drink to his lips, he got distracted by the fact that Alex was *still* talking.

"...so when you add all that up, it was pretty much a given I would tag along. But I have no idea why *he's* here." She hooked a thumb toward Mason. When Alex wrinkled her nose, the zinc oxide smeared across the bridge caught the running lights and glistened. She was the only person Bran knew who still used zinc oxide. "I say it's because he couldn't stand to be away from me," she finished impishly.

Mason's expression called Alex ten kinds of crazy, but he didn't say a word.

"Oh, goodie!" Alex clapped her hands. "He's gone back to being nonverbal. Happy, happy, joy, joy!"

Bran opened his mouth to tell them to stop poking at each other like children. But before he could say anything, a dull *pop, pop* echoed across the water, barely discernible above the snap of the mainsail as it tugged against the boom basket when a particularly strong gust of briny-smelling wind pulled the fabric tight.

The fine hairs on the back of Bran's neck stood on end, his adrenaline spiked, and hundreds of missions to the ass-ends of the earth flashed through his brain. If he lived ten thousand lifetimes, he'd recognize that sound for exactly what it was...

Automatic gunfire.

Pop! Pop, pop, pop! Another barrage carried over

the waves and slammed into his eardrums like percussion grenades.

"*Maddy!*" He hadn't realized he'd roared her name aloud until he saw Alex jump straight into Mason's lap and turn to stare at him with wide, frightened eyes.

"Huh? What?" she asked, then squawked when Mason hopped from his seat and bobbled her like a hot potato. Once Mason set her on her feet, she smacked him on the arm and glared. "What the heck was *that* all about?" she demanded. "You could've launched me overboard and—"

But that's all she managed before another unmistakable *pop* sounded over the water.

"What *is* that?" she asked, pushing her glasses up the medicated bridge of her nose.

"Gunfire," Mason gritted.

"*Gunfire?*" Alex's face went so white it was hard to see where the zinc oxide stopped and her skin started. "Wh-why? There isn't hunting on the Dry Tortugas, is there? I mean, what could anyone possibly hunt? There are only seabirds and turtles and…it's *dark*."

"That's not the sound of a fuckin' hunting rifle," Mason grumbled between clenched teeth, lifting his eyes to Bran. The look on Mason's face was one Bran knew all too well. It said one thing and one thing only: *Trouble*. The kind of trouble that separated men into two distinct categories: the quick and the dead.

Without conscious thought, Bran turned the key and engaged the catamaran's dual engines, adding their man-made horsepower to Mother Nature's wind power. The butterflies in his stomach grew lead wings and fell like rocks.

"Get the M4s!" he yelled, disgusted to hear his voice was nothing more than a reedy bark of sound, barely discernible over the roar of the engines and the *hiss* of the waves against the twin hulls as the sailboat picked up speed.

It must have been loud enough. With a hitch of his chin, Mason disappeared inside the cabin.

"What are M4s?" Alex called, blinking against the salt spray splashing over the deck as the catamaran plowed up one wave and down another.

Bran didn't answer. He couldn't. His pounding heart was sitting in the back of his throat, strangling him. He once again lifted the field glasses, but he couldn't see much of anything beyond the spray of white water kicked up by the outboard engine of a dinghy that had detached itself from the fishing boat and was now plowing toward the shore of Garden Key.

When Mason reappeared on the deck—two minutes later? Ten? Bran couldn't say; time was moving at a snail's pace—their trusty weapons were strapped to his back.

Now, it wasn't unusual for a boat to come equipped with firearms. The open oceans were the last great frontier, and it behooved a smart captain and crew to always be able to defend themselves. What *was* unusual was for a boat to be carrying fully automatic, gas-powered, 5.56 mm NATO round-firing pieces of death-dealing machinery, the kind of weapons strictly off-limits to civilians unless you bought them out of the back of a van or, in Bran's and Mason's case, unless you appropriated them from good ol' Uncle Sam—with the blessing of their CO, of course.

"Oh! My! *God!*" Alex screamed when she saw the rifles. "Where the heck did *those* come from?"

Bran barely spared her a glance. "Come on! *Come on!*" he yelled, punching the throttle as far as it would go and willing the sailboat to move faster.

It wasn't long, three seconds maybe, before he felt Mason's bulk on the steps leading to the captain's perch. Mason placed a hand on Bran's shoulder and leaned over him to kill the running lights.

Good idea. Don't know why I didn't think of it. Oh, right. Because all he'd been thinking was *Get to Maddy! Get to Maddy!*

"You need to ease off, bro," Mason said.

"Screw you," Bran grumbled, shrugging off Mason's heavy palm. "Maddy's on that island."

"I'm not trying to be a cocksucker here," Mason said, the next-to-last word sounding more like *cocksuckuh.* "But we go in there full tilt and guns hot, and we're likely to end up deader than fuckin' doornails."

"But Maddy—"

"I know, man." Mason nodded. "But we need to do this the right way. The *SEAL* way." Mason gave Bran's shoulder a squeeze that conveyed a million things at once: *Get your shit together. Don't worry, I got your back. Once more unto the breach, dear friend…*

Roger that. The SEAL way.

Bran managed a nod and throttled back the engines despite all his instincts screaming at him to do the opposite.

"Good." Mason said when the catamaran was no longer plowing hell-bent for leather toward Garden Key. "Now how do you want to play this?"

"Don't know," Bran admitted, his scalp on fire like every single one of his hairs had ripped out of their follicles. His lungs attempted to crawl into his throat to join his heart—*apparently it's a party in there*—and his mind was spinning out of control. "I don't—"

"Okay, okay." Mason hit the side of his heavy fist against Bran's shoulder. "So the way I see it, we got two options. Option one is we use the marine radio to call back to Wayfarer Island and tell LT there's a situation on Garden Key. We *should* still be within hailing range." His face said he wasn't sure about that last part. Truth to tell, Bran wasn't either. Marine radios weren't built to carry signals over great distances. They were meant to be used for close ship-to-ship communication. "Then LT can use the satphone on the island to call the Coast Guard on Key West."

"And after that?" Bran demanded. Each second they sat flapping their lips felt like an eternity. "We wait out here and twiddle our dicks until the authorities show up while who knows what happens to Maddy? Hell no. Plus, there's always a chance that they"—he punched a finger toward Garden Key and whoever the hell was firing off those weapons—"are monitoring the marine channels. If we use the marine radio to hail back to Wayfarer Island, they'll know help is on the way, and they could…" He couldn't even *countenance* the end of that sentence, much less voice it. If only they had a satphone onboard, they could make the call to Key West themselves and no one would be the wiser. *I wish.* But there was that old saying about wishing in one hand and shitting in the other and seeing which one filled up faster. "No way, *paisano*." He adamantly shook his head. "We hafta maintain radio silence until we know what we're dealing with."

"Hey!" Alex called from the deck. "What are you two talking about? Shouldn't we be—"

"Alex!" Mason bellowed, which was so unlike him that Bran actually flinched. "It would be wicked awesome if, for once in your life, you shut your chowderhole!"

Alex wasn't one to let something like that slide. But she was as taken aback by Mason's outburst as Bran was. She snapped her mouth shut, blinking rapidly behind the lenses of her glasses.

"Okay, so that leaves us with option two," Mason continued as if they hadn't been interrupted.

"Which is?"

"We need to get eyes and ears on that island. And I think I have a plan for how to do that."

"I'm listening" was what Bran said. What he was thinking was *I can't believe this is happening again!*

7:10 p.m. ...

I can't believe this is happenin' again! Maddy silently screamed.

She'd already been held hostage once. Surely that was enough for any one lifetime. And later—that is if she lived through this and *had* a later—she planned to have a very stern conversation with Fate or Destiny or the Big Man Upstairs, whichever one of them was responsible for this horseshit. But for right now, she had to concentrate everything she had on staying strong for the girls. Staying calm so they would cue off her and stay strong too.

Oh, and she also needed to keep from revisiting the corned beef sandwich she'd had for lunch all over the beach...

When Louisa glanced at her, Maddy rolled in her lips and nodded, hoping to convey confidence. *Concerned* confidence, but confidence nonetheless. She must have come close to hitting the mark because Louisa dipped her chin, squared her shoulders, and tightened her hold around Sally Mae, who was quietly sniffling and trying her best not to flat-out cry.

"Stop blubbering!" one of the four men who'd stormed the island thundered at Sally Mae. For a couple of seconds after the fishing vessel dropped anchor, Maddy and Ranger Rick had simply stood there like a couple of lollygaggers wondering who the new arrivals could be. Well...*Rick* had stood there wondering. Something had told Maddy it wasn't Bran. And since it *wasn't* Bran, any curiosity she'd had about the newcomers was overshadowed by the large crack of disappointment that opened up in her heart.

That large crack of disappointment had quickly been replaced by a huge fissure of terror when, through the gathering darkness, she'd watched four hooded figures board a dinghy and zoom toward her, white water rooster-tailing from their outboard engine and the sound of gunfire echoing across the beach as they aimed their weapons in the air.

"Get to the ranger's station!" Rick had yelled.

Despite a heart frozen with fear, Maddy had sprung into action, racing after him to the spot on the beach where the girls had been in the process of setting up their gear. She'd herded them in front of her on the mad dash to the tiny cottage at the end of the beach. They'd just piled through the front door—Rick making a beeline for the satellite phone in the corner—when the scary-looking masked gunmen wielding even scarier-looking machine guns burst in and ordered them all to halt.

"Run!" Maddy had screamed to the teens, throwing herself in the line of fire as the girls raced for the back door. But Louisa was the only one who made it out of the cottage. After a ten-minute chase around the tiny island, she'd been marched back to join the group already under guard. A few minutes after that, the gunmen had paraded them all back to the beach. Now the girls were huddled together, kept in a tight mass by two of the balaclava-wearing assailants.

They're just kids! Maddy wanted to scream, rage boiling in her chest like a teakettle getting ready to blow. *Stop pointin' those things at them!* But she wisely kept her mouth shut because a third gunman was keeping her dead center in his sights. As for the fourth masked man? Well, he was busy aiming the business end of his weapon at Rick.

"On your knees!" Masked Man Four yelled at Rick. "Get on your fucking knees!" He punctuated his order by jabbing Rick in the kidney with the barrel of his weapon, causing Rick to cry out.

"Lord Almighty! Take it easy!" Maddy yelled, unable to stop herself. "He'll do what you say! Just give him a chance!"

She nodded at Rick as he sank down, hands still raised above his head. Each of her breaths came hard and fast. Her knees felt as liquid as the tepid wave that crawled up the beach to swirl around her ankles for a couple of seconds, leaving a crab to scuttle after it when it retreated back across the sand.

"All of you, put your hands behind your backs!" Masked Man Four bellowed. Then he sucked his teeth like he had something stuck in them. It was a tic. A disgusting habit that left a sour taste on Maddy's tongue.

Or maybe that's just fear, she decided, complying with his command.

When she felt her captor tighten a zip tie around her wrists—his hands were warm, sweaty, but his touch chilled her to the bone—she was brought back around to her original thought…

I can't believe this is happenin' again!

"I said *shut up!*" The guy—correction: the *asshole*—who'd yelled at Sally Mae bellowed at the teen again, causing Sally Mae's mouth to gape open like an ugly wound even when no other sound emerged.

"Don't you holler at her!" Maddy shouted. Then she winced when Masked Man Four left Rick to take a menacing step in her direction.

Full darkness had fallen. The only light on the island glowed from the crescent moon, the few spotlights on the seawall surrounding the moat, which in turn surrounded the fort, and the small lighthouse atop the garrison that warned away passing vessels. But all combined, it was enough illumination to show the threat in the man's eyes as he leaned close.

"In case you missed it, honey…" His words were slightly muffled because the balaclava he wore was ninja style. The kind that covered everything but his eyes. Even so, she heard him clearly enough and thought, *Oh, no, he did* not *just honey me!* "You're not calling the shots here. *We* are. So keep that pretty mouth of yours shut, or I might be tempted to put it to better use." He sucked his teeth again, and Maddy was reminded of the sound a rattlesnake made when it readied itself to strike.

"Don't you h-hurt her!" Rick gritted.

Masked Man Four—apparently he was the leader since he was doing most of the talking—looked over at Rick, his eyes cold and dark and devoid of any human emotion. Rick swallowed and tried his best to hold the masked man's gaze. In the end, he couldn't manage it. He dropped his eyes to the sand in front of him, his dark hair shadowing his face.

"That's what I thought." Masked Man Four nodded, his voice cold enough to freeze an open flame. Then he turned his attention to his cohorts. "I think we're finally ready." *Suck, suck.* Maddy was fairly certain she was going to hear that sound in her nightmares.

"Time to head out to the boat?" The other man who was guarding the girls spoke for the first time, his Southern accent thick and telling of a youth spent south of the Mason-Dixon Line. If Maddy had to make a guess, she'd say Georgia or Alabama.

Of course, where he grew up wasn't important because... *The boat? Oh, sweet Jesus!* She knew the worst possible thing she could do was allow the masked men to take them to a secondary location. That was pretty much How To Survive Attempted Abduction 101.

"Please," she beseeched Masked Man Four. Like the Temptations sang, she wasn't too proud to beg. "If it's money you want—"

"I warned you what I'd do if you didn't keep your pretty mouth shut, didn't I?" *Suck, suck.* The barrel of Masked Man Four's machine gun was suddenly an inch from Maddy's nose. Her eyes crossed when she attempted to stare down its black throat.

It was hard to determine if the *whooshing* sounds she heard were the waves shushing against the beach or her own blood pounding in her ears. She stopped trying to figure it out when the strangest thing happened. Movement in the surf caught her attention. And if her hands hadn't been tied behind her back, she would've used them to rub her eyes.

Suddenly he was there.

Like the great god Poseidon himself rising from the sea, water sheeting off his dark head and broad shoulders. Her friend. Her hero. The man who had stormed into her life like a hurricane.

Bran...

Chapter 4

7:15 p.m. ...

"THROW AWAY YOUR WEAPONS, DICKHOLES!" BRAN BEL-lowed, aiming at the guy who was drawing down on Maddy's head.

Seeing her in mortal danger made something click inside him. Something that was black of heart and sharp of claw. Something he'd inherited from his bastard of a father.

It was a side of himself he tried to keep hidden, keep buried. But there were times like this when he gladly let it go free. It roared and slashed, filling him with deadly purpose.

Battle mode is what LT called it.

Bran simply called it his monster.

It consumed all the light and laughter in him and left only darkness and death. But it was what had kept him alive through too many blood-soaked missions to count. And *hopefully*, it was what was going to help him save the five innocent people on the beach.

"Bran!" Maddy choked, her Texas accent splitting his name into two syllables: *Brae-yan*. Her wide, heavily lashed eyes threatened to suck him in like a whirlpool when he gave her a cursory glance. "You came!"

I will always fly to your side with all the courage and destruction in my heart!

Whoa. Where the hell had *that* come from? But he knew. It was his monster. The thing was pure, red-eyed emotion.

He forced himself to ignore the catch in her voice and instead slid his gaze to the two men who'd been guarding the girls. They'd swung their SCAR-L rifles in his direction the instant he issued his command, and the way the dick-lickers handled the assault weapons told him they weren't amateurs.

But he already knew that.

For the first ten minutes after stealthily making landfall, he and Mason had slunk around the island, watching. Watching as the mysterious team assembled their hostages. Observing the way they carried themselves. Cataloging all those details both big and small that would eventually give them the advantage. Like... the short, mouthy dude favored his right knee. *There's an injury there that can be exploited.* Like...the asshole with the Southern accent had trouble using his nondominant left hand. *So if it comes down to CQB—*close quarters combat—*always approach from his weaker side.* All of this they'd filed away. And all the while formulating a plan. *This* plan.

"You drop *your* weapon!" the dude still drawing down on Maddy thundered. Bran knew two angry, red laser dots glowed on his chest. He imagined he could feel them there, boring, burning, inciting the darker side of him until his blood was a conflagration coursing through his veins, his heart a fiery fist that pounded flames through his chest.

"I'll give you one more chance!" he yelled, feeling the warm waves crashing against the backs of his calves.

A blade of seaweed slipped by his ankle, slick as an eel. "Drop your weapons and you might live!"

His finger twitched on the trigger. It would be so easy. Just a couple of pounds of pressure. Just a gentle contraction of familiar muscles against familiar resistance and *bang!* Done. One less evil piece of shit on the Earth.

"Ha!" The guy who seemed to be the leader cracked a laugh that echoed over the dark water. "In case you haven't noticed, asswipe, you're outnumbered!" He made a weird sucking noise against his teeth, like he was trying to remove a piece of stuck spinach.

Asswipe, eh? Careful, gavone, *or I might make you eat that insult along with that spinach.*

"I count four against one." Bran hitched one shoulder casually. "Which means you'll overwhelm and kill me in the end. But not before I take one of you with me." He jerked his chin toward Lead A-Hole. "I'm thinking I'll make *you* that one."

The man must have heard the truth in Bran's tone. Bran could see his throat work over a hard swallow behind the fabric of the balaclava.

That's right. Go ahead and make my day.

Before Lead A-Hole had a chance to respond, a red dot appeared on the chest of the man with the bum knee.

Mason. *Impeccable timing, my friend.*

"Uh-oh." Bran tsked. "I hate to hafta tell you… No, wait. I *love* having to tell you that the odds just swung in my favor."

"What the—?" The guy glanced down at the gleaming dot centered directly over his heart. Bran watched with satisfaction as his eyes widened. "What's going on here? Who *are* you motherfuckers?" He lifted his chin to Bran. "What are you doing here?"

"I could ask *you* the same questions," Maddy piped up. And *there* she was. The loudmouthed dynamo Bran had come to know and…lust after. Only, right now she needed to shove a sock in it. "Who are *you?* And what do you want with us?"

"None of that matters," Bran insisted. When Maddy turned to him, he sent her a look. Her lips flattened, the upper one protruding just past the lower. But she kept her mouth shut. That big, beautiful, Julia Roberts upside-down mouth of hers with the top lip plumper than the bottom. The mouth he'd kissed on that hot night three months ago. The mouth that…

You stupid pazzo, he scolded himself. *Now's not the time!*

"What *matters*," he continued, "is that you find your-selves in the middle of a crossfire situation. And judging by the way you jackholes carry those SCAR-Ls, you know a little bit about military tactics. Which means you *also* know that being caught in the middle of a crossfire situation means you could be dead as shit in about ten seconds if you don't *drop your weapons!*"

Maddy blinked rapidly, and then she did the damnd-est thing. She grinned. At him. And it was all blinding and brilliant and *you're my hero*.

Well, shit.

He watched as the leader glanced over at the guy sporting a shiny red dot on his chest. Bran decided to throw in a little more incentive. "Look. We don't wanna hurt you. We just want you to let these good people go. And then we'll let *you* go. No questions asked. So what'd'ya say you toss those rifles on the sand, hightail it back to your boat, and we'll forget this ever happened, *capisce*?"

Lead A-Hole darted a glance around, seeming to search for another way out. Part of Bran hoped he'd try something—the dark, angry, *bloodthirsty* part of him. But Maddy was downwind of a Category 5 shitstorm—a.k.a. having a full auto aimed at her cute nose—so the other part of him just wanted to get rid of these mysterious hooded men as bloodlessly and expediently as possible so he could run and gather her in his arms.

Which, when he took a tick to think about it, scared him spitless. That need to protect her. That need to touch her. That need to…

If I get my hands on her—when *I get my hands on her*—*I won't ever wanna let her go.*

A hot sense of possessiveness gripped him, which immediately sent a cold, spidery feeling crawling into his chest. He might have fallen victim to old memories if Lead A-Hole hadn't picked that moment to make a move. It was subtle. Just a slight sliding of his left foot behind his right. But Bran recognized the stance. His internal warning system flashed from yellow to red.

Sonofabastard's in a hurry to be a dangerous man.

Combat training and years of dodging bullets kicked in. Bran dropped to his knees in the surf at the same time Lead A-Hole swung his rifle in Bran's direction, pulling the trigger. A bullet whizzed by Bran's ear with a dull-sounding *zzziiippp* followed immediately by the booming report of the SCAR-L.

The trigger on Bran's M4A1 rifle was worn smooth. It felt like coming home when he squeezed it and the weapon bucked against his shoulder. The familiar smell of spent cordite perfumed the air as his bullet left his barrel.

He wasn't labeled one of the best sharpshooters ever to go through BUD/S training for nothing. His aim proved true, and his round buried itself in Lead A-Hole's wicked heart. The man's eyes flew wide, the whites shining eerily when he realized he was dead.

He had the wherewithal to wheeze "Can't breathe," and yank off his balaclava before he fell to his knees, gripping the hole in his chest. Dark blood spurted between his fingers with every ineffectual beat of his heart. And a face that was all-American GI Joe stared at Bran, mouth going slack, eyes going glassy. Then he tumbled onto his back, staring sightless into the star-studded sky.

I warned you, Bran thought.

The guy with the bum knee gaped at his fallen comrade. "You sorry *sonofabitch!*" he screeched at Bran, his lips moving behind the fabric of the balaclava, his eyes narrowed and filled with fury.

Bran wished he could say he was sorry. But he wasn't. The death of men who tried to kill him had ceased to make a dent in his psyche years ago. Not to mention he was completely convinced that any rat bastard who took women and children hostage at gunpoint deserved nothing better than a dirt nap.

He readied himself to dive beneath the surf to escape the bullet sure to leave Bum Knee's SCAR-L in the next second. But Mason came to his rescue, lighting up the sand at Bum Knee's feet. Mason didn't dare try for a body shot for fear of hitting one of the teenagers. And Bran was left with no clear line of sight either.

Damn!

"Get down! Get *down!*" Maddy screamed at the girls as she dropped to her knees.

Unfortunately, her call came too late. The remaining men each grabbed a girl, using her as a human shield against Bran while they turned and opened fire on Mason's position behind the seawall. Their rounds chewed up the aging masonry like it was made of Play-Doh. And Mason was left with no recourse but to do the ol' D and C—duck and cover.

Bran, on the other hand, surged through the surf toward Maddy in an attempt to gain a better firing position and, you know, *save the girl…*

7:19 p.m. …

Chaos…

That was Maddy's world. Even so, time seemed to slow to a lame man's crawl and she felt like she was seeing everything through one of those children's 3D View-Master toys. She wasn't pressing the little handle on the side to spin the disk of pictures, but the frames were still flicking in front of her unblinking eyes.

The body of the unmasked man lay on the sand beside her. Blood slowly seeped from his lifeless corpse and headed in a gruesome red river toward the waiting arms of the ocean.

Next picture…

The three gunmen rained lead death on the seawall as they pulled the girls with them up the beach and toward the narrow bridge that led across the moat into the fort.

Next picture…

Bran raced through the surf. His broad shoulders, exposed by his black tank top, flexed and bunched. His big thighs churned as he halved the distance between them.

Even in the chaos, she was struck by the sheer impact of him. Long, lean muscles made for endurance. Big, thick bones designed to keep him standing tall for decades. Deeply tanned skin that glowed with health and vigor and highlighted his Italian-American heritage. Her mind touched on a line she'd read from an Italian poet in college, Francesco Petrarca. He'd written, *Rarely do great beauty and great virtue dwell together*. But he couldn't have been more wrong. At least when it came to Brando Pallidino. Because Bran was all things beautiful and virtuous, a real-life, honest-to-God hero.

Glory be and hallelujah! She *needed* a hero to help her get the girls away from those awful men.

He skidded to a stop beside her. And then her world stopped doing that weird stop-action thing. Everything sprang into high definition. Including Bran's face.

Before he turned to take aim at the masked men, she caught a glimpse of his dark eyes, and her thundering heart ground to a halt, her blood turning to ice water in her veins. She recognized that look. It was the same one he'd worn the day he stormed her father's yacht and put a bullet in the brain of the terrorist holding her hostage. The look of a man who *had* killed and *would* kill again. A man filled with dark purpose. A man who…frightened her.

Which was silly. Bran was all things good and valiant. And yet…

She shuddered at the difference between *this* Bran and the one who talked her through her bad times, the one who liked to tease her and taunt her and fill her inbox with videos of Meat, the bulldog, snoring so loudly it vibrated the canine's jowls. It was almost like there were two Brans: Darling Bran and Deadly Bran.

"Flat on the ground!" he bellowed over his shoulder at her and Rick.

From the corner of her eye, Maddy saw the young park ranger face-plant. Bran in full-on SEAL mode was not the type of guy you ignored. And as much as she despised getting sand stuck between her teeth, she belly-flopped right alongside Rick. The beach was cold and wet and smelled of fish. The tiny, crushed shells interspersed with the sand scratched her cheek when she turned her head to keep her eyes focused on the helter-skelter scene.

"Let 'em go!" Bran thundered, his deep voice echoing over the dark water and bouncing against the brick walls of the fort and the seawall.

"Go fuck yourself, you sonofabitch!" the tyrant who'd been terrorizing Sally Mae, and who now held her in front of him, shouted between the intermittent volleys his cohorts sprayed at the seawall in an effort to pin down the Deep Six Salvage crewman who was obviously hiding there.

"Let the girls go, or end up like your friend here!" Bran yelled.

As if to punctuate his point, or else simply to add insult to injury, he nudged the dead man's body with his foot. The move caused fresh blood to erupt from the wide hole in the corpse's chest. More dribbled from his slack mouth to pool in the ear closest to Maddy. It was so dark and thick that it reflected the glow of the moon.

Jesus Christ and all his followers!

Once again her lunch was threatening an encore performance.

"I can knock the beak off a chicken at two hundred yards. Which means I'm gonna give you to the count of three to let that girl go! If you don't, I'll send you straight to your Maker with a bullet between your eyes! And then I'll do the same to your two friends!"

"You're bluffing!" the tyrant called, still easing Sally Mae backward. The girl's eyes begged Maddy for help. And it killed her that all she could do was lie there and watch. Her hands, still tied behind her back, curled into claws with the urge to scratch the tyrant's evil eyes right out of his head.

"I might be bluffing, you miserable, vomitous mass!" Bran yelled. *Oh, for heaven's sake. Really? He's quotin'* The Princess Bride? "But if you wanna test me," he added, "I'm your huckleberry!" *And now he's quotin'* Tombstone. "Last chance to let the girl go!"

The tyrant ignored him and continued to backpedal toward the fort.

True to his word, Bran began to count. "One!" The word exploded over the beach like an atom bomb. "Two!"

Maddy bit her tongue to keep from crying out. In the next second, Bran would let his bullets fly and she prayed he was as good as he claimed to be.

"Thr—"

Rat-a-tat-tat!

The sand around Bran's bare feet erupted with a hail of gunfire as the man holding Louisa suddenly turned his aim away from the seawall and opened up on Bran.

Bran spun like a top just as the fabric on the left leg of his cargo shorts shredded.

"No!" Maddy screamed when something hot and sticky sprayed across her face. Then the world went black. All the air was punched from her lungs. And a terrible, suffocating weight fell over her.

For a split second she wondered if she was dead. *Did I get shot in the head? Is this what the afterlife feels like? Dark, airless pressure?* But then familiar smells tunneled up her nose. Irish Spring soap and Tide laundry detergent. Bran...

He'd thrown himself on top of her, sacrificing himself to shield her from the melee of flying lead.

7:20 p.m. ...

Mason McCarthy had seen his fair share of wicked bad situations. And this one here qualified as a top ten. After watching the men and the way they carried themselves, he and Bran really thought that once the fuckheads found themselves in a crossfire situation, they would accept the offer to leave the island, no questions asked. Obviously, he and Bran had given them more credit for smarts than they deserved.

"Fuckin' hell," he cursed when another barrage of gunfire bit into the masonry behind his back. But he couldn't continue to take cover. Bran was in the open and needed his help.

Turkey-peeking around the corner of the seawall, Mason bellied out flat in the sand and gritted his teeth as he laid on his trigger, aiming for the ground at the feet of the masked men, hoping to draw all their fire in his direction and away from the trio on the beach.

It worked.

The seawall continued to take a beating from the assailants' lead as the end of his M4 flashed with orange lightning in return. The pressure against his shoulder, not to mention the growing warmth of the metal in his hands, felt wonderfully familiar.

Which just goes to show how far from normal *you are.*

He shook off the thought as soon as it hit him. Not because there wasn't truth in it. But because there *was*, and it had been one of his ex-wife's biggest beefs with him. Right behind *you're never home* and *you never talk to me.*

Ya-huh! On account of me being a fuckin' SEAL who goes on fuckin' missions that are fuckin' classified!

And she'd known that when she married him.

Of course, it'd all seemed very romantic while they were flush with hormones and having sex on every vertical and horizontal surface. But once the honeymoon was over and the hard part of being hitched to a covert operator set in, she'd quickly come to see how truly *un*romantic it was. He just wished she'd had the guts to divorce him before she turned to another. Because what her duplicity and faithlessness had left him with was a sore on his heart. An open, festering wound that refused to heal.

And what the fuck are you doing thinking about her at a time like this, chowderhead?

Right. What *was* he doing thinking about her? She was the past. And his present required all his attention.

He released his trigger for a second, looking for an
opening to take out one of the motherfuckers. He wasn't
as good a shot as Bran, but more times than not he could
hit what he was aiming at. Unfortunately, the three
assailants had made it to the bridge over the moat. And
they were smart enough to keep the teenagers in front
of them while they continued to lay down covering fire
aimed in his general direction.

"Fuckin' hell!" he cursed again.

He waited, counting each round that slammed into
the masonry above his head, each steady *thud* of his
heart, until the masked men stopped shooting to disappear into the arched entry of the fort. Then he jumped
up and zigzagged his way toward the beach in a classic
scoot-and-shoot crouched position. But there was no
need to shoot. Nothing breached the deafening silence of
the island except for the sound of the tide hissing against
the sand and the gentle breeze teasing the fronds of the
palm trees and making them rattle in delight.

"Bran!" he whispered, edging ever faster through the
sand. "Headed your way, bro!"

Of their own accord, his eyes traveled out over
the dark water. Out there, anchored far behind the
fort, was the catamaran. With the intrepid Alexandra
Merriweather on board—that is if she hadn't already
decided to set sail for Wayfarer Island like he'd told
her to if she thought there might be any trouble headed
her way.

Regardless of whichever outcome she was facing, she
was alone in facing it. And the poor woman had to be
terrified. She was a pocket-sized historian, for fuck's
sake, not some trained operator.

For one quick second, he was tempted to dive into the surf, swim out to her, and take her in his arms. But the impulse was fleeting. Firstly, because Alex might be a pocket-sized historian, but she was also completely brazen. So even if she *was* scared, she'd never let him see it, much less welcome his coddling. And secondly, because taking her in his arms, even for that brief moment on the catamaran when she'd jumped in his lap, had reminded him what it was to hold a woman. All soft curves and warm skin and sweet weight and…

He'd sworn off the fairer sex. Which was working out wickedly awesome for him, thank you very much. So he could totally do without being reminded of what he was missing. Especially when that reminder came with an adorable mop of curly red hair and freckles across her nose. Little Orphan Annie all grown up and ready for a man to show her what it was like to—

Aw, hell.

He shook the image of Alex away at the same time he skidded to a stop beside the people proned out on the beach. At first glance, he thought the blood on the sand beside Bran and Maddy's pancaked bodies was coming from the corpse sprawled alongside them. Then he realized it was draining from a wound on Bran's thigh.

"Fuckin' hell," he cursed for the third time.

Chapter 5

7:22 p.m. ...

IF BRAN'S THIGH WASN'T BARKING LIKE A BITCH IN HEAT, HE was sure he would appreciate the feel of the plump ass wiggling beneath him. As it was, he couldn't stop himself from growling impatiently, "Maddy! Stop squirming around, damnit!"

He was beginning to imagine himself a rodeo cowboy on a bucking bull. And if she kept gyrating, it wouldn't be long before his eight seconds were up.

"Get off me, Bran!" she howled, her sweet breath brushing his lips when she turned her head to look at him. "If you get yourself killed bein' all heroic and brave, I swear on my granddaddy's grave I'll murder you!"

He would have pointed out that what she said didn't make a bit of sense—*How do you murder someone who's already dead?*—but he felt Mason skid to a stop beside him, kicking cool sand onto the backs of his calves.

"Fuckin' hell," he heard the big Bostonian grumble.

Fuckin' hell is right. That's exactly where this plan of theirs had gone.

"They made it into the fort," Mason said. "Which means in about two minutes they'll gain the high ground and we'll be sitting ducks."

"Roger that," Bran agreed as he pushed away from

Maddy. He immediately missed her soft, feminine warmth. And his eyes automatically pinged down to the…ahem…not insubstantial derriere that'd been giving him such fits.

So sue him. He was a *guy,* after all. And for a petite woman, Maddy had an ass that wouldn't quit, the kind to make all the 'hood girls green with envy. Or as that pop singer Meghan Trainor liked to say, Maddy was *bringing booty back.*

Amen to that!

"Cut her loose," Mason said, pulling the matte-black Smith & Wesson Tanto blade from the clip on his waistband and moving toward the park ranger still face-first in the sand.

Bran shook away thoughts of Maddy's incredible ass and grabbed the K2 tactical folding knife from the sheath he'd strapped around his calf. Before he could put his blade to use, however, Maddy flipped on her side and pushed up to her knees, facing him. Her forehead and cheeks were speckled with blood.

If it was possible for a man to live after having his beating heart ripped out through his chest wall, Bran was doing it.

"You're hit!" he croaked at the same time she screamed, "He *shot* you!"

Her chin jerked back when she registered what he'd said. She looked down at herself, trying to locate her injury, then shook her head angrily. "I'm not hit, damnit! *You're* the one who's hit!"

"That's *your* blood on her face, numbnuts," Mason whispered.

"Oh, thank God." Relief hit Bran so hard he felt

dizzy. When he let his head fall back, the stars overhead spun in lazy circles.

"Thank God?" Maddy said. He lowered his chin to find her eyes blazing. "Thank *God*? Are you crazy? For the love of… Someone cut me loose!"

Before Bran could gather himself, Mason did the honors, skirting around Maddy to slice through her restraints. The minute she was free, her little hands landed on Bran's face.

The hairs on his arms lifted when her cool fingers smoothed over the skin of his cheeks, his lips, his chin. "Bran." His name sounded sweet on her tongue. "Oh, my sweet Jesus!" Her Texas twang turned the word *my* into an adorable-sounding *mah*.

Before he could suck in a breath, she gripped his thigh on either side of the deep furrow cutting through his flesh. A little pool of his blood was gathering on the sand, mixing with the blood of the man he'd eighty-sixed.

"What do I do?" she cried, her eyes beseeching. "Tell me what—"

"It's just a flesh wound," Mason said from beside them, having given the laceration a cursory glance.

"And who are you?" Maddy demanded, turning on the poor guy with a look hot enough to set his face on fire. "Monty Python?"

It hit Bran then. "Man, I really like you," he blurted.

Maddy turned to him, upside-down mouth hanging open in a little *O* that was far more tempting than he would have thought possible at a time like this. "I—" She hesitated. "I really like you too, Bran."

"You got a satphone in that ranger's station?" Mason asked the young ranger, ignoring them.

Bran was still absorbing the fact that Maddy had admitted to liking him, *really* liking him—*But she doesn't know the real you*, he reminded himself. *She doesn't know what you have inside you or what that means you're capable of*—when her fear-tinged expression turned to desperation.

"The ranger's station? But the girls!" She searched the exterior curtain wall as if she hoped to see the teenagers there. "We have to go get them!"

"First we hafta get off this beach," Bran told her, hating the way the pulse was hammering in her throat, hating that she was caught in the middle of a hostage situation. *Again*. "They could start taking potshots at us any minute, and storming the fort to save those girls will be a lot easier if Mason and I are both alive."

"Storming the fort will also be easier once we stop your bleeding," Mason added.

"Right." Maddy turned back to Bran. "Can you make it? You're bleedin' like a stuck pig."

He responded with a smirk. "I ain't got time to bleed."

"Would you stop doin' that?" She curled her plump top lip like Elvis. It was a gesture he remembered well. One that made strange things happen to the butterflies that had recently taken up residence in his stomach.

"Doing what?"

"Quotin' bad movies at a time like this!"

He gasped exaggeratedly. "You think *Predator* is a bad movie?"

Before she could answer, Mason told the park ranger, "Lead the way. But stay low."

Apparently Mason wasn't of a mind to hang around and discuss the merits of one of Arnold Schwarzenegger's better movies. Considering their current situation, Bran couldn't blame him.

Grabbing the dead man's weapon from where it had fallen on the beach, Bran slung the strap over his shoulder before reaching for his M4 and tactical blade. Once he'd shoved the latter into its sheath, he lumbered to his feet and offered a hand to Maddy. When her palm landed in his, he felt a jolt of awareness, like two wires on a car battery suddenly making a connection.

"Are you sure you can make it?" she asked again. Er…*demanded*, really. With her eyebrows pulled in a vee and her hands balled on her hips, it was definitely a demand. An adorable, *adorable* demand.

Before he could reassure her, Mason barked, "Go, go, go!" and they were all suddenly on the move.

Bran lifted his rifle, keeping his sights aimed at the fort and the large embrasures—the openings built into the side of the garrison to allow cannon fire—that peered out at the island and the surrounding waters like dark, malevolent eyes.

The short trip to the little cottage that was the ranger's station seemed to take an eternity. Bran figured that was partly due to the burning pain in his thigh. But it was also due to his acute—we're talking *absolute*—awareness of every move Maddy made. He sensed every stutter in her step. Was attuned to every breath she took. He imagined if he listened really closely, he could probably hear her heart beat.

This was how he remembered her, this…hyperawareness. And it was just one of the many reasons he hadn't wanted to come tonight.

In the three months since he'd last seen her, he'd been

able to convince himself he had imagined everything. Chalked up his overwhelming reaction to her to the extreme circumstances under which they'd met. But now that he was back by her side? There was no denying it. That pull, that draw was still there. Still thick in the air between them like a cloud of superpowered pheromones or some shit.

When they finally made it to the ranger's station, the quiet shuffle of feet scurrying up the stone steps sounded behind him. "Got you covered," Mason said. "Up and in."

When Bran turned to make his own way into the ranger's station, it was to see two things. The first was Mason on the little porch, leaning against the rail that could really use a coat or two of paint—the salty sea air was hell on exteriors—M4 raised and at the ready to provide cover fire should Bran need it. The second was Maddy's luscious ass at eye level. Had Bran not already been sporting a battle-field boner—adrenaline tended to make a man's stick and stones perk up—he would have sprung wood at the sight. Her hips swung back and forth with an enticingly feminine *tick-tock* when she hustled through the front door.

"Bran?" She spun around in the threshold. "Hurry!"

To jostle his brain around enough that it could tell his eyes to stop bugging out of their sockets, he had to shake his head like a dog shaking off water.

Oh man. He was in so much trouble. And only *some* of it was from the dick-lickers in the fort.

7:23 p.m. ...

Alexandra Merriweather didn't know which was worse. The horrifying sound of a real, live, honest-to-goodness

gun battle, or this. This oppressive, almost malig-
nant silence that seemed to be spreading with each
passing second.

"The silence is worse," she said aloud, just to hear
her own voice and not feel so alone.

When Mason and Bran had armed themselves to the
teeth before diving overboard, she'd thought she'd be fine
on her own. But now, in the midst of the eerie quiet, the
solitude was starting to get to her. The vastness of the sea
was daunting. The soft *clink, clink* of the rigging lines
against the steel mainmast sounded strangely sinister. And
the warm, humid air had become oppressive, pushing in
on her until it felt like her lungs were caught in a vise.

"You wait here," Mason had told her before donning
a pair of swim fins, his huge back flexing as he bent at
the waist. "The minute we know what's happening and
take control of the situation, we'll send up this flare."
He'd shown her the flare stick before shoving it into
a pocket of his cargo shorts. Then he'd slipped two
large…er…what she thought were called *magazines* full
of bullets into another pocket. Just…easy-peasy, as-you-
pleasey. No biggie. *Gulp*.

*I mean, come on. I knew they were Navy SEALs. But
the relevant word here is* were.

"When you see it," he said, straightening, "you sail
on over and get us. You got me?"

She nodded vigorously, unable to talk. Which might've
been a first.

He searched her eyes then, seeming to hesitate. In
those few seconds, she was able to locate her voice. "I
got you," she told him, her tone full of bravado she certainly didn't feel.

"But if you see another boat," he continued, his South Boston accent dropping the *r* sound off the end of the word *another*. "And I mean *any* boat headed your way, you start the engines and sail straight back to Wayfarer Island. On account of we don't know who's out here, and who's friend or foe. You don't take any chances—"

"But you and Bran—"

"No *buts*," he insisted, his eyes like flames. "You don't worry about us. We can handle ourselves."

She wanted to argue, unable to stand the thought of turning tail and running, leaving them all alone to face whatever fate waited for them on Garden Key. But arguing wasted precious time. Time when who knew what horrors were being perpetrated on that island. So she nodded and squared her shoulders. But inside she was saying, *This can't really be happening. This can't really be happening. This can't* really *be happening.*

When Mason chucked her on the chin with a scarred knuckle, she was forced to admit, *Okay, so it's really happening. Crap on a cracker!*

He pitched himself overboard. And she was left with nothing to do but watch him sink beneath the surface of the waves and contemplate the fact he'd *willingly* touched her for the very first time, and that their conversation had been the longest and most cordial of their acquaintance. Both struck her as unaccountably sad. Why did it take fully automatic weapons fire and a true life-and-death situation to make them stop taking digs at each other?

It was a question that filled her with a million conflicting emotions. On the one hand, Mason McCarthy was sullen and cantankerous and prone to growling at

her like a lion with a thorn stuck in his paw. On the
other hand, she couldn't ignore the appeal of his handsome face.

Oh, not handsome in the traditional sense. His forehead was too heavy, not to mention perpetually furrowed. His nose was too wide and listed slightly to the
left—evidence of a break he had never bothered to fix.
And his jaw? Well, his jaw was a mile wide. And if it
were any harder or more angular, it'd need to be carved
from granite.

But then there are his eyes. They were crystal blue.
Like the water around Wayfarer Island on a sunny,
windless day. *And his hair.* She sighed just thinking
about it. It was thick and shiny and inky black.

And that's before you get to his body. Whoa, momma,
what a body. He was so roped with muscle he could've
been a contender for the WWE. She could easily imagine him throwing an opponent against the ropes or choking out an adversary with his beefy forearm. In short,
Mason McCarthy cut a hard, forbidding figure. It was
like he'd been built for destruction.

Or something far more pleasurable.

See? Conflicting. That one word precisely described
their relationship.

Or in more expansive terms, her girl parts were super
interested in his boy parts. But every time he opened
his mouth—which, let's face it, wasn't very often; a
rock communicated more than he ever did—her brain
became very annoyed with him.

"Come on, Mason," she grumbled, lifting the binoculars he'd pressed into her hand. *Field glasses* he'd called
them. Through the magnified lenses, she could just

make out the back of the fort—Mason had instructed her to sail the boat nearly two miles out to sea. Now she scanned the redbrick expanse for movement. But there was nothing. Not a damn thing.

"Come *on*, Mason," she said again, grimacing at the hitch in her voice. When she felt something hot and wet slip down her cheek, she hastily brushed it away. Unfortunately, another drop replaced the first, and that's when she realized she was crying.

That's *also* when she realized just how much she'd come to care for the guys of Deep Six Salvage in the short time she'd been living and working with them. Not only were they men of rare courage and honor, but they were also incredibly…*good*.

That was the best way she knew to describe them. They were all *good* men—Mason's obvious aversion to her personality aside.

The truth was, they'd shown her more respect and consideration than she'd ever received from anyone. In grade school, she'd been teased unmercifully because she never played Red Rover on the playground, preferring instead to sit quietly under a tree and devour the stories in her history book. *And my Carrot Top hair, Casper the Ghost complexion, and Coke-bottle glasses didn't help, I'm sure.*

In high school, she was the butt of jokes because she was the latest of late bloomers. She didn't sprout breasts until she was nearly eighteen. *And it's not like they're anything to write home about even now.*

She thought she would find her tribe in college. But there weren't many girls—or *any*, really—who wanted to learn to read centuries' old scripts. And since she'd never gotten why keg stands were fun, she'd once again found herself the odd man…er…odd *woman* out.

Graduate school had proved to be a bit more accepting, filled with academic types who didn't begrudge her interests in antiquated documents and historical minutiae. But even so, her professors thought she was nuts to waste her time and the integrity of her doctoral dissertation trying to help a bunch of hairy, tattooed guys find a four-hundred-year-old fortune that had eluded treasure hunters for centuries. Her advisor had gone so far as to say, "If you were twice as smart, you'd still be an idiot for throwing in your lot with these men."

That hadn't stopped her from hopping on the first plane headed south. And she'd been surprised by how easy it'd been to convince the guys of Deep Six Salvage not only to let her stay, but to take her word for it when she said she thought they—and everyone who'd come before them—had been looking in the wrong place for the *Santa Cristina*. They hadn't called her crazy. They hadn't batted an eyelash at her youth or inexperience. Instead they'd sat down, listened to her arguments, and trusted her judgment.

And earlier, when they'd matched the hilt LT and Olivia found with Captain Bartolome Vargas's cutlass? Well, she'd crowed with victory not because she'd been proved *right*, but because she'd been beyond relieved that she hadn't steered these good men wrong. Even now, even scared out of her wits, a smile tilted her lips at the memory of LT swinging her around in a circle while Meat barked happily and L'il Bastard *cock-a-doodle-doo*-ed from his favorite spot on the porch railing outside the kitchen window.

It was strange, she realized, but at twenty-seven years old, and with a group of grizzled guys on a remote island, she finally, *finally* felt like she belonged. And it was *killing* her that she was twiddling her thumbs while two of those grizzled guys were risking their necks.

Grrr. Sitting tight, sitting *still* had never been something she excelled at.

Maybe I could just sail a little closer. If I don't use the engines, no one will hear me. Or…the Gulf Stream current blew by this side of the little island, right? And if she remembered correctly from the current map she'd taken a peek at two weeks ago, it should push her closer to Garden Key without her having to do more than pull anchor. By her recollection, the average speed of the current was four miles per hour. She was two miles away. So, in thirty minutes she could be setting foot on the island.

The idea was beyond tempting. But then what? It's not like she could help them do…whatever they were doing.

And speaking of…

"What *are* you guys doing?" she whispered, her fear morphing into impatience as the seconds ticked by. She liked the second emotion far better than the first. "And where the frick is that flare, Mason?"

Mason…

His name carried on the breeze. Hearing it filled her mind with a dozen familiar and conflicting emotions…

Chapter 6

7:25 p.m. ...

"DON'T YOU KEEP A FIRST AID KIT?" MADDY DEMANDED, rummaging through the drawers in the cramped little kitchenette with its green Formica countertops, opening whitewashed cupboards, and coming away empty-handed.

"Under the bed," Rick said.

Their first order of business after they barged into the little cottage was to get on the satellite phone and call in the cavalry. Or at least they'd *attempted* to make it their first order of business. They'd been thwarted, since the phone was smashed to bits, all its plastic parts and wires scattered in the corner like so much confetti. Same could be said for the marine radio.

"So *this* is happenin'," Maddy had whispered, staring in disbelief at the destruction and finally understanding why the guy with the Southern accent had stayed behind in the cottage for a while after the others had marched her, Rick, and the girls back to the beach.

Which left her the task of taking care of their *second* order of business: cleaning and dressing Bran's wound so they could all get back out there and rescue the girls.

The girls...

Donna, Louisa, Sally Mae...

Their names were on a loop inside Maddy's head.

And every second that ticked by increased her desperation tenfold. Not to mention her self-reproach…

If only she hadn't used the teens as an excuse to see Bran again, those three sweet girls would be home studying. But just like she'd been doing since she was old enough to climb onto the back of the sofa with a pillowcase tied around her neck cape-style, she'd leaped before she looked, plunging headlong into this let's-go-camping-on-the-Dry-Tortugas-in-celebration-of-your-scholarships scheme.

Although, in her own defense, even if she *had* looked first, there's no way she could have foreseen this… this…whatever the devil-lovin' hell this was.

"Where exactly?" she demanded again, down on her hands and knees beside Rick's twin bed with its wooden frame and red, white, and blue quilt. The only things she saw were sand and what, upon second glance, turned out to be a dusty stack of girlie magazines.

"Maddy, just grab that dish towel hanging on the refrigerator and the roll of duct tape on the table," Bran called to her from his spot by the little window on the side of the cottage.

He and Mason were keeping eyes on the entrance to the fort. Since it was the only way in and out of the structure, Maddy knew there was no way the masked men could spirit the girls onto their dinghy or their fishing boat without Bran and Mason seeing and stopping them. That should have had a calming effect on the boat-loads of adrenaline coursing through her veins.

It didn't.

She was wound tighter than a fiddle string.

Taking a quick glance at the dish towel in question,

she curled her lip. Like most young twentysomethings, Rick didn't appear to be too keen on laundry. The towel was stained with something brown and crusty.

"You!" She pushed up on her knees, pointing a finger at Bran and using one of the magazines to swat at the mosquito that landed on her thigh. "Zip it! I don't want to hear any of that tough-guy, don't-cry crap from you. And you!" She turned to point at Rick. "*Where* is the first aid kit? There's nothin' down here but a layer of sand and…" She held up the magazine so she could read the title in the low glow of the single bulb hanging from the center of the room. "Old copies of *Jugs*."

"Th-those aren't mine," Rick stuttered, his ears doing their Fourth of July thing again.

Any other time, she would have reveled in teasing him, just as she'd done when she was thirteen and caught her oldest brother with a *Playboy* centerfold tucked between his mattress and box springs. But right now all she cared about was seeing to Bran's leaking leg. "First. Aid. Kit." She enunciated each word with precision.

"F-far back corner by the footboard," Rick said.

She made a face that said, *Now, was that so hard?* before turning to scrounge under the bed again. "Aha!" she crowed when she found the red and white case just where Rick had said it would be.

When she spun around, it was to discover Bran's eyes zeroed in on her ass. She might have been embarrassed, or even insulted, but she was fully aware her rear end tended to draw scrutiny. Probably because it was, in the most genial of terms, *ample*. She hated it. Especially since she didn't have the boobs to match.

But what's a girl goin' to do?

Get the guy with the gun back on track, she assured herself as she scrambled to her feet and jogged to the little table in the center of the kitchenette.

"Bran, come sit down." She sprang the lid on the kit and found the bottle of peroxide inside. "And be quick about it." Each second the girls were alone out there with those masked men was one second too long.

"Wow. Anyone ever told you that you're incredibly bossy?" he asked.

"Don't act like you don't love it."

Silence reigned in the room for one second…two… three…

She made a face and glanced up at Bran. "Sorry," she said as he laid his machine gun and the machine gun he'd taken from the dead man on the table. They made metallic-sounding *clanks* against the cracked wooden top. "That's my standard comeback when my brothers accuse me of bein' overbearin'. So it just naturally slips out."

"It's okay." He shrugged, one corner of his mouth twitching. "I've never had a problem with a woman who knows what she wants and isn't afraid to ask for it."

Even as her heart stuttered, she narrowed her eyes. "Is that supposed to be a come-on?"

He lifted his hands and donned an innocent expression. "Wouldn't think of it."

"Hmm." She twisted her lips, not sure if she believed him. And quite honestly, part of her hoped he *was* coming on to her. She'd thought they were on the same page when it came to their burgeoning relationship. Then he hadn't answered her email and a million doubts had flooded in.

Twisting off the cap on the bottle of peroxide, she impatiently waited for Bran to take a seat. When he did, she breathed a sigh of relief. She didn't remember him being so *big*. And when he stood beside her, she was diminutive by comparison.

She didn't care for the sensation. Not when she needed to feel ten feet tall and capable of leaping buildings in a single bound. Or…at the very least capable of dealing with his wound without fainting dead away or puking all over him.

"This is probably goin' to burn like the fires of hell," she warned.

"Lemme have it."

She upended the bottle, pouring its contents over the gash that cut across the bottom half of his thigh. Had the bullet been lower, or higher, or an inch to the left, for that matter, they would have been in some serious— even more serious?—trouble. When the disinfectant hit the torn skin, it fizzed and bubbled. White foam turned pink as it mixed with his blood, and big blobs of the stuff dropped onto the unpolished wood floor.

Bran didn't utter a word. He simply sat there all Bran-like. His face showing not a flicker of pain. His lips never grimacing. A hiss never forming in his mouth.

That's okay. Maddy did all those things for him.

"I'm starting to wonder which of us is wounded," he said, tongue in cheek.

"Oh, piss on a log." She harrumphed, digging back into the first aid kit for more supplies. "I, uh…I think you're goin' to need stitches," she said when she pulled out the package of butterfly bandages. "These won't do the trick."

Bran looked down at the open gash, assessing it with a critical eye. "We could just wrap some gauze around it," he said.

Maddy made a face. "I may've been born at night, but it wasn't *last* night."

"I'm fine," he assured her.

Why do guys always do that? She'd had far too much experience with that whole keep-a-stiff-upper-lip nonsense from the men in her family to fall for Bran's baloney.

"So, you're tellin' me if we were sittin' in an emergency room somewhere, the doctor would just wrap some gauze around this thing"—she motioned to his thigh—"and send you on your merry way?"

"Well, no," he admitted. "But—"

"No buts." She searched through the kit for the suturing needle and thread. When she found them, she turned to Rick. "I'm assumin' you've had first aid trainin'." She held the wicked-looking curved needle aloft. "Mind doin' the honors?"

Rick squared his shoulders and pushed away from the counter in the little kitchenette to take the needle from her. The instant they were side by side, she could see the look on Rick's face again. That adoring puppy-dog look.

"I'm sorry about the girls," he whispered just for her ears. "I should've done more to…" He let the sentence dangle, shaking his head sorrowfully.

"You did everything exactly right," she murmured, squeezing his bicep and thanking her lucky stars that he was proving to have a level head on his shoulders, despite his age. "And when this is all over, I'm buyin' you a drink. A big one. With multiple shots of tequila and an umbrella."

His adoring puppy-dog look became decidedly less innocent as he searched her eyes. She shook her head and offered him a smile. One she hoped conveyed, *You're barkin' up the wrong tree, sweet pea. I'm currently a little hung up on the guy bleedin' all over your floor.*

And on that topic, when she glanced at Bran, it was to find his eyes narrowed, a considering expression wallpapered across his face. And…something more. Something that was hot and dark. Something she couldn't *quite* put her finger on. But just when she thought she might have figured it out, it was gone. And he was back to being cool, calm, and collected.

Classic Bran.

She was the *opposite* of cool, calm, and collected as she watched Rick kneel and place the needle near Bran's torn flesh. Her insides were mush, and acid burned the back of her throat. Since her patience was located near a spot you might call Rock Bottom, when Rick hesitated, she said, "What's the problem? Do you need—"

"I-I'm sorry." He shook his head. "I don't think I c-can do this."

He was absolutely *green*. And swaying like a willow in the wind. She hadn't had a lot of experience, but she'd say he was about…oh…ten seconds from lights-out.

Oh, for heaven's sake!

"Stop lookin' at the wound," she instructed him sternly. "Look at me and breathe."

When Rick glanced up at her, the look of self-reproach on his face had her taking pity on him. Poor guy hadn't asked for any of this. Point of fact, neither had *she*, but since she'd been through something similar before—and really, she *must* have a talk with Fate, Destiny, and/or the Big, Bearded Cheese—she was better prepared to deal with the situation.

"*I'll* do it." Bran grabbed the needle and thread from Rick.

The thought of him suturing his own flesh had Maddy blanching. "Are you kiddin' me?"

He flashed her the kind of focused, determined look you rarely saw. And when you did, it was usually on the face of a man who didn't back down no matter what. *He's* not *kiddin'*.

"Well, *someone* needs to fuckin' do it and get it the fuck over with," Mason said. "On account of we got three girls who need rescuing. Not to mention, Alex is still out there all by herself."

"You brought Alex with you?" Maddy asked.

Bran had told her about the indomitable young historian, and she was intrigued by the woman. Of course, right now she could do with *fewer* people being in mortal danger.

"She's anchored way out behind the fort," Bran told her, "waiting on our signal to sail closer." It occurred to Maddy that she hadn't considered how Bran and Mason had arrived on the island. Like the heroes they were, perhaps she'd assumed they flew in with the help of their superpowers. Then all thoughts zipped right out of her head when she saw Bran squeeze the two halves of his wound together. "Now," he said, "gimme a second while I—"

"Oh, for the love of…" She motioned for Rick to stand up and trade spots. "You can't stitch yourself."

Rick brushed by her, murmuring something to himself that sounded like recrimination.

"*Two* umbrellas," she smiled at him, giving his arm another friendly squeeze.

Before she could see if that look was back on his face, she dropped to her knees beside Bran's chair and snatched the needle and synthetic suturing thread from him. Their fingers brushed, just for an instant, but she jumped like a live current zapped her.

It'd been like this from the beginning. Or at least it'd been like this for *her*. When she looked up to gauge Bran's response, his face was a mask of ridiculous calmness. Which annoyed her for two reasons. The first was that it made all those doubts she'd been having swell to mammoth proportions. The second was that she judged the expression to be completely misplaced. You know, considering she was seconds away from going at him with a hooked needle, and that she had suddenly morphed into Lady Shimmy McShakyFingers.

"You ever done this before?" He cocked his head. Now was not the time to notice how his dark, wavy hair curled over the tops of his ears.

"Stitched a guy up?" She nodded and smiled. Then she shook her head. "Nope. But my grandma taught me how to sew on a button. Does that count?"

She'd meant it as a joke, but he just crossed his ridiculously muscled arms over his ridiculously wide chest and presented her with his oozing thigh like he had all the faith in the world in her.

Before she allowed herself to contemplate what she was doing—and who she was doing it *to*—she pushed the needle through the skin on one side of the wound.

She gulped and briefly squeezed her eyes shut when she had to muscle it through. Bran's tan flesh was thick and tough.

"See," he said, his deep voice absurdly steady, making a mockery of her trembling fingers. "That wasn't so bad, was it?"

She squinted up at him. "Shouldn't I be asking *you* that?"

"I'm fine," he assured her. *Again.*

"You keep sayin' that and I'll stop believin' you. Methinks he doth protest too much and whatnot." She wiped the back of one hand over her forehead. It came away damp with sweat and a smear of Bran's blood.

"Anyone ever tell you when you wear that particular expression, your nose and face all scrunched up, you look like a raisin with eyes?"

She blinked at him, mouth open. "Do you really think it's wise to insult a woman who's holdin' a needle this far away"—she held her fingers an inch apart—"from your Grand Master of Ceremonies?"

His white teeth glowed against the dark whiskers on his cheeks and chin when he flashed a smile. Bran seemed to sport a perpetual five-o'clock shadow. And his twinkling dark eyes, swarthy complexion, and shaggy hair made her realize once again how much he resembled a pirate of old. All he needed was a gold hoop earring and parrot.

He lifted a brow. "That's a good one. Maybe we should invite her over the next time we have our Who Can Come Up with the Best Euphemisms Contest. What'd'ya say, Mason?"

Bran had a way of making contractions out of multiple

words at once. Maddy figured it was because he was an East Coaster and they did everything fast, including talking. Not that she didn't have her own linguistic idiosyncrasies. She did a pretty mean *fixin' to* and *y'all*. Not to mention she usually dropped the *g*'s off the end of her words, but that was mostly because the *g* sound wasn't soft on the ear. And as anyone from Texas would tell you, the rounder and longer and softer words were, the better they sounded.

"And when I said you looked like a raisin with eyes," Bran continued, turning back to her, "I meant you looked like a really adorable raisin with really beautiful, gray, sea-after-a-storm eyes."

Maddy gaped at him. Now there was no denying it. He *was* coming on to her. Right? *Right?* Despite the direness of their situation, her inner Maddy let loose with an enthusiastic happy dance complete with hip shakes, finger guns, and maybe a few leaping heel clicks.

But before she could come back with some clever reply à la Joey Tribbiani—*How YOU doin'?*—Bran cupped her chin in his hand.

Whoa, Nelly.

Gone was the smile. Gone was the twinkling light in his eyes. Now his expression was serious as death. Just *flip!* As if he had some sort of internal switch that could change him from Teasing Bran to Terrifying Bran.

"Hey." His palm was warm and dry against her clammy skin, his calluses a gentle abrasion. "You're doing great. Just keep stitching and talking, and it'll be over before you know it."

Aha! Now she got his game. He wasn't coming on to

her so much as trying to distract her from the gruesomeness of her task. *Darnit.*

"I think I can accomplish the first," she admitted, swallowing the bile that climbed up the back of her throat when she pushed the two halves of his wound together before threading the needle and string through the flesh on the opposite side. "But the second might be askin' too much."

The new-penny smell of blood hung thick in the humid air. She ignored it, breathing out of her mouth as she tied off the first stitch. She tilted her chin, admiring her handiwork.

Not too shabby, even if I do say so myself. Grandma Bettie would be so proud.

"So, you sew," he said. "I'll talk."

"Deal," she agreed, going to work on the next suture. If she didn't think about what she was doing, she could pretend she was just stitching together two pieces of really tough, really leaky fabric.

"I'm sorry I didn't respond to your email," he said. Just like that.

She thought about herding him toward the end of the conversation the way a cattle dog herds a cow toward an open gate, with a bark and a few nips at his heels. But then she thought, *Why the hell not?* If he was willing to air their private business in front of two audience members, by God, so was she.

After she finished the third stitch, she lifted her eyes to his face. "I was wondering about that. And a little... *hurt*, I guess."

Chapter 7

7:29 p.m. ...

HURT.

The word rolled over Bran's heart like an Abrams tank, smashing the organ beneath its steel tracks.

"Maddy..." He whispered her name. "I..." He stopped himself from saying, *I woulda answered if the satellite dish hadn't blown down.* Because he wasn't sure that was the truth. And he was many things. But a liar wasn't one of them.

The muscles in the back of his neck tensed, and he ran his hand over them before blurting, "The truth is, I didn't decide to come 'til the last minute."

"*Why?*" She blinked up at him, her stormy eyes searching his face.

He didn't say anything, simply raised a brow and waited. Maddy was a smart cookie, so it didn't take her long to figure it out. He saw the moment shock and realization struck.

"Oh." She shook her head, frowning. "Sorry... I thought maybe we were... Because there was that thing on my father's yacht. And then the last three months we've... But...never mind. Doesn't matter. My bad."

Bran didn't know which he regretted more. Seeing that look on her face, or the burning mothersucker of a gash across his thigh.

On second thought, I do *know.* It was definitely her expression. His thigh would heal with time. But he'd never forget that he'd hurt Maddy. Hurt her, mislead her, and…embarrassed her in front of Mason and the park ranger.

"Maddy." He cupped her chin in his hand again. Partly to make her meet his eyes, and partly because he couldn't stop himself from touching her. Her skin was so soft and warm.

"Sure, I get it." She jerked her chin from his hand.

"Well, I sure as shit don't," said the park ranger whose embroidered name read "Rick." *Seriously? Ranger Rick?* He was once again in front of the kitchenette's counter. But he wasn't leaning against the Formica countertop. He was pacing back and forth. Back and forth. "I don't get anything about this." There was a slightly hysterical edge to his voice. "Who are those men? What are they doing here? And who in God's name are *you* guys?"

Bran stared down at the golden crown of Maddy's head glinting brightly in the dim light. His fingers itched to run through the strands of her short, silky hair. Then his fingers weren't itching to do anything but curl into fists. She no longer hesitated on his stitches, instead going after them like a dollar-a-day factory seamstress. He had to bite the inside of his cheek to keep from sucking in a harsh breath when the needle punctured fresh flesh.

He thought about asking her to take it easy, but she *had* made that comment about his Grand Master of Ceremonies—which he'd like to keep fully intact and sporting just the one hole. So he decided to keep his mouth shut and endure. And besides, he probably deserved it after the way he'd bungled things between them.

"I can't answer the first question," he told Ranger Rick, his eyes nearly crossing when Maddy hit a particularly tender spot. Sweat broke out across his brow and the back of his neck. "But if I had to guess, I'd say the answer to the second question is ransom. Maddy's family is beyond rich—we're talking Daddy Warbucks—and whoever these assholes are, they probably thought it'd be easy to snatch her from a remote island in the middle of the Gulf."

"There *was* an article that ran in the *Houston Chronicle* about me and the scholarship girls and this trip," Maddy said consideringly. "Anyone with an eye toward kidnapping could've seen it. I should've thought about that. I should've—"

"This isn't your fault," Bran assured her before turning back to Rick. "As for who *we* are…" He wagged a finger between himself and Mason. *Ow! Shit!*

He jumped. He couldn't help it. And instead of looking contrite, Maddy scowled at him.

"What did I tell you about that tough-guy, don't-cry crap?" she demanded. "Am I hurtin' you?"

"I'm f—"

She narrowed her eyes, daring him to say *I'm fine* one more time.

He cleared his throat and motioned with a hand toward his half-stitched wound. "Please continue."

She hesitated, turning her head to view him from the corner of her eye as if that might help her see through his bullshit. She must've been satisfied with what she saw—confirming he could have had a job on the stage—because after a second, she bent back to her work.

He blew out a covert breath and curled one hand around the edge of his chair, gripping the wood so hard he was surprised he didn't splinter it. "We're your neighbors," he told Ranger Rick through his clenched jaw.

"Huh?" Rick's youthful face scrunched up.

"We live on Wayfarer Island."

"Ah, the six retired Navy SEALs who are looking for the lost treasure of the *Santa Cristina*."

Bran lifted a brow.

"News travels fast in the Keys," Rick clarified.

Ain't that the truth?

Every time Bran made a supply run to Key West, some new stranger walked up to him and asked how the hunt was going. The Florida Keys were unique in that a person could disappear in them, just fall off the edge of the map as long as they kept a low profile. But keeping a low profile was damn near impossible when searching for a legendary treasure.

"But I don't understand," Ranger Rick said. He'd moved over to take Bran's position by the front window, but he wasn't watching the fort. He was eyeing Bran. "Why are you *here?* With machine guns? Killing people?" The young ranger had turned a milky shade of white at that last question. "I-I mean, that man out there…" Rick swallowed, and the sound his throat made was strangely loud inside the tight confines of the cottage despite the low rumble of the generator outside that supplied juice to the few electronics. "He *is* dead, right?"

"Graveyard dead," Bran admitted without a hint of remorse.

"Oh, forgive us," Rick murmured, crossing himself.

"Forgiveness is between him and God," Bran insisted. "It was my job to arrange the meeting."

"*Man on Fire*," Maddy blurted.

Despite everything, Bran felt himself smiling. *This* was their thing. Intoxicating physical chemistry, hurt feelings, and misunderstandings aside, they shared a mad love for the cinema.

"Huh?" Rick blinked, his face doing that scrunchy thing again.

"They're here because I invited them," Maddy said, forgoing an explanation for their brief tangent.

The blood loss was making Bran a little light-headed. And when he dragged in a steadying breath, Maddy's sweet scent—that intoxicating aroma of fruit and berries he remembered so well—invaded his nostrils, making him grip the seat for a whole new reason.

Why did he have such a reaction to her? And how was he supposed to continue to fight it?

By remembering what the alternative is.

Annnnndddddd…there was that.

"I was hopin' they'd stop by tonight and regale the girls with stories of the *Santa Cristina*," Maddy added.

Mention of the teenagers had her swallowing what Bran knew was a lump in her throat. But that's all she allowed. Just that tiny indication she wasn't as fine as she seemed.

"As for the machine guns…" she continued, only to trail off and bite her bottom lip when a particular stitch caused her trouble. She finally managed to tie off the thread—much to Bran's relief—and finished with, "You got me." She turned inquisitive eyes up to him. "Why *do* you guys run around Rambo-style all the time?"

"Old habits are hard to break," he allowed.

That seemed to be explanation enough because she nodded and turned back to finish the last two stitches.

"We were about two miles out when we heard the gunshots," Bran told Rick. "And we decided we better drop anchor, swim over, and investigate."

"So if you don't mind me asking," Rick said, "how is it that two Navy SEALs living on a remote island happen to know an oil heiress from Houston?"

The young park ranger's expression was a little... Was that jealousy Bran was seeing? Narrowing his eyes, he decided, *Yeah. It's jealousy.*

Which was sort of funny. Ranger Rick had probably only been legal for a couple of years. And to think Maddy would have any interest in a wet-behind-the-ears—

Although there *had* been the sweet smile she'd given the guy while they'd shared that whispered exchange a couple minutes ago. Not to mention the familiar way she'd squeezed his arm. And chicks were suckers for dimples, weren't they? Ranger Rick had the kind of dimples that could hold an ounce of liquid when he smiled. *The bastard.*

So maybe Maddy *was* interested in the young stud and—

Red edged into Bran's vision at the idea of Maddy in the ranger's arms. He could picture Rick kissing the soft skin on Maddy's throat. Imagine Maddy wrapping her arms around Rick's shoulders and arching into his caresses. And suddenly, the monster inside Bran roared to life, bringing with it a memory that snarled and snapped, nipping at the heels of his mind...

"Bran, baby," his mother whispered as she shoved him into the coat closet. "Be quiet, okay? And no matter what you hear, you don't come out." Her big, dark eyes were frantic, the soft skin around them showing fading bruises.

"Yes, Momma." He nodded, his lower lip quivering.

"You fuckin' bitch!" His father's voice boomed from the front of the house. "I saw the way you were looking at him!"

Bran burrowed back against the wall when his mother closed him in just as she had countless times before. Just as she surely would countless times to come. Darkness filled the closet. Only a thin sliver of light showed around the edges of the door, and the smell of old wool drifted down from the coats overhead to mix with the faint aroma of pee that lingered from the last time he was in here.

He'd tried to hold it. He'd pinched himself until he was bruised, bit his lip until he tasted blood, but eventually he hadn't been able to stand it. It had hurt so bad. And he'd had an accident all over the wood floor.

He would not have an accident this time. He would not make Momma clean him up when all he wanted her to do was lie on the sofa and watch Little House on the Prairie. *She smiled when she watched* Little House on the Prairie. *He figured it was because Pa Ingalls was always so nice. Pa Ingalls never screamed and hit. Pa Ingalls never pushed or shoved or called anyone bad names.*

When Bran grew up, he was going to be just like Pa. Not like Daddy. Never like Daddy…

"Donny." Momma's voice was soft and low. "Calm down, my love. Tell me what's wrong."

"What's wrong? What's *wrong*?" Daddy thundered, and Bran closed his eyes when Momma cried out at something Daddy did to her. "I saw the look you gave the mailman!"

"Donny, I swear I didn't—"

A sickening sound, a familiar sound, like the one Bran's basketball made when he tossed it against the side of the house, blasted through the door of the closet, followed closely by Momma's cries.

Bran curled into a ball on the floor. His legs to his chest. A terrible ache clutched at his belly until he thought he might throw up the macaroni and cheese Momma had made him for lunch. He covered his ears and willed himself not to be sick.

"Donny, please!" Momma begged. "I swear I didn't do anything! I love you! Only you!"

"You don't want the mailman?" Daddy demanded.

"Of course not, Donny! I don't know what you think you saw, but I promise you it was nothing. You're the only man for me."

For a long time everything was quiet. Bran could hear each of his breaths. They sounded funny. Like when he ran really fast for a really long time.

Then Daddy said, "Oh, Loraine!" And his voice was no longer raised. Instead it was kind of muffled like he'd taken a big bite of a peanut butter and jelly sandwich. "I didn't hurt you, did I? I didn't mean to hurt you. When I see you with another man, it just makes me so—"

"I know, Donny." Momma was using her feel-better voice. The same one Bran heard when he fell down and scraped his knee. "I know you didn't mean it."

Bran could hear the sound of kissing coming through the door. That meant Daddy was done. He wouldn't hit Momma anymore.

"You won't open the door to that man ever again," Daddy said between kisses. "You hear me, Loraine? You let him drop the letters in the box."

"Of course, Donny," Momma said.

For a long time, no sound breached the quiet except for the smack of kisses, the rustle of clothes, and Bran's catching breaths. Then Momma gasped, "Donny, we can't."

"Why not?" Daddy asked. "You got your period or something?"

"No." Momma's voice was halting, careful. "R-remember you told me I could take Bran to see a rerun of Bambi *at that theater in the South Ward?"*

"That's tonight?"

"Yes, that's tonight. You could come with us, Donny," Momma said, and Bran shook his head even though no one could see him.

"To a ridiculous cartoon about a bunch of silly animals? I'm a full-grown man, Loraine. I ain't got time for that kiddie shit." Bran blew out a relieved breath, wrinkling his nose because it smelled bad, like sour milk.

"But it's Bran's birthday and—"

"And I'll start celebrating with him when he's old enough to drink a beer and tell a good joke," Daddy said. "You go, Loraine." Then the sound of his work boots on the floor carried toward the front of the house.

"I'll head down to the pub and raise a toast to Bran's birthday with the boys."

Only after the front door slammed did Bran dare push up to his knees. And then the closet was opening and there was Momma, bending down to him. Her face wasn't bleeding this time, but a ring of purple bruises was forming on one side of her jaw.

"You ready to go watch Bambi, *birthday boy?"* she asked, smiling. But it wasn't her Little House on the Prairie smile. It was her fake smile.

"Can't we stay in?" That sick feeling in his stomach was swirling around and around.

"But you're turning five today," Momma said, her dark eyebrows pulled down. *"We can't stay in on your fifth birthday. We have to celebrate!"*

Bran wasn't sure what the word celebrate meant. But he was sure he wasn't going to like it. Still, if Momma wanted to go…

"Okay, Momma." He took her hand and let her lead him from the closet. *"But first I needa go potty."*

"Can you do it yourself or do you need me to help you?"

"I'm a big boy now," he told her, puffing out his chest. *"I can do it myself."*

"Okay," Momma said, playfully swatting his bottom when he turned toward the bathroom.

Closing the door behind him, Bran walked over to the toilet and lifted the lid. It smelled strongly of the cleaning stuff Momma used. She was always scrubbing. Daddy liked a clean house.

Bran waited a little while, long enough to fool his mother into thinking he was peeing, before he flushed.

The moment the toilet made its loud whooshing *noise, he bent over and threw up every last bite of his macaroni and cheese…*

"It's a long and sordid tale," Maddy said, dragging Bran back to the present.

"Sorry." He shook his head, trying to jostle away the sense of impotent rage that always came with memories of his miserable childhood. "What's a long and sordid tale?"

"How we know each other," she said, digging back into the medical kit to pull out a rolled length of Ace bandage. While he'd been sucked down Memory Lane, Maddy had finished stitching him up.

His chin jerked back, his brows drawing together. "It's not *sordid*," he insisted.

"Well, then it's just a *long* tale. One we don't have time for." When she bent down to grab the loose end of the bandage she'd wrapped around his leg, her warm breath fanned the inside of his thigh. She might as well have wrapped her amazing mouth around the head of his dick the way his shaft pulsed with delight.

He must've jumped or sucked in a sharp breath or something, because she looked up at him sharply. "Now how in hellfire did *that* hurt? I didn't even *do* anything."

"Uh…sorry," he told her, disgusted to hear his voice was little more than a gravelly croak. "Just a…a…phantom pain, I guess."

She curled her lip before finishing her work, using the little metal cleats that came with the Ace bandage to secure the loose end. Then she sat back on her heels, cocking her head.

"I think it should hold," she declared, her expression tinged with satisfaction.

He pushed to a stand—happy his loose cargo shorts disguised the semi he had going—and tested the strength of his leg as well as the integrity of the dressing. Both held up surprisingly well.

One more mark in the Maddy Powers plus column.

Like she needed one. By his calculations, when it came to Maddy, every mark landed in the plus column. "It's good," he told her. "Thank you." Then, without thinking, he reached to hoist her up.

The minute they were palm-to-palm, a flash of awareness blazed through him and he nearly lost his balance. He hoped to cover his stumble by making a grab for his weapon.

He must not have been all that successful at hiding what he was feeling—contradicting his earlier thought that he could have a job on the stage—because Rick narrowed his eyes and blurted, "So, are you two, like, an item or what?"

Bran's spine did its best impression of a ramrod.

"No. We aren't an item. We're just…"

What are we exactly? Not mere acquaintances. Those hundreds of emails and those few heart-to-heart phone conversations had pushed them far beyond such an insipid term. *Friends, maybe?* But that implied a strictly platonic relationship. And even though there was only that one kiss between them—that one *amazing* kiss— every time they touched it was obvious they were more than just *friends*.

So, what? How to define them?

"We're…um…pen pals," he finished. And the minute

the words were out of his mouth, he wanted to call them back.

And the trophy for Asshat of the Year goes to… Bran Pallidino! Otherwise known as King Dipshit from Dipshit Island!

Mason made a strangled noise like he'd accidentally swallowed his tongue. Maddy just narrowed her eyes at him. And Rick nodded enthusiastically and said, "Oh, that's good." The underlying *because I'm hot to trot and looking to fill that slot* was so obvious the guy might as well have said the words aloud.

"Oh yeah?" *Is that my voice that sounds more like the growl of a grizzly bear?* "Why is that good?"

Rick's Adam's apple bobbed in his throat. "Uh…" He glanced sheepishly at Maddy. "I just meant that…" He trailed off when something outside suddenly snagged his attention.

"What is it?" Bran demanded, marching over to nudge Rick aside so he could see. He assured himself he didn't use more force than was necessary, but the wide-eyed look on the ranger's face called him a big fat liar.

"I…" Rick swallowed again, backing away from Bran as he hitched his chin toward the window. But he didn't say anything more. Too scared Bran might point the business end of his M4 at his head, maybe? And why wouldn't Rick be scared, given the way Bran was acting?

Shiiiiittt!

And *this* was why Bran insisted his relationship with Maddy remain exactly as it was. She provoked the part of him he was most ashamed of.

"One of the girls just crossed the bridge and is headed our way," Mason said, his big shoulders tense as he angled his rifle through the open front door and scanned the face of the fort for additional movement.

"One of the girls?" Maddy's voice broke, the sound of the fear she'd been holding at bay bubbling up through the crack.

Bran could feel her come up beside him. She spotted the blond girl with the ponytail hustling over a little dune at the same time he did.

"It's Sally Mae!" she cried, throwing an arm around his waist and hugging him tight. "Oh, thank heavens she's okay!"

Her relief, her excitement was catching. So even though he knew better, he hugged her back. Just as he'd suspected, the instant he had her in his arms, he didn't want to let her go.

Chapter 8

"Oh, come on!" Maddy huffed. "It's not like I asked you to skin your neighbor's cat. So you can stop with the googly eyes. I just asked to come with y'all to rescue Donna and Louisa."

"No." Bran shook his head while sliding out the magazine on his machine gun to check how many bullets he had left. Or at least that's what Maddy assumed he was doing since that's the reason the movies always gave for that particular move.

Sally Mae had managed to escape her captor's clutches when he was dragging her across the grassy parade grounds inside the fort. The way Sally Mae told it, a bit of cat and mouse had ensued with him chasing her, and her hiding in various places before she was eventually able to make it to the entrance. Her pursuer had stopped there, not daring to follow her further. And after seeing the light on in the ranger's station, Sally Mae had headed straight for it. Now she was sitting on Rick's bed, drinking the bottle of water Maddy had pressed into her hand and watching them with wide, red-rimmed eyes. But she was especially watching Bran, who was being obstinate and tyrannical and...and...*male*.

Truly, Maddy was tempted to smack the handsome right off his face. Of course, if she was being totally honest with herself, some of her temper might have a smidge to do with that whole "pen pals" comment.

I mean, pen pals? Really?

If he believed that, he was crazier than a catfish carrying a canteen, as her grandma used to say.

"Those girls out there don't know you from Adam." She pointed to the front door. When he simply lifted a brow, she curled her finger into a fist. "What if they don't understand that you've come to save them?" she continued, infusing her voice with determination. "And what if that causes them to do somethin' silly? Like, not obey your orders? Or run off the first chance they get? Or… or…" She searched her brain frantically, but it'd run out of examples. "Or somethin' else equally foolish?" she finished with far less *oomph* than she would have liked.

"That's a lotta hypotheticals," he said.

Her jaw clenched. It would be so easy. Just *pow!* And there would go the handsome. In her fantasies, at least. In real life, he'd probably look even *more* tough and delectable with a fat lip. *Ugh.*

He slammed the magazine back into his weapon. The move made his biceps bunch, drawing Maddy's attention to the tattoo inked onto the skin on the inside of his forearm. *For RL* the scrolling black letters read. And she knew it was both a testament and a promise to a fallen teammate. Rusty Lawrence's horrific and untimely death was the reason Bran and the others had retired early from the Navy. And their pledge to Rusty to live life to its fullest was the reason they were all now determined to find the lost treasure of the *Santa Cristina*.

And see! That's not the kind of stuff people who are mere pen pals share with each other!

As soon as she had the thought, she brushed it away. *Stay on target. Stay on target.* Right. When all else fails, fall back on Star Wars references.

"Bran…" She took a step toward him. Up close, she was struck again by just how powerful he was. Big enough to hunt a bear with a switch. *Another of Grandma Bettie's favorites.* A smarter gal would've taken one look at his scowl and backed down. But Maddy had been dealing with overgrown buttheads her whole life. "I know the ins and outs of Fort Jefferson. I have a mental blueprint"—she tapped her temple—"right up here."

"And how's that?" Bran asked, but she could tell he wasn't really interested. He was just humoring her while he planted his foot on the kitchen chair and checked the knife strapped to his calf.

"I studied up," she said. "I was plannin' to give the girls an in-depth tour and history lesson tomorrow."

And there you go! This trip wasn't totally about me bein' selfish and wantin' to get within spittin' distance of you. I was goin' to make it educational too.

Her conscience immediately answered with a snidely worded, *Whatever you have to tell yourself to sleep at night, sister.*

Sometimes her conscience really needed her smarty-pants ass kicked.

"No," Bran said again. Just that single syllable spoken with the utmost authority.

Maddy wanted to shove her hands on her hips and scream, *Well, who the hell died and made you King Shit?* But she'd learned long ago that another old saying was true: It was easier to catch a fly with honey than vinegar.

She batted her lashes and pasted on a false smile. "So you're tellin' me you already know you need to be careful around the northeast side of the fort's parade grounds?"

A muscle ticked in his jaw. She could see him struggling. Finally, he gritted, "No. Why there?"

"Because there's a weird openin' in an old magazine house that the bad guys could easily pop out of." She tried not to sound smug. She wasn't sure she managed it. And given that was the case, she reckoned, *Oh, what the hell. Might as well press my luck.* "And do you know the placement of all the old gun rooms?"

He shook his head and shrugged. "But this won't be the first time we've had to go into a situation blind." He turned to Mason. "You ready?"

"What's the plan when we find them?" Mason asked.

"Well, we already tried the carrot. So let's give 'em the stick, what'd'ya say?"

Mason nodded. "My thoughts exactly."

Bran turned to Rick, leveling on the young ranger a hard look, one he'd probably perfected in places and in situations he'd just as soon forget. "Now, like I told you, if anyone but me, Mason, or those girls comes through this door, you don't hesitate. You shoulder that rifle and let 'em have it." He tilted his head toward the machine gun he had taken from the bad guy. Bran had quickly gone over how to operate the weapon with Rick, all the while handling the rifle as easily and familiarly as if it were his own.

"I'll hold down the fort," Rick said, weapon in hand, his handsome face contorting. "No pun intended."

When Bran and Mason turned for the door, Maddy's

frustration turned to desperation. She clutched Bran's forearm. The heat coming off his skin was nearly enough to burn her.

"Please let me come," she pleaded. She couldn't stand the thought of staying safe inside the ranger's station while Bran and Mason were out risking their hides. Besides, she truly believed she could be an asset. And if Bran would just take a moment to consider—

"No," he said, going for a world record or something.

"Ugh!" She threw her hands in the air. "No? *No? That's your favorite word, isn't it?"

"It's a classic," he told her calmly, succeeding in making her more irate. "So much simpler than, say, *ain't gonna happen* or *not a chance in hell*."

Mason made a move toward the two of them, and Maddy's irk boiled over. "You"—she swung on the big man—"shut up. I'm warnin' you."

Mason held his hands in the air. "I didn't say anything."

"Doesn't matter. I heard you thinkin' from three feet away."

"That a fact?" Mason lifted one black eyebrow, his startlingly blue eyes sparkling in the light from the bulb.

"Yes, that's a fact."

"Then you must've heard me thinking you're absolutely right."

Maddy was nodding before he finished. "That's right. And I could really do without you—" She stopped so suddenly she was surprised her vocal cords didn't leave skid marks on her throat. "I'm sorry." She did a double take. "Did you just say you think I'm right?"

"Let Miss Maddy go with y'all," Sally Mae piped

up. "If it was me out there with those men"—her voice hitched, but her chin was held high—"I wouldn't be fixin' to trust anyone but her to come and get me."

Maddy sent her a grateful smile before turning back to Bran. She didn't have to say *Well, what do you have to say to that?* She made sure her eyebrows did the talking for her.

With a curse, Bran turned to Mason. "You really think this is a good idea?"

Mason shrugged. "None of this is good." The man had a way of making the obvious sound strangely discerning. "But I think it'll be *better* with someone who knows the grounds. Besides, if those guys are still hoping to hold her for ransom, they're not likely to take any potshots in her direction."

"Good. Yes." Maddy nodded. "I hadn't thought of that. I can totally be your shield. She fisted her hands on her hips and turned to Bran. "Looks like you're outvoted."

A muscle was twitching beside his lips. "This isn't a democracy."

"Oh, come on!" She'd tried the honey. It hadn't worked. So bring on the vinegar. "Don't be such a pigheaded…uh…pig." *Great. Brilliant, Maddy.* "Unless you can come up with two reasons why I shouldn't come along, I'm comin'. No matter what you say."

"You don't know how to fight." He lifted a finger. "You don't have a weapon." Up went a second finger.

"Name *ten* reasons," she challenged, pretty sure steam was pouring from her nose.

"Fine," he agreed after a long, tense standoff where they waged a bloody battle with only their eyes. "You can come." Maddy beat back the urge to holler

Victory is mine! "But you do exactly as I say when I say it."

"Roger that." She realized she'd mimicked his standard comeback when he narrowed his eyes. "Um…what I meant was ten-four." She had to curl her fingers around the hems of her shorts to keep from saluting.

"Christ, this is gonna come back to bite me on the ass," he muttered before turning to Mason. "You want me to lead the way?"

"Now where's the fun in that?" Mason said, and Maddy knew from the emails she'd exchanged with Bran that the phrase was their old SEAL Team motto.

"Then be my guest." Bran motioned toward the door before turning back to Maddy. "You stick to my six like a bad rash, you hear me?"

"You got it." She threaded her fingers through his belt loop when he followed Mason out the door. With a "six" as fine as Bran's, sticking to it wasn't a hardship.

~~~

7:41 p.m.…

"Well, here's another fine mess we've gotten ourselves into," Bran whispered to Mason, trying to forget that Maddy's little fingers were still twisted around his belt loop. Her knuckles had brushed against his lower back with each step they'd taken to their current position, which was hiding behind a bramble bush a few yards from the spot where the body of that teeth-sucking shit-for-brains lay cooling on the sand.

The imposing redbrick walls of Fort Jefferson filled their vision. Ninety percent of Bran was already second-guessing bringing Maddy along. It was the ninety percent that, in the cold light of the moon, considered her a liability, not to mention a goddamned distraction. As for the remaining ten percent? Well, *that* part of him growled with feral approval every time she as much as breathed. So just for the record, that ten percent part of him was a complete and utter imbecile.

"This sucks," Mason muttered, scanning the bridge over the seawater moat.

"Roger that." The heat of the night pressed down on Bran's shoulders like a pair of strong hands, making him feel like he was carrying more of a load than just his weapon. He gritted his teeth when Maddy pushed up on tiptoe behind him to see over his shoulder. Her warm breath fanned his ear and raised the hairs along the back of his neck. He swatted at his ear and turned to scowl at her.

"I can't see," she whispered. "You're blockin' my view."

And because he didn't want her to know how shaken he was by her nearness, by her touch, he decided to play it cool. Play it smart. Give her exactly what she'd come to expect from him. "Babe"—he turned and flashed her an exaggerated wink—"I *am* the view."

Even in the low glow of the spotlights on the seawall and the occasional flash of the lighthouse, he could see her roll her eyes and fight a grin. "And *there's* the Bran I've come to know and love. Hi there. I've been missin' you tonight."

Hearing the word *love* on her lips in reference to him had him swallowing hard and searching frantically for some pithy reply. He couldn't come up with one, so he went with the decidedly *un*pithy reply of a silent scowl.

Maddy considered him for a second before shaking her head and releasing his belt buckle. He heaved a sigh of relief when her knuckles were no longer pressing against his back. "He always like this?" she whispered to Mason.

"Like what?" Mason asked.

"Dr. Jekyll and Mr. Hyde."

"Pretty much."

"I think they make meds for that."

"Mmmph."

"You two realize I'm standing right here, right?" Bran demanded in an incredulous whisper.

"Right," Mason said. "So how do you want to handle the fatal funnel?"

"That sounds ominous." Maddy curled her lip. "What's a fatal funnel?"

"It's when you enter through a narrow space, like a hallway or an alley or a damned bridge through an archway, and you're silhouetted against the entry point to the defenders inside," Bran explained. "That's the *funnel* part, anyway. I suspect the *fatal* part is self-explanatory."

He heard her gulp. *Yeah. You got it, babe.*

"And considering no one took any shots at us as we were making our way here," he whispered to Mason, "that probably means the dickheads are holed up inside with a defensible position, biding their time and just waiting for us to go on the offensive. Makes sense. Considering they're in a goddamned *fort*, which was built for exactly that strategy."

"Wish there was another way in," Mason muttered. "Maybe we could swim around back and try to scale the seawall and then the curtain wall. Get in that way."

"Maybe," Bran mused, turning to Maddy and looking her up and down. He frowned when he did some quick muscle-mass to body-weight calculations.

"What?" she demanded. "What's with the face?"

"I was born with it," he said drolly. Yeah. He was definitely Jekyll and Hyde. "And I was once again asking myself why I decided to let you come along, because no way are those scrawny arms of yours"—he dipped his chin toward the set of lithely muscled biceps under discussion— "strong enough to get you up that curtain wall. Not unless you get bitten by an irradiated spider between here and there and suddenly turn into Spider-Woman."

"How awesome would *that* be?" Maddy feigned wonder. "And just so you know," she continued, "you agreed to let me come along because I know another way into the fort." She batted her lashes so fervently he was surprised he didn't feel a breeze.

He and Mason exchanged a look. Mason was the one to say, "Do tell, Miss Powers."

"The reason they call this place the *Dry*"—she made quote marks with her fingers—"Tortugas is because there's no natural fresh water available anywhere on the islands. So when they were buildin' this fort, they had to construct large cisterns to catch rainwater and store it."

"Same thing we do on Wayfarer Island," Bran told her. "So what?"

"So this fort was built with over sixteen *million* bricks. Just think about that for a second. Sixteen million bricks on top of shiftin' sands."

"Is this history lesson headed somewhere?"

She gave him a look that promised pain to some of his softer body parts. He wisely snapped his mouth shut.

"The main reason this fort was never finished," she continued, "is because the mammoth weight of the structure kept crushin' the cisterns, allowin' seawater to seep in and contaminate the freshwater."

The wind chose that moment to kick up. And the lighthouse made its revolution, briefly flashing over the beach and illuminating Maddy's hair until it sparkled like corn silk.

Bran regretted not asking Ranger Rick if he had a ball cap she could borrow. He *also* regretted not considering that *before* they made their way along the beach to this bush.

"Over the years," Maddy continued, "the crack in the foundation of the fort and the cistern grew. It's big enough to swim through. It's against park rules, of course. But there have been a few folks who've done it and posted pictures on the Internet."

"And you know where this fissure in the foundation that leads to the cistern is?" he asked.

"Southwest wall. Between the two corner gun rooms."

Bran tried to convince himself there was a better way. One that didn't involve dragging Maddy through an underwater tunnel.

"You have that thinkin' line between your eyebrows." She pursed her lips. "Which usually doesn't bode well for me."

He searched her face, looking for…he wasn't sure what. But all he saw in her eyes was stony resolve. And maybe a little desperation. She was willing to risk it all, her life even, on a chance to save those girls. "Okay, then," he said before turning to Mason. "Thoughts?"

Mason nodded. "Worth a try."

Bran blew out a breath at the same time he ran a hand through his hair. It was stiff with salt and still damp in places. "Well, you know what the SEALs say, right?"

"Where's the fun in that?" Maddy offered.

It struck him just how much Maddy knew about him. How much she knew *him*. He'd let her in. He'd let her get close. Too close. And in doing so, he'd let himself fall. Just a little. Or maybe a lot? He wasn't sure. What he *was* sure of was that he had to stop the downward trajectory now, before it was too late.

"That's our *Team* motto," he told her. "The SEAL motto is something different."

"So then what do the SEALs say?"

"The only easy day was yesterday," he told her.

"Hooyah," Mason said, shouldering his weapon and quartering the area in front of them, preparing to make a move.

When Bran looked back at Maddy, she jerked her chin in a quick, businesslike fashion. She was ready to jump into the fray without a second thought.

God help me. She's too brave by half.

"Hold up, Mason," he said, setting his M4 aside and grabbing the hem of his tank top. Since the last time he'd seen Maddy, he'd entertained about two thousand fantasies surrounding the events that might lead to him taking his clothes off for her. But nothing he imagined had been anything like this.

Chapter 9

7:43 p.m. ...

"I'M SORRY," MADDY WHISPERED WHEN BRAN WHIPPED OFF his tank top and started wrapping it around her head. "What's happenin' right now?"

"Your hair is gonna get us killed," he said. His broad chest with its smattering of crinkly dark hair was an inch from her nose. She was absolutely drowning in his scent. And the silver piece of eight caught her eye where it lay between his flexing pectoral muscles, glinting in the moonlight.

H-h-holy mackerel, he was hotter than a two-dollar pistol. Literally and figuratively. He radiated heat like a blast furnace. And he was straight-up, panties-on-the-floor, legs-in-the-air, have-at-me-big-boy sssssmokin' sexy.

Considering she was dealing with wildly celebrating hormones and fifty shades of scrambled gray matter, it was amazing she had the wherewithal to come up with the super articulate reply of "Huh?"

"I said your hair is gonna get us all killed."

Uh-huh. So she *had* heard him correctly the first time. Unfortunately, the second time was *not* a charm. His words still didn't make a lick of sense.

"How in God's name is my *hair* goin' to get us killed?" she whispered as he continued to fashion a makeshift turban. "I mean, my brothers told me it was a crime against coiffures, but surely it hasn't crossed the line into bein' fatal."

Bran stopped what he was doing to glance down at her. "I like your hair," he said simply. No artifice. "But it's too bright," he told her, getting back to the business of tucking a piece of the damp fabric above her left ear. "It shines like a candle against the night. We don't need it drawing unwanted attention."

She was only listening with half an ear. Why, you ask? Well, because his nipple was suddenly right… frickin'…*there*. Staring at her. Daring her. She blew out a ragged breath and watched, fascinated, as the flat brown disk furled tight around the little bud in the center, making it poke up proudly.

Bran sucked in a startled breath. Then he pulled away, checking his handiwork and *not* meeting her eyes.

Aha! She felt like pointing a finger at his nose. *And you think we're just pen pals?*

"We've gotten rusty," Mason mumbled, looking over his shoulder and giving Maddy the once-over. "We should've thought of that before we left the ranger's station."

"I know." Bran frowned. Then he shook his head and picked up his big, deadly gun, checking something on the side before tugging the strap over his shoulder. "You ready?" he asked her, finally meeting her eyes. To her great annoyance, his face didn't show an ounce of the excitement and hunger that had passed between them ten seconds ago. He did, however, wince and make a grab for his wounded thigh.

"Question is," she said, "are you?"

"I'm fine."

She flayed him with a look.

"It just twinges every once in a while," he assured her. "Now, we're gonna head toward that southwest corner. And we're gonna do it double time. You gotta stay close." Staying close to Bran had never been a problem. "This is where things could get hairy." She liked hair, especially the smattering across Bran's chest. "We'll be totally exposed 'til we reach the moat." *Exposed? Have I mentioned that Bran is now shirtless?*

"I understand." She nodded, the weight of her improvised turban making the move feel awkward. As for the weight of the task ahead of them? Well, not to put too fine a point on it, but it didn't get any more real than this. And if they were about to drown in a dark tunnel or get filled full of lead once they managed to make it inside the fort, she had one final point to make.

"But before we go," she whispered, stopping Bran with a hand on his forearm, "there's somethin' I need to do."

"What's that?"

She grabbed his big shoulders and went up on tiptoe. "This," she said before slamming her mouth over the top of his.

She didn't stop there. She took advantage of his slack-jawed surprise by sliding her tongue between his teeth. His breath was hot and sweet, just like she remembered. His lips masculine and firm. She remembered that, too. Her own lips tingled at the contact, every single nerve ending *zinging* with approval.

Bran stiffened against her. Just went ahead and did his best impression of a two-by-four. *Hello, Mr. Wood!*

But the act only lasted a second. Because his rigidity morphed into a subtle quiver. Which, in turn, became… *Whoa, Nelly!* The sound that emanated from the back of his throat couldn't be described as anything other than a low growl. And suddenly, his arms were around her, crushing her to him.

Somehow, without her knowing exactly how, their roles reversed. Just like that, she was no longer the aggressor. He was. And, oh, she'd never enjoyed being aggressed—*Is that even a word?*—so much in her life. His warm, wet tongue plunged into her mouth, invading and plundering like a marauder of old, a real-life pirate come to whisk her away with his dark eyes and even darker desires.

Over the past few months, she'd thought maybe she'd exaggerated the mastery he'd displayed during that one brief kiss they'd shared aboard her father's yacht. Thought maybe the shock and adrenaline of the day had somehow skewed her perception of his skill.

Huh-uh. No siree.

Bran was the most accomplished kisser she'd ever had the privilege of kissing. It was all perfectly timed licks and sucks and nips. She could have gone on making love to his amazing mouth forever, but her pesky conscience tapped her on the shoulder and reminded her that it was her responsibility…nay…her *duty* to go save those girls.

Tick-tock, sister, it said.

She pushed out of Bran's embrace and rolled in her lips, savoring the taste of him. If she weren't mistaken, at some point during their exchange a puppeteer had connected strings to her knees and was now tugging on those strings, making her legs shiver and quake.

Bran breathed like he'd run a race. His pulse beat a rapid tattoo in the side of his neck. And his eyes were hot and fierce on her face.

Then, as if all of that weren't delightful enough, he did something completely wonderful. He reached down and adjusted himself, drawing her eye to the rather impressive package housed behind the fly of his cargo shorts. There was no denying her effect on him. *And hello, Mr.* WOOD!

She couldn't help herself. She donned a cheeky grin. "And *that* was for tellin' Rick we were just pen pals."

7:59 p.m....

"Seven feet down and about three feet wide the whole way," Mason said, wiping the seawater from his eyes.

"Tight squeeze," Bran murmured, bobbing gently in the bath-warm waters of the moat. Their journey across the beach had been miraculously uneventful. Well...as uneventful as it could be considering he'd been recovering from that mind-blowing kiss Maddy had laid on him. The woman knew how to prove a point, that was for sure.

And, damnit! That makes me like her even more.

It was officially official—when it came to Madison Powers, he was one sorry SOB. Completely incapable of controlling himself. Which was the whole mothersucking problem, wasn't it? Little did she know it, but her stunt behind that bush proved *his* point too.

"But not too tight a squeeze," Mason added. "The problem might be the distance."

"Tough, eh?" Bran asked.

"Not for me." Mason shook his head, water droplets flying from the ends of his wet hair. "And definitely not for you. But I don't know about her." He jerked his chin toward Maddy, who was dog-paddling in the water beside them.

"We could do a couple of time tests on her lung capacity," Bran suggested.

Mason shook his head. "I don't know about you, but I'm feeling like our luck has got to be running out." Together they glanced up at the embrasures in the brick facade above them. The black holes were empty of the masked men *and* their weapons. But how long would that last?

"This conversation is weirder than a three-dollar bill," Maddy declared quietly.

The turban he'd tied around her head had come undone on the swim through the moat. She was now wearing his tank top like a wedding veil, the neck hole wrapped around her forehead and the rest of it trailing down her neck and back to float atop the gently lapping water. The light was dimmer here in the shadow of the fort, but there was still enough illumination to show that the dried blood spatter that had stained her cheeks and forehead was washed away, leaving her skin clean and clear.

Beautiful, he thought. What he *said* was, "Mason thinks you might not be able to hold your breath long enough to make the swim through the crack in the foundation and up into the cistern."

"I'll have you know I'm the Powers Pool Party Breath-Holding Champ," she declared, water dripping from the tips of her long, inky lashes. For a platinum blond, Maddy had surprisingly dark eyebrows and eyelashes. It made Bran wonder if she was a natural towhead or if her Marilyn Monroe tresses came out of a bottle.

There's one way to find out, the voice in his head whispered. He studiously ignored it. Mostly because it was a jackass. But also because he knew that nothing lay down that particular path but trouble.

"I can make twenty feet, no problem," she asserted. "So let's do this thing already. This moat is startin' to give me the heebie-jeebies. Did y'all know when they used the fort as a prison in the eighteen hundreds, someone kept a ten-foot shark in here?"

He opened his mouth to assure her there were no sharks in the moat now. But before he could say anything, she blinked and made a face. A weird gurgling sounded at the back of her throat.

"What?" he demanded, all his protective instincts jumping to the fore. His M4 was strapped to his back, but his muscles bunched, ready to swing it over his head.

"Something just touched my foot," she whispered, and a line from that old English rock band sprang to mind: *a whiter shade of pale*. That definitely described what had happened to her complexion. Before Bran could tell her it was probably nothing—a fish or an eel or even just a piece of seaweed—she was splashing toward him like a lunatic, her eyes wide, her mouth contorted in a grimace.

"There it was again!" she croaked, climbing on top of him, her bare feet finding footholds on his knees and hip bones, her hands clawing at his shoulders and head until he was shoved under water.

Now usually, he would welcome a woman's legs going over his shoulders and her breasts smashing his nose. But not while he was treading water. For a couple of seconds, they sank into the dark void before he had the wherewithal to kick and stroke toward the surface. He came up sputtering and sucking in oxygen that was heavy with the berry-sweet scent of her lotion and the subtler aroma of luscious, warm female.

"Little help here." His words were muffled by Maddy's sopping T-shirt and the soft cushion of her boobs. Her calf pressed against the barrel of his M4, digging the metal into his back.

"You're on your own with this one, bro," Mason said. And even though Bran couldn't see Mason's expression—what with Maddy attached to his head like one of those facehugger creatures from the *Alien* movies—there was no mistaking the exasperation in his teammate's voice.

So much for having a brother's back, Bran thought uncharitably as he doggy-paddled to the side of the fort. He managed to get a toehold in the mortar and a hand-hold on a piece of cracked masonry above the waterline.

Once he secured them and caught his breath, he muttered into her chest, "So you're telling me you don't bat a lash when a gun is aimed at your head. And you don't hesitate for a second to stitch up a gnarly-looking wound. And swimming through a pitch-black underwater tunnel doesn't give you a moment's hesitation. But something brushes your foot and suddenly you go all girlie on me?"

"What can I say?" Maddy's whispered words were muffled since her thighs were suctioned against his ears. "Things in the water, especially slimy things or scaly things or *toothy* things, rate a ten out of ten on my squick-o-meter." *Squick-o-meter?* That was a new one. "And am I the only one who keeps hearin' the theme from *Jaws*? Da-dum. Da-dum. Da-dum…"

She was clutching double fistfuls of Bran's hair. And every second or so, another follicle pulled loose, causing tears to burn at the backs of his eyes. Then something brushed by his leg. Something big. Something scaly. Something he thought he might recognize given all the hours and days he'd spent in the ocean.

He didn't jump when a tail fin slapped against his calf. He didn't panic. But that was definitely an uptick in his heart rate. And he was certainly having a difficult time breathing. Of course, the latter was likely attributed to Maddy.

He carefully snaked a hand between her left thigh and his right ear, breaking the vise she had on his head. "Damnit, Maddy!" he grumbled impatiently, turning his head so as *not* to talk into her breastal region. Any other night, he would breathe her in and maybe—okay, *definitely*—open his mouth and taste her. But right now it made carrying on a conversation, not to mention *concentrating* on the conversation, more than a bit…uh…*arduous*. To Mason he said, "I think we may have a problem."

"Barracuda, you think?" Mason asked and Bran wasn't surprised the ol' Boston boy had already come to the same conclusion. Obviously the fish was testing them all, nudging and brushing and trying to determine if they might be good to eat.

And the blood on my shorts and seeping through my bandage sure isn't helping matters.

"If I had to guess," he agreed.

"Likely it's been stuck in here for a few days," Mason speculated. "Since the last storm made waves big enough to carry it over the seawall."

"Not good news," Bran said unnecessarily. Barracudas didn't usually attack humans. But there was no telling what a six-foot, one-hundred-pound, trapped, *hungry* fish was capable of.

"You gotta get off my shoulders," Bran told Maddy. "But I want you to stay between me and the fort wall. Be careful of the barnacles." Because those could do almost as much damage as the fish.

"Did I hear y'all mention somethin' about a barracuda?" she asked, not budging an inch.

"Could be," Mason said. "Feels like it every time it rubs against me."

Great. Way to reassure her, gavone.

"Hey," he said, trying to offer some comfort. "Barracuda attacks aren't usually deadly. Not like shark attacks can be." Of course, with a set of dagger-like teeth made for digging into prey and ripping away chunks of flesh, the fish could score some serious devastation. Just *thinking* about what the creature could do to Maddy's soft, perfect skin…

He was suddenly sick, the Gatorade he'd had earlier turning sour in his stomach.

"Good, great," Maddy said, slipping off his shoulders and quietly splashing into the tepid water. "All the same, what do you say to us blowin' this Popsicle stand and gettin' our asses inside the fort?"

"You sure you can do this?" he asked.

"Does the Tin Man have a sheet-metal dick?" she responded.

Brave…

Once again the word whispered through his head. Because contrary to what some people believed, bravery wasn't about *not* being afraid to do something. It was about *being* afraid to do something and still doing it anyway.

He would not have thought it was possible for his estimation of Maddy to grow any more. But right then and there, it did. Madison Marie Powers, oil heiress, philanthropist, Texas tornado disguised in a tiny teacup package, was one of the most courageous individuals he'd ever met. Which was saying something considering he'd made a career of working with the bravest sonsofbitches on the planet.

And then something else occurred to him. It wasn't *just* his estimation of her that had grown, so had his feelings. What he'd thought were simple *lust* and *like* abruptly felt bigger. Wider. Deeper. *More*.

Chapter 10

"MASON FIRST. YOU SECOND. AND I'LL BE THE CABOOSE ON this train," Bran said, and Maddy tried with her whole heart to project courage even though she was feeling about as yellow as mustard with half the bite.

It wasn't the upcoming swim that gave her the willies. It was the thought of the barracuda that had her blood running through her veins in a river colder than a cast-iron commode—another of Grandma Bettie's faves.

It's in here. With us. And it's hungry.

When her teeth threatened to chatter, she clenched her jaw so tight she reckoned she heard a molar crack.

She glanced into the water, trying to see the silver flash of the fish. And barring that, she hoped to get a gander at the crack in the foundation of the fort. Unfortunately, neither worked. The barracuda was probably hanging back, suspended in the water, completely motionless in that terrifying way only predators of the deep could pull off. *Brrrrr.* And the tunnel? Well, it was down there. Somewhere unseen beneath all that dark water. And was it her imagination, or was it suddenly whispering up at her, "Abandon all hope, ye who enter here!"

"Use your arms to pull yourself along," Mason instructed, his Beantown accent making it sound like *use yah ahms ta pull yahself along*. He could've stepped into a scene in *Good Will Hunting* without missing a beat. "And if you get scared down there, just keep going. Don't turn back. Turning back is the worst thing you could do."

"Got it," she managed around the Rock of Gibraltar-sized lump that had grown in the back of her throat. "Use my arms. No turnin' back."

Holy moly. That last part sounds ominous.

"Ready?" Bran asked. He was paddling behind her, providing a barrier between her and the waiting barracuda. She was so grateful she could kiss him.

Oh, wait. I already did that. And it was better than good, it was gggrrrreat! In fact, she was determined to repeat the exercise. Repeatedly. But preferably under less dire circumstances.

"I was born ready." She was pleased to discover her voice wasn't shivering like the rest of her.

Bran flashed his pirate smile. "Woman, you got more guts than—"

"You can string on a fence," she finished for him.

"What?" He cocked his head.

"It's somethin' my daddy always says to me. 'You got more guts than you can string on a fence.'" She made a face. "What's *implied* there is that my bravado usually outweighs my brains." Not waiting on either Bran or Mason to agree or disagree with the sentiment, she continued, "That being the case, let's make like a stump-tailed cow at fly time, and get busy gettin' it done."

"I know that last part was English." Mason frowned. "But I'm not sure I understood it."

Apparently he didn't care to be enlightened because

he sank low in the water, only his face above the gently lapping surface. She watched him blow out a big, blustery breath and suck in an even larger one. Then he just...disappeared. Allowed the water—the *inhabited* water—to swallow him up.

"Your turn," Bran said.

She nodded, ignoring all the inner bells and whistles warning her that what she was about to do was completely, totally, utterly bonkers. It wasn't too difficult, considering she'd been ignoring those inner bells and whistles most of her life. *Leap before you look*. Her father said she should have the phrase tattooed across her forehead. Maybe after tonight, she'd take the suggestion seriously.

Mimicking Mason's moves, she kicked away from the side of the fort and allowed herself to sink into the moat until the warm water covered everything but her face. With her ears submerged, the *glug-glug* of the liquid moving against the side of the structure was both muted and strangely amplified.

Blowing out a huge breath, she then sucked in as much air as she could. Sucked until her lungs couldn't hold another drop. Sucked until her nose was filled with the distinctly ocean-y smell of the barnacles clinging to the side of the fort wall: fish and shells and algae and...death.

She hoped that last bit wasn't portentous of anything as she dove beneath the surface, kicking hard to propel herself downward, her hands gently rubbing along the rough masonry in search of the opening. She wasn't sure why she kept her eyes open in the stinging salt water. It's not like she could see anything. But then, suddenly, she did. An inkier blackness within all the blackness, right before her probing fingers sank into a hollow.

Here goes, she thought as she pulled herself into the narrow tunnel. *This one's for the girls.*

It was a mantra she repeated as she hauled herself along, finding handholds in the bricks and the slimy sea life that made its home in the craggy walls. Maddy didn't *begin* to want to know what was slipping beneath her fingers. Nor did she want to contemplate the seconds ticking by.

Twenty feet? Really? It was beginning to feel more like two hundred.

Then again, time flies when you're havin' fun!

She redoubled her efforts, adding a few soft kicks to the work her arms were doing. She *softly* kicked because she didn't want to smack into the walls of the fissure. The tunnel was tighter than a skeeter's butthole—she couldn't imagine how Mason and Bran were able to shoulder their way through—and no telling how stable the centuries' old brickwork was. Lord knows, she didn't want to trigger a cave-in. Also, she didn't want to boot Bran in his handsome mug.

She couldn't feel him. And she certainly couldn't see him. But he said he'd be right behind her, and Bran was nothing if not a man of his word. It gave her the confidence, the calm to keep pushing ahead.

At least for a while.

Five seconds stretched to ten. Ten seconds quickly became twenty. The water inside the tunnel was cooler than that in the moat. It softly brushed against her cheeks and hair, slipping down the collar of her T-shirt to slide across her breasts and belly like intrusive, chilly hands.

Come on. Come on…

Where was the cistern? Why hadn't she reached it? Surely she'd gone twenty feet by now. *Surely!*

Her lungs burned. Her heart rate spiked, trying to push oxygen that wasn't there through her bloodstream.

Did I take a wrong turn? Could the tunnel have forked?

She kicked and pulled, kicked and pulled, her motions becoming more desperate as oxygen deprivation set in. All her instincts yelled at her. *Turn back!* But she fought them off, pushing, pulling, propelling herself forward. Ever forward.

Where's Bran? I took a wrong turn! Somehow I—

Space...

Big, beautiful, wide-open space. She was free-floating in the cistern. *Finally!*

She kicked toward the surface with all her might. Her fingers became claws, tearing at the water. The beat of her heart was a ferocious roar in her ears. Her lungs spasmed, desperate to suck in air.

Uh-oh. Had she gotten mixed up in all that cool, wet blackness when she exited the fissure? Was she swimming down instead of up?

Oh Lord! Oh shit! Oh—

Her mouth opened in a silent scream. Briny water rushed in, triggering her gag reflex. Spots of light flashed in front of her unblinking eyes, but they weren't bioluminescent sea creatures. They were hallucinations conjured up by her under-oxygenated brain as her synapses misfired.

She stopped to turn around. Surely she was swimming down. She had to be. She would have reached the surface by now! But before she could switch directions, a hard arm came around her middle.

In an instant she was propelled through the water. Bran's muscled legs kicked. His free arm stroked. He was a human torpedo dragging her along for the ride. Good thing, because she was done.

Out of juice.

Out of air.

Out of time. And then…

"Uhhhhh!" They breached the surface just as her convulsing lungs overrode her willpower and forced her to suck in bright, brilliant oxygen…along with a fair amount of liquid.

She immediately folded in half, hacking and coughing and trying to clear the spray from her lungs. The sound of her struggle echoed through the cistern, bouncing around the brick walls. Bran slammed a wide-palmed hand over her mouth.

"Shhhhh," he hissed, his lips moving against her ear, his hot breath burning along her cheek. "Just breathe, babe."

Uh-huh. Breathe. Right.

Problem was, she couldn't. Not without hacking up a lung. And if she did that, the resulting sound could reso-nate through the cistern and out into the parade grounds, alerting their enemies to their presence.

For Pete's sake, Maddy! Could you be *any more of a pain in the ass?*

Going on instinct, she spun in Bran's embrace, wrap-ping her legs around his waist and burying her nose in the crook of his neck. Her stomach contracted around the need to cough. Her lungs quaked. But she managed to execute a muted throat-clearing thing that she further muffled against Bran's tough flesh. It wasn't exactly a silent exercise. But neither was it sure to bring the bad guys down on their heads.

Again and again, she repeated the process. Each odd inhale and exhale felt gritty, like she'd pulled sand into her lungs instead of water. But after a few seconds, she was able to suck air through her nose without her diaphragm trying to send it hacking back out into the warm, dense atmosphere.

Her senses returned. She could hear the gentle *slap-slap* of the water against the sides of the brick structure. She could smell the clean, masculine scent of Bran beneath the thin layer of seawater that coated his skin. She could feel his heavy pulse beating beneath her lips, a drumbeat she could set her watch to. And even though she couldn't see—the darkness inside the cistern was complete—she knew at some point Bran had swum them to the edge. She could sense the tall, damp walls of the water tank rising overhead. With one arm still wrapped securely around her waist, he was holding on to something that allowed them to float freely, effortlessly in the water.

For a while, she allowed herself to revel. Revel in being alive. Revel in being able to breathe. Revel in feeling momentarily safe and secure inside Bran's embrace—she'd stuck herself to him like a whole sleeve of plastic wrap; if there was a fraction of an inch of space between their bodies, she couldn't feel it. She closed her eyes against the darkness and simply…*was*. No thoughts. No fears. Just her. Just him. Just being. Just touching.

And then it happened…

Bran's pulse kicked up. His chest expanded on a deep

breath. And he stilled against her, all his muscles contracting at once. She knew what caused the change. It was the same thing that happened any time they touched. Sudden, intimate…*awareness*.

The smooth firmness of his skin beneath her lips tempted her to taste. She fought the need for a whole two seconds. It was two seconds she was extremely proud of, just to be clear. But then she couldn't stand it. She opened her lips over his hammering pulse-point and flicked her tongue against his hot flesh.

Male. That was the word that flittered through her brain as Bran's sweet, salty taste exploded on her tongue. He was all man. From top to bottom. Inside and out. And when she was touching him, kissing him, she was every bit a woman. Completely aware that she had breasts and a womb. Both ached, throbbed, *yearned*.

Bran sucked in a ragged breath at the second pass of her tongue. "Maddy," he rumbled, lowering his chin until his lips moved against her ear. The arm around her waist became a wide, warm hand that crept lower, lower, *lower* until he was palming her ass, kneading and caressing and moving her against him in that age-old rhythm that rubbed her swelling sex against the seam of her shorts.

Her nipples tightened into painful buds. Her clitoris throbbed, rejoicing in the sudden friction. And his response, his inability to pretend they were just pen pals when they were together like this, emboldened her. She closed her mouth over his pulse and sucked. Bran started to quiver. A telltale sign of what would happen next. He'd snap. Suddenly *he* would be the one running the show, not her. *He* would be the one making her moan.

He would be the one making her shiver. *He* would be the conqueror and she the conquered. And she would love every minute of it.

But before Bran had the chance to go all...*Bran* on her, Mason cleared his throat. The sound carried from somewhere over on the opposite wall of the cistern and accomplished two things. It reminded Maddy that she and Bran weren't alone and that they still had a very important job to do.

The girls...

Holy shit! How could she have forgotten for even a moment? But she knew. It was six-plus feet of tough-as-nails hotness that started with a *B* and ended with a *ran*. Whenever she was in his arms, she forgot she even had a name.

Chapter 11

8:10 p.m. ...

REGRETS WERE LIKE CHICKENS. THEY ALWAYS CAME HOME to roost. And right now, Bran's chicken coop was full.

Hiding behind the old gunpowder magazine house inside the parade grounds in the center of the fort, he regretted not making it clear to Maddy weeks ago that he wasn't the kind of guy she should set her cap on. He regretted letting her think there was more to their relationship than there was or ever could be. And he regretted that he was continuing to foster that belief, that *hope*, every damn time she got near him. Because despite his best intentions, he just couldn't keep his stupid hands to himself.

One look from her pretty eyes, one touch of her soft hands, one taste of her sweet lips, and he was a goner. Just done. *Finito*. He forgot all the reasons why he shouldn't be with her, all the reasons why he *couldn't* be with her, because the monster inside him took over. And it had only three goals: claim, conquer, consummate.

"We better find those girls fast," Mason murmured, interrupting Bran's pity party. Which was just as well. It wasn't like Bran was having a good time there anyway. "Or Bran and I are going to run out of clothes."

Bran was aiming his weapon at the interior of the curtain wall behind them. The fort was basically a hexagonal-shaped, two-tiered wall that surrounded a patch of land called the parade grounds. The latter had been the site of the soldiers' and officers' quarters and a few other small buildings. From the outside, the fort looked like a two-story brick wall dotted by small embrasures. But from the inside, you could see the curtain wall was actually made up of a double tier of arched rooms called casemates.

So many places to hide behind and fire from, Bran thought, giving the line of casemates a slow, deliberate scan through his scope. A battlefield survey, it was called. A move used when everything was important, every nuance and shadow of grave concern because everything could be either threat or salvation.

The operator in him didn't like his position, exposed on one side to all those yawning casemates. Especially since his backup was busy whipping his gray T-shirt over his head and handing it to Maddy, momentarily unable to help him keep watch.

"Sorry," Maddy whispered. "I think I lost Bran's tank top somewhere in the cistern." She hooked the neck hole of Mason's wet T-shirt over her head, effectively covering her hair.

"So what are we looking at when we step out from behind this gunpowder magazine?" Mason whispered, quickly rearming himself.

"Let me just take a quick gander and get my bearin's," she said, darting a fast look around the edge of the building before ducking back and flattening herself against the cool brick wall. The light of the moon and stars, when paired with the soft glow of the spotlights outside, was enough to make everything visible if not perfectly clear.

And bringing her along. That was *another* of his
regrets. Because she shouldn't be turkey-peeking around
corners in an attempt to guess where armed men might
be hiding. She shouldn't be smack-dab in the middle of
a situation that could very easily go pear-shaped. She
shouldn't be seconds away from potentially finding herself staring down the wrong end of a gun.

Even though she's probably used to it by now.

And that was another thing. Was it just him? Or
did trouble seem to follow her around like a yappy
little lapdog?

"So," she whispered, unaware of his thoughts, "to our
left is the cistern. We know the girls aren't there, so no
use checkin'. Directly in front of us will be the little house
they used as the officers' quarters. That's a possibility.
But there are a lot of windows and doors, which I would
think means it'd be hard to defend. It wouldn't be my first
choice of hideouts. Across the parade grounds is another
gunpowder magazine house. We'll probably need to scout
that. It'll be tricky, though. It has that weird openin' I was
tellin' y'all about. To the left of the magazine house are
the ruins of the soldiers' barracks. They wouldn't make
very good hidin' spots. We can probably skip them."

She took a breath from her long, impressive list.
Obviously, she hadn't been kidding when she said she'd
done her due diligence before coming here.

"Honestly," she continued, "if it were me wantin' to
find a defensible position where I could corral two teenagers, I'd choose that far north casemate. From there
you can see across the parade grounds to the bridge and
anyone enterin' the fort. It's protected on three sides by
thick walls, which means the only worry is the openin'."

"Get a load of General fuckin' Patton here." There was a fair bit of respect in Mason's tone. "*Now* are you glad we brought her along?"

Bran opened his mouth to say, *Hell no!* But before he could, Maddy whispered, "Let me check one more thing." She darted her head around the corner again. But this time, she didn't immediately pull back. Instead, she went stock-still.

Bran chanced taking his eyes off his sights and the arched holes of the dark casemates to dart her a quick glance. "What is it," he demanded, maybe a little too loudly. All the hairs on his body were waving around like semaphore flags, warning him of impending danger. "What'd'ya see?"

Now Maddy jerked back, flattening herself against the bricks. "The men." Bran's ears caught the panic in her voice. And when she turned to him, her eyes were wide and unblinking. "They're crossin' the parade grounds and headed our way." She lifted trembling fingers to her lips. "Alone! What did they do with the girls?"

8:13 p.m....

"Get inside the magazine house." Bran barked the order and it was a verbal slap. Then there was the heat in his eyes. It was enough to set Maddy's soul ablaze.

Death and destruction. She'd been trying to find the right words to describe that particular look that sometimes came over his face, and it suddenly occurred to her. He was death and destruction personified.

Oh no. No, no, no...

"You can't kill them," she whispered desperately.

The way he moved closer to the corner of the gunpowder magazine house told her he wasn't paying her a lick of attention. "Bran," she whispered, grabbing his forearm. "You can't kill them."

"No?" He lifted his weapon. It effectively jerked his arm from her grasp. "Watch me."

"Not until we know what they did with the girls," she pleaded. It was a tiny island, but there were lots of places to squirrel away two teenagers—or hide their bodies. *No. No, don't even think about that! They're not dead. They can't be dead!* "Bran, listen to me. We need to—"

"I won't ask you again, Maddy." He briefly met her eyes, and she found herself backing away from him. She wasn't sure why. Bran would never hurt her. But in that moment, instinct took over. Like a gazelle darting away from a recently fed lion, there was no real danger, but the urge to flee was there nonetheless.

He narrowed his eyes. In the dim light, she thought she saw a strange emotion flicker across his face. He almost looked…*anguished*. But then his expression changed, morphing back into that whole death-and-destruction. "Get in the magazine house. Now!" he hissed.

He didn't wait for her to comply. He grabbed her arm and dragged her toward the open doorway, shoving her inside—not cruelly, but not very gently either. For the first time in her life, she understood how the term *man*handling came about. He was a man. And he was definitely handling her.

"But if it's *me* they want," she insisted, "I could offer myself up, and then maybe they'll tell us where—"

"Stay." He pointed a long, blunt finger so close to her nose that she went cross-eyed trying to focus on it.

Now, normally Maddy would come back with some wiseass remark along the lines of *Hey, bucko! In case the lack of pointed ears didn't give me away, I'm not a German shepherd*. But she was too scared to be her usual sarcastic self. Scared of what had happened to the girls. Scared of what was about to happen to Bran and Mason in the next couple of minutes.

When Bran turned and darted out of the magazine house, there was a part of her that longed to follow him. The part of her that hated, loathed, and utterly despised being reduced to the little woman who sat in the corner painting her toenails. But the *other* part of her, the far smaller yet far wiser part of her, piped up and told her she had no business interfering in whatever they planned to do.

She glanced around the dark interior of the structure, looking for something. She didn't know what. Anything. Something she could use to help. Something she could use to defend herself if all hell broke loose and somehow those three masked men managed to get past the two Navy SEALs—*heaven forbid*. But there was nothing. Just a small, dark room that smelled of old mortar, damp bricks, and dirt.

Wait. There!

Her eyes adjusted and she spied a shadow in the corner. It was long and thin and propped against the wall.

Scurrying over, she discovered it was an old piece of driftwood about three feet long. It was dry and cracked, but it felt sturdy enough to survive one or two good whacks upside the heads of the bad guys, should she need to use it that way. The tip was sharp. Stake-sharp. It could be used that way too. And even though it was ridiculous—you didn't bring a knife to a gunfight, much less a brittle piece of driftwood—she felt better once she was armed.

Then she heard it...

The quiet *clink* of metal against metal. The muted *crunch* of boots on dirt.

The bad guys.

Maddy held her breath and pressed back against the brick wall beside the door. The old mortar was cool, and for a moment her mind drifted to the men who had fired the bricks and laid them. They were all dead now, left to the pages of history books. Their testament to life was a decaying ruin in the middle of nowhere. But at least they *had* a testament.

What would *her* testament be?

Please, not the deaths of two innocent girls, Lord. Please!

She turned her head and strained her ears so hard it was a wonder she didn't burst an eardrum. More boots on uneven earth. A hissed exchange of words she couldn't make out. The sound of someone tripping and cursing.

They were close.

"Damnit, Dustin," one of the men, the one with the Southern drawl, said. "That bum knee of yours is a problem. Rory should've never let you come on this job."

Who is Rory? What job? Her kidnapping?

"Fuck you, Luke. Just cover me for a second." It was the tyrant talking. Maddy's jaw clenched at the same time her fingers tightened around the piece of driftwood. She thought she felt a splinter sink into the pad of her thumb, but couldn't be sure. Not with her attention eagle-eye focused on the men and their whispered conversation.

Well, it was focused on that and the distinct *lack* of sound coming from either Bran or Mason. Their silence was unsettling.

The Angel of Death comes on silent wings…

It was a line from a poem she'd read somewhere. But never had it made as much sense as it did in this moment.

But the girls! she wanted to yell. *We need to know about the girls!* Instead, she bit her bottom lip, welcoming the pain that grounded her.

Tick-tock went her internal clock. *Lub-dub* went her thundering heart. *Drip-drop* went a bead of sweat from her temple to her shoulder.

Jesus Christ and all his followers! What's happenin' out there?

She didn't have long to wait for the answer.

"This whole thing is shot to shit," Luke of the Southern accent griped.

"No, it's *not*," Dustin the Tyrant insisted. "Just because those two meatheads decided to hole up in the ranger's station instead of trying to rescue the girls, that doesn't mean we can't still do the job." There he went again, using that word. *Job*. "We just have to get to the boat and—Fuck!" he yelled, causing Maddy to jump. Then his voice dropped to an angry grumble. "Something told me I might be staring down the black hole of your gun again before this night was over."

"Tit for tat, dicksmack, since I recall you pointing that SCAR-L at me on the beach." *Bran*. "Where are the girls?" he demanded.

Maddy stopped breathing as she waited on the answer. Her stomach knotted like someone twisting a wet towel until the fabric screamed with the strain.

"How the hell did y'all get in here?" Southern Accent Luke demanded. "We been watchin' the entryway—"

"Where are the girls?" Bran's voice held a world of menace.

"We didn't hurt them," the one called Dustin said.

"Good," Bran answered. "Then toss your weapons my way and tell me where they are."

For a second, none of the men responded. Finally, the Southerner said, "Once we do that, what's stoppin' ya from lightin' us up?"

"Guess you'll just hafta trust me," Bran said.

"Fuck that," the tyrant spat. "And fuck you."

"Oh, eh." Bran laughed. "Not even on your birthday, sunshine."

"We're not giving you our weapons, asshole," the tyrant snarled.

"What we have here," Bran said, and Maddy silently finished the sentence with him, "is a failure to communicate." *Cool Hand Luke*.

"I could drop you where you stand," Dustin the Tyrant warned.

"I'd so like to see you try," Bran answered with a feral-sounding snort.

Maddy wanted to scream her head off. *Enough with the dick-measurin' contest, you idiots!*

But she didn't scream. In fact nobody screamed. Not a word was spoken. Not a breath was taken. The island itself seemed to be holding perfectly still, waiting, anticipating. She couldn't see the moon from inside the gunpowder magazine house, but she knew it was shining down on the men, a watchful spectator of events to come.

Finally, Bran said, "Look, I'm being magnanimous here and giving you two choices. You can drop your weapons, tell us where you've stashed the girls, and leave this island alive and well. Or you can keep your weapons, keep your secrets, and leave this island in a body bag. I'm happy either way."

"You seem to be miscountin' again," the Southerner piped up. "There's three of us and only one of you."

"Man, you seriously need to get your eyes checked." Mason's low voice rumbled from the opposite direction. Maddy reckoned he'd skirted around the other side of the magazine house to come up behind the bad guys. He and Bran were quite a pair. And, boy howdy, she was glad they were on her side.

"Shit," the third guy cursed, probably after having glanced over his shoulder to find Mason taking aim at his head.

Yessiree, boys, Maddy thought with a savage, frantic sort of glee. *That's what you might call bein' stuck between a rock and a hard place*. Bran being the rock and Mason being the hard place, of course.

"Don't try it," Bran rumbled. His voice had all the gravity and solemnity of someone speaking at a funeral.

Try what? Oh! She *so* wanted to peek her head out and see what the heckfire was going on.

"I'm serious," Bran continued. "I won't hesitate to turn you into an organ donor. There's a real shortage of assholes lately, so I hear."

And Maddy suddenly had the distinct urge not only to peek her head out, but to march out there and wring Bran's neck. He was baiting them. Egging them on almost as if he *wanted* a reason to—*BOOM!* The sound of a shot echoed around the fort and inside the magazine house like an exploding cannonball. She was pretty sure her heart exploded right along with it.

Chapter 12

8:15 p.m. ...

THE GUY WITH THE BAD KNEE IS A GRADE-A, DOUBLE-D *douche canoe*.

That was the thought that spun through Mason's brain when the fuckface squeezed off a shot that flew by Bran's head and stuck in the brick corner of the old gunpowder magazine house.

Bran returned fire without flinching. Two shots. Both hit Bad Knee center mass, dropping the man in under two seconds.

Mason sighted down his barrel as he readied himself to take out the remaining masked men. But they took one look at their buddy and tossed their rifles to the ground.

Now, not every decision Mason had ever made in the midst of a gun battle was one of moral clarity. But this one was. There was no way he could justify shooting two unarmed men.

"Whoa! Whoa! Whoa!" the one who sounded like he should be skinning squirrels and sipping sweet tea on a porch swing yelled when Bran swung the business end of his M4 in his direction. "We're unarmed!" He and his pal threw their hands in the air. "Don't shoot!"

Should've given that advice to your buddy, fucknuts.

"Dustin!" Southern Boy shouted, glancing at his

squirming friend who was flat on his back, writhing and clutching at the wounds in his chest.

"Forget it," Mason told him. "He's a dead man. He just doesn't know it yet."

When Bran aimed to kill, he didn't miss. It was just one of the many things Mason loved about his brother-in-arms.

"Damnit!" the third guy screamed. "I didn't sign up for any of this shit. It was supposed to be an easy snatch-and-grab. It was supposed to be—"

"Shut up!" Southern Boy snarled.

"Screw you, Luke!"

"Why don't you both shut the fuck up," Mason grumbled, having heard enough. *An easy snatch-and-grab?* So this *had* been about kidnapping.

"I'd listen to him if I were you," Bran said, skirting around Bad Knee, kicking his dropped SCAR-L away, and not sparing the dying man a glance. It wasn't that Mason and Bran were unmoved by death and killing. It's just that very early in their SEAL careers they'd learned that sometimes there was nothing to do but put rabid dogs down.

"And while you're listening to him," Bran said, "you can tell us where you've hidden those girls."

"Well, which is it?" Southern Boy asked. Even though Mason couldn't see his face because of the balaclava, he was pretty sure by the sound of Southern Boy's voice that he was sneering. "Do ya want us to do what that jackhole says and shut the fuck up? Or do ya want us to tell you where the girls are? I'm gettin' mixed signals here."

Bran glanced over the man's shoulder at Mason,

raised brow saying, *Can you believe this bozo?* When he turned his attention to Southern Boy, he said, "Wise guy, eh? Well, wise guy, unless you fancy a round in your shoulder, you'll stop with the lip service and answer my goddamned question."

"We really didn't hurt them," the second half of the duo answered quickly. "We tied them up—"

"I told ya to shut up!" Southern Boy screeched. "Those girls are our only bargainin'—"

His sidekick ignored him and went on as if he hadn't spoken. "They're in the far north casemate on the second floor and—"

"Shut up! Shut up! *Shut up!*" Southern Boy was apoplectic.

"Thank you," Bran said. "Now, both of you get down on your knees and put your hands behind your heads."

"B-but," the chatty man stuttered, "earlier you told us we could leave and—"

"Sorry, *gavone*," Bran told him. "That ship sailed. And then it sank. Now, on your knees."

They hesitated and Mason rolled his eyes. He contemplated swinging his M4 like a baseball bat at the backs of their knees. The longer they fought against the inevitable, the longer he had to wait to send up that flare.

And the longer Alex is alone out there.

He hadn't stopped thinking about her—worrying about her—since the moment he'd chucked himself overboard the catamaran. Then again, she'd pretty much been a plague on his brain since she exploded onto Wayfarer Island like the pint-sized bombshell she was.

Bran proved he was suffering a similar fate—having a woman on the brain—when, instead of insisting the masked assholes do as he told them, he yelled over his shoulder, "Maddy? Y'okay in there?"

For a couple of seconds no sound emerged from the gunpowder magazine house. Then Maddy poked her head around the corner. She held a piece of driftwood aloft like a baseball bat.

"Bran?" She scooted out from behind the building, glanced at the unarmed men, and swallowed. "Can I go find the girls?"

Her firm chin and straight back were a testament to her mettle, but Mason heard the tremor in her voice. And even under the dim light of the moon, he could see that her complexion was so pale she looked like she'd been to the blood drive but hadn't been given the requisite post-donation cookie and juice.

He wondered if he'd ever met a woman as dauntless and determined as Maddy Powers.

Alex, a voice whispered inside his head. Ya-huh. Sure. Alex was what you would call dauntless and determined…if you were prone to understatement.

And fuckin' hell! Were *all* his thoughts going to lead back to her tonight?

"Wait 'til we—" Bran began, and the masked men took advantage of his distraction.

"Run!" Southern Boy shouted, taking off like a shot toward the fort's arched entryway. His cohort bolted after him.

Mason swung his weapon in their direction and took aim. But he didn't pull the trigger. Once again he drew the line at shooting unarmed men in the back.

"Let 'em go," Bran said.

Mason didn't take his eyes off the targets as his breathing slowed right along with his heart rate. His finger twitched on the trigger. "I could wing them. Or take out a knee." Apparently, he was having a knee fixation tonight. *Odd*.

"No need," Bran said as the duo zigzagged their way across the parade grounds.

"But what if they're going to the ranger's station to—" Maddy started, only to be cut off by Bran.

"They're dumb, but they're not that dumb," he said. "They're outnumbered and weaponless." He nodded to the SCAR-L rifles lying in the dirt. "Dollars to doughnuts they're making a beeline straight to their boat. But don't worry, even then they won't get far."

"What do you mean?" Maddy asked, skirting the body of Bad Knee to come stand beside Bran.

When she reached for his hand, Mason saw Bran stiffen. But that only lasted a split second. Then it was like something inside Bran broke loose and he curled his fingers through Maddy's, dragging her close to his side. The look on Maddy's face when she glanced at Bran was one Mason recognized. Longing and hero-worship and…something more.

It was the something more that worried him.

Bran didn't believe in happily-ever-afters. Which meant at some point in the near future, that bouquet of heart-shaped balloons flying above Maddy's head would inevitably meet the sharp pins of Bran's unshakeable resolve.

This'll get ugly, Mason thought as he lowered his weapon and swung the strap of his rifle over his shoulder. The metal of the weapon was cool where it rested against his bare back, the weight comforting.

"While I was in the surf, watching and waiting to see what the masked assholes were getting up to," Bran said, "Mason snuck aboard their fishing boat to disable their radio and satellite phone. Rule number one for any successful battle is knock out the enemy's communications. While he was there, he cut a hole in their fuel line. Rule number two for any successful battle is to block any avenue of escape. They'll make it *maybe* a mile or two before they run outta gas. You didn't *really* think I was serious when I told them they could leave the island no questions asked, did you?"

"Well...I...:" Maddy blinked. "I reckon I did."

"Much to learn you still have," Bran said, doing a pretty spot-on impression of Yoda.

A smile more radiant than the lighthouse's glow spread across Maddy's face.

Going to get so fuckin' ugly, Mason thought again. Aloud he asked, "So what now?"

"Now, Maddy and I go get the girls," Bran said, just as the sound of an outboard engine sputtered to life. Fuckheads One and Two were on their way to nowhere fast. "You still got that flare handy?"

Mason reached into his pocket to remove the flare stick.

"Good." Bran dipped his chin. "If Alex is still out there, it's time to bring her in."

Mason was overcome by the urge to run up to the parapets and fire off the flare, but he managed to keep his cool. They had a plan to make. "If she is still out there, you think we should load everyone up on the catamaran and sail back to Wayfarer Island?" He'd seen just about all he'd wanted to see of Garden Key and Fort Jefferson, thanks.

"Not sure that's a good idea." A concerned line sliced between Bran's eyebrows. "Bum Knee kept calling this a *job*. Which means this wasn't their brainiac scheme but someone else's. They won't be able to call that someone else with their coms down. But the thought that there are others involved makes my asshole pinch. Being out on the open ocean when we aren't sure who else might be skulking about…" He trailed off.

"Ya-huh." Mason nodded. "Better to be inside a fuckin' fort should whoever hired them get tired of waiting on their call and decide to come investigate."

"My thoughts exactly," Bran agreed. "Hopefully the marine radio on the catamaran will be able to reach Wayfarer Island. If so, we'll have LT make a satphone call to the Coast Guard on Key West and tell 'em to get their asses here ASAP." Before Mason could raise the issue of the wrench that might get thrown into that plan, Bran addressed it himself. "Sure, whoever those asswipes are working for might hear our call over the marine channels, but so what? Again, we'll have the high ground, we'll be inside a fort, and we're not lacking in weapons. I think the odds are in our favor should anyone attempt to make landfall here on Garden Key."

"Agreed," Mason said. "And if Alex *isn't* out there, then hopefully she's well on her way back home and the end result will be the same. A satphone call back to Key West and Coast Guard to the rescue."

"You got it, *paisano*." Bran dipped his chin.

But there was one last hitch. And even though the flare stick was burning a hole in Mason's hand, he forced calm and asked the final question. "What if the marine radio isn't strong enough to reach home?"

"Then we stay holed up in the fort until the fast ferry or a floatplane arrives tomorrow."

"Right." Mason nodded. And then he couldn't stand it a second longer. He turned and ran for the nearest casemate and the stairs that led up to the top of the parapets. As his legs chewed up the distance, his fisted heart seemed to pound out a name in Morse code against his ribs.

Alex...

She was the thorn in his side. The bane of his existence. But he hoped she hadn't set sail for Wayfarer Island. Because everything that was anything inside him desperately needed to see her and make sure she was okay.

———

8:17 p.m. ...

"It's takin' too long," Gene insisted.

For the last hour, he had been trying to pace a hole through the deck of the yacht, and it was starting to drive Tony in-fucking-sane. The fact that he was on his third cocktail should've meant the sharp edges of his nerves were smoothed over by top-shelf scotch, but to his dismay, they were not. He was so wired it was a wonder he wasn't shooting sparks from his ass.

And Gene wasn't helping, damnit!

"Sit down, Gene," he snarled, not hiding the impatience in his voice.

"Screw you, Tony," Gene snapped, whipping off his

Stetson to run his shaky fingers through his thinning hair. The ocean breeze blowing across the back of the motor yacht caught the sweaty strands and lifted them in hunks. "I don't take orders. And I'm tellin' you, it's takin' too goddamn long. Somethin' is wrong. You get on that satellite phone, call up *your guys*"—when Gene stressed those two words, Tony squeezed his highball glass so hard it was a miracle he didn't shatter it—"and get a situation report right now."

"I'm not going to do that, Gene," he said as calmly as he could.

"The hell you say!" Gene thundered, his blood pressure boiling so hot and fast that his face flushed ruddy in the overhead light, his eyes going bloodshot in an instant. "In case you've forgotten, *Anthony*, we're partners in this. And she's my fuckin'—"

"I won't call them." Tony cut him off and waited to see if that vein snaking up the center of Gene's forehead would blow. It pulsed frantically for a couple of seconds, but seemed to hold. "We need to stick to the plan. And the plan is I wait for them to call me. I won't disturb them before then. Who knows what they're dealing with? They could have run into some kind of issue."

All the blood drained from Gene's face as he stopped pacing to glare at Tony. "Like what?" he demanded. "What possible issue could a group of highly trained, armed men run into on a remote island filled with nothin' but three teenage girls, one woman, and a guy who decided to make a career out of huggin' trees?"

"If I knew the answer to that," Tony told him, feeling the vein in his *own* forehead pulse menacingly, "we wouldn't be having this conversation, would we?

Now sit down, Gene. I'm sure everything is fine and
the phone will be ringing any minute to tell us they've
got them. Then they'll sail Maddy and the girls out to
international waters and call in the ransom, just like we
planned. The ball will be rolling into our court."

"I don't know…" Gene shook his head.

Tony glanced over his shoulder at the man who
covertly poked his head around the door leading into the
cabin. Gene thought he was just another one of Tony's
guys, brought onboard to help pilot the little yacht. And
that was true. That was *part* of his job description. The
other part of his job description was that he would help
Tony implement Plan B, should the need arise.

The man lifted an inquiring brow and Tony subtly
shook his head. *Not yet. Let's give it a little more time.*

8:35 p.m.…

Alex tossed the anchor overboard and watched it sink to
the shallow, sandy bottom. She'd sailed the catamaran
to within forty feet of the beach on Garden Key, and
on an impulse she decided to forgo using the dinghy to
make it the rest of the way.

It'll take too much time.

Tucking her glasses into the front pocket of her shorts,
she pinched her nose and chucked herself over the side
of the sailboat, hitting the water like a lead anvil—
gracefulness had never been her strong suit. The sea was
colder than she anticipated when it rolled over her head.
The average water temperature in the Gulf of Mexico
this time of year was anywhere between sixty-five and

seventy-five degrees. But the raised goose bumps on her bare arms and legs told her this particular spot was far below the norm.

She came up sputtering.

"Oh, for fuck's sake," she heard Mason curse. Sound traveled easily on the water. "Of all the crazy-assed—"

She wasn't sure how he ended that sentence. She was too busy stroking for shore. With every second that passed, with every inch she gained toward the beach, the composure she'd managed to don in the last few minutes slipped away.

Ninety minutes…

Ninety minutes! That's how long she'd been forced to sit out there, desperate to know what was happening after they'd gone overboard. Longing to help. Terrified out of her mind.

Ninety minutes of conjuring up a million horrible scenarios that ended with Mason and Bran dead or dying—after all, there had been all that gunfire right at the start. Ninety minutes of wringing her hands and tearing out her hair and deciding to pull anchor and set sail to help, only to remind herself that Mason had told her to stay put. Ninety minutes of pacing. Ninety minutes of peering through the binoculars. Ninety minutes of angry crying that turned into scared crying that inevitably gave way to frustrated crying. And around and around it'd gone in a vicious circle.

And then, after all that crying and pacing and hair-pulling and hand-wringing and second-guessing had come the three gunshots. Just three. *Bam!* Followed by *boom, boom!* Then more silence. Silence that was eventually broken by the roar of an outboard engine grumbling to a start. That had lasted all of about fifteen seconds before the deeper sound of inboard engines resounded across the open water. Through the binoculars, she'd watched the fishing boat emerge from around the side of the fort and zoom away from the island, its twin motors frothing up white water that played havoc with the dingy trailing behind the boat on a long rope.

It was then she'd *really* had a meltdown of near-nuclear proportions. Because she'd known with one-hundred-percent certainty that Mason and Bran weren't on that boat. No way would they have left her floating alone without a word.

They're dead.

Her heart had shattered, just...*crash*. And a million sharp pieces had shredded her soul. And then she'd seen it...

It had risen above the brick parapets, glorious and golden and bright beside the light of the low-hanging moon. The flare.

He's alive! They're alive!

She'd raced to start the sailboat's engines. And when she'd rounded the island, and through the binoculars saw Mason waiting for her on the beach—all big and strong and *alive*, his shaggy black hair glinting in the glow from the lighthouse, his granite jaw set at that stern, uncompromising angle—she'd wondered if it was possible for a person to die from sheer joy and relief.

"Damnit, Alex," Mason said now, his voice shockingly close.

She splashed to a stop, coughing on the seawater that invaded her mouth when it opened in a shocked *O*. He'd waded away from the beach to meet her and was standing in water up to his chest. The waves toyed with the silver piece of eight he and all the rest of the Deep Six Salvage guys wore around their necks.

Even without her glasses on, she could see his expression wasn't exactly welcoming. Neither were his words. "You couldn't bring the dinghy with you? Now I have to swim out to the—"

She didn't let him finish. She was so happy to see his sourpuss face and hear his cantankerous complaints that she swam straight into his arms, squeezing him until he grunted. Burying her nose in shoulder, she breathed in the unique scent of him. Watercolor paints and coconut oil.

Yes, big, bad Mason McCarthy was an artist. That's how he'd gotten the SEAL nom de guerre of "Monet." Though she rarely heard the others actually call him that. Maybe because watching him sit on that little stool with his easel and his paint palette was like watching an elephant perform *The Nutcracker*. It simply boggled the mind.

She gave him another heartfelt squeeze and decided it was sort of like hugging a sack of potatoes. He was all hard and lumpy…and hot. "What happened to your shirt?"

Not that she was complaining. Mason McCarthy in the semi-buff was quite a sight to behold.

She pulled back to find he had the strangest look on his face. It wasn't derisive or sarcastic. It wasn't even mildly annoyed. Nope. It was…*shocked*. Or pained, maybe?

"What?" She peered into the water around them. "Did you step on a jellyfish or something?"

"No." A muscle ticked in his jaw.

And then it occurred to her… "Is Bran okay? Oh, for

the love of… He's not hurt, is he?" The roar of her heart sounded like a waterfall in her ears.

"No." Now his eye was twitching.

"Madison Powers? Is she okay?"

"Yes."

"And the girls?"

"Fine."

"So what is it?" she demanded. "Why do you look like someone shoved a porcupine up your ass?"

"Don't," he said, reaching behind his back to unhook her ankles. Then he unwound her arms from around his neck and gently pushed her away.

"And Monsieur Monosyllable strikes again!" she said, frowning and treading water beside him.

"I need to get to the catamaran and try to use the marine radio to call back to Wayfarer Island."

"But—"

"No buts." He cut her off, wading further into the sea.

"But aren't you going to tell me what's going on?" All those happy, sparkly feelings she'd been having were starting to wear off. She was reminded why she and Mason didn't get along. It was because he was the most *impossible* man. "After almost an hour and a half, I think I deserve an explan—"

"Later," he muttered, stroking toward the sailboat.

"Wow!" she called after him. "How is it you've never been voted Mr. Personality? I mean, with conversational chops like that?"

He didn't turn back. Didn't stop swimming. Simply ignored her and kept stroking across the tops of the waves, his huge arms and massive shoulders making the exercise look effortless.

So…same ol', same ol'.

And why that should cause an ache to form somewhere in the vicinity of her heart, she didn't know. Or maybe she just didn't *want* to know.

Yup! And there they are. Right on schedule.

All her conflicting feelings were back in full force.

Chapter 13

8:51 p.m.…

"IT'S EMPTY," ALEX SAID AFTER PEERING INTO THE PARK
ranger's refrigerator, causing Bran to bite the inside of
his cheek.

After he and Maddy rescued the missing girls—
thankfully, they'd been precisely where the masked
asshole said they'd be, scared but unharmed and terribly
happy to see Maddy—they'd trudged from the fort and
across the bridge, intending to gather Rick and Sally
Mae before heading back to the fort to keep watch. But
about halfway down the beach, they saw Alex wading
onto the sand.

After the introductions had been made and Alex had
been brought up to speed on the events of the night, she
proceeded to do what she did best: jabber nonstop and
make herself right at home.

"I mean, I've never seen a fridge this empty," she
said, shaking her head in wonder. Her riot of curls was
drying and poking out every which way until it looked
like she'd gone through hell in a high wind.

"It's not *empty*," Ranger Rick assured her, leaning
against the Formica countertop. "It's just…slim pickings."

"Slim pickings?" Alex glanced from him to the
refrigerator, back to Rick, and then back to the refrigerator. "It's like *The Grapes of Wrath* in here."

Bran snorted, happy for the levity Alex brought to the situation. It helped him feel more like his usual self. The monster having been safely tucked away. Its claws sheathed. Its fangs filed.

He blew out a deep breath that immediately strangled in his throat when Maddy walked over to him and laced her fingers through his. She'd passed out water bottles and comforted the teens as best she could. But now, to his complete dismay, she gravitated toward his side and acted like that whole hand-holding thing after the standoff by the gunpowder magazine house wasn't a onetime deal.

He'd allowed it then because she'd seemed to need it, seemed to need his physical touch for reassurance. But now? Well, now, if he let her hold his hand it would mean…something it *shouldn't*.

"What do you usually eat?" Alex asked Rick, dragging Bran from his thoughts. He extricated his hand from Maddy's by pretending he needed to check something on the side of his M4. Cowardly? Sure. But at least it got the job done. And never mind that the skin of his palm missed the feel of hers against it.

"Mostly PB and J," Rick said.

"Oh, good!" Alex beamed. "One of my faves." She reached into the refrigerator and grabbed the jar of strawberry jelly from the middle shelf. Turning, she brandished it triumphantly and asked, "So where are the PB and the bread to go along with this J?"

Rick opened the breadbox and pulled out a loaf of classic white Wonder Bread. He passed it to Alex and opened a cupboard door to take down a half-empty jar of Jif.

"Thank you." She gave him a toothy smile that, unless Bran was mistaken, made Rick blush. It hit Bran then... Alex was pretty. In a wholesome, quirky kind of way.

Huh. How about that?

And even though he tried to convince himself otherwise, he was happy Rick had somebody besides Maddy to flash his dastardly dimples at.

"So who's hungry?" Alex turned to the three teenagers sitting on the bed.

Bran glanced at the girls. They'd been put through the wringer, and it showed in the circles under their eyes and the paleness of their cheeks. *Poor kids. No one should hafta see what they've seen. Not at their age.* And he should know. He'd been there, done that. And if there was a T-shirt involved, he wanted no part of it.

"Anyone?" Alex prodded when the teens just stared at her and blinked. "No? Really?" She looked perplexed. "Is it because of peanut allergies? Because they say that one point four percent of all Americans have peanut allergies. Or maybe...are you guys gluten free?"

God help them all if any of the girls *were* gluten free because Alex probably had some mind-numbing statistic to spout. Lucky for him—for all of them, really—the girls shook their heads and Alex was forced to turn her attention to Rick. "How about you? Can I make you a sandwich?"

The park ranger looked at the peanut butter Alex was slathering onto a slice of bread the way you looked at a dead bird your cat proudly presented you with. *Thank you. Barf.* He declined with a vigorous headshake.

Alex's expression was the same one she would have worn if Ranger Rick had been growing extra pairs of hands from his ears. She eventually shrugged and turned to Bran and Maddy by the front door. "How about you guys? Surely, after all that running and swimming and shooting, you're both starving."

"She's kiddin', right?" Maddy asked from the side of her mouth.

"Not at all," Bran assured her quietly. Louder he said, "I think you're on your own, Alex."

"So you're all telling me I'm the only one who eats when she's stressed out?" She shoved the peanut-butter-smeared slice of bread into her mouth.

"And when she's happy or excited or bored or..." Bran let the sentence dangle.

Alex pinned him with a look. "What are you saying? That I'm always eating?"

"If the current squirrel cheeks and the Pop-Tart wrappers strewn around your bedroom back home are anything to go by," he said.

"Hmph," Alex grunted, loading up another slice of bread with peanut butter. This time she added jelly before folding it in half and taking a monster bite. "You're just jealous," she garbled around a mouthful. "Because I've got a metabolism that would make—"

"Does she ever stop talkin'?" Maddy whispered conspiratorially.

Bran raised a brow. "That's a little like the crocodile telling the alligator he has too many teeth, doncha think, Mouthy McGee?"

Maddy grinned at him. *Really* grinned at him. And he was so happy to see something on her face besides fear or anguish or grief that he was tempted to scoop her up and press a kiss to that grin. While he was at it, he'd suck that plump top lip of hers straight into his mouth and lave it with his tongue until she met him stroke for stroke.

What the hell are you thinking, dickhead?

"My momma always said I could talk the hair off a dog. But I swear," Maddy said below her breath, "I think Alex has me beat."

"You get used to it after a while," he assured her, absently squeezing his thigh, trying to rub away the dull, annoying ache of his wound. "Eventually it starts to sound like the teacher in the Charlie Brown cartoon."

Maddy snorted.

"Are you guys whispering about me over there?" Alex demanded.

And because Bran *was* feeling more like himself, it was easy to fall back into his usual habits. "This just in, Alex." He lifted a hand to an imaginary earpiece like he was a national newscaster. "Galileo reports you're not *actually* the center of the universe."

Alex pulled a face, still chewing. "Smart-ass." At some point she'd rubbed the zinc oxide from her nose so the smattering of freckles across the bridge stood out in sharp relief.

The sound of the outboard engine on the catamaran's little dinghy growled to a start, and Bran turned to the open door to watch Mason motor the rubber craft from the sailboat to the beach. Then Mason pulled the dinghy onto the sand and hustled to the ranger's station, taking the steps two at a time and shouldering his way past Bran only to blink against the dull brightness inside.

"You're eating." Mason frowned at Alex once his eyes had adjusted. "Should've known."

Alex didn't bristle or take offense. She grinned and held out the last of her peanut butter and jelly sandwich.

Mason hesitated for a whole half second before accepting it. He shoved the entire thing in his mouth. "Thanks. I'm starving."

"See." Alex waved a hand at Mason. "*This* man has sense."

Bran rolled his eyes. "So did the signal work? Were you able to get LT on the marine radio?" he asked Mason.

"Ya-huh." Mason nodded, motioning for Alex to make him another sandwich. She snapped him a salute before slathering peanut butter onto a fresh slice of bread. "I gave him the skinny, and he put in a satellite call to the Coast Guard station on Key West."

"And?" Bran prompted when Mason stopped to accept the sandwich Alex handed him. Between the two of them, Ranger Rick would soon be eaten out of house and home. Bran knew from experience since somehow it had become his job to keep the cupboards and refrigerator on Wayfarer Island stocked—probably because he was the only one who cooked—and the endeavor was proving to be a full-time occupation.

"And LT says the closest Coast Guard cutter is three fuckin' hours out," Mason said, shoving half the sandwich into his face. When he realized there were underage ears listening in, he turned to the teenagers who were blinking and eyeing him with awe. Bran couldn't blame the girls. Mason was as big as a Mack truck and twice as tough-looking, what with his M4 slung over his shoulder and a huge Celtic cross tattoo stretched across his mammoth back. "Uh...pardon my French, ladies," he garbled around his PB and J.

"Three hours." Bran made a face.

Mason nodded and chewed. "We're supposed to hang tight until they get here. Oh, and by the way, I had to convince LT not to power up the Otter and head in our direction." He was referring to the single-engine, propeller-driven floatplane that Romeo, one of their teammates, had purchased soon after moving to Wayfarer Island.

Amusement and affection for his best friend warmed Bran's heart. "That shouldn't have taken too much convincing since he doesn't know how to fly the damned thing." He winced and turned to the teenagers. "Pardon *my* French, ladies."

"I think he was thinking he'd wing it." Mason snorted around another huge bite. "But he eventually agreed it was probably best if he didn't try to become a pilot in one night. He's going to hang out by the radio in case we need to relay any additional information."

Bran nodded, then looked around the room. "So that's it then. We wait."

"In the fort," Mason added for the benefit of those who weren't privy to the plan. "At least that's where all of you guys will hole up. I'll keep vigil on the cat." He used their abbreviation for the catamaran. "Just in case the Coast Guard tries to reach us on the marine radio once they get closer."

"I'll help you man the radio," Alex piped up.

"F-for fuck's sake, why?" Mason sputtered. He grimaced as he peeked at the group of girls. "Sorry. I'm not used to having kids around."

"Hey, man. We're not kids," the dark-haired girl named Louisa said, her Spanish accent barely noticeable.

"And we're pretty proficient in the use of profanity. So you can stop apologizing."

Mason lifted his eyebrows. "Duly noted." Then he turned back to Alex. "Manning the radio is a one-man job."

"But I wouldn't want you to get lonely out there on the sailboat," Alex said. "And I wouldn't want you dozing off either. I'll be there to provide company and keep you awake."

"No." Mason adamantly shook his head. "You need to go with Maddy and the girls into the fort. Stay safe in there while Bran and Rick"—he tilted his head toward the park ranger—"keep watch from the parapets."

"Wow," Maddy blurted from beside Bran. "Do you even hear yourself?"

"Huh?" Mason frowned at her. "What do you mean?"

"I mean the fact that this plan of yours *reeks* of machismo and misogyny." She crossed her arms and thrust out her chin.

Uh-oh. Danger, Will Robinson, Bran thought.

"Well said, sister suffragette." Alex raised a fist like she was auditioning to be the next leader of the Black Panthers.

Mason opened his mouth. Closed it. Opened it again. Then closed it again. He started blinking like he had something in his eyes.

When Mason had been silent for too long, Maddy shoved her hands on her hips. "You have a way of *not* sayin' anything louder than anyone else on the planet. Has anyone ever told you that?"

"You can really hear the gears grinding up there, can't you?" Alex motioned toward Mason's head.

Mason turned to Bran. "Little help here?"

"No way." Bran shook his head. "You're on your own with this one, bro." They were the same words Mason had used when Bran asked for help in the moat.

Mason sent him a look that promised slow, painful retribution. Bran didn't care. Any pain he suffered later would be totally worth it. Mason was the kind of man even tough guys called *Mister*. So seeing him squirm beneath the blistering stare of two women wasn't something Bran often, or *ever*, got the chance to do.

Where's a bowl of popcorn when I need it? Suddenly, his appetite had returned.

"Look," Mason said. "It's just a fact that it'll be better for everyone if you ladies stay out of the way where we don't have to worry about you."

Oh, it's like watching a slow-motion train wreck!

"Um, yeah." Maddy's eyes flashed, her cheeks going rosy red. When she was in full-on pique, she was that kind of beautiful. The discombobulating kind. "If we've suddenly changed the definition of the word *fact* into *shit you just made up*. I'm done being told to sit in the corner and paint my toenails."

"Huh?" Mason shook his head in confusion.

"It's like you can *see* the stupidity cloud handing over his head, am I right?" Alex lisped. A sure sign she was really enjoying herself.

"I don't understand," Mason said, a muscle ticking under his left eye.

When Maddy said, "Obviously," two of the teenagers snickered.

"We could take him out back and try to beat some sense into him," Alex suggested.

Bran snorted. The idea was so absurd. Like hearing a second grader challenge a senior to a fistfight. *Jungle gym. Three p.m. No backsies.*

He sobered immediately, however, when Alex turned on him. "What's that, Bran?"

"Yeah," Maddy demanded, her gray eyes sparkling. "You want some of this?"

Oh, she had no idea how *much* he wanted some of that. *All* of that, in fact. And *that* thought was enough to convince him it was past time he put an end to this incredibly entertaining tête-à-tête. "So what would you ladies suggest be your jobs for the next three hours?" he inquired.

"Alex can help Mason man the radio, and me and the girls will join you and Rick on lookout duty," Maddy told him. "Girls, grab some more water bottles. We're headed to the fort."

When Mason joined Bran by the front door, he mumbled, "I don't know how it happened. I thought I was doing a hell of a job in the driver's seat and then *wham!* The wheels went flying off the bus."

Bran chuckled and slapped Mason on the back.

"I'll trade you places," Mason suggested, and it was the first time Bran had ever seen pleading in the big guy's eyes. "You can sit by the radio and let Alex keep *you* company."

As enticing as it was to separate himself from Maddy and all her sweet, curvy, kissable temptations, Bran couldn't imagine spending three hours alone with Alex. His eardrums wouldn't survive it.

"I'd rather put on a life jacket lined with razor blades and jump into a pool of rubbing alcohol," he said.

"But—"

"I'd rather jab sharpened pencils into my eyes."

"But—"

"I'd rather eat three-day-old road kill."

"I get it," Mason grumbled. "You're not trading places."

Bran grinned. "What was your first clue?"

"Go fuck yourself," Mason muttered, shouldering his way through the door.

"Tempting!" Bran called after him. "I do have great legs!"

Mason mumbled something Bran couldn't make out while he jogged down the three steps.

"He does that so well," Alex said.

Bran glanced over to see she'd joined him in the doorway. But she wasn't looking at him. Oh, no. She only had eyes for Mason.

Uh…Mason's *ass,* if Bran was correctly tracking the trajectory of her gaze.

"I thought you didn't like him." He eyed her curiously.

"Can't stand the talk," she admitted, then made a face. "Or the *no* talk, which is usually the case. But, man, do I *love* the walk."

"No shit?" Bran chuckled. "Have you ever thought of telling *him* that?"

Alex pushed her glasses up the bridge of her nose. "I've considered it." She shrugged. "But the one time I opened my mouth to say something to him, my brain got really agitated and started shouting, *No! Don't do it! It'll be awful!* Which totally offended my mouth. And then it took two weeks for my brain and my mouth to make up and become friends again. Which meant I spent the first week saying things I hadn't thought about. And the second week thinking about things I never got up the nerve to say. It was just awful. Terrible. I never want to go through that again. So…yeah. No." She shook her head and wrinkled her nose. "I'm sorry. What was the question again?"

"I've forgotten," he said, his head spinning because he'd inadvertently hopped on the carnival ride known as Alex Merriweather's Motor Mouth.

"Mason! Wait!" Maddy darted past them and ran down the steps to catch Mason on the beach. "Your shirt! I forgot to give it back to you."

Mason took the gray T-shirt from her, handing her his rifle so he could tug the garment over his head.

"Well, now *that's* a pity," Louisa said as she and others pushed past Bran and Alex to gather on the front porch. Bran was overwhelmed by the smells of lip balm, body butter, and hair gel. A million high-school memories swirled through his head. "That man should never wear a shirt."

Alex nodded. "Preach it, sister."

"And he should be bronzed for posterity," Louisa added. "So generations of women can appreciate his magnificence. Like Michelangelo's statue of David."

Alex answered with an "Amen!"

"I'm gonna be sick to my stomach," Bran complained. "You." He pointed at Louisa. "You're too young to be saying things like that about a man who's old enough to be your father."

"Right," Louisa scoffed. "If he started having kids at, like, what? Sixteen?"

"It's a biological possibility," Bran insisted. "And

you." He narrowed his gaze on Alex. "You shouldn't be encouraging the delinquency of minors."

"No need to be jealous, dude." The brunette with the Jersey accent and the tough-girl piercings grinned at him. Maddy had introduced her as Donna. "We think you're totes adorbs too."

He shook his head. "I'm sorry?"

"Totally adorable," she clarified. "Like an older, taller, hotter version of Benjamin Ciaramello."

"Who?" he was amazed to find himself asking.

"Ah, come on. You know," Sally Mae drawled. "He played a high school football player on *Friday Night Lights*. The TV show, not the movie."

"Really?" Alex asked. She glanced at Bran, her eyes narrowed, her expression considering. "Yup. I guess I can see it. Around the eyes and mouth, maybe. Hey, isn't that show a little retro for you guys? I mean, it was popular when *I* was in high school."

"We stream it on Netflix," Louisa said. "Mostly to catch shirtless Taylor Kitsch moments."

"Ah." Alex nodded again. "Yes. Those *are* nice, aren't they?"

"What did I just say about contributing to the delinquency of minors?" Bran asked, completely disconcerted to be standing within earshot of this ridiculous conversation.

"Relax, Rambo," Alex said. "It's just girl talk."

"Yeah." Louisa grinned at him, her dark eyes glinting. "Talking about shirtless guys is pretty much de rigueur for the seventeen-year-old set."

"Good use of an SAT word." Donna slapped her a high five.

"So don't *you* go putting a shirt on, too, *si?*" Louisa continued, batting her lashes. "You shirtless is by far the best thing that's happened to any of us tonight."

Bran sputtered as Alex hee-hawed beside him like a crazed donkey.

"*You,*" he said again, this time pointing at Alex's nose. "Cut it out."

"Hey, I'm just—"

Before Alex could finish, Sally Mae piped up with, "Are y'all really Navy SEALs?"

He turned to the blond, ponytailed teenager. "*Former* Navy SEALs," he corrected. "Who told you that?"

"Miss Maddy," Donna answered. "She said you were the baddest of the bad, and we didn't have to worry about a thing as long as you're protecting us."

"Man, that's hot," Louisa said.

"*He's* hot," Sally Mae added.

"Yo, they're *both* hot," Donna finished. "The big one in a fierce, scary kind of way. And *this* one"—she tilted her chin toward Bran—"in a dreamy kind of way."

Bran felt a muscle twitching in his jaw. And when Sally Mae asked, "Are y'all the ones who took out Bin Laden?" he turned and pointed his finger at Maddy. "Madison Powers!" he thundered.

"What?" She blinked at him from the beach.

"Control your charges!"

The teens dissolved into giggles and Maddy shook her head with exasperation. "Come on, girls!" she called. "Leave Grumpy Gus alone."

"Don't you mean hot, shirtless Grumpy Gus?" Donna hooted as they traipsed down the stairs to join Maddy and Mason on the beach.

"I need a shower," Bran told Alex. "I feel dirty."

Alex rolled her eyes. "I think you'll survive."

Rick exited the cottage, looking a little incongruous in his khaki shorts and shirt with the SCAR-L rifle slung over his shoulder. But Bran had to give it to the guy. He'd comported himself pretty well, all things considered.

Now, if only the little shit would stop looking at Maddy with all that yearning and lust in his eyes...

"So how's it going with Maddy?" Alex broke into his thoughts, clicking off the light inside the cottage and closing the door behind them.

"So far it's been just great," he said sarcastically, watching Rick jog down the steps and join Maddy and the girls. When Rick placed a hand on Maddy's arm, leaning close to whisper something in her ear, the thing inside Bran unsheathed its claws and bared its fangs.

Alex pursed her lips. "I'm not talking about the creepy masked men and the gun battles, doofus. I'm talking about...you know. Like, *how's it going with Maddy?* How is it seeing her again? She's prettier than she looks in her online pictures. And pluckier too. Although you can't really tell pluckiness from Internet photos, can you? No. That's ridiculous. But my point is, I can see why you're all goo-goo, gah-gah over her. So?"

"I'm sorry." He used her earlier words against her. "What was the question again?"

"So how's it going with Maddy?"

"In how many languages can I say *none of your god-damned business*?"

"Because when you look at her," Alex continued as if he hadn't spoken, "the expression in your eyes says *I'll take a slice of that* along with *and how about some right goddamned now on the side*."

"You better go catch up with Mason." He hated that his feelings for Maddy were so obvious. "He's liable to take off in the dinghy and make you swim out to the catamaran."

"Uh…change the subject much, Señor Subject Changer?" She pursed her lips.

"It'd serve you right," he continued. "Since you didn't bring the dinghy with you the first time around."

"So, how's it going with you and Maddy?"

He gritted his teeth. "You're like a dog with a bone."

"I'll take that as a compliment."

"You shouldn't," he insisted as the motor on the dinghy's outboard engine grumbled to life.

Alex's eyes rounded.

"Told you." He smiled in vindication.

"Ugh!" Alex threw her hands in the air. "He is the most *impossible* man!"

As she ran down the steps and across the beach, Bran was left with no recourse but to follow Maddy and the ranger as they herded the teenagers toward the bridge. All the while he tried *not* to think about how much he wanted Maddy. How much he *craved* her.

It was an exercise in futility, of course. Because no matter how he tried not to watch the swing of her plump ass in those cutoff shorts, he found his eyes glued there time and again. And no matter how often he told his lips to *just forget about it already*, they continued to throb with the memory of her kiss.

And talk about throbbing… His lips weren't the only body part suffering the affliction.

Damnit! Maddy was driving him crazy. Totally nuts. And when she turned to smile at him over her shoulder, her pretty eyes sparkling in the glow of the moon and stars and the spotlights, he seriously considered taking Mason up on his offer of trading places.

Eardrums be damned!

Chapter 14

8:54 p.m. ...

RING! RING!

When the satellite phone came to life, Tony nearly dropped his fourth scotch and soda in his rush to answer it. Punching the talk button with one hand and setting his drink on the end table with the other, he said two words: "I'm listening."

The response that echoed through the receiver sent chills cascading over his entire body. "We have a problem."

Tony swallowed and glanced at Gene who had stopped his incessant pacing to skirt the molded fiber-glass coffee table and hover over him where he sat on the end of the sofa. Careful to keep his face blank even though his stomach was trying its best to make the scotch reverse directions, he managed to say evenly, "What kind?"

It took every ounce of willpower he possessed not to grab his highball glass and hurl it against the bulk-head as he listened to Rory Gellman—his former high school buddy turned Army Ranger turned high-priced mercenary—tell him that two of the four men who'd stormed Garden Key were dead. And that the remaining two men had been forced to limp back in their dinghy to the trawler Rory was using as a base of operations when their fishing boat ran out of fuel.

Tony gritted his teeth so hard he heard them creak. "What happened?"

"Apparently there are two armed men on the island," Rory said. "And my guys are saying they're highly trained."

"Shit," Tony cursed, belying his calm demeanor.

That had Gene demanding, "What? Damnit, Tony! What's happenin'?"

Tony scowled up at Gene and raised a hand for silence. Into the phone, he said, "Who are they, Rory?"

"Hell if I know," Rory answered. "You checked the logs just like I did. No one but Miss Powers and the girls was supposed to be camping on Garden Key tonight."

"Shit," Tony cursed again, his mind racing. Was it possible Madison Powers had hired an armed escort without telling anyone? And then he quickly decided it didn't matter. He had bigger things to worry about.

"Can the two you lost be traced back to you?" he asked, holding his breath. Because if those guys could lead back to Rory, and if Rory could lead back to Tony…

"What do you mean the two that were lost?" Gene thundered. "*Who* was lost? The girls?"

"Shut up and sit down!" Tony yelled right back. "I'm handling this!" Into the satphone he said, "Go on."

"All the authorities would have to do is run their prints," Rory admitted. "We were all in the services, so our profiles are in the government databases. And that brings me back to the *really* bad news. One of those two mystery men on the island got hold of a radio. I'm not sure how, but I suspect they had a boat anchored somewhere. A few minutes ago, right before my guys showed up, he put in a call over marine channel sixteen to some asshole on a nearby island who used a satellite phone to call the Coast Guard in Key West."

"*Shit!*" Tony roared, ignoring the sputtering sound Gene was making. The ocean breeze had been blowing across the back of the yacht, keeping his temper cooled, but now it suddenly felt hot and oppressive. "We have to go back and get the bodies."

"The *bodies*!" Gene howled, stumbling back and nearly losing his footing on the stairs that led down to the small swim deck on the back of the boat.

"I have a second group willing to go in and do exactly that," Rory assured him. "And they'll finish the job with Miss Powers and the girls too. But to do that, my men will need to take out the two murderous assholes guarding that island. And I know you said you didn't want any bloodshed, but—"

"Forget that," Tony snarled, not hesitating. "Do it. Whatever it takes."

"Quadruple the pay, right?" Rory asked. "You said if things went haywire, then we'd get—"

Impatience skittered across Tony's nerve endings. "Damnit, Rory!" he thundered. "When in all our years together have you ever known me to go back on my word? Besides, it's your ass on the line as much as it is mine if the authorities get their hands on the bodies of your men."

"Consider it done then," Rory said. "Just know it'll take some time. The place is a fort, so I can't use standard tactics. I'll have to put my men in the water and have them sneak onto the island, past the seawall, through the moat, and then inside the curtain wall."

"Just hurry," Tony snarled. "You don't want the Coast Guard getting there before you."

"According to the radio transmission, we should have some time," Rory assured him. "The closest cutter is a few hours out."

"Good. Great. Call me when it's done." And with that, he signed off and faced Gene.

"Wh-what the hell is goin' on, Tony?" All the color had drained from Gene's face. And by the time Tony filled Gene in on what had transpired on the island, Gene's paleness had taken on a definite bluish tinge.

"So…" Gene said, only to stop and swallow and suck in a ragged breath. "We just…we just have to cut our losses, right?"

Oh! Tony wanted to reach up and strangle him. *Cut our losses? Cut our losses! Are you nuts?*

"Wrong," he gritted. "We see it through."

"See it through?" Gene asked incredulously. "How the hell do you plan to—"

"I *told* you I prepared for every contingency." Tony fisted his hands so tightly he knew he was ruining his latest manicure and leaving crescent moon cuts on his palms.

"You prepared for there to be two armed men on the island who—"

"Not *that* precisely," Tony interrupted again. "But something, *anything*, like it. My guys are sending in a second team."

Gene blinked and drew back as if Tony's words had physical force behind them. "A *second* team?"

Tony nodded. "A larger, better-armed team."

"*Better armed?*" Gene spat the words as if they tasted rancid on his tongue. He grabbed the phone and thrust it at Tony's face. "Call them back! Tell them it's off! It's too dangerous!"

Tony slid a glance to the man standing by the cabin door and subtly dipped his chin. The mercenary began a stealthy journey in their direction.

"It's done, Gene," Tony said, reaching nonchalantly for his highball glass. "The wheels are already in motion."

"Well, apply the goddamned brakes!" Gene yelled, his voice echoing over the gently lapping waves. "You can't be serious about sendin' in more men. They could turn that island into a war zone!"

"If that's what it takes to get the job done." Tony took a sip of his drink, grimacing because the melting ice had watered it down.

"If that's what it t-takes?" Gene sputtered, his face having gone from blue to fire-engine red. That vein in his forehead was pulsing again.

"Yes!" Tony yelled, having reached the end of his patience. His nerves were shot. His certainty of success had dropped from one hundred percent to something more like fifty-fifty. And Gene was such an idiot that he actually thought they could call it off. "Even if we can't get Maddy and the girls, we have to retrieve those dead bodies. Don't you *get* that? Don't you understand? If the authorities get their hands on those bodies, they'll lead back to Rory. Rory leads back to me. I lead back to *you*. If we don't finish this, we won't just be looking at a failed business, we'll be looking at an eight-by-ten!"

"I don't care!" Gene shrieked. "Maddy's on that island!"

"You may not care!" Tony screamed, pushing to his feet and forcing Gene to stumble back. "But I do! I'm not losing everything just because you don't have the stomach to follow through when the going gets tough!"

"No!" Gene bellowed and lunged for him, hands curled into claws.

Rory's man moved like a flash, tackling Gene to the deck before Gene could lay a finger on Tony.

"Get off me!" Gene howled, writhing ineffectually as the mercenary yanked Gene's arms behind his back and secured them with the bright-orange zip tie he pulled from the pocket of his shorts.

"Take him down to one of the berths," Tony said, looking at the Stetson that had flown off Gene's head to land at his feet. With a curl of his lip, he kicked it off the back of the boat and watched the waves happily embrace it, tugging it along in the direction of their tidal pull. "Tie him to the bed and gag him."

───⟨⟨⟩⟩───

8:59 p.m. …

"Okay, so y'all keep your eyes peeled for any approachin' boats. I'll go help Bran keep an eye on things over by the lighthouse," Maddy told the girls once she found them a spot atop the parapets where they had an unobstructed view of the sea around the island.

"Right, Miss Maddy," Louisa said. "You go help Bran over on the other side. Because your face on his face will be *so* helpful."

"L-Louisa Sanchez," Maddy sputtered. "Of all the things to say."

"Do ya deny it?" Sally Mae asked, leaning back against an old cannon that no longer had the ability to defend the crumbling garrison. There was enough light filtering up from the spotlight on the seawall below them to show the teasing glint in the girl's eyes. It gave Maddy hope that the teens wouldn't be *too* scarred by what they'd experienced this night.

Kids are resilient, right? They bounce back?

"Deny what?" she asked as innocently as she could, picking at a loose thread on the hem of her T-shirt.

"Deny that you're hot to trot for SEAL McStudly," Donna said.

Maddy pulled a face. "Am I that obvious?"

"Totally," Donna said. "But, yo, that's okay, Miss Maddy. He's that obvious too. Way to go. Big-time score. He's super hot."

"Wait a minute. Wait a minute." Maddy patted the air. "Are y'all sayin' you think Bran…"

She didn't finish. She wasn't sure how to. *Do y'all think Bran really likes me?* just sounded so…high school girls' locker room.

Well, look who you're talkin' to.

"Wants to butter your muffin?" Sally Mae said, causing Maddy to blink. "Yes. We definitely think he wants to do just that."

"Sally Mae Winchester! And here I thought you were the shy one!"

Sally Mae snickered.

"Good Lord." Maddy shook her head. "Your parents are goin' to kill me. Not only did I nearly get y'all kidnapped, but I also got you talkin' about butter and muffins. Which…ew. That's a disgustin' euphemism when you stop and think about it. But more important, it's official. I am the *worst* chaperone in the history of the world. The *universe*!"

"Please," Louisa scoffed. "We've known about

buttered muffins for quite some time. In fact, I venture to guess some of us have even had our muff—"

"La-la-la!" Maddy sang, plugging her ears. "I'm ignorin' all y'all. You don't exist. This conversation never happened."

"Come on, Miss Maddy," Sally Mae said after Maddy dropped her hands. "After everything that's happened tonight, don't we deserve a little fun?"

And suddenly all Maddy's guilt and self-reproach bubbled to the surface, making the skin across her face and shoulders itch. "I'm so sorry, girls. Sorry for everything."

"It's not your fault," Louisa was quick to assure her, grabbing her hand.

Maddy squeezed her fingers. "But I chose this island adventure because I…because I…"

"Wanted to get close to SEAL McStudly," Donna finished for her. "Yo, that took us about two seconds to figure out once we saw you with him."

"And we certainly don't blame ya for it," Sally Mae piped up. "After all, the man is a triple threat."

"What does that mean?" Maddy asked.

"Tall, dark, and handsome," the three of them chimed at once.

Maddy made a face. "I know, right? It should be against the law or somethin'. Two out of the three? Sure. But three out of the three?"

"So go on," Louisa encouraged. "Go make like Paula Abdul."

"I'm afraid to ask…"

"Get your groove on."

"Were you even *alive* when that song came out?" she demanded.

"We are the digital generation," Sally Mae said. "All media, past and present, is at our fingertips."

"I don't know whether to be terrified or impressed," Maddy admitted.

"Do you guys suddenly get the impression she's stalling?" Donna interjected.

"You're totally right," Louisa agreed. "Hey, Miss Maddy, Colonel Sanders called. He wants you back on the job."

Maddy blinked. "And now I'm lost again."

"You know"—Louisa rolled her hand—"Colonel Sanders. Kentucky Fried Chicken?"

"Yeah. So?"

"So we're sayin' that now that ya know SEAL McStudly wants to butter your muffin, you're bein' a total chicken," Sally Mae finished.

"I'm *not* being a chicken," Maddy insisted.

"Then go make like Paula Abdul," Louisa challenged.

"I am goin' to help him with *lookout* duty," Maddy insisted haughtily, sniffing like the Queen of England. "There will be *no* Paula Abdul-ing about it."

"*Bok, bok, bok!*" Louisa said.

"Fine! I'm goin'!" Maddy turned on her heels and fled like the lily-livered coward she was. When the sound of giggles followed her, a grin tugged at her lips. It was good hearing the teens laughing.

Even if it is at my expense.

Careful on the worn bricks, she made her journey along the top of the parapets, thinking about what the girls had said and feeling a sense of vindication. Despite Bran trying to pretend like there was nothing between them, it was obvious to everyone—including three teens—that, in fact, there *was*.

Fueled by that knowledge, she lifted her face to the warm wind. The sea had a particular aroma at night. There were still the smells of salt water and fish. But underneath that was something sweeter. Something older. Something darker and more mysterious.

At night the sea smells like the secrets it holds, her father told her when she was eleven and commented on the phenomenon. *Like lost souls and fantastical creatures and the sunken treasure of millennia.*

Maddy had always fancied that explanation.

She breathed deep and thought of the treasure that Bran and his friends were hunting. The *Santa Cristina*. The holy grail of sunken Spanish shipwrecks. It was so romantic. So exciting. So…Bran-like.

She blinked as the lighthouse made its revolution, momentarily blinding her. But when her eyesight returned, she located Rick at his post atop the west wall. The barrel of the machine gun rested against his shoulder, and he marched back and forth in a tight pattern, reminding her of an old-timey soldier.

Biting her lip, she started in his direction. Not once since this whole hellacious night began had she stopped to ask him how he was doing, if he was okay—probably because he'd been such a trouper about everything—but she planned to remedy that right now. Except, when she stopped beside him, he beat her to the punch.

"Are you okay?" The moonlight showed the concern in his eyes.

Lord, he's adorable. If I were ten years younger…

You wouldn't have a chance at Bran, her conscience reminded her.

Right-O. Plus, you couldn't pay her to repeat her

early twenties. She'd been so young and silly, caught up in college and sorority functions and her boyfriend who, although he'd been a really nice guy, was more interested in going to see local bands play than he was in going to class and making sure his parents' money was well spent. It wasn't until she went to work for her father that she came to realize the true meaning of life, which, as far as she could figure, was about living each day to its fullest and helping your fellow man along the way as best you could.

"Shouldn't I be askin' *you* that?" She gave Rick a self-deprecating smile.

"Why?" He frowned.

"Well, because you're a park ranger, not a commando. Yet here you are on guard duty with a machine gun in hand."

"Says the oil heiress who swam through an underwater tunnel and withstood two standoffs at gunpoint."

"Touché." Her smile turned genuine.

Of course, it dimmed a bit when she saw that look come over his face again. Not wanting to give him the wrong idea, she shook her head and said, "Well…I guess I better finish my rounds and check on Bran."

Rick's expression fell. "I'm sure he's fine. After all, he *is* a commando."

"All the same," she said, skirting by Rick and giving his arm a companionable squeeze along the way. With that one touch, she hoped to convey her thanks for all he had done and at the same time let him know that friendship is all that would, all that *could*, ever be between them.

She didn't check his expression to see if it worked—not really wanting to know if it *didn't*—and instead

turned her gaze to Bran. He was leaning against the side
of the lighthouse, one knee bent to take the weight off
his wounded leg, his arms crossed over his spectacularly
bare chest. He'd stopped to grab one of the sleeping
bags off the beach. It was folded in half and acting as
a pallet for his mean-looking rifle and the rifles of the
two men who were stranded out on their fishing boat
somewhere. The starlight reflecting off the surrounding
waves seemed to make love to his skin, kissing it and
caressing it in undulating patterns until it looked alive
and healthy and vibrant. And the medallion he wore
around his neck caught the moonlight and glinted, a
beacon calling her to him.

Triple threat indeed, she thought as she picked her
way toward Bran. The ground atop the fort walls was
uneven. The years had deposited sand and soil over the
bricks, allowing grass and a few sticker bushes to take
hold and grow.

On the subject of sticker bushes…

She had one stuck in the base of her thumb. *Well, not
a sticker. A splinter.* The irritating little foreigner burned
and itched, and she absently tried squeezing it out. But
that only seemed to anger the thing.

Then the *last* thing she was thinking about was her
impaled hand. Because suddenly, she was standing in
front of Bran, and there was a warm, wicked gleam in
his eyes when he turned away from the sea. It punched
the breath right out of her.

It really should *be illegal.*

Chapter 15

9:04 p.m.…

"THE GIRLS OKAY?" BRAN ASKED.

"Full of piss and vinegar," Maddy managed, disgusted at how breathless her voice sounded.

"They are quite the trio." A lock of hair fell over his brow, but he didn't brush it back. Just stood there looking big and hot and completely, quintessentially *male*. She tucked her hands into her pockets to keep from touching him.

"So, now that we're alone," he said, getting right to it, "there's something I wanna talk to you about."

Here it comes.

He rolled in his lips, hesitating, then, "I owe you a blanket apology for…a lot of things. But mostly for giving you the wrong impression about me." He rubbed a hand over the back of his neck. "About *us*."

His words might have cut into her like knives had she not just had that conversation with the girls. Now she was armed with rope and was determined to give him just enough to hang himself.

"And what impression would that be?" she asked curiously.

"That we're more than just—"

"Pen pals?" she finished for him, batting her lashes.

He pulled a face. "Okay. So that was a total asshole thing to say."

"Total asshole," she agreed.

"And you've already proved your point. No need to keep busting my balls."

"Aw, shucks." She pouted playfully. "And here ball-bustin' is one of my favorite pastimes."

He grinned. Then the light in his eyes dimmed, like dark clouds suddenly boiling across a sunny sky. "I shoulda told Ranger Rick the Prick the truth. I shoulda told him we're *friends*. I mean, I—"

"I'm sorry." She cut him off and cocked her head. "What has he ever done to deserve *that* nickname?"

A look that very closely resembled jealousy flashed across Bran's face, proving his whole "friends" argument was a big-O load of horseshit that belonged right alongside the stinking pile of cow patties that was his "pen pals" proclamation.

"Nothing," he admitted. And was she imagining it, or had his expression turned churlish? "He just rubs me the wrong way."

"Is that because he's cute and sweet and funny and—"

"Young and dumb and full of—"

"Do *not* finish that sentence." She held up a hand and curled her lip in disgust.

"But it's true," he insisted.

"Let's get back to the point."

"That we're friends?" He tilted his head against the lighthouse and watched her from beneath hooded lids.

"Mmm." She nodded. "The point that we're *friends*"— she made air quotes—"who can't seem to keep their hands or their tongues to themselves for more than ten minutes at a time."

"And *that's* where the apology comes in," Bran

insisted, his tone as sharp as broken glass. "'Cause I *should* keep my hands and my tongue to myself."

"Why?" She reckoned she'd just about given him all the rope he needed. It was time to fashion the noose. "It's not like I *want* you to keep them to yourself. In fact, I'm pretty partial to you *not* keepin' them to yourself."

He shook his head and chuckled, rubbing a hand over the back of his neck again. "You don't beat around the bush, do you?"

"I was raised on a steady no-bullshit diet," she informed him. "Just a whiff of the stuff turns my stomach."

"Gotcha." He nodded. "No bullshit. But don't say I didn't warn you."

Maddy's heart was running around like a wild mustang, because they were about to get to the crux of the issue.

He pushed away from the lighthouse to stand at his full height. It forced her to tilt her chin way back. "The honest-to-God truth of the matter is I like you," he said. "Like, really *like* you. As a person."

She blinked at him for a good three seconds. It was the second time tonight he'd said that. But this time felt different. It was as if *liking* her was something that caused great confusion, or great discomfort.

"Well…" she said slowly, "I guess that's better than likin' me as a zucchini or a roll of dental floss or—"

"I'm being real here, Maddy."

She studied the determined set of his jaw, the earnest light in his eyes. "I can see you are. But I guess I'm failin' to grasp your point. You like me. I like you. So what's the problem?"

His jaw sawed back and forth, his dark beard stubble

an undulating shadow across his cheeks. "The problem is I *want* you too. Whenever I'm near you, I'm aware of every breath you take, every move you make, every—"

"Bond I break?" she cut in. His words were *exactly* what she wanted to hear, but his tone told her they shouldn't be. "Are you about to break into song? Because if you are, there are better ones in the Police's catalog. I'm partial to 'Roxanne' myself, but you could always go with—"

"Damnit, Maddy!" His deep voice thundered over the fort and had them both glancing surreptitiously at Rick and the girls.

"Everything okay over there?" Rick shouted, his question carrying on the warm breeze, his concerned face momentarily spotlighted as the lighthouse made a revolution in his direction.

"Mind your own fu—" Bran managed to get in before Maddy yelled over him, "We're fine!" She turned to gift Bran with her very best stink eye. He cleared his throat and yelled, "Yeah! We're fine!"

Rick hesitated for one second, two. The lighthouse passed by him, plunging him into a silver shadow of moonlight. Then he nodded and went back to his pacing.

"Remember, Miss Maddy!" Louisa called, popping her dark head over the top of the old cannon. "When in doubt, take Paula's advice!"

Maddy felt her cheeks heat.

"Who's Paula?" Bran asked.

"Never mind that." She waved him off. "Where were we? Oh yeah." She snapped her fingers. *Ow. Note to self: no finger snapping. It angers the splinter.* "You were talkin' about that crazy physical attraction that crackles between us like a lightnin' strike from the clear blue sky every time we touch."

He screwed his eyes shut and shook his head. "You're killing me."

"You don't agree?"

"No," he said, opening his eyes to pin her like a bug to corkboard with his dark, marauding stare. "I absolutely agree."

A fat sense of vindication filled her, stretching her skin. She hadn't been crazy. She hadn't been imagining things. What she was feeling wasn't one-sided. "So I ask again, what's the problem?"

He blew out a breath, glancing over at Rick. Then he made an impatient sound and motioned for her to follow him around to the back of the lighthouse. She picked her way over the ground and settled into the shadow of the small structure.

"So the problem," he said "is there's this mutual like and this mutual lust and…well…never the two shall meet."

Her chin jerked back. "In what world? Because in *this* world you pretty much described what happens at the beginnin' of a beautiful relation—"

"In *my* world," he interrupted.

Frustration simmered inside her. "You're goin' to need to explain yourself a little better, bucko. Or else give me your copy of the Bran Code Talk Translation Manual because it seems I inadvertently left mine at home."

"You really are a smart-ass, you know that?"

"So my brothers tell me."

He shook his head and stared at the sand and bricks beneath his feet. "So here's the deal." He planted his hands on his hips and lifted his chin only enough to stare at her through the fan of his too-thick-for-a-boy-much-less-a-man eyelashes. "I'm gonna explain myself in no uncertain terms. But that's gonna require me asking you a really personal question."

She blinked. "Okay."

"How many men have you slept with?"

Plop! And that, ladies and gentlemen, would be the sound of Maddy's jaw hitting the ground at her feet. "Wow!" Her cheeks were on fire. We're talking five-alarm. "I'm not the only one who doesn't beat around the bush."

"I warned you." It was hard to tell for sure in the semidarkness, but she thought she saw him lift a challenging eyebrow. "So? How many?"

She considered equivocating, but knew if she did, she might never get to the bottom of whatever had him hesitating to take their relationship to the next level. She thrust out her chin and blurted, "Three."

"Three?" He said the word like it was foreign to him.

"Yep. Three." She nodded, and started ticking off names on her fingers. "There was Jake Reynolds, who I dated my last two years of high school. Brent Thomas, my college boyfriend. And finally, Winston St. James, who worked for my father for a while, and who I nearly married until we both realized we were far better friends than we were lovers and decided to call off the engagement."

"Three," Bran said again.

"Yep. Three," she repeated.

"Three?" He shook his head really quickly like maybe a gnat had flown in his ear.

"What?" she demanded. "You can count, right? Why do you keep repeatin' the number?"

"'Cause it's worse than I thought."

"I beg your pardon!" She bristled. If she'd been a hen, her feathers would be puffed out a foot from her body. "In case you didn't get the memo, you big Neanderthal, slut-shamin' went out in the nineties. We millennials grant women the same sexual rights, privileges, and powers of choice that men have enjoyed since the dawn of time, and I—"

"I meant *only* three," he said, cutting her off. "That might as well be zero. And you're nearly thirty."

"In eight months!" she squawked, taking the chicken bit to a whole new level. This entire conversation had gotten off on the exit to Crazy Town and was now circling the square. "And hasn't anyone ever told you never to talk about a woman's age? That's rule number two right behind don't bring up politics or religion in polite company!"

"So in twenty-nine years and four months," he said, ignoring her outburst, "you've only slept with three men."

"Well," she huffed, "I mean you can't really count the first couple of decades, right? So it's like I've slept with three men in—"

"And you were in long-term relationships with all of them," he interrupted. His inflection made it sound like a statement instead of a question, but she answered him anyway.

"Well, duh. *Of course* I was in long-term relation-ships with all of them."

He pointed a finger at her nose. "And *that's* why we can't act on all that crazy physical attraction that crackles between us, as you so aptly put it. 'Cause you have sex with men you're in relationships with. And I don't do relationships. *Ever*."

That's what this was all about? If she rolled her eyes any harder, she was afraid they might get stuck backward.

"Right," she scoffed. "So says every commitment-phobic man right before he finds the right person and *poof!* Suddenly he's in a relationship."

"Maybe so." He shrugged. "But that's not the case with me. *Ever*."

"You're startin' to sound like a broken record."

"Just trying to make sure what I'm saying sinks in."

She cocked her head, studying him for a minute. "You're tellin' me that you've *never* had a romantic relationship? Not once in all your thirty-four years?" She knew her tone was disbelieving. She couldn't help it. She *didn't* believe him. He was too handsome, too *wonderful* to have escaped all the hooks women must've thrown his way since the moment he passed puberty.

"Nope."

"Not even a will-you-go-with-me, puppy love, hold-hands-at-recess thing back when you were in elementary school?"

He shook his head. "Nope."

"No first love in high school? A girl you still sometimes think back on with sepia-toned fondness?"

"Not a one."

"How about a woman who you would visit for a little… um…R & R when you'd get leave from the Navy?"

He pursed his lips.

"Aha!" She pointed at his face. "I knew it! You *have* been in a relationship."

"Women," he said.

"What's that?"

"Plural. As in a couple dozen different women I'd rotate through depending on my location and their schedules."

She began blinking so rapidly that the world looked like it was caught under a strobe light. "A couple *dozen*?" She nearly strangled on the last word.

"Give or take." He shrugged.

"S-so…" She shook her head. "I guess…that begs the question: Just how many people have *you* slept with?"

Even in the shadows, she could see the line that formed between his eyebrows. "I don't know."

"S-so…" She had to shake her head again to make her tongue work properly. "You don't *know*?"

"I've never counted."

"S-so…" Okay, now *she* was the broken record. "You've never *counted*?"

"Stop repeating everything I say in the form of a question," he said, the line between his eyebrows deepening.

"Can you at least… I don't know…" She made a rolling motion with her hand. "Ballpark it for me?"

He screwed up his face and seemed to be making a mental tally. Two seconds stretched to five. Five stretched to ten. Out on the pilings somewhere, a roosting seagull took offense to something its neighbor did, screeching its displeasure. The lighthouse overhead clicked mechanically every time it made a full rotation. Beneath them, the fort groaned, shifting with the sands like an old man trying to find a more comfortable position.

"Do you need an abacus?" she demanded when she couldn't stand it anymore. *I mean, really?*

He shook his head. "Do people still use those?"

"A calculator then?"

"Look," he said, rolling his eyes like *she* was the insane one. She was *so* close to whacking him upside the head that she had to recross her arms. "All I can say for sure is the number is more than you can count on your fingers and toes. But less than the population of Miami."

"*Gross!*" She curled her lip.

"Hey!" he barked in affront. "I thought you said slut-shaming went out in the nineties."

"Sorry." She held up a hand. "You're absolutely right. It's not my place to judge. Just…" She wrinkled her nose. "Are you…um…up to date on all your shots?"

The look he gave her was withering. "I'm not a dog."

"Well, that's obviously not true," she muttered. "You're a *horn*dog." And then a thought occurred. "Or is it somethin' else? Are you a…" She glanced around as if worried someone might be listening in before lowering her voice. "Are you a sex addict? Are you under-goin' treatment? Is that why you—"

"I'm not a sex addict!" he whispered impatiently.

She turned her head and narrowed her eyes. "How can you be sure? Have you ever consulted a professional?"

He blew out a huge, windy sigh and she could tell he was hanging on to his patience by a thin, red hair. "I am *not* a sex addict," he insisted. "Do I enjoy sex? Undoubtedly. But I don't *have* to have it. In fact, there were times when I was away on long missions that I went *months* without it."

"Whole *months?*" she stressed sarcastically. "Wow! I think the Catholic Church might want to sign you up for an honorary priesthood. Whole *months!*"

"And I know I don't need shots 'cause the Navy

tested us. And also because I've always been extremely careful," he continued as if she hadn't spoken. "No glove, no love, as they say."

"Who says that?"

"I don't know!" His exasperation was showing. *Join the club.* "Everyone!"

"If you say so."

"I *do* say so. And the reason I've had so many sexual partners is 'cause I'm a healthy thirty-four-year-old man with a healthy thirty-four-year-old man's appetites who has refused to get into romantic entanglements. Which means I'm relegated to one-night stands and brief repeat performances with women who share my take on the whole sex-versus-relationship thing."

When she didn't respond, simply because she wasn't sure *how* to respond—she was still trying to wrap her mind around Mr. Casanova here and whether she was shocked, offended, impressed, or what—he sighed and added, "You're the first woman I've been friends with, Maddy. And I wanna *keep* you as a friend. The first thing I do in the mornings is check my email, and it's the last thing I do at night. I look forward to our talks, our jokes, our end-of-day wrap-ups. Hell, I even like our arguments."

Warmth spread in her belly like the hot toddies her daddy liked to sip at Christmastime. "Since when do we argue?"

"Uh, every time you try to convince me *Silence of the Lambs* should rank higher than *Shawshank Redemption* in a tally of the one hundred greatest movies of all time."

"Excuse me," she said, immediately distracted by the old disagreement. "But *Silence of the Lambs* won five Academy Awards. How many did *Shawshank Redemption* win?"

"It was nominated for seven."

"Yes," she allowed. "But how many did it *win?*"

"You cannot base the merits of a movie simply on the number of awards it—" He shook his head and karate chopped the air. "Never mind. My point is I like you, Maddy. I know I'm repeating myself, but I'm doing it because I don't think you fully understand how huge it is for me to say that. I *like* you. So no matter how much I want you, no matter how much I dream about screwing your brains out"—*That sounds good; let's do that*—"I refuse to do anything about it because I value your friendship more than I want another hot roll in the hay."

She was missing something. The pieces were there, but she had yet to put the puzzle together. "I don't understand. Why can't we do both? Why can't we be friends *and* screw each other's brains out? Isn't that how most—"

"'Cause you're gonna want something more than that. You're gonna want a *relationship*." He said the word like it was foul. "And I'm not gonna give it to you. *Ever.* I'll never be your boyfriend, much less anything more."

Wow. And there it was. The truth. Finally.

You asked for it, her conscience reminded her.

Yes. Yes, she had. Which proved she was an idiot.

A hollow feeling opened up inside her, yawning and stretching, filling her up and emptying her out at the same time. Not wanting him to see how off balance she was, she said flippantly, "Well…when you put it *that* way, I guess I see your point."

He blinked at her for a full five seconds. Then the tension in his shoulders relaxed. "So," he said, "friends then?"

She pasted on a false smile. "Friends," she agreed, extending her hand.

He looked down at her offering like it might be a turd floating in his cereal. But after a moment's hesitation, he grasped her fingers in his warm palm.

The second he did, she understood his reluctance. *Sparks, baby.* Huge, massive, immediate sparks that ignited her blood and dizzied her brain. He quickly released her hand, and the skin on her palm tingled with phantom sensation.

"Good thing this friendship of ours is usually separated by the Gulf of Mexico, am I right?" he joked, once again leaning against the lighthouse, resuming his non-chalant stance, arms crossed, one knee bent.

"I guess so," she managed even though she was reeling from his recent revelations.

Chapter 16

"SO HOW ARE YOU DOING, *FRIEND*?" BRAN STRESSED THE last word.

"Don't overdo it," Maddy warned. She propped her back against the cool, black metal of the lighthouse's facade and mimicked his stance by pressing one foot against the base. She covertly flattened a hand to her chest, hoping to push closed the black hole opening inside her and swallowing all the dreams—*pipe* dreams, apparently—she'd had for the past three months.

It didn't work. Which forced her to fall back on her most tried-and-true method of self-preservation: humor. "I'm still tryin' to get over my disappointment that you're not goin' to let me touch your pickle."

He swallowed like the thought of her hands on him caused his throat to close up. Then he managed to play along. "Never refer to a man's package as a pickle. It brings to mind a baby gherkin, and that's not at all flattering."

"Sausage then," she countered.

A muscle started ticking in his jaw, and any humor he'd tried to portray drained from his face. Was she completely evil to take delight in torturing him? Probably. But she couldn't stop herself. As he'd told one of the masked gunmen, *Tit for tat, dicksmack.* If she was going to be miserable because he had some ridiculous standing rule about relationships, if she was going to be denied the joy of what could be between them if only he weren't such a confounding idiot, he needed to suffer a little too. *Fair is fair*.

"Don't say sausage either," he grumbled.

"Okay," she agreed. "I'm willin' to allow for kielbasa, but anything bigger than that and you're just foolin' yourself."

"Maddy," he groaned, adjusting his stance. When her eyes pinged down to the front of his shorts, she realized all this naming of his nether region had caused the area to perk up. And maybe kielbasa *was* the best comparison.

Oh! How she longed to find out for herself.

But he didn't do relationships. And she didn't do casual sex. So they'd reached an impasse. Or at least she *thought* they had. Then an idea began to gestate. A scary, crazy, sort of…*intriguing* idea. With its birth, the emptiness inside her shrank.

"Fine," she told Bran, her mind racing over possibilities. "No more talk of your man meat or the fact that I was lookin' forward to—"

He lifted a hand. "Stop right there."

"You're no fun," she declared.

"And you're relentlessly wicked," he countered.

"I'll get you, my pretty," she cackled, mimicking the Wicked Witch of the West. "And your little dog too!" Only, in her mind, she decided that *dog* was a euphemism for his pickle. His sausage. His kielbasa.

He grinned at her, having no idea of the devilish thoughts spinning through her brain. Then his expression turned serious. "How *are* you, Maddy? Really.

How are you holding up? 'Cause I know you were just starting to get over the hijacking on your father's yacht. Is this gonna set you back?"

Okay, so apparently fun time was over. She could have dodged the question and kept up the lark, but they'd never been anything but forthright with each other.

"Who knows?" She sighed. "I didn't expect to experience such an aftershock three months ago. I thought I was okay and then *bam!* The nightmares and the cold sweats started. So…" She shrugged. "I guess we'll just have to wait and see."

"But for right now?"

"I'm okay." When he lifted an eyebrow, she tossed her hands in the air. "What can I say? I feel like I woke up this mornin', stepped in quicksand, then fought my way free only to have a two-ton anvil land on my head. I'm tired. The kind that can't be fixed with sleep. The kind that's bone deep. The kind that comes when you realize so many people are willin' to do bad things for power or money or…or…whatever."

He let his head fall back against the lighthouse. It made a soft *bong*-ing sound when it hit the metal. "It's a cruel world."

She glanced at his perfect profile. "Meanin' a cruel world begets cruel men?"

"And cruel women."

She raised an eyebrow. "Are you tryin' to tell me somethin'?"

He snorted. "Babe, there isn't a cruel bone in your whole body. Now, sarcastic bones? Ball-busting bones? You're lousy with those."

"I don't know about that," she admitted, turning to

stare out at the dark waves. The moon kissed their peaks, making them shimmer in the light. Somewhere out there were the last two men who had tried to do wrong here tonight. "After the hijacking three months ago, I feel like a poisonous seed was planted inside me and now it's grown into a bloodthirsty tree." When he turned to her, she went on. "I wasn't sorry to see those men killed tonight. And I *was* sorry when those last two got away. Surely that speaks of cruelty."

"Nah. You're just human. There's a difference."

"I'm not sure I see it."

He pursed his lips as if trying to arrange his thoughts. Finally, he said, "A cruel person is violent to achieve some self-serving end or to satisfy some sadistic need to inflict pain on another. Resorting to violence to defend yourself or those who are depending on you to defend them, wishing to put a period on a man's life to make sure he doesn't put a period on yours, is simply human."

The way he said it, with such conviction, suddenly reminded her of how he'd behaved toward the masked men during the second standoff. Baiting them almost as if he *wanted* them to give him a reason to pull his trigger.

"And which one are you?" she asked, absently picking at the splinter in the base of her thumb. "Cruel or simply human?"

"I'm both."

The quick way he answered made her chin jerk back. Then, she thought about it. "I reckon all the men in your line of work…uh…*previous* line of work probably feel that way after a time."

He shrugged one large shoulder. "Maybe. But I was born that way, not made that way by good ol' Uncle Sam."

"What do you mean?"

"I mean I inherited my cruel streak from my father." His eyes were lazy and half-lidded in the shadow of the lighthouse; nothing moved on him but the hair across his brow when a soft breeze decided to ruffle it. But she knew he was watching her reaction intently. "It's stamped into my DNA," he finished.

She swallowed, careful to keep her expression calm. After the hundreds of emails, she would have said she knew Bran. But she was beginning to realize she'd just scratched the surface of him. And right now he was showing her what lay underneath all the charm and wit and swagger.

Inherited my cruel streak from my father…

It could mean so many things.

"It's funny," he said, but there was no humor in his voice. "I have this wonderful life and all these friends who are *more* than friends, they're family, 'cause I chose to become a SEAL. And I chose to become a SEAL because of him, that rotten, brutal bastard. So, it's like he's the alpha and omega of my life. Responsible for all the bad shit and all the good shit too."

Maddy didn't know what to do with her hands. If she kept picking at her splinter, she might dig a hole through her hand. And she didn't dare reach for him. Not when his casual stance belied the tension running through him. She thought if she cocked an ear, she might hear the gentle *hum* of him, like he was a recently plucked piano wire. She settled on simply tucking her fingers back into her pockets.

"I thought you told me you became a SEAL because you worked on that fishin' boat in high school and you fell in love with the ocean," she said, then grimaced, wanting to grab all her words and shove them back into her mouth. Here he was, opening himself up, and she was…what? Nitpicking details?

Well done, Maddy, you dimwit. Jeez.

"I joined the *Navy* 'cause I loved the ocean," he corrected. "I became a *SEAL* because of the meanness in me, the *violence* in me. It needed an outlet. And I figured if I had to be Donny Pallidino's kid"—he bit off the name like uttering it aloud was offensive—"the least I could do was try to make something good come out of it."

She couldn't stand it anymore. "What…" She stopped, feeling like she was teetering on the precipice of something huge and dark and dangerous. And then she did what she'd been doing her whole life. She leaped. "What did he *do* to you, Bran?"

—◦◦◦—

9:15 p.m.…

Sometimes you hafta let the blow fall by degrees…

Bran had heard that somewhere once. At the time, he thought it was good advice. But now, looking at Maddy, at her big, sympathetic eyes, he knew it was better to let the hammer come down all at once. One fatal blow that would obliterate any illusions she had about him.

Earlier, behind the gunpowder magazine house, she'd caught a glimpse. He saw it in her eyes. The fear. The burgeoning recognition of what was in him. Now it was time to pull back the curtain completely and show her the reality behind the Not-So-Great-and-Powerful Oz.

"Except for once, he didn't do a damned thing to me," he said. "My mother always made sure of that. But he beat the shit outta her on a fairly regular basis."

"Oh, Bran." Maddy's hand landed on his arm. At first contact, a *zing* of electricity shot up his spine. *Lightning strike from the clear blue sky. She's got that right.* "I…" She swallowed and shook her head. "I'm so sorry."

He squeezed her fingers before gently removing her hand from his arm. He couldn't think when she touched him. And he needed to think. He needed to make her understand why he was the way he was. Why he couldn't give her what she wanted.

"It's okay. No, really," he assured her when she vigorously shook her head. "Like I said, my past brought me to my present. And my present is pretty spectacular. I have friends and a home and"—he looked at her— "*friends*," he repeated.

And all those feelings he had for her that went *beyond* friendship and lust? Well, he'd just keep them to himself. Keep them locked away safe and sound where he could take them out and cherish them during those times he was alone and quiet. During those times when he allowed himself to think about, to *dream* about… *what if?*

She nodded her understanding, her expression sad. "Is that why you've kept women at arm's length? Because you're afraid of letting anyone close, afraid if you do you'll become like your father?"

Afraid I'll become like my father? Babe, I already am *like my father.*

"Don't delude yourself, Maddy. I've kept women at arm's length because that's exactly where I want them."

She searched his face, her gray eyes reflecting the moonlight bouncing off the waves. When she reached up to smooth a lock of hair back from his forehead, he stilled and held his breath. But her touch was feather-light. And then it was gone.

"And not wantin' anything more…you don't think that has something to do with what you think is stamped into your DNA?" Her voice was low and husky, perhaps a bit beseeching.

The truth is I was never even tempted. Not until you… "Unquestionably," he said with determination, not sure who he was trying more to convince, himself or her.

"Oh, Bran." Her hand landed on his forearm again, making him grit his teeth. "You are more than your father's son. You have a huge heart and a loyal, steadfast character. That combination always wins the day."

If only that were true.

But he knew better.

He knew it was possible for a man to have both dark and light living inside him. He knew that sometimes, no matter how he might wish it otherwise, the darkness overwhelmed the light. He knew because it happened every time he'd stepped onto a battlefield.

And there was one more thing he knew. *The human heart, more than anything else, can be utterly, entirely deceitful.*

"Love is like liquor," he explained. "Some people can handle it, use it to make a bad day good or a boring party fun. They can take it or leave it. Let it loosen 'em up and give them a rosy glow. And then there are the others.

The ones who *can't* handle it, because when they try, it finds all the bad in 'em and makes it worse. They can't take it or leave it because it consumes them from the inside out. It doesn't loosen 'em up; it winds them tight. It doesn't give 'em a rosy glow; it wakes up the darkness inside. I've seen the latter. I *am* the latter."

"But—"

"And like an alcoholic"—he kept on like she hadn't tried to interrupt—"the only way I know to stay true, stay sober, stay *me*, is to make sure I avoid the thing that temps me the most."

She searched his face for a long time, trying to find a weakness in him, a crack that she could exploit, a way to try to convince him he was wrong. But eventually her expression fell, her eyes dulling with sadness. "Well... then I'm sorry for you," she said haltingly. "Because I've always thought of life as a treasure hunt, and if in the end you have someone to share your life with, then you've found wealth beyond—"

"But I *have* people to share my life with," he cut her off. He didn't want her pity. "That's been my point all along. I have *friends*. And I have *real* treasure to hunt. LT and Olivia found the hilt of a cutlass today."

"All hail the king of the really bad sequiturs." She twisted her lips, and he ignored what the gesture did to the top one, making it plump and pucker. Or at least he *tried* to ignore it. The pulse in his pants told him he was only marginally successful. Of course, his arousal withered like a grape left too long on the vine when she blurted, "Will you at least tell me how long it lasted before we change the subject?"

He knew to what *it* she was referring. "'Til I was

fifteen and big enough to stand up to him," he said. "Or at least until I *thought* I was big enough to stand up to him."

She blinked rapidly. Her little chin trembled. "That's the 'except for the once' you were talking about." And there it was. The pity he didn't want. "So, what…" She stopped and swallowed. "What happened when you were fifteen?"

He inhaled deeply, rolling in his lips. The memory of that day was sharp and painful, like a box covered in switchblades that cut his fingers when he opened it. And he *hated* talking about his childhood. Never did, in fact. But he'd started this so she'd understand what he was, *who* he was. And he couldn't do her the disservice of not finishing it.

"It was a half day at school. Parent-teacher conferences, I think." He frowned. "Or maybe it was a professional day for the teachers? Anyway, it was a half day." And he could still remember it clearly. The crunch of the hard-packed snow under his boots on the walk home. The sweet promise of spring in the cloudless blue sky even though the winter wind still nipped at his nose. The barbecue place on the corner had been winding down after the afternoon rush, but the smoldering smell of its smokers still perfumed the air.

"After lunch, I walked home and climbed the steps to my front porch. And that's when I heard 'em. Those sounds that were the soundtrack of my childhood." He shuddered even now, even after almost twenty years. "It'd been a while because my father had stopped beating on Mom when I was home."

"Why?"

He made a face and rubbed his hand over the back of his neck, staring out at the silvery stars dotting the black blanket of the sky. "Probably 'cause when I was twelve I stole Joey Santorini's father's shotgun off their mantel and hid it in the coat closet where my mom stashed me when Dad whaled on her. So the next time he started in, I popped out, shoved both barrels in his face, and swore if I ever saw him lay a hand on Mom again, I'd blow his fuckin' brains out."

"Oh, Bran." Maddy blinked rapidly, her bottom lip quivering ever so slightly.

Bran had to look away. "Yeah, well, he wrestled the gun from me and took it back to Joey's dad, but I think the warning stuck. I think he believed me when I said if I ever *saw*"—he stressed the word—"him lay a finger on Mom again, I'd kill him. After that, he was careful to only give her a beating when I wasn't around. Not that I wouldn't have killed him even without *seeing*"—again with the emphasis—"but Mom was always there to stop me after the fact."

"Jesus," Maddy said.

Yeah. Not even close, babe. There's a special corner of hell where the devil keeps my father.

He shrugged. "Anyway, I came home from school early and heard Dad going at her…"

"Donny, please!" Bran's mother screamed as he climbed the steps of the porch. The bright winter afternoon was ruined by the crash of something inside the house. "It's not what you think! I love you!"

Bran dropped his backpack on the porch, his hands clenched into fists, blood on fire.

I warned him! I *warned* him!

He wasn't thinking when he wrenched open the screen door and ran inside to see his mother cringing on the floor by the coffee table, a fresh black eye swelling on her pretty face, a cut near her left temple oozing blood over her ear and shoulder. His father stood above her, face contorted in an evil sneer, ham hock of a fist raised and ready to fly.

"No!" Bran screamed, dismayed when his vocal cords cracked. "You bastard! I told you I'd kill you!" He flew at his father with all the rage inside him.

"Bran, no!" his mother yelled. "Oh, please, God! No, Bran!"

Bran barely heard her over the roar of his fury. He landed the first punch and, to his delight, it whipped his father's head back.

"How does that feel?" he screeched, his mind numb and at the same time bubbling over with hatred. "How does your own medicine taste?"

Pow! *He hit the sonofabitch again, this time in the stomach, and watched with vicious glee as his father wheezed and doubled over.*

Finally! His old man was getting his due! And Bran was giving it to him! The ache in his knuckles felt wonderful when he landed another blow on his father's ear. Blood exploded near his dad's temple from the keys Bran hadn't realized he'd still been holding. He reveled in the sight, wished he could drink it in and spit it back into his father's face.

Red had eased into Bran's vision upon hearing his mother's scream. And now he was seeing the world through a crimson film. His heart beat with a terrible rhythm. His lungs burned with vengeance until every breath he took was a hot wind that whipped the fire of his wrath ever higher.

He lost himself. Stopped being Bran and became a thing that punched and kicked, that bit and clawed, that rejoiced in every drop of blood and every grunt of agony. He wanted to hurt. He wanted to maim. He wanted to kill.

His father caught him with a punch below his left eye, and it felt like his entire face exploded. Pain radiated up into his head and scrambled his brains. Another blow landed on his jaw, knocking him off his feet. He fell onto the wood floor with enough force to make his tailbone cry out in misery.

"You little bastard!" his father yelled, spittle flying from his sneering mouth. Bran saw it then. The monster that was wearing his father's flesh like a skin suit. The ugly, evil thing whose eyes glowed with fury and the ravenous need to hurt.

Bran recognized it because the same thing was inside him, staring out, wanting to smash his father's face over and over and over again until there was nothing left.

"Fuck you!" he yelled, kicking his father's knee and grinning when his father howled. The grin slipped from his face when his dad booted him in the mouth. His lips split. Blood gushed over his tongue and down his throat.

"No, Donny! Don't you dare!" his mother yelled, and Bran looked up to see her launch herself onto his father's back, clawing at his face.

Through the haze of misery, Bran's macabre grin returned. It was the first time his mother had fought back. The first time she'd dared raise a hand to big Donny Pallidino.

He wanted to yell, "Good for you, Mom! Good for you!" But his mouth was a mess. And then his father reared back with one of his steel-toed kickers and booted Bran in the head near his right temple.

That was it.

Lights out.

Bran emerged from the memory like he always did. The anger boiling inside him until his skin bubbled. But when he looked at Maddy, at the wetness making her big eyes appear even larger, the monster immediately pulled back until it left no trace of its passing. Not even a shadow.

"So there you have it." He shuddered, not surprised to hear his voice had gone hoarse. He'd relived that day a million times in his mind. But speaking the words aloud… That was different. "That's my wreckage."

"Oh, Bran." Maddy choked on his name, her nose red and shiny. She seemed to hesitate, unsure of what to do or say next. Then she leapt at him, wrapping her arms around his neck and going up on tiptoe to press her head against his shoulder.

His initial reaction was to shove her away. Shove away the temptation she represented. But for the first time in their history together, her touch didn't awaken his libido. Instead, it awakened the boy in him. The boy who hadn't been held in a woman's arms for any reason other than sex since the last time his mother had hugged him. The boy who, until this very moment, hadn't realized how much he'd *missed* the affection, the soothing feel of a sympathetic touch, the sweet peace that came from caring for someone and knowing they cared for him too.

This was why he couldn't ruin their friendship.

Because *this* was sweet and innocent. *This* was good. And he hadn't had much of that in his life.

His arms went around her. He buried his nose in her short hair, squeezing his eyes shut. When he breathed deep, he took her scent into him. Maddy. Wonderful Maddy. His friend. His…*confidante*.

"I w-wish there w-was somethin' I could say to make it b-better." A hot tear escaped her eye and seared his bare skin, but he welcomed the burn. Maybe because he had no more tears to shed himself, and it felt good she was sharing hers in some small way.

"Just having you here"—his breath ruffled her hair until it tickled his lips—"just having you listen and understand is enough."

Her arms tightened around his neck and he suddenly thought, *Yeah. We can really do this. We can really be friends*. And it was a precious gift. He would cherish it, protect it, treasure it.

"And that was the only time it happened?" Maddy pushed back to look at him. Her eyes were red. Her cheeks splotchy. At some point she'd shoved her finger in an electrical socket because her hair was standing out in a million directions in chunky platinum tufts.

And she's never looked lovelier.

"When I got outta the hospital," he told her, his hands around her slim waist, the ring finger on his left hand touching her warm flesh where her T-shirt rode above the hem of her shorts, "she moved us into a shelter for victims of domestic violence."

"Brave woman," Maddy said.

Bran cocked his head. "Huh," he mused. "Yeah, I guess… I guess she was. In a way. But she was *sick* too.

They both were. His sickness was his unrelieved jealousy and his ability to hurt the only person who meant anything in his life. And hers was her unfaltering love for him, her inability to see that all the bad things in him outweighed the good."

"But she loved *you* more." One lone tear clung to Maddy's lower lashes. It caught a shaft of starlight and shimmered like a tiny, liquid diamond. Cupping her face, he used his thumb to tenderly brush it away.

"You think?" he asked.

"I *know*." Her little chin jutted out. "Because she stayed for all those years. But the minute he hurt you, she got out."

"Yeah." He nodded slowly. *And that ultimately proved to be her undoing. Maybe if I had—*

But no. If he'd learned anything, it was that *maybe if* thoughts were a waste of energy. He couldn't change what had happened then any more than he could change who he was now. Some things just *were*, no matter how hard he might wish they *weren't*.

"Is she…" Maddy bit her top lip and his eyes focused on the gesture so quickly and so directly that he felt like a dog on point. The libido that hadn't woken upon her touch opened its eyes and stretched. He willed it back to sleep, not wanting to lose the sweet, innocent intimacy of their embrace.

"Is she still alive?" Maddy finally finished, releasing her lip. But it was too late. The damage was done. All his nerve endings were tingling. His muscles clenched with interest at her nearness. Her *femaleness*.

He could have curbed his burgeoning desire, he supposed, by giving her the whole sordid answer to her question. But he wasn't ready to go that far. Wasn't ready to share with her just how bad it had really been. So he gave her the Cliff's Notes version and ignored the voice in his head that accused him of being a coward.

"No," he told her.

"Oh, Bran." Maddy reached up and cupped his face with both hands. Her fingers were cool and gentle. He was insanely aware of just how vulnerable her mouth looked. How ripe and succulent and ready to be ravaged. "I'm so sorry."

He should have felt the same sorrow. But his hurts were old, calloused over, and though they still plagued him, the pain had dulled. Besides, *want* of her was on him now. *Need* of her. And all he could think about was claiming her lips in a kiss that would blow everything he'd just asked her for, their truce, their *friendship*, clean out of the water.

"Thanks," he murmured, trying to decide if there was a way to extricate himself without making it obvious that he'd once again fallen victim to the passion between them.

"And him?" she asked tentatively, catching her top lip between her teeth again. His dick flexed hungrily at the sight.

"Dead too," he said, dismayed that even thoughts of his father couldn't dampen his burgeoning lust.

"Oh, Bran!" she said—it seemed to be a running theme tonight—and threw her arms around his neck. *That* seemed to be a running theme too.

Unlike the last time, it wasn't the boy in him who exalted in her embrace. *Oh, no.* It was the *man.* The man who couldn't deny the feel of her small, soft breasts smashed against his chest. The man who was eagle-eye focused on the warmth of her soft thighs pressed next to his.

And then it hit him. Her thighs. *His* thigh. It was the perfect excuse!

He hissed in a breath.

"What is it?" she demanded. "What's wrong?"

"My leg," he said, shuddering in relief when she immediately stepped back. "Adrenaline is an awesome painkiller. But mine has worn off."

"Oh." She glanced down at the dressing peeking from beneath the bloodstained leg of his cargo shorts. It was looking a little worse for wear, the Ace bandage damp and smeared with grime. And he'd probably go straight to hell for lying to her. It didn't hurt any more now than it had all night. *But in a life filled with transgressions, what's one more?*

"Did I…" She wrung her hands. "Did I bump into it when I—"

"No," he assured her. "It wasn't you." *It's me. It's all me. Everything that's wrong, everything that can never be, that's all me.*

"I should've brought the first aid kit." She shook her head at herself. "We could go back to the ranger's station and—"

"No." The idea of going back to the ranger's station where there was an empty bed was as terrifying as it was tempting. "The pain will subside in a second."

"Well, at least let me check it." And then, before he could stop her, she was down on her knees in front of him.

Chapter 17

9:22 p.m.…

Maddy reached for the little metal cleats holding Bran's Ace bandage in place. But she dropped her hands when she saw her fingers were shaking so badly that she reckoned if she tried to perform her Florence Nightingale routine, she'd bumble the whole gosh-darned thing.

The story he'd told… *Sweet heavens…*

She didn't know what to ask, what to say, what to *do*. And she was completely overwhelmed by a whole host of emotions. There was sorrow for all he'd endured. Anger at the savagery of a world that had forced him to withstand it all. Helplessness that there was nothing she could do to change what had happened. And sadness that because of his past, she would never get the chance to find out if he was…the one.

And there it was. She'd been avoiding putting a name to it. The one. *Her* one.

Except…he wasn't. He didn't *want* to be. He wouldn't *let* himself be. Because of all he'd endured. Because of all this savage world had forced him to withstand. Because there was nothing she could do to change what had happened.

And around and around it goes…

She screwed her eyes closed and mourned the

loss of him. Which was silly. She'd never had him to begin with.

But I had the hope *of him.*

Opening her eyes, she reached for the soiled Ace bandage, but Bran's voice, so soft and low, stopped her. "Please leave it."

She glanced up and their gazes collided. Just... *wham!* It was a blow that nearly knocked her on her ass. She flung out a hand to steady herself against the side of the lighthouse. She wasn't sure what she'd expected to see in his face, but it certainly wasn't bone-deep, soul-deep hunger. The kind of hunger that started wars, toppled kingdoms, and changed the history of the world. The kind of hunger that was saved for women like Cleopatra and Helen of Troy, not for Madison Powers.

All her pain and sorrow and regret were momentarily scorched away by the fire burning in his dark eyes. Every hair on her head stood up as if she'd grabbed hold of a live wire. And her skin felt ten degrees too hot, so hot she wondered if she was feverish, delirious, imagining things.

"Bran?" Was that her voice? She'd never heard it so husky.

"Sorry," he gritted, his jaw sawing back and forth. "It's just that you were..." He swallowed, his Adam's apple bobbing in his throat. "You were pressed up against me a second ago. And you're so soft. And so sweet. And so...*everything*." Her heart grew wings and flew right out of her chest. "And now you're down on your knees in front of me. And we might be friends, but I'm also a red-blooded man, babe."

And now her stupid heart wasn't just flying, it was doing loopty loops. She jumped to her feet. The idea she'd been toying with earlier solidified in her head. She knew what she wanted to do. Knew what she *had* to do. It was the only option left to her.

"Friends with benefits," she blurted.

Bran had a way of going completely still that was unnerving and slightly...*predatory*. A smarter woman might have backed away from the danger flashing in his eyes. *She* took a step closer, closing the distance between them until they were toe-to-toe.

"W-what?" he asked slowly, a muscle ticking frantically in his wide jaw.

"We should be friends with benefits," she said, lifting her chin even higher.

She could tell the idea shocked him by the slight narrowing of his eyes, the way the muscles in his face seemed to tighten. But beneath that shock was intrigue and maybe, just maybe...excitement. She decided to press her case.

"Look," she said. "There's all this...*tension* between us. This crazy, *sexual* tension, right?"

He didn't say anything, just stood there, stock-still, like he was afraid any sudden movement and *whoops!* his penis would accidentally slip into her vagina.

Not that I'd complain.

"So let's scratch the itch," she said. "Let's solve this mystery. Let's make like Nike and *just do it*. And then once we've *done it*, all the curiosity and tension will ease and we can focus on what's important, bein' friends."

He shook his head slowly at first. Then he picked up speed.

"Why not?" she demanded, fisting her hands on her hips. "It just makes good sense."

At least it did to her. Because he was in her blood, like a disease. A wonderful disease. And she wasn't sure she could recover from him any other way. She needed to know. Know *him*. Like getting a vaccination. She needed an infusion of the live virus so she could eventually become immune.

But he didn't seem to get it. She decided to change tactics. "Unless…you're worried it won't be any good and then it'll make things weird between us." She screwed up her face as if she really thought this might be a possibility.

"It'll be good," he gritted.

"Well, I figured as much," she allowed charitably. "What with all the practice you've had. Unless…" she said again, cocking her head.

"Unless what?"

"Unless the reason you've had so many one-night stands isn't because *you* wanted it that way, but because your partners wanted it that way. Oh, Lord Almighty. You don't do that weird jackhammer thing, do you?" When he lifted a brow, she clarified. "The one that's all *bam, bam, bam!*" She clapped her hands together to illustrate her point and was reminded of the splinter. "No real finesse and definitely no real friction on any of the parts that need it. Or, ew…" She made an awful face. "Are you one of those guys who thinks a clitoris is like a magical *go* button and all you have to do is give it a quick flick and assume that should be enough to—"

"It'll be *good*," he insisted. And now the muscle in his jaw was twitching fast enough to beat the band.

"Care to put your money where your mouth is?" she

challenged, batting her lashes, knowing the best way to goad a man into doing something was to challenge his prowess.

Four older brothers, remember?

"Maddy." The way he said her name, emphasis on both syllables, had her coming right back at him with a slow "Bran." She made sure to thicken her accent, splitting his name into two parts and stressing both.

"Are you trying to seduce me?" His voice was so dry and hoarse it sounded like someone had shoved a wad of cotton down his throat.

"Nope," she assured him, glancing pointedly at the bulge straining his fly. *Well, hello again, Mr. Wood. So nice to see you!* "By the looks of things, that's already done."

He expression turned pained. Then he reached down to adjust himself.

When Maddy saw his wide-palmed hand grab the thickness of his shaft through the fabric of his cargo shorts, her throat dried up. *Who is this person with the cotton?* Heat spread across her chest, tightening her nipples.

There was nothing sexier than watching a man touch himself and knowing you were the cause of his excitement. She'd *dreamed* of this moment, fantasized about it. And she stared with a watering mouth and aching core as he gritted his teeth, sucking in a breath like his touch brought both pleasure and pain. When he found a position he liked, he released himself and Maddy blew out a ragged breath.

"Next time," she told him, licking her lips, "let me do that for you."

"Maddy." He emphasized her name the same way as before. So, same as before, she met him with "Bran."

"You're not a friends-with-benefits kinda woman," he insisted.

"You're right," she admitted. "Sex always equals commitment for me. *Eventually*. Which is why I'm proposin' we become friends with benefits just once. Just tonight."

So she was Paula Abdul-ing it after all. Those three girls were too smart for their britches. "And after tonight?" His pulse was pounding in his neck. *Her* pulse was pounding decidedly lower.

"After tonight we go back to the present state of affairs. Friends. Email buddies. *Pen pals*." She grinned evilly when she used the phrase he would probably prefer she struck from her vocabulary. "With all the appropriate itches havin' been fully scratched. If we can't have it all, at least we can have this. And besides, maybe it'll make things better between us. Easier. Make the friendship that much stronger."

Her heart stuttered when he didn't say anything for a ridiculously long time. Just stood there looking at her. Try as she might, she couldn't read his expression. The man gave new meaning to the term *poker face*. But finally he said, "What if you end up regretting it?"

"Anything's possible," she admitted. Her conscience had been poking her on the shoulder during the entire conversation, trying to tell her something important. She'd studiously ignored it. Instead, she took a running jump. "But, honey, the worst mistake beats the hell out of never tryin'."

~~~

9:28 p.m. . . .

Bran could hear the belief buried like a land mine

beneath Maddy's persuasive tone. And he was terrified
that one false move would have him stepping on it and
blowing his friggin' legs off.

No matter how he looked at the situation, he was
screwed. If he didn't agree to give this one-night-only
thing a go, he'd hurt her. *Again*. Reject her. *Again*. But if
he agreed, there was a chance that tomorrow morning, in
the cold light of day, she'd realize she really *wasn't* okay
with the concept. In which case, he'd hurt her. *Again*.

He looked around, trying to figure out if by some
small chance there was a third option. Unfortunately,
the only thing that met his searching gaze was the long
hexagonal circle of the fort's parapets, the dark sea, and
the lip that Maddy once again caught between her teeth.

Everything inside him was pushing him, needling
him, damn near hitting him over the head with a rubber
mallet to give Maddy what she wanted. One scenario
guaranteed her hurt feelings, and the other one only
guaranteed a *chance* of her hurt feelings, right? Right.

And now you're rationalizing.

Damnit, he was. The soil of abstinence was oh-so-
fertile ground for a breakdown of self-restraint.

Zero-dark-thirty read the display on his diver's
watch. *Don't be a fool,* warned his brain. *Trust me and
give me one night,* said her liquid mercury eyes.

"Bran?" she finally said when he'd been quiet for too
long. And even the way she said his name was a turn-on.
"Say somethin'," she insisted, her voice deliciously low
and throaty.

"I don't wanna step on my dick here," he managed. "So
I figure I'm better off keeping my damn mouth shut." And
that was the third option he'd so desperately been searching

for. Neither Door A nor Door B, but Door C. Behind which was shut-up-and-hope-it-all-miraculously-goes-away.

Her expression turned impish. "Well, I wholeheartedly agree with that first thing. I don't want you steppin' on your dick since I have plans for it that require it bein' in top-notch shape."

He made a weak, strangled sound at the back of his throat. He was now harder than those nights when he'd lain in bed and jerked off while looking at the picture of her he'd found on the Internet—the one where she was in a short, black cocktail dress that showed off her flawless back and the high, tight curve of her ass. The one where her head was turned over her shoulder and she was grinning wickedly at whoever had snapped the photo.

"But I don't agree with the second thing," she continued, completely unaware he was teetering on the brink of what was likely to turn into a medical condition if he didn't do something quick. "You keepin' your mouth shut isn't an option. Tell me what you're thinkin'."

What he was thinking? What he was *thinking*? He was thinking her deal probably made about as much sense as a cool spring breeze, but it was just as sweet and delicious and alluring.

"So what happens if we do this tonight, but instead of banking the fire, it only stokes it?" he demanded. He got the distinct impression that one-and-done wouldn't cut it when it came to Maddy. In fact, he didn't know if a-thousand-and-done would cut it. Not when there were a million things he wanted to do to her. A million things he wanted to share with her. A million things he wanted to learn about her and teach her about himself.

"Well, then we'll have the Gulf of Mexico between

us," she said, shrugging. "Just like you said. Surely all that water and distance will be enough to bank any lingerin' conflagration."

The more she talked, the more she chipped away at the foundation of his reason. Particularly since he knew that *if* he did this, he'd have something real and wonderful to take out and cherish during those quiet times, those alone times when he allowed himself to touch upon the feelings he had for her, when he allowed himself to think about, to *dream* about, *what if*.

"You tempt me." And that was the understatement of the damned millennium. "But, I…" He stopped there. For some reason he couldn't force out the words.

"Nothin' will change between us," she swore, grabbing his hands and squeezing. Her touch affected him like it always did, making him hyperaware of the coolness of her fingers, the softness of her palms, the delicate feel of the bones in her hands. "Good or bad, fire stoked or banked, I will remain your friend. I swear it."

His heart skipped a beat. Was it possible? Possible to have his cake and eat it too? Possible to know Maddy as a lover *and* a friend?

It seemed too good to be true. But, oh, how he *wanted* it to be true. He'd never wanted anything more in his life. Before he'd made the conscious decision to open his mouth, he heard himself asking, "You promise?" And there was so much longing in his tone. So much *desperate* longing.

"Cross my heart and hope not to die of anything but bliss." She grinned and winked.

He snorted. But he couldn't tell if it was with humor or surrender. When he squeezed her hands, something that looked very much like pain flickered across her face.

Is she changing her mind? Is she second-guessing herself now that I'm on the verge of agreeing?

"What is it?" A muscle ticked in his jaw. "Maddy, if you're not sure, you need to tell me right now because—"

"No." She pulled her hands from his grasp. He felt the desertion of her touch like a blow to his solar plexus. "It's not that. I have this splinter. See?" She held her hand in front of his face and he blinked, trying to focus on the angry red circle of skin at the base of her thumb. In the center was a line of gray buried beneath the surface. "I tried to pull it out, but—"

He didn't hear the rest of her sentence. He was too busy turning her hand toward what little light glowed up from a nearby spotlight. And never let it be said that he couldn't roll with the punches. One second he was inches away from Don Juan-ing her and scooping her into his arms. The next second he was forced to slip back into the role of friend—a.k.a. Splinter Remover.

"Hold still," he told her, squeezing the skin around the splinter in an effort to push it out.

"*Ssssss,*" she hissed.

He stopped and, on impulse, bent to press a kiss to the irritated flesh. "Sorry," he said into her hand, loving the way her fingers curled around his face like she was trying to hold on to his words. "I never wanna hurt you, Maddy."

They both knew he was talking about much more than the splinter. Her free hand smoothed a lock of hair back from his face, her fingers running through the strands and sending ripples of sensation across his scalp and down his spine.

"I know that." Her voice was hoarse. For a couple of seconds neither of them moved, neither of them spoke. Finally, she said, "Just leave it. It's in too deep. I'm goin' to need—"

"If you leave it, it could just work its way in further. And then you'll be in real trouble. This is gonna sting," he warned.

"No pain, no gain, right?" She lifted her chin and squared her shoulders. His little soldier ready to bear the brunt of battlefield surgery. And she *was* his. For this one night she'd promised to be his.

Anticipation nipped at the nape of his neck, urging him to hurry up and finish the job so they could get back to...*friends with benefits*. Even the phrase made him feel primed, pumped, and raring to go.

"Stop me if it gets too bad." He once again squeezed the soft flesh around the splinter, cursing the sucker to hell and back for having the extremely bad sense to mar Maddy's perfect skin.

The end of the sliver poked through to the surface, but no matter how hard he squeezed, the rest refused to budge. He tried to pull it out, but his fingers were too thick and blunt.

"I gotta use my teeth," he said before lifting her palm to his mouth.

She gasped when his breath caressed the center of her hand, but it had nothing to do with pain and everything to do with the current of want, of need, of *desire* that arced between them.

Using the sensitive pads of his lips, he located the

splinter. Then he grabbed hold of it with his teeth, and as gently as he could, as slowly as he could so as not to break it off, he pulled it from her tender flesh and turned to spit it on the ground.

"Ohhh, that feels a million times better," she whispered, which made him contemplate the million *other* things he could do to her that'd feel even better than that.

He lifted his eyes to her face, and when their gazes met, electricity jumped in the air around them, sparking, sizzling, washing over them in voltaic waves until she gasped and he...*throbbed*.

For a while they just looked at each other. Wanting each other. *Aware* of each other. Poised to take the next step together, but neither of them moving a muscle. Maybe because it felt so big.

Finally, through trembling lips she said, "You can live a hundred years and never really *live* one minute if fear of what *could* happen, what *might* happen prevents you from goin' after what you want. Tonight, I want *you*, Bran."

She didn't give him time to respond. She didn't give him time to argue—not that he would; he was past that. She grabbed his ears, went up on tiptoe, and dragged his head down for a kiss that was so hot it burned away his ability to think, his ability to reason, his ability to do anything but meet her lick for lick, nip for nip, and stroke for deep, wet, penetrating stroke.

Chapter 18

MADDY MAY HAVE BEEN THE ONE TO INITIATE THE KISS, BUT it didn't take long—two seconds, maybe—before Bran was leading the way.

He was the kind of kisser who reveled. The kind of kisser who took his time. A hedonist. A glutton. A *master*.

She let herself surrender.

"Bran," she whispered when he came up for air sometime later—two minutes? Ten? Time had ceased to exist in its usual state—and kissed the corner of her mouth. Her nose. Her cheeks. Her chin. Peppering her with quick, biting caresses that were as much about the need to claim every inch of her, brand every inch of her, as they were about pleasure or lust.

Her whole body was humming. His kisses alone were better than any full-on sex she'd ever had. Her skin was sensitized to every brush of his fingers, every touch of his lips, every warm sweep of his breath.

"Say it again," he murmured, nuzzling her ear. His teeth gently tugged on her lobe until her eyes crossed and her toes curled from the thrill of it. "I love it when you say my name."

"Bran," she said huskily, giggling and moaning when the pressure on her earlobe increased. A gentle nip, a soft warning that he was barely keeping himself in check.

She knew what would come next. Knew he would let the raider, the conqueror, the *plunderer* go free.

She wanted that. Oh, how she wanted that. To be raided. To be conquered. To be plundered and made his. His...woman.

Just for tonight, her conscience warned.

But she wouldn't think about that. Like Scarlett O'Hara, she was determined to think about that tomorrow. *Tomorrow is another day*.

"Again," he moaned, reaching around to palm her ass.

Turning her face into his, she was pleased with the throaty, sexy sound of her voice when she whispered softly, "Bran."

"Fuck *me*," he moaned, pulling her tight against him, forcing her up on tiptoe. He ground her swollen sex against the steely rod of his erection, and the warm sea breeze at her back underscored just how hot he was against her front. A living flame. And like a moth, she sought to fly even closer.

"I think that's our agreement, right?" She caught her breath when he dipped to grab her knee and lift her leg high around his waist, opening her to him, to the bump and grind of his hips as he stroked into her, rubbing, rubbing, *rubbing* his hard length against the seam of her shorts and the distended bud of her clitoris. Sensation sizzled. Friction fizzed. Nerve endings rejoiced and begged for more.

"Yesss." The word hissed from between his lips, circling sensuously inside her ear. "I feel how hot you are for me, Maddy. Are you wet too?"

"God, yes," she admitted even though it shocked and titillated her to do so. She'd asked for this. *Demanded* it actually. And she'd be damned if she allowed any inhibitions to stop her from enjoying every single second.

She was determined to do whatever she could, what-ever it took, to make this something he'd never forget. To make herself stand head and shoulders above the crowd of women he'd had before her. To make him think twice about abandoning what they could have together if only—

Whoa there, sister, her conscience cautioned. *If that's what this is all about, then you better stop it right now.*

Of course anything else her conscience said was drowned out by the low sound of approval that rumbled from the back of Bran's throat. "Good," he whispered, still stroking, still teasing. "I want you wet. I want you so wet you drench me when I put myself inside you."

He didn't give her time to answer that thoroughly wicked comment, instead catching her mouth in a kiss so drugging it left her dazed and confused, unable to concentrate on anything other than the terrible ache between her thighs and the friction he was providing that just…wasn't…quite…enough.

She needed bare flesh on bare flesh. She needed fin-gers and tongues and lips and teeth and…his cock. *Holy hell,* she needed his cock. The hard column of flesh that pressed insistently against her, the steely rod of pleasure that promised so much more to come.

Put yourself inside me now! she wanted to scream. But all she managed was "Bran, I want…"

"What?" he said against her mouth, nibbling on her top lip. He sucked the sensitive pad between his teeth and laved it with his hot tongue as if demonstrating how he would suck and lick other parts of her. "What'd'ya want, Maddy? Tell me."

"Should we go to the ranger's station first?" she

asked even though she dreaded the time it would take to walk there. Time when his hand wouldn't be kneading her ass and working her over his throbbing hardness. Time when his skilled mouth wouldn't be showing her the wonderful world of kissing without limits or reticence.

"No time for that," he said.

Great minds…

"But, where—" That's all she managed before he dropped her leg and pushed out of her arms. Her body ached with the loss. Her womanhood throbbed for friction that was no longer there. And she was so dizzy she had to thrust out a hand to steady herself against the metal skin of the lighthouse.

Bran leaned around the lighthouse and yelled, "Girls! Rick! Eyes on the entire perimeter for a while, okay? If you see anything, and I mean *anything*, yell at the top of your lungs! I gotta duck into the lighthouse for a bit and take care of something!"

Maddy didn't hear Rick respond—*I gotta take care of somethin'? Really? Does Bran think he's foolin' anyone with that?*—but she should've known the girls wouldn't stay quiet. Which was why she just shook her head and waved off Bran's curious look when Donna hollered, "Yo, Miss Maddy! Way to go!"

Later, she might blush at the thought that Rick and the girls knew *she* was the "something" Bran had to take care of. But right now, she had to concentrate to keep up when Bran grabbed her hand and led her along the base of the lighthouse. She made it three steps, three wobbly steps before her traitorous knees gave out on her.

Weightlessness.

That's what she experienced when Bran scooped her into his arms. She barely had time to marvel at his strength, at the easy way he carried her despite his injured leg and the fact that she was a far cry from a size two, before he bent to move the weapons from the spot atop the sleeping bag. Carefully propping them against the wall of the lighthouse, butts down, barrels up, he retrieved the sleeping bag, shook it out, and reached for the handle to the door. When he yanked it open, it made a deep groaning noise, its hinges rusty and tight from years battling the salty sea air.

This is it, she thought. *This is the place.*

The place where she'd *finally* know him. All of him. Know what made him gasp, what made him moan.

She squinted against the dimness to see the interior of the lighthouse was nothing more than a circular room with an uneven wood floor. It was empty of everything but a metal ladder that led up to a trapdoor in the ceiling, behind which she assumed was the light fixture and all the mechanical whatnot. A gentle *whirring* drifted down from above. It grew louder when Bran kicked the door closed and they were engulfed in warm, humid darkness.

It wasn't a featherbed with silk sheets. It wasn't a hot tub with fragrant bubbles. But it was theirs. Their little hideaway. Their refuge from the world outside and any second thoughts about the repercussions of their decision. In a word, it was *perfect.* A place without place. A time without time.

"Maddy," he whispered, slowly lowering her to the ground so that she was aware of every inch of him on the descent. The heavy muscles in his chest. The impossible hardness of his stomach. The thick length of him unabashedly throbbing and flexing against her.

Her world condensed down to this room. To the two of them. Right here. Right now. Nothing else mattered. Nothing but this man who was broken and bitter. Who was equally fearless and funny. Who could promise her nothing, but who meant everything.

"Say it again," she whispered, her voice echoing softly in the dark when her feet hit the floor. "I like it when you say my name too."

His Jersey accent did something wonderful to it. Making it harder sounding. Tougher sounding. *Erotic* sounding. When he said *Maddy*, she wasn't a silly Southern belle. She was a temptress, a seductress, a siren.

"Maddy," he said huskily, and she groaned, feeling passion fill her until it pushed against her ribs, her backbone, until her whole being ached with the enormity of it.

Then he was gone. Just like that. Her hands grasped at the darkness but came away empty. Her flesh chilled upon the absence of his intense heat. Then she heard the sleeping bag *shush* when it hit the wood floor. And suddenly he was back, herding her backward, using his big body and his superior strength to pin her against the wall. The metal was cool at her back as he reclaimed her lips in a kiss so lazy and long and thorough that by the time he allowed her to come up for air, she'd forgotten how to breathe.

"I wanna make this about you," he said, leaving a string of kisses across her cheek and back to her ear. "Tell me what you want, Maddy. Tell me how you wanna be touched. How you wanna be kissed. How you wanna be fucked."

With her eyesight gone, all her other senses were enhanced. For the first time she could hear the subtler bass notes in his sexy baritone, smell the lighter scent of suntan lotion underneath the salt water and Irish Spring soap clinging to his flesh, and taste the lingering flavor of a sports drink beneath the natural sweetness of his breath.

"Tell me all your fantasies, Maddy," he continued, pressing his forehead to hers and running one finger down her cheek and over to her mouth so he could feel her swollen, parted lips. Feel her words when she finally gave them to him. "Tell me so I can make 'em all come true."

"Bran," she moaned. He shuddered when her breath feathered over his finger, like it'd burned him, but the pain was so good. The temptation to suck the digit inside her mouth, to take a part of him inside her, was too much. So she did exactly that and was rewarded when his uninjured thigh thrust between her legs, pushing high, lifting her on tiptoe. She rubbed herself against him even as she sucked.

"You're so damned sexy," he whispered before replacing his finger with his tongue, spearing deep over and over again. "Tell me, Maddy," he insisted again. She was so wet she had to have soaked through her shorts and into his. "Tell me, damnit," he growled when she didn't answer him. He nipped her bottom lip. A warning. A gentle reminder that, when it came to this, he made all the rules.

"S-suck on my pulse point," she stuttered.

He immediately obeyed, his hot lips closing over the spot on her neck where her heart hammered close to the surface of her skin. His hot tongue laved sweetly before he sucked deeply. And it was like an invisible string was connected from that spot on her neck to the swollen bundle of nerves between her legs.

"Touch me," she rasped, running her hands over his big shoulders, amazed at the hardness of his muscles, at the density of his bones, at the smooth firmness of his warm skin. He felt exactly like what he was. A big, strong, very *manly* man. And everything that was female in her delighted in the differences between them. His hard to her soft. His rough to her smooth. His toughness to her tenderness.

"Where?" His voice was low and demanding. "Where do you want me to touch you?"

Everywhere. But he wasn't an octopus. So she started with something she'd been dreaming about for months. "My b-breasts," she managed, her breath catching when a low grumble vibrated at the back of his throat.

And then his hand inched beneath the hem of her T-shirt, his palm skating up her stomach, over her ribs. Higher. Higher. Ever higher. The calluses on his palm were wonderfully abrasive, adding one more delightful sensation to the already heady mix.

Part of her wanted to tell him, *Hurry the hell up!* Her nipples were so hard they hurt. Her breasts were heavy and aching for his caresses. But another part of her reveled in the exquisite torture. In the exquisite waiting and wanting and anticipation of—

"Good Lord," she groaned when he cupped her right breast, plumping it high, his thumb rasping over the distended tip and creating a delicious friction even through the satin of her bra.

"You're so fuckin' sweet," he said, reclaiming her mouth. His lips were swollen yet firm. His tongue bold and unapologetic.

"More," she begged him, her hips moving of their own accord, thrusting over his thigh, seeking more friction. Faster. Harder. Her heart pounded. Her blood roared. She was a thing now. A being entirely comprised of want. Of need. Of *hunger*.

"I'll give you more," he promised. "I'll give you everything."

That's exactly what she wanted. All of this. All of him.

Bran tugged her T-shirt top over her head. With a flick of his fingers, he unsnapped the front closure on her bra. "Damn," he cursed.

"What?" she panted, barely able to think the words, much less form them. "What is it?"

"I wish it weren't so dark," he said as he cupped her breasts in his hot, callused palms. His thumbs reverently brushed over the painfully erect tips, and she hissed her pain. Her pleasure. "I wanna see you. I've dreamed of seeing you for so long."

He caught her nipples between his thumbs and forefingers and softly plucked. He should've been a musician, a surgeon, something that would make use of his crazy talented hands. The pleasure twanging in her breasts made her hips work faster over his thigh. The delectable friction was building to a fever pitch. Soon. Soon it would be enough.

"Describe them to me," he rasped, alternately feathering his fingers over the hard points and gently pinching them. She was bombarded by sensation, by ever-burgeoning bliss. *Close. So close.* "Are they brown like berries? Red like cherries?" His voice was thick with passion.

"Pink," she managed, though she hadn't the first clue how her vocal cords were still working. "Light pink. Like cotton candy."

"Mmm," he hummed against her lips. "I bet they taste as sweet."

And then he dipped his head to catch one taut peak between his warm lips. She moaned and speared her hands into his hair, pulling him closer, catching her lip between her teeth when his hot tongue rasped over her nipple.

"Delicious," he murmured. "Just as I suspected."

Maddy couldn't respond. Her orgasm was barreling toward her at full speed now, sending pulses of pleasure down her spine, into her breasts, and through her womb.

Bran must have sensed how close she was. "Wait, Maddy. Shit. I wanna—"

"No!" she whispered deliriously when suddenly he was…gone. His lips left her breast with a suctioned *pop*. His thigh and the wonderful friction it provided vanished from between her legs. "Bran! Please!" She blindly reached for him, her searching fingers finding the impenetrable wall of his chest. The crinkly hair there tickled her palms. She felt her way up to his shoulders, digging her fingers into his muscles, desperate to pull him back to her.

"Shhh, Maddy," he said, allowing her to draw him close. "I'm gonna get you there. But I wanna feel you come the first time. Please, Maddy. Let me feel you."

"Hurry, Bran," she begged.

She thought she heard him chuckle. Thought she

heard him call her an *impatient little minx* but she couldn't be sure. Her blood was pounding in her ears and every ounce of her attention was focused on the hand Bran snaked between their bodies. He popped the button on her shorts. Her zipper made a subtle *scrrrr-ritching* sound when he tugged it down.

"Yes," she whispered when his long, thick fingers speared down the front of her panties. He parted her swollen folds.

"*Fungule,*" he moaned. "You're so damned wet."

"As requested," she said, delighted to hear him growl before he reclaimed her lips, using his teeth and tongue to play with her mouth even as his knowledgeable fingers played with her sex. He strummed her clitoris again and again. Rubbing, rubbing, *rubbing* just right.

He definitely didn't treat it like a *go* button. Oh, no.

"You like that," he whispered into her mouth.

"Yes," was all she managed.

"Do you want my fingers inside you?"

"Yes."

"Do you—"

"Damnit, Bran!" She grabbed his head, biting his bottom lip in her frustration, in her urgency. "Yes, yes, *yes!*"

This time she was sure he chuckled. But the laugh died in his throat when he pressed one finger inside her. She'd waited so long for that kind of stimulation, to be penetrated, to be filled, that her body gripped him fiercely.

"Just let me—" He didn't finish. He didn't need to. She'd let him do anything. Including letting him work a second finger inside her until she was stretched and full. Nerves that had been crying out for stimulation got exactly that.

"Bran…" She breathed his name when he pumped slowly. And then her ability to talk eluded her when slow pumping became faster, harder. In and out. Over and over again. The wet sounds of sex whispered inside the lighthouse, sliding against the metal walls and inside Maddy's ears.

"Now, Maddy," he said. "Now, babe. I want you to come for me. I wanna feel it."

He ground the heel of his palm into the top of her sex, abrading her clitoris while simultaneously reaching up with his free hand to pinch her nipple. The instant he did, Maddy did as instructed. She muffled her scream in the crook of his shoulder and went off like an atom bomb, her orgasm blowing wave after wave of sweet, exquisite ecstasy through her until she lost track of where she was. Who she was. *What* she was other than a thing that was pure, incandescent bliss…

Chapter 19

10:02 p.m. ...

BRAN WENT OFF IN HIS SHORTS.

Or at least it *felt* like he did. His dick pulsed rhythmically when Maddy's body clamped around his fingers until his knuckles rubbed together. Then again, the throbbing, insistent ache of his balls drawn up tight against his body proved he hadn't pulled the fifteen-year-old-boy-copping-his-first-feel routine, after all. He was still fully loaded, locked, stocked, and ready to rock. In the timeless words of Mr. Mellencamp, he *hurt so good*.

"That's it, babe," he encouraged when he could find his voice. He wiggled his fingers in a come-hither motion, rubbing the rough patch of swollen flesh inside her. "Ride it out."

And she did. For long, *torturous* moments.

"Dear Lord," she said huskily when the last shudders of orgasm washed through her, her body easing around him, her hands relaxing their grip on his shoulders. She had turned liquid in his arms, sinuous, warm, so utterly soft in her repletion.

"I wanna taste you, Maddy," he whispered in her ear. He only had this one night, and he needed to experience it all. No shortcuts. No exits. The entire journey from start to finish. All the sights and sounds and smells and flavors of it.

Close as they were, with his fingers still buried inside her, he had no trouble feeling the shudder that shook her small frame. For a second he thought maybe he'd embarrassed her with his crudeness, his unapologetic honesty. But then she planted a kiss on his jaw near his ear and whispered, "So what's stoppin' you?"

Maddy was everything he'd hoped she'd be. Sweet, receptive, passionate, and a little bit raunchy. And funny. Even in the midst of sex, she was still funny. And fascinating. The most fascinating woman he'd ever met.

What has she done to me? This Texas tornado in a teacup package?

But he knew.

She had wormed her way into his life, into his dreams, and into his…heart.

And there it was. The flash of insight nearly blinded him with its brilliance. All those feelings he had for her that went beyond friendship and lust, those feelings that were bigger, deeper, wider were really all just *one* feeling. The simplest and most complex feeling of all.

Love.

He loved her.

He was *in love* with her. Little by little, day by day, email by email, he'd fallen more. And it'd happened so slowly, so subtly, that he hadn't understood until right now.

So where does that leave me?

And perhaps it was a day for epiphanies because as soon as he asked himself the question, he knew the answer. It left him with this. This moment right here and now. This one time to hold the woman of his heart in his arms.

And by God, I refuse to waste one minute thinking about what tomorrow will bring.

Slowly, inexorably slowly, he slipped his fingers from her body. Loving the way her inner muscles grasped at him. The air inside the lighthouse was warm and damp. But it still felt cool against his fingers when he lifted them to his mouth, his nostrils flaring at the scent that coated them. The scent of her. The scent of passion and completion.

Even though she couldn't see what he was doing, he could tell she knew by the soft, mewling sound she made. And when he put his fingers in his mouth, her taste exploded on his tongue. Tart and sweet. Salty and delicious. It was the unmistakable flavor of hot, healthy, satisfied woman. And he could no more hold back his animal-like sound of approval than he could hold back the tide.

Maddy's voice was husky when she whispered, "And now it's your turn, sailor. What is it you say? Tit for tat?"

Before he knew what she was about, the button on his cargo shorts sprang open under her dexterous fingers. His zipper followed suit. And then Maddy's cool, soft hands were inside the front of his boxer shorts and closing around his hot, throbbing shaft.

He groaned and had to brace his palms against the metal wall on either side of her head to keep himself upright. His dick pulsed hard. Once. Twice. Three times.

"You're quite a handful, aren't you?" Maddy murmured, nibbling on his jaw, then alternating nips with sweet, wet kisses.

Roger that. Not that he was one of those guys hung up on size, but he was pretty sure his dick was ten feet tall and bulletproof. At least it was in *this* moment.

He could have made some witty reply to that effect, but his tongue hit the top of his mouth and stayed there when she used her thumb to spread his own wetness over his super-sensitive head and down the length of his shaft. Then he nearly swallowed his tongue when she fisted him firmly and began pumping.

"So," she breathed against his lips, "tell me how *you* want to be kissed. How *you* want to be touched. How *you* want to be fucked."

Raunchy and sexy and determined to give as good as she'd gotten. That was Maddy. Wonderful, remarkable Maddy.

"K-kiss my chest," he managed. "My n-nipples are sensitive."

When her soft mouth landed on the flat disk of his left nipple, his areola contracted, forcing the center to form a tight bead.

"Ah, hell," he groaned when her tongue lapped at his tip, flicking it softly. Each twang echoed down into his dick. And then she closed her lips over him and sucked, pulled deep. If there was any light, he knew he'd see her cheeks hollowing out. Below, she tightened her fist around him and pumped in a rhythm that matched the cadenced suction of her mouth.

It was too much. Too good. His hips jerked forward. He curled his fingers into the metal of the wall, anchoring himself to the moment. Fighting off the orgasm that threatened to explode from him with just one more lick. One more suck. One more stroke.

He didn't want to come. Not yet. He wanted to luxuriate in her bold, unmerciful ministrations for a while longer.

"Tug my balls down," he rasped, his breath sawing from his lungs, his stomach muscles contracting. "Quick, Maddy, or you're gonna make me c-come."

"I *want* you to come," she murmured around his nipple. "I want to feel you spill into my hands, all hot and wet and slippery."

"Fuck. *Me*," he groaned at each naughty wording coming out of an upside-down mouth that he knew looked deceivingly sweet and innocent.

"Now, Bran," she said, echoing his earlier words back to him. "I want you to come for me. I want to feel it."

Bran had been taking orders most of his adult life. But none had ever been as erotic or carnal as the ones Maddy issued. Lightning hit the base of his spine. His hips worked back and forth in a rhythm that was a counterpoint to the push and pull of her sweet, soft hand. Higher and higher he climbed. Tighter and faster she tugged.

And then it happened.

His orgasm burst from him. Lights flashed behind his screwed-tight lids. Pleasure rolled over him in wave after body-shaking wave. He spilled his desire into her hands.

He thought he whispered her name, but couldn't be sure. He thought he was still on his feet, but couldn't be sure of that either. The only thing he *was* sure of was that he was coming harder, faster, longer than he ever had before. Because it was Maddy.

Maddy, Maddy, Maddy...Her name was a refrain inside his mind. *Maddy...sweet, wonderful Maddy...*

———

10:10 p.m. . . .

"I think Bran and Maddy might be soul mates," Alex said.

And it was the one trillionth statement or observation she'd made since they parked themselves at the small, molded fiberglass table on the back of the catamaran. Mason should know. He'd kept count. And while just about everything else she'd jabbered on about hadn't inspired any responses from him, he felt compelled to answer this one.

"The concept of soul mates is crap," he told her, lowering the field glasses he'd been using to keep an eye on the ocean around them. He adjusted the knob on the marine radio he'd moved from inside the small galley, and static briefly echoed over the line. "Hollywood invented it to sell tickets to Rachel McAdams movies." When Alex just blinked at him, he narrowed his eyes and demanded, "What?"

"I'm trying to decide if you really spoke or if exhaustion has me hallucinating."

He harrumphed.

"Okay," she nodded. "So not hallucinating then. There's no way I could recreate that certain…je ne sais quoi that echoes through your special brand of caveman-esque grunt. It really is quite something, you know? It's like, with one word that isn't even a word, you're able to convey annoyance, frustration, disapproval, and dismissal."

"Alex—"

"And since when do you watch Rachel McAdams movies?"

He shook his head. "I never said I *did*."

Had he *really* jumped for joy when he saw the catamaran sail toward the island after he set off the flare? Had he really been happier than he could remember being in…well…forever when she dropped anchor and jumped overboard to start swimming in his direction?

To his consternation, the answer was *yes* to both questions.

Alex is nothing but a pain in my ass. What the fuck was I thinking?

"Sure you did," she challenged, her eyes twinkling behind the lenses of her glasses. "You said soul mates were invented by Hollywood to sell tickets to Rachel McAdams movies. Which means you must've *seen* a few to make that summary judgment."

"You're missing my point." He hadn't been thinking. That was the only explanation. Or at least he hadn't been thinking with the head atop his shoulders.

"I don't think I am." She placed her elbow on the table, cupping her chin in her palm. "You like Rachel McAdams movies. Admit it. So which is your favorite? Most people are partial to *The Notebook*, but I like *The Time Traveler's Wife* the best."

"I *don't* watch Rachel McAdams movies," he grumbled, though he had watched *The Time Traveler's Wife*. But only because he liked the paranormal, science-fiction aspect of it.

"Well, why not?" she demanded, her deep auburn eyebrows pulling down in a vee.

"Because I have these things," he told her.

"What things?"

"They're called a dick and balls."

"Oh, big macho man." She waved her hands. "Has to act all rough and tough, like he doesn't enjoy a good star-crossed lovers story just as much as the rest of us."

"Now *that's* something I believe in," he told her, leaning back in the molded fiberglass seat and lifting the field glasses to do another quick scan of the dark horizon.

"What?" she asked. "Star-crossed lovers?"

"Nah." He shook his head. "Just *lovers* in general. I believe in hormones and animal magnetism and the biological urge to mate."

She studied him for a second, blinking slowly. "So you're saying…what? That there's no such thing as love? Only sex?"

Hearing the word, just the *word*, come out of her mouth made his shorts feel too tight.

"I'm just saying there's no such thing as soul mates." He shifted in his seat, trying to find a more comfortable position. "I'm saying there's lust that leads to love. And love that leads to lust on rare occasions. But mostly there's *just* lust that burns hot and fizzles fast."

"Wow." She wrinkled her nose. "You're a real romantic."

There was a time… "Hey." He shrugged, feigning far more indifference than he felt. "You asked. It's not my fault you don't like the answer."

"Point taken," she allowed with a bob of her eyebrows.

They were ever mobile, those eyebrows of hers. And he couldn't help but wonder if they felt as soft and sleek as they looked. He curled his fingers around the edge of the table to keep from reaching to find out.

She started peeling the orange she'd grabbed from

the galley, and his attention shifted from her eyebrows to her hands, to the swift, efficient movements they made. He was instantly mesmerized. The soft moonlight streaming down from above seemed to highlight just how graceful and small they were. Narrow palms. Thin fingers. Short, unpainted nails that showed half-moon shapes up by her cuticles.

Pretty.

Alex had pretty hands.

Which made sense, he supposed, since the rest of her wasn't too hard to look at either. Oh, not that Alex ever flaunted her cute, all-American-girl appearance. Quite the contrary. She didn't seem to care that her curly hair was usually sticking out every which way. She didn't wear revealing clothing that showed off her delicately curved figure. And she hid the most amazing green eyes he'd ever seen behind a dark pair of tortoiseshell glasses.

Nevertheless, there was no mistaking how attractive she was. It was always there. Staring him in the face. Taunting him.

And maybe that was why he was always so short with her. Because he could have ignored any woman who strutted her stuff. But it was impossible to ignore a woman who didn't seem to know or care she even *had* stuff.

Or maybe I'm short with her because she drives me crazy. There was always that possibility.

"Orange?" She held out a peeled half to him.

"Sure." He accepted her offering. One thing about her that *didn't* drive him bonkers was the fact that she fed him. Always. "Thanks."

For a couple of seconds they sat in blissful silence. The only time Mason knew Alex to keep quiet was when she had food stuffed in her mouth, which, thankfully, was quite often. But he should have known the reprieve wouldn't last for long.

"So which kind do you think Bran and Maddy are?" she asked.

"What do you mean?"

"People where lust turns into love? Or people where love turns into lust? Because they've been cultivating this friendship for months, which leads me to think they're the latter. Then again, seeing them together is like walking into a welding factory." When he cocked his head, she wiggled her eyebrows. "I'm talking sparks, baby. So *that* leads me to think it's the former. I guess it's that whole chicken-and-egg thing. One of the quintessential mysteries of life. Although maybe you have more insight. After all, you were there when they first met."

He blinked. "What was the question again?"

She narrowed her eyes. "Why is it no one can ever follow my line of inquiry?"

"Maybe because after you ask something, you keep talking for five minutes, and by the time you're finished, people have forgotten the initial query."

"Well, then *people* should learn to focus."

"Consider me a camera," he told her, a grin tugging at the corners of his lips. Despite all the ways she exasperated him, it was fun keeping up with her lightning-fast mind.

She blinked at him. "I can't tell if you're serious or just being a smart-ass."

"Can't I be a serious smart-ass?"

"We've gone off the rails."

"You act like that's something new for you."

"The *question*," she stressed, "is whether you think Bran and Maddy are the kind of people where lust turns to love or vice versa."

"Neither," he said, popping an orange slice into his mouth. "Theirs is a lust-only situation."

"How can you be so sure?" she asked curiously, taking a bite of orange. A drop of juice landed on her lip, and she absently licked it away. He gritted his teeth when the sight of her pink tongue caused an ache to form low in his belly.

"Because I know Bran," he said, looking away from her. "And he won't let love into the equation."

"Why not?"

He turned back to stare at her the way he would stare at a blank wall. "He just won't."

He and Bran were peas in a pod in that respect. They both agreed that there were two kinds of love. The kind that flourished and left both parties stronger for its presence; the *rare* kind of love. And the kind that destroyed and made both parties weaker and warier for having experienced it; the more *common* kind of love. Turned out, neither one of them cared to play the odds on the former because both of them had already experienced the carnage left behind from the latter.

"Does it have something to do with his father or the way he was raised?" Alex asked.

And now Mason's stomach ached for a whole new reason. "What the fuck do you know about that?"

"Nothing," Alex said, blinking warily. "I just heard LT say something to Romeo once about Bran being the way he is because he was afraid of becoming like his bastard of a father, so I figured…" She let the sentence dangle.

"LT should keep his fuckin' mouth shut," Mason grumbled. They all had baggage. *All* of them. As far as Mason was concerned, they had an unspoken agreement never to talk about it.

"Is that your nice way of telling me it's none of my business?"

"Was I being nice? I wasn't trying to be."

"Exchanged smart-ass for wiseass, huh?" Alex twisted her lips, and Mason noticed for the first time how small and plump they were. A rosebud mouth, he thought it was called. "Does Dorothy Parker know about you?"

"Who?" He was still distracted by her mouth. *How is it so red when she isn't wearing any lipstick?*

"You know." Alex furrowed her brow. "Dorothy Parker. Queen of the snappy comeback? No?"

He shook his head.

She blew out a disbelieving breath. "Remind me to educate you once we get back to Wayfarer Island. Some of her satire, even though it's fifty years old, is better than anything anyone is writing today. She's super sarcastic. I think you'll like her."

"Mmmph," he said, then a thought occurred to him. "Wait, she's a writer? But you said you only read for educational or research purposes, never for enjoyment. If I remember correctly, you watch *Sex and the City* for enjoyment."

"Well, that whole no-reading-for-enjoyment rule doesn't apply to Dorothy Parker." Alex narrowed her eyes. "And do I detect a hint of judgment in your voice? Don't tell me you have a problem with Rachel McAdams movies *and*"—she stressed the word—"*Sex and the City*. Because I'll be forced to agree with Maddy's earlier assessment that you're a big, ol' misogynist." She popped another orange slice between her succulent lips.

To distract himself, he did the same, savoring the burst of tartness on his tongue. "For your information," he said sullenly, "I have no opinion of *Sex and the City*. I've never seen a single episode."

Her eyes rounded behind her glasses, and he was struck by the deep, saturated hue of her irises. They reminded him of the wet jungles of the Amazon or the vibrant stands of bamboo in the Sagano Forest of Japan. Kelly green. Luck o' the Irish green. *Gorgeous* green. "Seriously?" she asked. "Not even a clip?"

"Nuh-uh."

"Forget Dorothy Parker," she said. "We have to remedy your *Sex and the City* deficit first. We'll fire up the laptop and do a marathon the minute we get back. I know you passed on the offer earlier tonight. But this time I'm not taking no for an answer. Besides"—she grinned and bobbed her eyebrows—"you'll like it. Did I mention the boobs and boinking?"

He really wished she would stop talking about boobs and boinking. Every time she did, his mind immediately conjured up images of *her* boobs, and what *she'd* look like boi—

He shook his head, refusing to finish the thought. "Which begs the question," he said. "Why do *you* like it?" And then it occurred to him. "Unless…are you…" His mouth was suddenly dry as a desert. He slid another slice of orange between his lips and chewed to wet his whistle. "Do you…ahem…bat for the home team?" Was it possible he'd read her wrong these last few months? "Or maybe you're a switch-hitter?"

His gaydar was usually spot-on. But maybe his long, self-imposed dry spell had caused his systems to go wonky.

Alex frowned. "Your baseball jargon is flying right over my head. English, please."

He wasn't sure how else to ask the question except to just…ask it. And was it totally crazy he wasn't certain what he wanted the answer to be? If she *was* batting for the home team, it definitely solved the little problem he seemed to be having with her, the one that made him question his self-imposed moratorium on all things sporting that double-X chromosome. Then again, he couldn't help thinking, *But that'd be a crying shame.* In his not-so-humble opinion, Alex's dainty *femaleness* seemed to cry out for a male counterpart.

"Do you like girls?" he blurted.

"Of course," she said.

Holy fuck.

"I like girls, guys, transgender, transsexual, or any type of person you can think of," she said. Despite his best efforts, he couldn't stop his eyes from widening. "I just like *people*. They're endlessly fascinating and… Oh my God! I just realized you're asking if I'm a lesbian!"

He didn't say anything, choosing instead to sit and wait. There were two things he knew beyond a shadow of a doubt. One was that the sun would rise tomorrow in the east. The other was that there really wasn't much need to talk when Alex was around. She was completely capable of carrying on whole conversations by herself.

And I'm cracked because I enjoy it. The sound of her

voice was soothing. And that lisp she developed when she got really worked up? Well, it was nothing short of adorable.

"*No*," she said emphatically. "I am *not* a lesbian. Not even close." She made a face. "Wait. I didn't mean for it to sound that way. I'd be proud to be a lesbian. If I were a lesbian. Which I'm not. I like boys…er…guys. I mean *men*. I like *men*. Well, not *all* men. But in a general sexual sense I prefer the male to… Oh, for Chrissakes, I feel like I'm digging myself in deeper with every word."

And he was totally content to watch her shovel. He took another bite of orange and watched her shift uncomfortably in her seat. She tilted her head and pushed her glasses up the bridge of her nose. For some reason, that gesture always got to him. And now that she'd unequivocally declared she liked boys…guys… *men*—inside he was quaking with laughter—it was worse. His blood started speeding, spinning, rushing like his heart was a clock that was wound too tight.

"Why did you think I was a lesbian?" she asked, peeling another slice of orange from her half, but not popping it in her mouth. "Is it because I don't wear makeup? Because just so you know, I usually *do* wear makeup when I'm not living on an island that requires me to slather on sunscreen.

"Or is it because I don't run around in a bikini the way Olivia does? If it is, then I would like to state that the reason I wear a one-piece is the same reason I don't wear makeup. My skin is really fair, and if I wear a one-piece that's just that much more surface area I don't have to rub sunscreen into." She frowned. "Or maybe it's the unpainted nails and the baggy shorts and…

Wow. I really *don't* put out a very girlie vibe, do I? That would explain some things."

When her face looked like it was ready to crumble, Mason figured it was time he opened his mouth. "I think you're *very* girlie," he reassured her.

"You do?" She blinked at him. *Fuck, yeah, I do.* "Then why did you ask me if I was... Oh!" She had a laugh like a shotgun. It blasted out of her and echoed across the boat and over the water. "Because I said I like *Sex and the City* for all the boobs and the boinking. Yup." She nodded. "I can see how that might give you the wrong impression."

He simply lifted a brow.

"But just so we're clear, I watch *Sex and the City* for two reasons. Firstly, I like the female camaraderie on the show since I never had sisters or even really close girlfriends." She stopped to toss another orange slice in her mouth. "And secondly, I find it educational since recently I've decided it's time to take a lover."

Mason wasn't sure, but he thought perhaps the bottom had fallen out of the sailboat.

Chapter 20

"AND I FIGURE I CAN USE ALL THE POINTERS I C-CAN..."
Alex stuttered to a stop when she realized Mason
looked like he was about two seconds from keeling
over in a dead faint. If she wasn't mistaken, that ruddy
color riding high on his cheeks was there because he'd
stopped breathing.

Well, crap on a cracker. What's with him?

She barely had time to ask herself the question before
she knew the answer. She slammed a hand over her
mouth. "Sorry," she said through her fingers, feeling like
someone had dumped a bucket of hot water over her head
so that heat washed down the entire length of her. "That
was a definitely a case of TMI, wasn't it?" She winced.

"And I know we don't have the kind of relationship
where we can talk about lovers, past, present, or future.
But in my defense, I'm not a very secretive person. And
that added to the fact that I tend to suffer from a severe
case of verbal diarrhea means sometimes I just unload
without thinking. Sorry," she said again, seriously considering chucking herself overboard so the ocean could
cool the embarrassment from her skin. "I can't believe
I... Maybe I'm having an aneurysm."

She screwed up her face and waited for him to say
something to diminish the tension in the air, to put her

at ease. But he remained stubbornly mute. *Go figure.* And since she and silence had never been on friendly terms, she found herself saying, "And I know it might have sounded like I was propositioning you when I said I was determined to take a lover. But I wasn't. Not that I don't think you'd make a good one." He started blinking rapidly. "I mean, come *on.*" She waved a hand in his general direction. "You're, like, the very definition of *man.* So it stands to reason you'd be good at doing that quintessentially *man* thing."

His eyes were bugging out of his head. Scared they might pop out and go rolling across the table, she hurriedly added, "But you don't really like me. And the truth is, sometimes I'm not so sure I really like you. You're rude and grouchy, and you *never* talk. I think you've said more words to me tonight than in the two and a half months I've known you. So even if I *do* look at you and think bow-chicka-wow-wow, I'm not sure—"

He started choking. She assumed it was on a slice of orange. Startled, she scooted around the bench seat and whacked him on the back.

"Fuckin'-A," he wheezed. "You're about to punch a hole through my spine."

"Well, excuse me for trying to help." She frowned at him.

"Stop talking." He continued to wheeze. His eyes were watering.

"Sure, sure." She nodded. "My pleasure." She ground her teeth and picked up the discarded orange peel. Then, unable to stop herself, she said, "Look." When he glared at her, his face a study in frustration, she rolled her eyes. "Just let me say my piece and then I'll stop talking. I swear."

There was a muscle twitching beneath his eye, and she was worried now that she might give *him* an aneurysm, but she just needed to get this last bit out.

"When I said I was ready to take a lover, I was talking in the general sense. Not about anyone in particular." She firmed her chin. "And the reason I'm approaching it so pragmatically is because I've tried doing it the usual way, but it hasn't worked out."

She could have stopped there. But, as always, she figured, *In for a penny, in for a pound*. If she was going to open up her raincoat and show him the goods, she might as well stand there and let him take a good, long gander.

"See, I was a super-late bloomer in high school," she explained, thinking back on Johnny Gallagher, the hottest boy in school, and the way he'd always ruffled her hair like she was his kid sister instead of someone he'd consider taking to the prom. Mason reminded her a little bit of Johnny. Same black hair. Similar blue eyes. Apparently she had a type. *Who knew?* Of course, right now she'd settle for a brown-eyed blond. Anyone who could get the job done.

"No boys were interested in flat-chested Alex Merriweather, I can assure you," she said. "And then in college I was so focused on my studies that I really didn't give much thought to guys or getting laid. And then there was grad school and research, and *that's* when it started to occur to me that maybe I should really try to make this thing happen. But it was too late."

Mason's face was almost purple now, but she was certain she saw his left eyebrow quirk with interest. It was all the encouragement she needed.

"I mean, it's fine to tell a guy you're a virgin when

you're eighteen, right? They take it as a challenge, considering the average American loses their virginity at seventeen. Only twelve percent of twenty- to twenty-four-year-olds are still virgins." Yes, she'd done the research. And like everything else she happened to read, the facts and figures had stuck in her head. "That stat drops to less than five percent for women between the ages of twenty-five and twenty-nine. *Five percent!*"

She realized she was rambling and reined herself in. "Which means that if I try telling a man I'm still a virgin at twenty-seven, he assumes I'm some sort of religious fanatic, frigid freak, or a woman itching to get hitched. For the record"—she skewered him with a look when he seemed like he might have something to say to that— "I'm none of those."

There. Done. Now, say something!

But he pulled a classic Mason and just continued to sit there, staring at her as if she were a six-headed alien.

Before she knew it, her mouth was open and going again. "I'm watching *Sex and the City* so I'll know what to do when I *do* finally take a lover." She held up a hand. "And, yes, in case you were wondering, I've learned my lesson. No more virginal confessions. Are you sure you don't want me to whack you on the back again?"

I mean, that must be the most stubborn orange slice in the history of the world.

"Y-you're a *virgin*?" he managed in a strangled voice. *He speaks!* Thank goodness. Even *she* had a limit as to how long she could carry on a one-sided conversation.

"And *see*." She pointed a finger at him. "That right there is my whole point. Just look at you looking at me like I have some sort of disease. If I could take a picture of your face right now I'd frame it and whip it out as the precise explanation of why it's imperative I get a man in bed tout de suite."

"N-not any of the Deep Six crew," he said, still wheezing.

"Nah," she assured him. "They're too much like my brothers for me to set my sights on them." She cocked her head and narrowed her eyes. "Well, except for *you*. We've never really gotten all that friendly. Why is that, do you suppose?"

"I need a drink," he said by way of answer.

She watched him push up from the bench and stagger into the galley. When he reappeared in the doorway, he was guzzling a bottle of water.

Figuring he wasn't going to answer her question, she decided she'd outline her strategy for him in the hope that he'd offer a second opinion on her plan. It was a small hope, given his propensity for aphasia, but she was a gambler by nature and had won on low odds before. "I'm thinking I should tag along with Romeo or Uncle John the next time they make a Key West run. How hard can it be to pick up a tourist in a bar? I mean"—she frowned down at her black T-shirt with the red lettering that read: *History…don't make me repeat myself*—"I clean up pretty good when I try. What do you think?"

After he'd drained the contents of the bottle, he took a deep breath that made his chest expand to ridiculous proportions. "Your virginity…" He shook his head, still looking slightly ragged. "It isn't something you should give away to some random fucknuts you pick up at a bar." *Ya pick up atta bah* was how his accent made the sentence sound. She did so *love* how hearing him talk brought to mind Ivy League schools, crisp fall leaves, and steaming clam chowder. Which was one more reason his usual mutism annoyed her.

"Why not?" she demanded.

Now he just looked exasperated…or constipated. She wasn't sure which. "Because it's *special*!" he bellowed, throwing his hands in the air. "You should save it for someone you at least *like*."

"Are you volunteering?" And it was beyond satisfying to watch his chin jerk back and listen to him sputter.

"B-but you just admitted that you *don't* like me."

"Not so." She shook her head. "I said there are *times* when I'm not *sure* if I like you. That's totally different."

He blinked. And while he was blinking, the silence on the boat stretched. It was broken only by the *slap-slap* of the waves between the twin hulls. Finally, he opened his mouth. She leaned across the table, eagerly awaiting his reply. *Are my beaver teeth showing?* But to her disappointment, he snapped it shut again and grumbled, "I need another drink."

When he turned back into the galley, she studied the wide V-shape of his torso, feeling a bit giddy that she'd managed to throw him for a loop. A man of Mason's size didn't get tossed around too often. And that meant she gave herself major kudos for accomplishing the feat.

Then it occurred to her that maybe asking him to volunteer wasn't so completely ludicrous after all.

I mean, I'm a girl. He's a guy. I'm not looking for love and neither is he. So it'll be completely objective, scientific even.

Hmm. The longer she thought about it, the more intrigued she became.

"Do you find me attractive?" she asked when he reappeared in the doorway with a second bottle of water. She watched his reaction closely. Of course, she didn't have to watch *too* closely since his jaw hanging open was hard to miss. He choked again.

The man has some sort of throat problem apparently.

"It's a really simple question," she told him conversationally. "And don't worry about hurting my feelings. I'm a big girl. I can take anything you tell me."

And she convinced herself that was the truth, even though her insides were quivering around like pudding. She was *nervous. Why am I nervous?* Oh, right. Because she was putting herself out there and asking big, burly Mason McCarthy if he fancied her bod the same way she fancied his.

"So?" she prompted when he just stood there blinking at her. *Is he nearsighted or something? Did sand get in his eyes?*

"Sorry." He shook his head. "What was the question again?"

"Ugh." She blew out an exasperated breath. "How many times am I going to be asked that tonight?"

He must've thought it was a rhetorical question, because he didn't answer her, simply continued to play the part of a blinking mute.

"Do. You. Find. Me. Attractive?" She enunciated each word and punctuated the end of the question with a quick flutter of her lashes.

A muscle ticked beneath his eye again. It was joined by another in his jaw. And for a while she thought he wasn't going to answer her at all. But then he muttered, "Yes."

It was just the one word. No elaboration. But it was all she needed to hear. "Then it's perfect!" she said, grinning and clapping her hands.

"How do you figure?"

"Well, because you think *I'm* attractive and I think *you're* attractive." She began ticking off the reasons on her fingers. "You're not some stranger at a bar. I know you. And you know me. And considering we don't really get along in our everyday lives, there's no chance we'll develop any of those pesky romantic feelings for one another, so it'll just be a physical thing. What do you say? Do you want to be my first?"

He choked again.

Does he have a medical condition?

She started to ask him if he'd seen a doctor recently when the radio on the table squawked to life. "Garden Key, Garden Key, this is Captain Andrew Webber with the United States Coast Guard transmitting on—"

Alex stopped listening to the rest of the transmission. She was too busy trying to turn her eyeballs into laser beams so she could fry the radio.

Could the timing be any worse?

Mason marched over and grabbed the handset. "We copy you, Captain Webber," he said. "This is Senior Chief…uh…" He stopped and shook his head. "I mean this is Mason McCarthy of Wayfarer Island and Deep Six Salvage Company. We're happy as hell to hear your voice. You're earlier than we expected. Over?"

"Rrrrroger that, Senior Chief McCarthy," the captain responded, doing Mason the service of addressing him by his Naval rank. One thing Alex had learned in the short time she'd been on Wayfarer Island was that military men, regardless of which branch of the armed services they worked for, always treated each other with due respect. "Headquarters usually errs on the side of caution. When I got the call you all needed some help, I figured I better blow the cobwebs out of the engines. Over?"

"Copy that," Mason said. "We appreciate the effort."

"Rrrrroger that, Senior Chief. We're ten minutes out and closing fast. Over and out."

Mason placed the handset back on the cradle and turned to her. "What?"

"I hope you don't think this means you don't have to answer my question."

Mason pointed to the surrounding sea like the Coast Guard was pulling up beside them right now. "The authorities are almost here."

She narrowed her eyes. "What came out of your mouth was *The authorities are almost here*. But I'm pretty sure that's *Saved by the bell* I see written all over your face."

10:21 p.m....

"I come here to chew bubble gum and kick ass," Bran said. Maddy waited on the closing line and quietly mouthed it along with him. "And I'm all outta bubble gum."

"*They Live*," she said, pumping a fist when Bran chuckled and told her, "Damn, you're good."

They'd spread the sleeping bag out on the rough wood floor, undressed, and now lay side by side. Temporarily sated after the initial sexual frenzy, they'd started playing one of their old games, quoting the most badass movie lines they could think of and making the other person try to guess the title of the film. Only they'd added a new dimension to their play. For every title they guessed correctly, the other person had to kiss whichever body part the winner wanted.

It went without saying that any satiation they may have enjoyed was quickly disappearing. Touch by touch, kiss by kiss, deep wet suck by deep wet suck, they were rebuilding their aching desire to new heights.

Maddy's thighs quivered, her skin was slick with sweat, and the tips of her breasts were so hard she didn't know how much more she could stand. She just knew she wanted, wanted, *wanted*. Wanted sex. Wanted him. Wanted…everything.

Everything he could give her and all the things he'd sworn to withhold.

Told you this was dangerous, her conscience whispered. *You'll never be satisfied with only this*.

And for the first time since she'd taken the leap, she didn't ignore her inner voice. It was right. She *wasn't* going to be satisfied with only this. This one night. But she'd made her bed, and now she was forced to lie in it.

"I really thought I had you that time," he said, nuzzling her neck and absently caressing her breast. His callused fingers created a wonderful friction every time they feathered over the aching point. "So where next?" he asked, his breath hot against her skin. "We've already seen to your neck and your belly and your breasts…"

He pinched her nipple for emphasis. The pleasure was so sharp, so keen, her heels dug into the cotton lining of the sleeping bag.

"*Ssss*," she hissed. *Too fast. Too fast. Draw it out. Savor it.* But she couldn't stop the force of the sensations thundering through her. They were too big. Too intense. Too *insistent*. "I guess there's only one place left then."

"Your elbows?" he whispered teasingly.

"Bran," she said, drawing out his name just the way he liked.

He opened his mouth over her pulse point and sucked. "Say it again."

"Bran," she whispered over and over as he made his way down her body. Kissing her collarbone, her breasts, her belly, her hip bones. His mouth was hot and sweet; his lips were firm and determined. Her blood bubbled close to the surface of her skin everywhere they touched.

And then her lungs seized up. Because he was *there*. Hovering right above her throbbing sex. She buried her fingers in his hair when he grabbed her ankles and bent her legs until her feet were where he wanted them, on either side of her ass. The position opened her to him completely. And she shivered when the warm air of the room rushed over her most private parts.

"God, I've been dreaming of doing this for three months," he said.

You aren't the only one.

And then he put his mouth on her. Even in the stygian darkness his aim proved true. His lips closed around the bundle of nerves at the top of her sex and gently tested its boundaries. A sweet suck here. A soft probe there. Every touch was erotic, felt not only at the point of contact but higher, traveling up her channel, making her sex ache.

"Sweet Jesus," she groaned, pleasure slamming into her like a wrecking ball. Over and over. Determined to tear her down before his mastery built her back up.

Her body arched, seeking more, ever more. But he stopped her writhing by wrapping one big hand around her thigh and holding her down. He used his other hand to gently spread her tender folds and slip first one, and then a second finger deep inside her.

"Mmm," he hummed at the same time he curled his fingers upward, touching some magical spot that, until tonight, she hadn't even been aware she had.

And talk about a go button. If there was such a thing on a woman's body, that was it.

He pressed her clitoris with his tongue then, creating counterpoints of pressure, one from the inside, one from the outside, and her orgasm immediately threatened to overtake her.

"Bran!" Her voice hitched on his name.

He didn't answer her, simply used his fingers to rub that wonderful spot, used his tongue to lave the aching button and...*boom, boom, BOOM!* Her thighs snapped around his head as blow after blow of undulating rapture rolled over her. Again and again she was hammered. Until lights flashed behind her squeezed-tight lids. Until her whole body contracted around itself, around him, around the red-hot pleasure he pressed on her...

Chapter 21

10:26 p.m. …

BRAN DELIGHTED IN MADDY'S RELEASE. NOT THAT HE hadn't *always* taken joy in a woman's pleasure, but there was something completely sublime about having Maddy in his arms. Maybe it was because she was so damned responsive. So unashamed and eager.

The dear, sweet woman approached physical pleasure with the same joie de vivre that she approached life. Just…all in. No holds barred. Balls to the friggin' wall. And it was beautiful.

So beautiful, in fact, that he wished with his whole heart that it wasn't so dark in the lighthouse. Because he wanted to *see* her in all her carnal glory. Wanted to see the flush of completion on her dewy skin. Wanted to see how pink and swollen she was between her legs. Wanted to see the color of the little landing strip of pubic hair that crowned the top of her sex.

Platinum like her hair? Dark brown like her eyelashes and eyebrows? Something in between?

There were still a million things he wanted to see, wanted to do, wanted to experience. *There's just not enough time. There'll never be enough time!*

He pushed the thought away as soon as he had it. He couldn't dwell on what he *didn't* have. Not now. Dwelling would come later.

"That was…*wow*," Maddy said. "You're quite good at that."

The sound of her throaty laugh went all through him. His beautiful, responsive, naughty Maddy coming down from the heights of ecstasy as only she could, with grace and humor and praise.

Pressing one last kiss on her, he gently removed his hand and pushed up to his knees between her thighs. Even though he couldn't see it, he could feel the heavy bounce of his cock and knew it was standing nearly vertical.

Maddy must've sensed it too, because he heard her breath catch. "How bad do you want me?" she asked impishly.

"So bad," he said, finding her hand and guiding it to his shaft. She made an appreciative sound when she curled her fingers around him. "I came so hard in your soft, eager hands earlier. But I'm so swollen and achy I don't feel like I've come in a year. *This* is what you do to me. You feel that?"

He moved her hand to the base of his shaft, using his fingers to show her where to touch him so she'd feel the heavy pulse that fed his cock and had it standing straight.

"Mmm," she murmured. "So big and hard, yet satiny soft." She angled him toward her entrance, toward the hot, quivering flesh he'd just had in his mouth and hands. "Please, Bran," she pleaded. "Feelin' you like this has me achin' again. I want you to fill me up. Come inside me. Come inside me *now*."

Her husky voice and dirty words made his balls clench. He didn't want to go off like a geyser the minute he entered her. He wanted this to last. He couldn't have forever, but he hoped to have more than a few measly seconds.

Once he had himself under some semblance of control, once the ache wasn't so acute, he bent forward and allowed her to guide him to her entrance. He shuddered when the hot, swollen crown of his dick slipped through her tender folds. His bare toes curled. His hips flexed forward ever so slightly until the tip of him was snugged inside her.

"Holy shit," he gritted. "I've never felt anything so good in my life. You're so warm and wet and soft and—"

He stilled, letting his head fall back. *Hell!* He suddenly realized *why* nothing had ever felt so good. Well, besides the fact that it was *Maddy* beneath him. *Maddy* hooking her heels behind his ass in an effort to drag his hips forward. *Maddy, Maddy, sexy, completely unprotected Maddy!*

"Bran?" Her voice was a syrupy sweet temptation in the darkness. "What is it? What's wrong?"

"N-no…" He had to stop and clear his throat. At some point his vocal cords had shredded. "No condom," he finally managed.

He wasn't sure if he wanted to scream or cry. *Maybe both.* What he *was* sure of was that he couldn't force himself to pull back, to break the delicate connection of their bodies. It was too good. Too sweet. Too perfect.

He suddenly knew what all the fuss was about when it came to love and sex and no barriers. The combination of the three transcended the mere physical and slipped into what he could only describe as spiritual. And although he considered himself a lapsed Catholic at best, he would swear that right then and there he was connected to Maddy in a deeply fundamental way that encompassed his entire being. Heart, body, and soul. If he'd ever doubted it before, he didn't doubt it now. There must be a God. Because what other than a divine being could have created two things so perfectly matched for each other?

"So are you goin' to pull those pistols or whistle Dixie?" Maddy's voice reached out to him, jerking him from his thoughts.

"What?" He groaned when she scooted back and broke their delicate connection. He mourned the loss of it like he'd mourn the loss of a piece of himself.

"Play the game, Bran," she teased. "So you can tell *me* which body part *you* want kissed next. With no condom…" She let the sentence dangle. Instead of finishing it, she repeated the line, "You goin' to pull those pistols or whistle Dixie?"

"Too easy," he told her, his hips swinging forward when she used her nails to graze the supersensitive skin of his shaft. "*The Outlaw Josie Wales.*"

"Right," she said and he could hear the sateen side of the sleeping bag whisper against the rough wood floorboards as she changed positions.

Then her hot breath feathered over his swollen crown and he nearly died on the spot. He thought maybe he *did* die, the little death as the French called it, when her silky tongue darted out to taste him.

"Maddy, s-stop," he gritted, catching her sweet face between his hands and forcing her maddening mouth away from him.

"Why?" Her voice was so low he had to strain to hear it above the gentle *whir* of the lighthouse motor spinning overhead.

"I wanna be inside you the next time I come," he said. He'd gotten a look at heaven, at what it could be like to join himself to the woman he loved, and now nothing else would do.

"But we don't have a con—"

"Get dressed," he told her, pushing to his feet. "We're switching places with Mason and Alex. There are condoms on the sailboat. And bonus: There's *light* on the sailboat. 'Cause, Maddy, when I make you come with my cock, I wanna *see* you."

In typical Maddy form, she made his heart swell and a smile pull at his lips when she said, "Well, when you put it *that* way…"

11:21 p.m. …

"We have a problem."

Tony squeezed the satellite phone so hard the casing made an ominous crackling sound. "For fuck's sake, Rory!" he bellowed, his breath strangling in his lungs. "Again?"

"Hey!" Rory yelled back so loud that Tony had to hold the receiver away from his ear. "You're the one who screwed the pooch on this deal and didn't know there would be some sort of security contingent traveling with Miss Powers. I'm just trying to clean up the mess *your* poor Intel has gotten us into."

Tony didn't point out that there was no way he could have known Maddy had hired bodyguards and that *four* of Rory's guys had been bested by *two* no-names. Playing the blame game wasn't going to do either of them any good. So he blew out a deep breath and asked as calmly as he could, "What's happened now?"

Little white lights were blinking in his field of vision. Either he was ten seconds away from having a stroke, or that was his future...his *fortune* slipping away in front of his eyes.

"I had my men in the water ready to climb the outer seawall of the fort when I picked up a radio transmission from the Coast Guard on the open channel. They arrived earlier than expected."

"Shit."

"My guys hung around for a bit, waiting to see if they might get an opening. But the Coast Guard didn't waste any time loading everyone on the island onto the cutter—and that includes the two bodies."

"Shit, shit, *shit!*" This time Tony didn't squelch the urge to hurl his highball glass against the bulkhead. To his fury, it didn't shatter. Simply made a thumping sound before hitting the deck and rolling under the teakwood coffee table.

Will nothing go my way tonight?

"Cool your jets," Rory said, and if Tony wasn't mistaken, there was a note of smugness in his tone. "I've got a plan. We can still make this thing work, but it'll be messy."

And by *messy*, Tony knew that Rory meant *bloody*.

"It's *already* messy," he snarled. "I'm listening."

"It requires you to pull anchor and bust ass my way."

"You mean *toward* the Coast Guard cutter?" Tony asked incredulously.

"Sort of," Tony said, then proceeded to lay out his scheme.

Tony walked over to the little side bar on shaky legs and poured himself a stiff drink with trembling hands. Straight scotch. No soda. He needed some pure, high-octane liquid courage if he was going to help Rory implement this last-ditch effort.

~~~

11:31 p.m....

"This might seem like a crazy question," Alex said. "Especially considering we're standing here on the deck of a Coast Guard cutter with three teenage girls bunked in the cabin below us and two mysterious dead men zipped into body bags and getting stiff in the hold, but how large is it?"

Maddy turned away from her view of Garden Key and the golden glow of the lighthouse that blinked its warning over the surrounding ocean. After Bran and Mason gave the Coast Guard the lowdown on what had happened, told them of the two men who'd escaped and the unknown *someone* who'd hired them to do the mysterious *job,* the captain of the cutter decided the best way to insure the safety of everyone was to load up and head back to Key West.

Maddy wasn't complaining. *Hell no.* She wanted nothing more than to see those three sweet girls back home with their families. But there *was* a part of her that wished the Coast Guard could've held back, oh, say, half an hour longer. She and Bran had just run hand in hand onto the beach, ready to switch places with Mason and Alex, when the cutter arrived and dropped anchor.

So where does that leave us now? she wondered. *Is*

our one-night stand over? Would Bran expect her to hold up her end of the bargain and go back to treating him the same as she'd treated him before, like a friend, like a...*pen pal*?

But we didn't even get to do the deed! she railed silently, ignoring any inner arguments about what exactly constituted *sexual relations*. For one thing, she wasn't Bill Clinton. And for another, she'd assumed when she made the deal with Bran to scratch their itch that he'd understood she meant full-on penetration. Him inside her. Sex. Sex. And *more* sex until they expired from either starvation or dehydration, or both.

Oh, like you'd be satisfied even then? her conscience insisted. *You are* so *foolin' yourself, sister.*

"Earth to Maddy." Alex snapped her fingers in front of Maddy's unblinking eyes. "In case you missed it, that was the conversational baton I just passed you."

"Sorry." She shook her head. The Coast Guard cutter had picked up speed, and the wind played with Alex's curly hair until it was standing out about a mile from her head. "What was the question again?"

"I'm cursed!" Alex threw her hands in the air.

"Huh?"

"Never mind." Alex waved her off. "I was asking how large it is. The cloud hanging over my head. I'm afraid to look."

Maddy leaned against the rail, absently noting the *shhh-shhh* sound of the waves washing against the hull. The wind was cooler out on the ocean than it had been on the island. It helped to blow some of the haze from her head. "Okay, I'll bite. *Why* is there a cloud hangin' over your head?"

"Because I have the worst taste in men," Alex declared with a jerk of her chin. "Or at least I have no clue how to judge them. It's like I have an internal compass that points straight at Mr. Wrong. Except I don't *know* he's Mr. Wrong until I go and make a fool of myself in front of him."

Ah. Man trouble. I can relate. "I'm assumin' we're talkin' about Mason?" When Alex blinked at her, Maddy said, "I see the way you look at him."

Alex narrowed her eyes. "And how do I look at him?"

Maddy bit the inside of her cheek to keep from grinning. "Like he's a big, juicy piece of man meat and you're sharpenin' your knife and fork."

Alex groaned. "That obvious, huh?"

"Only to anyone with eyes," Maddy assured her.

"Great."

"So…um…what happened? If you don't mind me askin'?" She was happy to talk about, to *think* about, something besides her and Bran and what was left undone between them.

Alex shrugged. "I sort of…er…well, I kind of asked Mason to be my lover."

Maddy blinked for a couple of seconds, then burst out laughing. "Apparently tonight is ladies' choice."

"What's that supposed to mean?" When Alex scrunched up her nose, all her freckles melded together.

"I propositioned Bran too," she admitted.

"Well, no duh." Alex shoved her glasses up the bridge of her nose with a terse finger. "I mean, talk about *obvious*. All those smoldering stares you two have been exchanging since you walked out of the fort are impossible to miss. I'm lucky my hair hasn't combusted in the crossfire."

And that gave Maddy hope that Bran *wasn't* under the impression their deal was done. Her body hummed with the memory of all they'd shared in the lighthouse and warmed with images of what she hoped to share with him still.

"The only question is," Alex continued, "did he jump on you *before* you finished propositioning him, or did he behave like a gentleman and wait a whole two seconds *after* you'd finished the sentence?"

"I…um…I take by your tone that between the two of us we're battin' five hundred?" Maddy asked cautiously.

"Why is everyone using baseball jargon with me tonight?" Alex gestured toward her baggy T-shirt with its history slogan, her two-sizes-too-big shorts, and the KEEN hiking sandal/shoe thingies on her feet. "Do I *look* like a sports fan?"

No. She looked exactly like what she was. An academic with a penchant for fashion faux pas. What Maddy wouldn't *give* to get Alex in Eduardo's chair. Her stylist was an artist, and Alex was a blank canvas.

"It means," Maddy clarified, "that I take it he didn't agree to your offer."

Alex slow-blinked at her. "If by not agreeing to my offer you mean nearly swallowing his tongue and now refusing to talk to me, then yup."

"Well, maybe that's a good thing," Maddy speculated. "Nearly swallowin' his tongue and refusin' to talk to you isn't a *no*."

"It might as well be." Alex's expression was sullen. "I think he's just too much of a good guy to reject me straight out, so he's falling back on his patented Mute Mason act."

Maddy didn't know what to say to that so she kept her mouth shut.

Alex frowned at her. "So maybe his act isn't so patented after all because you're doing a fairly good job of it yourself."

"Alex—"

"But enough about me." Alex waved her off again. "Let's talk more about you."

Maddy was instantly wary. "What about me?"

"Would you categorize this thing you have with Bran as a love thing that turned into a lust thing or vice versa?"

"I'm sorry, what?"

"Would you"—Alex lifted her voice above the wind blowing over the deck—"categorize this thing you have with—"

"I heard you." Maddy cut her off, looking around at the two crewmen who were across the deck checking some sort of rigging. "I'm just not sure I understand the question."

"Oh"—Alex nodded—"right. So, during the wait for the Coast Guard to arrive, Mason and I were talking about you and Bran."

Maddy's wariness increased. "Um...*why?*"

"Common ground, I guess." Alex shrugged as if the reason was inconsequential. "Something he would actually open his mouth and discuss. Anyway, I want you to settle an argument we had." Alex reached up to pull out a lock of hair that was stuck in her mouth. The cutter was moving at a pretty good clip now, and Maddy grabbed the railing to brace herself when a larger-than-usual wave caused the ship to list.

Alex stumbled and steadied herself without so much as a break in conversation. "See, Mason said that when two people meet, three things can happen." She raised her voice to be heard over the wind and waves. "Lust can turn into love. Love can turn into lust. Or lust can just stay lust until it eventually fizzles out. So, which it is for you and Bran? Love follows lust, or lust follows love?"

"I-I…" Maddy had to stop to clear her throat. Suddenly the sea was calling to her. *Just jump in! Just jump in and escape the situation!* But she'd never been one for the open ocean; it gave her the willies. So she looked around, hoping there was a hatch in the deck she could slip into.

"Don't tell me you don't know," Alex said. "You were looking down the wrong end of a gun tonight. Which I've been told makes a person see things very clearly."

It wasn't a hatch that opened up. It was a door leading into the interior of the cutter.

"Maddy!" Bran called from the threshold. "Can I have a word with you?"

Oh, you wonderful man with your perfect timin'! "Be right there!" she hollered back.

It wasn't that she didn't want to answer Alex's question because it was super-duper *personal*. It was more that she didn't want to answer because, the way Alex posed the question, it was like Alex thought it was a foregone conclusion that *love* was part of the Bran-Maddy equation.

And Maddy refused to do that math. She feared the solution would be too painful.

"Go on then," Alex said when she turned back. "Let Bran dip his doodle."

Maddy lifted a brow, glad the wind was cool enough to wick away the heat spreading across her cheeks. "Don't think I've ever heard that one before."

"Dunk his dingus?" Alex grinned.

Now *Maddy* was the one nearly swallowing her tongue. "I think you've been livin' on Wayfarer Island too long. You've picked up their bad habit of inventin' ridiculous euphemisms."

Alex gave her a shove. "At least *one* of us should get laid tonight."

"I seriously doubt Bran—"

"And I seriously doubt you seriously doubt anything," Alex cut in. "I mean, just look at his face. He'd have to be juggling sex toys and a bottle of lube to look hornier. Now *go!*"

This time when Alex gave her a shove, Maddy didn't hesitate to cross the deck toward Bran. Mostly because she was terrified of what might come out of Alex's mouth next. Bran quickly closed the door behind her, and the sound of the wind and the waves was replaced by the rhythmic hum of the cutter's big engines. The stairwell they were standing in was painted bright white except for the metal treads that led down into the belly of the boat. Those had neon-yellow strips of antislip material running lengthwise across them.

When Bran reached into his pocket, he didn't pull out a clutch of sex toys or a bottle of lube. But it was close. He yanked out a long strip of condoms. "Snagged these from the ship's medic when he was redressing my wound. And the captain said Mason and I could bunk out in his private cabin for a few hours to rest and recuperate, but as luck would have it, Mason says he's gonna hang out up on the bridge." Bran was talking so fast, he could've given Alex a run for her money. "So what'd'ya say? Wanna join me in the captain's quarters?"

"First of all"—Maddy held up a hand—"how *is* your wound? Are you in much pain?"

"Nah." Bran shook his head. "The medic gave me a shot of antibiotics and a local anesthetic, so I'm feeling great." He wiggled his eyebrows and grinned his pirate smile.

And there he is, my modern-day marauder.

Except he wasn't hers. Not after tonight. That void that had appeared inside her earlier was back, growing steadily until she wondered if she might tumble in and be consumed by it. She forced a smile and asked, "And second of all, a whole strip of condoms? Isn't the ride to Key West less than three hours?"

"I'm an ambitious man," he told her.

"Wow." She shook her head. "That Alex is sharp as a tack."

"Wha'd'ya mean?"

"Never mind," she said. "So where's this private bunk you speak of?"

"Follow me," he said, leering at her before tromping down the stairs. His steps made *bong-bong* noises on the metal treads.

Why does that sound so familiar?

Oh, right. It's the noise an empty heart makes when it beats.

The same noise *her* heart was making...

Chapter 22

"WHY DO I GET THE IMPRESSION I'M BEIN' STALKED BY A BIG, hungry beast?" Maddy said, spinning and pressing her back against the bulkhead.

The captain's cabin was a tiny room just big enough to house a twin-size bed and one small desk. Not exactly what Bran would have *wished* for his first time with Maddy.

But beggars can't be choosers.

"Probably 'cause you *are*," he told her, unbuttoning his shorts and yanking down his zipper. He stepped out of his shorts and boxers and kicked them aside, then bent to unhook the knife and sheath from around his calf. Standing in front of her in nothing but the fresh bandage, he watched her eyes widen.

"Wow!" she said, catching her top lip between her teeth. His dick jumped at the sight, bobbing unabashedly in front of him. "I think you just set a land speed record for droppin' trou."

"Send my name to Guinness." He stalked toward her. "I don't have nearly enough time to do to you all the things I still wanna do to you. So I refuse to waste one single moment on the boring task of undressing."

"Well, in that case..."

He stopped in his tracks when Maddy whipped her

T-shirt over her head and unhooked her bra in one fell swoop. Her shorts and panties hit the floor a second later, and his tongue glued itself to the roof of his mouth.

What the hell is that wheezing sound?

Then he realized it was him. The air was leaving his lungs like a couple of balloons with slow leaks because Maddy was, in a word, *gorgeous*. Pale skin and high, small breasts. A thin waist that flared to dramatically curvy hips.

And now his mouth was watering. Which was handy. It helped unstick his tongue.

"It's lighter than I thought it'd be," he said.

"What is?"

"Your pubic hair," he told her and watched her brow furrow as she ducked her chin and glanced down at the little line of hair that created a landing strip above her plump, swollen lips. "I thought it'd be dark like your eyebrows. But it's blond. Not quite as blond as your hair, but pretty close."

"You've been thinkin' about my pubic hair?" she asked incredulously. Then she raked in a startled breath when he closed the distance between them.

Her smooth belly welcomed the hardness of his shaft. Her tight nipples abraded the hair on his chest. Just as with any time they touched, a strong voltage seemed to crackle over his skin.

Warm. She was so damned warm. *Soft.* So unbearably soft. He wanted to make her warmer and softer still. Love her so long and so hard she became putty in his arms.

"I've been thinking about *everything* about you," he admitted, then silenced whatever reply she might have made with a kiss.

11:37 p.m. ...

Maddy moaned when Bran's tongue speared deep. His hands were on her breasts, softly kneading, his fingers gently strumming. As for *her* hands? They were everywhere. His thick hair. His broad shoulders. His flexing back.

She wanted to touch all of him. Learn every single one of his textures. Hard and smooth. Rough and warm. The more she touched, the hotter he burned, the louder he growled, the more urgent his mouth became.

"Let me just..." He trailed off and worked a hand between her back and the wall, palming one globe of her ass and lifting her slightly so he could rub himself against her. "God, you're soft," he whispered, sliding his tongue into her ear as a drop of passion oozed from his tip and left a warm, slick spot above her belly button.

Between her thighs she was already wet. Ready. So ready. She'd *been* ready for months. Maybe she'd been ready for this, for *him,* her whole life.

"Bran," she whispered against his scratchy cheek between wet, biting kisses along his jaw. "Please make lo—" She stopped herself before she could say *Make love to me*. Instead she finished with "Make this night somethin' I'll never forget."

"Maddy, I—" He stopped himself too, and her heart clenched. She felt like something important, something portentous was dangling off the edge of his tongue.

"What?" she demanded. "What is it?"

"You're beautiful," he whispered, nuzzling his nose

near her temple, breathing her in. "You're the most beautiful woman I've ever seen."

It wasn't exactly what she expected to hear. Perhaps it wasn't exactly what she *hoped* to hear. But it was still pretty darn good.

In Bran's arms she *felt* beautiful. The way he held her, so gently yet so desperately. The way he kissed her, like he wanted to devour her whole. The way his big body shivered when she touched him.

Yes, with him she *was* beautiful.

"Please, Bran." She reached between them to palm his hot, hard length, kissing his chin, delighting in the prickly stubble that tickled her lips. He groaned when she stroked his shaft. He was so thick she couldn't close her fist around him. And his heavy veins pulsed against the pads of her fingers, keeping his member stiff and engorged. "You're ready. I'm ready. I don't want to wait anymore."

It was all the invitation he needed. With a hungry moan, he picked her up and sat her atop the desk. *Eep!* The metal was cold against her bare bottom. *Oh, heavens to Betsy, yes!* His mouth was hot against her lips.

"Stay right there." His voice was full of desire. "Don't move an inch."

The air inside the little room was warm and humid. A thin layer of sweat dampened his skin and made it glow with health and vigor.

And he calls me beautiful? He was the gorgeous one.

She had to curl her hands around the lip of the desk to keep from reaching for him when he backed away to grab his shorts and pull out the strip of condoms he'd stuffed in the pocket. Every move made his muscles ripple. He sported more than his fair share of scars, she noticed. Little badges of bravery. But they only seemed to highlight his perfect proportions. Tan skin, broad shoulders, and lean hips. Legs, chest, and belly lightly dusted with hair. He looked like he should grace the cover of a men's fitness magazine.

A dirty men's fitness magazine, she thought a bit giddily, watching him rip open a condom packet with his teeth.

There was no ignoring the column of male flesh jutting from between his thighs. It was long and thick, roped with veins, and so flushed with blood it was nearly purple. The glans was large and flaring and seemed to pulse when he fisted the condom down his length.

That part of him was gorgeous too. In a blatant, unabashedly *male* way.

Hell, even his testicles, large and heavy and pulled up tight beneath the thick base of his shaft were—

Whoa, Nelly. All thought fled her head because suddenly he was there. Standing between her spread thighs and using his thumb to bend himself toward her waiting entrance.

"Scoot to the very edge," he instructed hoarsely, his eyes nearly black with passion.

She didn't hesitate to comply, propping one heel on a drawer handle and the other on the seat of the chair sitting next to the desk.

"So soft and pretty," he said, stroking his flaring head through her juices, coating himself and the latex covering him. He stopped for a moment to gently slap his plump glans against her throbbing clitoris before he finally—*glory be and hallelujah!*—disappeared the tiniest bit inside her.

"Lord, yesss," she hissed, her body grabbing at him, sucking at him. Her hiss turned into a groan when he refused to stroke deeper. Frowning, she hooked her heels behind his ass to drag him closer. She needed to be filled. Stretched. Completed.

"Slow, Maddy," he gritted between his teeth. "The first time only happens once. I wanna see it all. Experience it all. Watch, Maddy. Watch us."

And despite her thundering heart and struggling lungs, she looked down to see him slowly, ever so slowly, impale her. His shaft looked huge between her thighs, deeply hued compared to her blushing pink.

Oh, Jesus, help me. She'd been with three men—*which isn't zero, no matter what he says*—but nothing had prepared her for this. For him. Because she was rather small and he was rather large and—

Oh, oh, oh!

Inch by incredible inch he pressed deeper, spread her wider, filled her up until there was no part of her he wasn't touching. And then, with a grunt and forceful jab against the resistance of her body, he seated himself to the hilt.

Holy hell, she'd done it. She'd taken all of him.

But just barely…

His hot head smashed against her cervix, making her belly feel full and achy. Her channel was stretched until the pleasure bordered on pain. She felt like she deserved a trophy. Or at least a high five.

"So tight," Bran whispered, his chest heaving.

A drop of sweat rolled down the side of his tan neck, pooling in the hollow above his collarbone. She wanted to lean forward and lick it away, take a bit of his salty, male essence inside her. But she couldn't move. She barely dared to breathe.

"Y'okay?" he asked, hooking a finger beneath her chin and forcing her to meet his eyes. They were sparkling and dark, half-lidded and lazy. Bedroom eyes. *Hubba, hubba*.

"J-just go s-slow at first," she panted. "I need t-to—"

"Anything," he whispered, catching her mouth in a blindingly sensual kiss. "Anything you want, Maddy."

And then he began to move.

Just a bit. Just a subtle stroke that slid his shaft an inch out and then back in. Maddy was suddenly aware of nerve endings she hadn't known existed. All of her was touched by him, caressed by him, seemingly *surrounded* by him even though she was the one holding him inside.

"Again," she said, opening her mouth wider for his kiss, opening her legs wider for his cock.

"As many times as you want," he promised, stroking again. Again and again and again. Each one a little longer. Each one a little harder. Each one better than the one before until Maddy lost the ability to see. Lost the ability to hear. Lost the ability to do anything but feel the delicious friction he created with every retreat and advance, with every thrust and parry.

"Bran…" She said his name breathlessly over and over in cadence to the rhythm he set, meeting him stroke for stroke, their bodies slapping together as they strove for that ultimate pinnacle.

Sweat slicked their skin. Their breaths grew ragged. The tension increased. And Maddy had no idea how long he made love to her, driving her up, higher and higher. She just knew she wanted it to go on forever.

But then he snaked a hand between their rocking bodies and used the rough pad of his thumb to press the bundle of nerves at the top of her sex, and her orgasm built to a fever pitch. It lit her up, burned her down. Her body flexed and flowered and readied itself for the inevitable.

"Yes, Maddy," he encouraged. "Yes, babe. That's it. Come for me. Come all around me."

And Lord help her, she did. Her whole being disintegrated into an ecstasy unlike anything she'd ever known.

12:02 a.m....

Bran had never seen anything as gorgeous as Maddy in the throes of rapture. Her head was thrown back, her pretty breasts upthrust, and her beautiful upside-down mouth open in a soundless scream. Her body gripped his, her inner muscles squeezing and contracting and fluttering along his length. It was exotic. Erotic. And at the same time so fundamental that he felt it not just in his cock, but in his bones. In the fabric of his soul.

This was what it was all about. Man and woman coming together to make a more perfect whole. He worked her, stroked her, kept the pleasure and the friction going in an attempt to hang on to that perfection for as long as possible even though it caused his own orgasm to threaten deep in his groin.

With everything he was, he fought off completion. Gritted his teeth. Ran through the roster of the 2009 New York Yankees—as a Newark New Jerseyan that was his team, and they'd been particularly great that year. But it wasn't enough. Her body milked him, seeming to draw his orgasm closer, closer, ever closer.

No, damnit! Not yet!

He'd fantasized about this moment, dreamed of it for so long. And in all his fantasies, in all his dreams, he was taking her from behind. Again that pop song came to mind. *All the right junk in all the right places*. That description fit Maddy to a T. And as a bona fide, self-titled ass man, he was determined to watch the round globes of her butt bounce while he slammed his passion into her over and over again. Until he couldn't stand it. Until the whole world condensed down to the point where their two bodies connected. Until he spilled all his lust, all his *love* inside her.

So when her body went from gripping and sucking to merely trembling, he sent up a silent prayer of thanks that he was able to stave off climax and wasted no time plucking her from the desk—she squealed her surprise—and spinning her around. He bent her forward over the surface and used his feet to spread her legs wide.

Just as he'd known, her bare ass was a wonder to behold. He smacked it just to hear her yelp, just to see the sweet flesh jiggle seductively. She turned to glare at him, still panting.

"Gorgeous," he told her, rubbing a hand over her plump bottom to sooth the sting of his smack.

Her skin was hot and dewed with sweat, smooth and creamy. Her sex was smoother and creamier still. He could see it open to him below the curves of her butt, teasing him, tormenting him. A siren's call of woman to man.

With gritted teeth, he fisted the base of his dick and

angled himself down, stroking slowly into the hot welcome of her body, watching his length disappear inside her, feeling every nuance of her channel, memorizing each detail of their joining.

"Sweet Jesus!" she moaned as he filled her, stretched her tight.

He set a rhythm sure to build her release even as it tantalized his own. The sound of their bodies slapping together was the sweetest music he'd ever heard. The smell of hot skin and sex the headiest of perfumes. And all the while he loved her, he kneaded her luscious ass. Watching her skin grow flush with renewed desire. Tightening his jaw at the sight of his shaft turning shiny with her juices.

It was heaven.

It was hell.

It was better, hotter, more glorious than all his fantasies, all his dreams had ever been.

Then he heard the telltale catch at the back of her throat. She was there, once more teetering on the brink. He quickened his thrusts and reached around to play with the hard points of her breasts. Gently biting her shoulder, he closed his eyes and let the sensations roll over him, through him. So that this time, when she threw herself off the erotic cliffs, he gladly let her take him with her.

Chapter 23

12:35 a.m.…

"SO WHY DID YOU BECOME A MOVIE BUFF?" BRAN ASKED curiously, wondering why he'd never thought to ask before.

They were stretched out on the little twin bed, his arm under her head, her leg thrown over his unwounded thigh. And even though his fingers were going numb, he couldn't make himself move. Lying with Maddy was the closest thing to nirvana he'd ever known.

"Hmm," she murmured. "I guess I've never thought about it before." She absently played with his nipple. Every time she feathered her fingers across the hardened tip, blood surged to his cock.

He glanced at his watch.

Damn. Just two more hours.

Long enough for him to make love to her two, maybe three more times.

But two or three more times wasn't going to be enough. Just as he'd feared, a thousand times wasn't going to be enough.

"But I guess it probably has somethin' to do with me bein' the only girl in the family," she mused. "And the youngest to boot. Watchin' movies was the only way I could get my brothers to hang out with me. I didn't hunt or play football, but I could do a pretty mean *Footloose* dance. I've got the moves," she assured him, pinching his nipple and making his toes curl.

"Don't I know it." He slapped her ass.

She squealed, her eyes threatening murder. He smacked a kiss on her mouth and soothed the sting of his hand with a gentle caress. *Soft.* She was so unspeakably soft. He couldn't get over it. Couldn't stop touching her. Couldn't stop *wanting* her.

Twisting her lips, she tucked her head beneath his chin and lifted her thigh higher. It brushed the base of his semi-hard shaft. Of course, his erection withered a bit when she asked, "So why did *you* become a movie buff?"

He could have evaded the question, he supposed, kept the tone light and flirty. But he didn't. "Desperation," he told her.

She pushed up on one elbow to stare at him. Her eyes were soft and warm, like summer storm clouds swirling in a hot sky. "What does *that* mean?"

"It means I started sneaking into my local movie the-ater 'cause it was a warm place to sleep in the winter and a cool place to sleep in the summer. After my parents died, and after I ran away from my third foster home because the middle-aged, chain-smoking woman there kept trying to come into my bedroom at night, I took to the streets."

"Good Lord, Bran." She searched his face.

"It wasn't as bad as you think," he assured her. "I couch-surfed in the homes of friends. I worked odd jobs and spent time in the library studying for my GED. Sleeping at the movie theater was always a last resort. And I found I actually *liked* watching all those movies. At night, after closing, I'd go into the storage room and shuffle through the old reels. I think I watched every one they had from *Doctor Zhivago* to *The Matrix*."

She smoothed the hair back from his forehead. He closed his eyes and leaned into her hand, loving the feel of her. Loving *her*.

When he opened his eyes, it was to find a question burning in hers. He knew what it was before she asked it.

"Murder-suicide," he told her and watched her throat work over a hard swallow. They were just two words. Alone they were awful. Put together they were reprehensible. "After a month in the shelter, Dad convinced Mom to come and talk things over."

And why did you go, Mom? Why? It was a question he continued to ask himself even though he already knew the agonizing answer. She'd gone because she couldn't stay away. As sick as it was, as perverse as it was, she'd loved his father. Loved *all* of him. The good, the bad, and the ugly.

But she hadn't known just how *bad and ugly Dad could be.*

Bran had known. Even then, he'd known because the same badness, the same ugliness lived in him.

"Remember that shotgun I told you I borrowed from Joey Santorini's father?" He watched Maddy nod jerkily. "Well, my father used one barrel on my mother and the other on himself. And you wanna know the crazy thing?"

She swallowed, a lone tear sliding down her delicate cheek.

"She was *happy*. Before she hopped on the bus, she was wearing her *Little House on the Prairie* smile."

Maddy blinked, not understanding. And as he explained, the memory of that day, the last time he ever saw his mother, washed over him…

"Don't go, Mom," he pleaded, grabbing her hand.

Spring had arrived early, and even though the leaves hadn't bloomed on the trees, the sun was warm and bright. It reflected in his mother's dark eyes when she smiled at him.

He grimaced because it was her real smile. Not her fake one. And it wasn't for him. It was for his rat bastard of a father. To make matters worse, she'd put on her best dress and had splurged on new lipstick for the occasion.

"Bran, baby." She pulled him into a hug. He was taller than she was now. Bigger too. But he still felt like a child in her arms. "I hafta go."

"Why?" he demanded, bitterly pushing out of her embrace. "Why do you have to go?"

She shook her head. "I know you don't understand, but the bad parts of him don't outweigh the good. I love him, Bran. And if there's a chance…" She drifted off, not finishing the sentence.

Frustration and fury were twin fires in Bran's chest. They licked flames into his face. "What's wrong with you?" he demanded hoarsely. "How can you still love him after…after…" He didn't finish. He was too busy angrily wiping away tears that made his eyes feel like they were filled with fine-grained sand.

His mother placed gentle hands on his cheeks. "Because that's how love works," she whispered. "No matter what, it doesn't go away. It remains part of you. Forever. Someday you'll understand."

"No, I won't," he swore, disgusted when his voice

broke and more impotent tears filled his eyes. "*Because if love is what you say it is, if it makes a man beat his wife—*"

"*Brando Pallidino,*" *she tsked, glancing around the bus stop.* "*Keep your voice down.*" *But they were alone on the sidewalk, the garbage truck across the way and the lonely sparrow chirping on a nearby limb their only audience.*

"*If it makes a woman stay with a husband who calls her names,*" *he went on like she hadn't spoken,* "*and is so eaten up with jealousy that he can't help but hurt her, then I want no part of it.*"

"*Don't blame that on love, baby.*" *Her expression was sad.* "*That doesn't have anything to do with love. It has to do with…*" *She paused to drag in a deep breath.* "*Your daddy didn't have it easy growing up. There were things that…*" *She didn't finish, just shook her head again.*

"*And that makes it* okay?" *He blinked at her, realizing just how…*crazy *she was, how deluded. And* blind. *She didn't see. She'd never see.*

"*It doesn't make it okay,*" *she told him.* "*But it should give you comfort to know that when you fall in love, it'll be different for you because* you're *different from him. Different from me too.*"

Bran stumbled away from her. "*You're wrong about a lotta things, but you're* really *wrong about that,*" *he told her as the crosstown bus turned the corner and rumbled in their direction.* "*What's in him is in me too.*" *He beat a closed fist against his chest.* "*All that fury. All that rage. I got it too, Momma.*" *Some of it was flaming inside him even now, shouting for his father's head on a pike.*

"*No.*" *She let her gaze run over his flaring nostrils*

and bloodshot eyes. "You're all our good parts, Bran, and none of our bad. You're all our loyalty and none of our jealousy. All our courage and none of our cowardice. I thank God every day for that."

She was deranged. Completely, utterly deranged. He had all of their bad parts in him, and he opened his mouth to tell her as much, tell her she didn't have the first fucking clue, but with a squeal of air brakes, the bus stopped beside them and the door popped wide with a squeak and a shhhh of sound.

Panic set in. His heart skipped a beat. "Let me come with you," he begged, a dark sense of foreboding wrapping cold fingers around his throat until he could barely breathe. "Let me—"

"Your father and I need some time alone," she said, cutting him off.

"But—"

"Bran." She grabbed his hands, giving them a squeeze. "Please stay. I'll be—"

"In or out, lady?" the bus driver called, chewing noisily on a monster-sized piece of pink gum. He blew a bubble bigger than his face as he waited on Bran's mother's reply.

"In!" she yelled, hopping onto the bus's first step. Before she turned away to pay for her ticket, she smiled down at Bran, the hem of her new dress tangling around her slim ankles as the wind suddenly blew up with serious intent. But it wasn't the breeze that made Bran nervous. It was whatever he sensed was following close on its heels. "Don't worry, baby." She smiled so sweetly, with so much…hope in her eyes. "I'll be back before you know it."

"And that was the last time I saw her," he said, coming out of the memory slowly, like a person wading to shore.

Maddy lovingly stroked his hair. "I'm so sorry."

When it came to his past, Bran had formed a psychological callus—at least that's what the Navy headshrinker had called it. But Maddy had no such protection. Tears rolled freely down her soft cheeks to drip from her chin and land on his chest, right above his heart. Each hot, salty drop felt like a benediction. Was he fanciful to think maybe they'd be enough to wash all the blackness inside him clean?

He pulled her down so he could kiss her tears, sip their saltiness between his lips. "I didn't tell you so you'd feel sorry for me," he whispered. "I told you 'cause you're my friend. My *true* friend. And I want you to…*know*. To know…*me*."

She pushed away and opened her mouth to say something, but the cutter abruptly changed course, nearly toppling them from the bed.

"What in blue blazes?" she huffed, dragging the backs of her hands over her wet cheeks before wincing and looking down at his bandage. "Did I bump into—"

"No," he cut her off, glancing toward the door. Everything in him wanted to stay here in this warm room, in this warm bed, talking, making love. Unfortunately, his operator's sixth sense told him something was up. A familiar sensation prickled over his skin like an icy kiss of cold wind.

A hard knock sounded on the metal door. "I hate to disturb you guys," Mason said from the opposite side, "but we've got a fuckin' situation up here. I think you should both come to the bridge."

Bran exchanged a look with Maddy. She didn't have to say anything. Her thoughts were written all over her face: *Not again.*

"What's up?" he called to Mason, his body nearly crying out at the loss of contact with Maddy's warm skin when he slid from the bed to grab his boxers and shorts.

"Picked up a Mayday from a nearby motor yacht," Mason said through the door. "Apparently two guys in a dinghy boarded it about an hour ago, roughed up a couple of the folks onboard, and took off again after they stole some fuel cans."

Bran and Maddy exchanged another look. This one said: *Two men in a dinghy? That's no coincidence.* Apparently after the fishing boat ran out of gas, they'd used the skiff to go in search of more. He hadn't banked on that. Regretted not putting bullets in their brains when he had the chance.

"They're requesting emergency medical help and Webber has to oblige," Mason continued.

When Maddy bent to grab her clothes, Bran got an eyeful of her plump ass. It didn't matter what was happening, who was talking, or where they were. He zeroed in on the round hemispheres like a heat-seeking missile.

She turned and caught him staring—his tongue hanging down around his knees—and shook her head. Her eyes were still red and puffy, but there was a grin twitching her lips. "Stop givin' me the Big Bad Wolf, all-the-better-to-eat-you-with-my-dear stare right now, or we'll never leave this room."

"Would that be such a bad thing?" Bran whispered, buttoning his shorts over his burgeoning erection. One look at Maddy's bare butt and he was raring to go. Bad guys in dinghies and teammates standing outside the door be damned!

She got a pained look on her face. "We'll be right there!" she called to Mason. Then she stepped into her panties and fastened her bra, covering up all her beautiful, feminine flesh.

And now *he* was the one who felt the need to cry.

1:08 a.m....

"I got a bad feeling about this," Maddy heard Bran whisper to Mason.

Mason grunted his agreement.

"What did he say?" Alex asked Maddy from the side of her mouth.

They were standing shoulder to shoulder on the bridge, watching as four of the six crew members on the Coast Guard boat scrambled around the deck, throwing over bumpers in preparation for tying up next to the motor yacht, which was the kind of ship owned by the one-percenters of the world but not the one percent of the one-percenters. With a main deck for seating, dining, and a small galley, and a lower level that was likely separated into a couple of cramped cabins, the vessel was nice without being ostentatious like her father's yacht, the *Black Gold*.

Running lights on both ships cast a cool, dim glow over the dark water surrounding them. And Maddy noticed two of the people on the motor yacht were standing on the narrow front deck, watching the activity aboard the cutter. They were both men, both dressed in what she'd come to recognize as standard yachting wear—Polo shirts and blindingly white shorts—and neither of them seemed to be injured. For that, she breathed a sigh of relief and hoped whoever *was* injured wasn't hurt terribly bad.

"He said he's got a bad feelin' about this," she whispered to Alex, watching how the two yachters caught the ropes the Coast Guard crew tossed them, quickly and efficiently tethering the vessels together.

Alex frowned. "Looks legit to me," she said.

"Me too," Maddy agreed. "But if something is wigglin' their antennas…" She hooked a thumb toward Mason and Bran and let the sentence dangle.

"Captain," Bran turned to Webber, a man whose leather face and sun-bleached hair spoke of a lifetime at sea. "I'm gonna take the women belowdecks, and then Mason and I will assume a defensive position, if you don't mind."

Webber, behind the controls in the captain's chair, narrowed his eyes. "You see something that makes you think this isn't a real Mayday call?" he asked.

"Nope." Bran shook his head. "But not too long ago I was in a situation where a Mayday ended up in a shitload of bloodshed, and there was nothing to make me think it wasn't on the up-and-up until the moment guns were blazing." Sure enough. Maddy had been there too. And in this case she fully supported the *History…don't make me repeat myself* slogan on Alex's shirt. "Let's just say that since then I'd rather err on the side of caution. Have you…uh…have you checked the radar?"

"Nothing showing up for miles around but a fishing trawler," Webber reported, motioning with a finger toward the radar screen. "There's no sign of the dinghy. The two goons are probably out of range by now."

"Right." Bran nodded. "But I'd still feel better if we covered all our bases."

For three ticks of the clock Webber regarded him. Then he dipped his chin. "Do what you have to do to set your mind at ease, sailor."

Bran nodded his thanks before shepherding Alex and Maddy through the door of the bridge.

"So what does *assume a defensive position* mean?" Maddy asked, her heart rate spiking as they tromped down the stairs into the belly of the cutter.

"It means we're gonna arm you ladies to the teeth, leave you with the girls, and play ourselves a little game of watch-and-wait," Bran explained, motioning them toward the ship's small galley. "If all is aboveboard? Great. If not, we'll be ready."

"Arm us?" Alex squeaked. "Just so we're clear, I've never held a gun in my life."

"It's easier than it looks," Mason muttered from the back of the pack.

"Oh, so *now* you're talking to me?" Alex demanded, craning her head around to lift a brow in Mason's direction.

Maddy ignored them, instead looking at the weapons arranged atop the pristine white dropcloth draped over the galley's metal trestle table. Bran and Mason's machine guns, as well as the machine guns the bad guys had left on Garden Key, were in a neat row, paper tags tied around their triggers.

"We were surrendering them as evidence," Bran explained.

Evidence. Of the carnage that is this night.

"Where is Rick?" Alex asked, reminding Maddy of the young man who'd been dragged into this nightmare with her. "Shouldn't we be arming him too? Or better yet, shouldn't we be arming him *instead*? I'm sure he'd be much better than me when it comes to—"

"He went down in the hold ten minutes ago to check on the bodies and make sure that one-eighty we did didn't jostle them loose and have them rolling across the floor," Bran explained.

Ew, Maddy thought, bile climbing into her throat.

"Ew," Alex said, making a face and proving the two of them had more in common than jabber jaws.

"So for right now, you're it," Mason told Alex, grabbing one of the weapons, ripping off the tag, and handing it to her. She held it in front of her like it might be a live grenade.

Bran slammed a magazine into his machine gun and then threw the strap over his shoulder before presenting Maddy with one of the remaining weapons. The assault rifle was heavier than she imagined. The metal was cool and menacing to the touch. Unlike Alex, she *had* held a gun before. But never one like this. One that felt like pure, raw, unrepentant death.

She tried her best to hide her revulsion and her shaking hands as she went through the instructions Bran quickly listed. How to change it from safety mode to firing mode? Check. How to slam in a new magazine when the old one ran dry? Check, check. How to *aim and spray*, as he called it? Triple check.

And triple gulp too.

She shivered and thought she heard Alex's teeth chatter behind her as the four of them quickly made

their way down the narrow hall, stopping in front of
the door to the crew's quarters where the teenagers
slept soundly.

*They've been through enough tonight, don't you
think, Lord?* Maddy sent up a silent prayer. *How about
givin' them a break, okay?*

"Hopefully this is nothing," Bran said, his dark eyes
fierce. Death and destruction. That look was back.

She shook her head. "You don't really believe that."

He leaned down to press a kiss to her lips. Then he
grabbed her chin between his thumb and forefinger
and stared hard into her eyes. "If things go bad, you do
whatever it takes to protect yourself, you get me? No
hesitation. Hesitation will get you killed."

"O-okay." She nodded, her breaths coming hard and
fast. Fear was alive inside her, crawling through her
chest like a poisonous spider on a sticky web.

"What? No kiss for me, Mason?" Alex asked the big
man, batting her lashes.

Maddy turned to see Mason chuck Alex on the chin.

"I guess that'll have to do," Alex said with a wry
twist of her lips.

And then she and Alex were left to watch the bravest
men on the planet run off to do their parts to save the
day. *Again.*

"So lust that led to love, or love that led to lust?"
Alex whispered after Bran and Mason disappeared up
the stairwell.

Maddy gave her the stink eye. "You're like a dog
with a damned bone."

"So I've been told," Alex said when Maddy grabbed
the door handle. "But humor me, okay? I need to take

my mind off the fact that I'm holding a fully automatic rifle in my hands."

Maddy paused before opening the door. And maybe it was the adrenaline. Maybe it was the nerves and the worry and the fear. But before she made the conscious decision to confess a truth, *the* truth, the one she'd known for quite a while now but had been afraid to admit even to herself, she blurted, "I don't know which came first. It's all lust and love, and love and lust. Has been since the beginnin'. At least for me."

"I knew it!" Alex shot a fist in the air.

Chapter 24

1:12 a.m....

"SO FAR, SO GOOD," MASON MUTTERED.

"Here's hoping," Bran replied.

He and Mason were hiding behind the bridge house, bellied on the deck and peeking around the corner to watch the activity on both boats. The eighty-seven-foot Marine Protector Class patrol ship was one of the smaller cutters in the Coast Guard's fleet. Still, it was larger than the yacht. Larger and lower in the water since it was built for speed. Which meant the yacht's deck was approximately two feet above the cutter's, giving those onboard the cruising boat the high ground.

Which I don't like a damned bit.

Bran watched as the Coast Guard's medic climbed onto the yacht, medical kit in hand, two members of the cutter's crew following him. The sound of the men chatting carried over the water. The air smelled of marine fuel and antifouling paint. The running lights on both vessels lit the decks in a friendly, half-light glow. Everything appeared A-okay, nothing but apple pie.

Bran's finger tightened on his trigger. *There's just something...*

He narrowed his eyes and looked through his scope, zeroing in on the faces of the two men on the deck of the motor yacht. "What do they look like to you?" he whispered to Mason.

"Like more than your average overfed, over-coiffed millionaires," Mason mumbled. "Check out the tattoo on the forearm of the one on the left. Looks like Airborne Ranger ink to me."

Sure as shit. There was no mistaking the grinning skull tattoo. "And if I'm not mistaken," he said, "the other one has *Semper Fi* inked on his bicep. I can only make out the bottom of the words below his sleeve, but..."

"The few. The proud," Mason grumbled the U.S. Marine motto. "Who the hell *are* these guys?"

"Mercs." Bran spat out the shortened form of the word *mercenaries*. Before he could say more, the sound of metal clinking against metal reached his ears. Mason heard it too. They flipped onto their backs in time to see two guys in hooded wet suits pulling themselves aboard the cutter, weapons in hand.

"What the fuck?" Mason asked.

It's another one of tonight's running themes.

Normally Bran wasn't the type to shoot first and ask questions later. But he'd seen too much over the last few hours, *heard* too much, to think these *cazzos* were up to anything good.

"Light 'em up," he snarled before laying on his trigger.

———

1:13 a.m....

The *crack* and *pop* of gunfire sounded from above, and a piece of dry ice slid from the nape of Maddy's neck all the way down her spine to the top of her tailbone. Or at least it felt like one did. Every inch of her skin prickled, and her heart froze into a useless chunk.

I can't believe this is happenin' again! Her sense of déjà vu from three months ago was only slightly keener than her sense of astonishment. *Another false Mayday? It's like a flippin' epidemic! Do bad guys get together to go over tactics, or what?*

"Wh-what's happening?" Louisa called out in the semi-dark room. Maddy and Alex had tiptoed inside, hoping not to disturb the girls. Hoping there'd be no *reason* to disturb them.

So much for that, Maddy thought, flipping on the lights, scared and angry and incredulous and...*scared*. Sally Mae and Donna came awake with gasps and confused mutterings, blinking against the sudden glare.

"What's happening, Miss Maddy?" Louisa asked again, pulling the plain gray coverlet up to her chin and looking no older than half a minute with her hair all mussed and her dark eyes taking up her whole face.

Maddy firmed her shoulders and tightened her grip on the machine gun. As calmly as she could, she said, "Girls, I need y'all to get out of those bunks and pull off the mattresses. Huddle up against that back wall and tip the mattresses in front of you so they create a barrier."

"Are they back?" Sally Mae asked, horror and disbelief filling her big, blue eyes. Maddy was reminded of the movie *Poltergeist* and little Carol Anne turning away from the television to utter creepily, *They're heeeere.* Another piece of dry ice formed and slid down her spine.

"I can't say for sure," Maddy told her. "But I think so, sweetheart. Now hurry. Do as I say."

Boom! Boom! Boom!

Another volley of shots echoed from above. With soft squeals, the girls scrambled from the bunks to do her bidding.

They don't deserve this. They don't deserve any of—

She didn't finish her thought before a man burst into the room like he'd been blown there from an explosion outside. Maddy spun and aimed. She cried out when she saw Rick standing in the doorway.

"For Chrissakes!" Alex yelled, lowering her weapon and lifting a shaky hand to her mouth. "I almost—" She stopped and swallowed, breathing heavily. "I almost shot you."

"You're not the only one," Maddy assured her, her own hands quaking so hard that the metal clip on the rifle's strap rattled.

"What's happening?" Rick asked, his face so white he almost looked dead.

Dead... Right. Which begs the question, who's dead on deck? Who's shootin' and who's been shot?

Maddy refused to contemplate the answers. "No clue," she told him before turning back to the teenagers. "Hurry, girls. The mattresses." Then back to Rick, "There are more rifles on the table in the galley. Go get one and come back here to help us guard the girls."

"O-okay." Rick turned and ran from the room, muttering either an expletive or a prayer under his breath. She wasn't sure which.

"And be sure to knock next time so we know it's you!" Alex yelled before the door slammed shut with a loud *bang* that had everyone in the room jumping. To herself Alex said, "It's crazy to think about the fact that

a bullet travels twenty-five-hundred feet per second.
That's something like seventeen hundred miles per hour,
faster than the speed of sound. So if I shoot him the next
time he comes in the door, he'll probably be dead before
I even hear the shot."

She looked around the room, her face chalk white.
"Sorry," she said. "I tend to spout facts when I'm
stressed unless…there's something else I can fill my
mouth with. Does anyone have any food? No?" She
rolled in her lips and turned back toward the door.

Maddy blew out a shaky breath, sour with the smell
of fear, then jumped again when a loud *bwarrrr-bwarrr*
sawed across the deck above them.

She closed her eyes and made a deal with God.

*Let him live, Lord. Let him live, and I'll keep my end
of the bargain. Let him live, and I'll never make him
choose between my friendship and my love. Just…let
him live.*

1:14 a.m….

"On the right! On the right!" Bran bellowed to the Coast
Guardsman standing at the 50-caliber machine gun
mounted on a swivel on the portside of the bow.

No sooner had Bran and Mason watched the dead
bodies of the men who'd been trying to sneak aboard
the cutter slip back into the sea than the sound of return
gunfire echoed from the cruising boat. Only it *hadn't*
been return gunfire. At least the shooters hadn't returned
fire at Bran and Mason.

Instead, the yachtsmen had pulled pistols and

carelessly put bullets into the brains of the medic and the Guardsmen who'd boarded with him. Bran had peeked around the corner of the cutter's bridge house in time to see blood spraying from their skulls as their bodies crumpled to the deck.

One of the Coasties still on the cutter had screamed his rage before rushing over to the closest 50-cal. and letting loose with a barrage of lead that chewed up the side of the yacht and took down one of the mercs. The Guardsman was still laying on the trigger, doing his damndest to destroy the vessel all by himself.

The *ping-ping* of empty shell casings was a sweet melody compared to the loud roar of the weapon. The smell of spent gunpowder hung heavy in the air.

"On your right!" Bran bellowed again, flaying his vocal cords in an effort to be heard. The merc the Guardsman had missed was bellied up to the edge of the yacht's deck, aiming his pistol straight at the head of the Coastie. And Bran didn't have a shot. Because of the angle, the Guardsman's head kept slipping into his line of fire.

"Mason!" he yelled over his shoulder. Mason had moved to the back end of the bridge house. "You got a shot?"

"Negative!" Mason yelled back.

"Shit," Bran cursed, once again sighting through his scope. "Come on! Come on!" he gritted between his teeth. "Keep your head to the left. Just keep your god-damn head to your left!"

Bran's heart slowed. The breath left his lungs on a hot breeze. And the world around him disappeared until there was nothing. Nothing but the two-inch piece of real estate between the eyes of the mercenary when the Guardsman finally shifted left.

Boom! He squeezed his trigger. His bullet flew true, plowing into the merc's skull and killing him instantly. But it was too late. The mercenary got off his shot. And the Coastie dropped to the deck, clutching his neck as dark, wet blood spurted between his fingers.

"Damnit!" Bran yelled. Then, "Mason! Cover me!"

Bran waited until Mason raced back to him before scooting from behind the bridge house to snake his way across the deck towards the writhing Guardsman. After the roar of the 50-cal., the silence that hung over both ships was eerie, weighty, like that inside a casket six feet below freshly shoveled earth. It was made even more macabre when the wounded man began to gurgle.

Bran slung his M4 across his back and grabbed the Coastie beneath both arms. As quickly as he could, bare feet sliding on the slick deck, he dragged the man backward, toward what little safety the far side of the bridge house provided.

"P-please help," the Guardsman burbled, blood staining his lips.

"I'm doing my best, buddy," Bran told him, grunting as he finally managed to heave the wounded man around the corner.

He was down on his knees a second later. "Let me see." He gently removed the Coastie's hands. Carnage met Bran's eyes and a hard stone of remorse settled low in his gut. Carefully applying pressure to the awful wound on the man's neck, he looked up to see the muscle beneath Mason's eye twitching. They both knew a mortal injury when they saw one. The Guardsman only had a minute or two of this world left in him, and then he'd be on to the next.

"H-help me," the Coastie pleaded again.

Bran gave him the only help, the only *comfort* he could. "You are one brave sonofabitch jumping on that saw gun like you did. May have saved everyone on this boat."

The man's eyes focused on Bran's face, wide and terrified. "Am I—" He coughed on the blood filling his mouth. It left slick, dark droplets over his face. "Am I dying?" he garbled.

"You've got a shredded carotid artery," Bran told him, having learned it was better to give a dead man the truth. Somehow it lessened the fear and sped up the journey to acceptance. "Is there anything you want me to tell anyone? Anything you want me to do?"

For a second, the brave Coastie searched his face as if hoping he misheard. Then he said, "T-tell my wife and kids—" More coughing. More blood. "I love them."

"I will," Bran vowed, feeling the man's blood pumping hot and heavy against his hands. The Guardsman's life was slipping through his fingers. "I'll tell 'em you were a hero. And that your last thoughts were of them."

"I d-don't—" Now the man was struggling to breathe, struggling to hold on to that last, waning vestige of life. The fabric of Bran's already tattered soul shredded just a little more. He could not believe he once again found himself ferrying a fine man to the other side. "I don't want to…to die…"

With those awful words, the courageous Guardsman breathed his last. His eyes went opaque as the life left them, his skin gray and already cooling from lack of blood. Bran gently removed his hands from the man's ruined neck and wiped the blood on his shorts. His jaw clenched so hard he was surprised he didn't shatter his teeth.

"Fuckin' hell," Mason muttered, still standing over them, weapon raised, guard up.

"I thought we were finished watching good men die," Bran said. "I'd *hoped* we were finished." He took a second, a moment of silence for the fallen sailor, before asking, "So how many friendlies we got left?"

"At most two," Mason said. "The captain and one more."

"And we have no idea how many mercs are still out here."

"I say we untie, start the engines, and get the fuck out of here."

"Roger that," Bran agreed, pushing to his feet just as movement at the back of the boat near the ramp where the Coasties launched their rescue dinghy caught his attention. "Behind you!" he yelled, grabbing for the M4 strapped to his back.

A sound around the corner of the bridge house told him he didn't have time to get his weapon in the ready position. Mason bellied out and opened up on the two men sneaking aboard the back of the boat at the same time Bran spun and slapped the barrel of a SCAR-L away from his head just as it peeked around the corner and aimed. The metal was cold and wet against the side of his hand, and the rifle hit the deck with a clatter before skidding toward the railing.

Bran barely had time to brace himself before his would-be assassin let loose with a bloodcurdling scream and launched himself. The two of them slammed onto the deck in a tangle of arms and legs as the sound of two rounds *zzzzzipped* through the air beside them.

As Mason laid down a covering fire, keeping the assailants at the back of the boat pinned, Bran fought to gain the upper hand with all the rage and fury inside him. Still rolling across the deck, he yanked his knife from the sheath around his calf. With a grunt and twist, he was able to end up atop his attacker. He didn't hesitate. He plunged the blade straight toward the merc's heart, but the man grabbed his wrist at the last moment and stayed the deathblow.

"Who *are* you guys?" the mercenary gritted as they both struggled to control the direction of the blade.

It's the dude with the Southern accent. Bran would recognize that voice anywhere.

"I'm the last guy you'll ever see," he snarled, putting his full weight against the hilt of the blade, ignoring the ache in his thigh. The local anesthetic the medic— the now *dead* medic—had given him was wearing off. "Brought to you courtesy of the United States Navy."

"Please," Southern Accent begged, his eyes wide and frightened inside the holes of the balaclava he still wore. "You wouldn't kill a brother in arms, would you? I was Navy too."

The tip of Bran's knife pierced the merc's flesh. Tears welled in the villain's eyes. "You're no brother of mine." The monster was alive inside Bran. It yelled for blood. For death. For vengeance in the name of the brave Coast Guardsman who was dead on the deck not two feet away. "You sold your soul to the devil, dickhole. And I'm here to collect."

With that, Bran twisted slightly to the merc's left, toward the man's nondominant hand, and was rewarded when his blade cut deeper. Deeper still. The mercenary tried to buck him off, tried to twist away, but it was no use. Bran's knife slipped between the man's ribs and pierced his black heart, blood bubbling around the blade, the sound of the mercenary's scream slicing through the humid air before quieting to an open-mouthed wheeze.

Bran didn't wait for the light to dim in the merc's eyes before jumping to help Mason, swinging his M4 over his head. But Mason didn't need his help. He'd already taken out the men who'd tried to board the vessel. Well...*one* of them anyway. The other was crawling across the deck, leaving a bloody path like a slug's trail in his wake.

Mason walked up behind him, M4 trained, and yelled, "Stay where you are, motherfucker!"

The man flipped onto his back, revealing the pistol in his hands. But he didn't have time to squeeze off a round before Mason drilled one right between his eyes at the same time Bran squeezed his trigger, his round hitting the merc center mass.

Mason looked down at the blood oozing up through the man's wet-suit-clad chest and twisted his lips. "Thanks for the assist." He glanced over his shoulder at Bran. "But I had that one."

Bran shrugged and cocked his ears, straining to hear the sound of more swimmers in the water, or more men trying to slip stealthily aboard the cutter. But nothing breached the stillness except for the gentle lapping of the waves and the soft *thump-thump* of the boats rocking together.

The seconds ticked by. His breath held. And just when he thought it might be over, a voice split the odd peace of the night, sending an icy chill skittering down his spine.

"Madison Powers! Come out right now, and no one else has to die!"

———

1:15 a.m....

"Mmm! Mmmm!" Gene grunted behind the length of duct tape covering his mouth. He struggled against his restraints and Tony's death grip. For such a wiry old fart he was amazingly strong. Luckily Tony had three inches and thirty pounds on him, so he was able to muscle Gene closer to the rail of the yacht's back deck without losing his hold.

"Shut up, Gene!" he snarled, pressing the pistol tighter against Gene's temple and making sure to keep Gene in front of him.

Fifteen minutes...

Rory would arrive to implement Plan D in minutes.

Plan C had been for Tony to call in a Mayday. Once the Coast Guard cutter arrived to provide aid, the six armed men Rory had deposited on the yacht and in the surrounding waters would take out the Guardsmen and the two mystery men while Tony remained belowdecks with Gene. Then Rory's guys would retrieve the bodies, grab Maddy and the girls, sink the cutter to destroy any evidence that might remain, and proceed with the original ransom scheme.

It was risky as hell. But Rory had assured Tony *this* plan would be a slam dunk.

Some slam dunk.

As far as Tony could figure from the number of bodies littering the decks or floating in the sea around the two boats, all of Rory's men were either dead or dying.

This *newest* plan was devised during the quick, desperate phone call Tony had made when he realized their third attempt to secure Maddy and the teenagers and take back the bodies was going to hell in a handbasket. He had called for Rory to sail over as quickly as he could with the two men he'd kept with him as well as the two rocket launchers he had onboard.

"Stall them!" Rory's voice had shouted through the satellite phone's receiver, the sound of the trawler's engines loud in the background but not nearly as loud as the Coast Guard's mammoth machine gun as it set about chewing away chunks of the anchored yacht.

"And how would you suggest I do that?" Tony had screeched, cowering beside the bed in the main cabin, his ears ringing from the sound of the big gun. He reached for the bottle of scotch he'd brought down with him. Twisting off the cap, he took a healthy slug. The liquor burned his throat and belly, but he appreciated the heat. It told him he was still alive.

How much longer will that *last?*

"Grab Gene and drag him out on the deck," Rory said. "Act like you're holding him hostage. Pretend to ransom his life for the money you need."

"But Maddy will see. She'll know that I—"

Rory kept talking right over him. "They'll hold their fire, and that'll give me time to get there and blow them out of the water. Consign them to the devil and the deep blue sea."

"Blow them out of the water? But Maddy—"

"Doesn't matter," Rory said, his tone ice cold.

A shiver of dread rippled over Tony's skin, raising the hairs on his body. "What do you mean?"

"*Come on*, Tony," Rory spat, yelling something over his shoulder at one of his guys before turning back to the phone. "It's over. You need to forget about the damned ransom money and start thinking about a quick cleanup that'll leave no trace and *no* witnesses who might lead back to us."

Shit! He knew Rory was right, but it was impossible to accept. This was supposed to have been *easy*, a piece of cake. A quick snatch-and-grab. A fast ransom, and voilà, the company he and Gene had started would once again have full coffers, and once all the new ventures were up and running, *Tony* would get his just reward. Namely, money. Boatloads of it. We're talking Rockefeller wealth.

He racked his brain for a way to turn it all around, to get back on track. But the scotch was muddling his mind. Either that, or the truth was there *was* no way to get back on track. *It's over. I'm ruined! And all because of those two mysterious assholes!*

He'd wanted to scream. He'd wanted to kick. He'd wanted to *kill*. But the only thing he could do was acquiesce to Rory's final solution, grab Gene, and head out on deck.

"Maddy Powers!" he called now. It was the third time he'd repeated the words since towing Gene topside. "Come out and see who I have with me!"

Chapter 25

1:16 a.m....

"Don't go," Alex pleaded, grabbing Maddy's arm when she reached for the door handle.

Maddy glanced back to find Alex's gaze beseeching. Rick wore the same expression. For that matter, so did the three teens peeking over the wall of mattresses.

It's not like I want *to go*, she thought. What she said was "I *have* to." Her knees and hands and stomach were quivering. And the only good thing she could say about the latter was that she could now affirm with one-hundred-percent certainty that the corned beef had finally digested. If it hadn't, it would be all over the floor of the crew's quarters. "What if whoever is up there is talkin' about Bran or Mason when he says no one else has to die?" she asked.

Alex pushed up her glasses and swung the strap of the machine gun over her shoulder. "Then I'm coming with you."

"No. Stay with the girls." Maddy turned to include Rick. "*Both* of you."

Before they could argue—*no time for that*—Maddy pulled open the door, leading with the barrel of the weapon in her hands because she hadn't the first clue who or what might be waiting for her on the other side.

A pitiful mewling sound, like that of an abandoned kitten, burst from her when she saw *Bran* was waiting for her. Big, bad, still-breathing Bran.

She launched herself at him, overcome with joy, with gratitude—*thank you, Lord!*—that none of those bullets that had sounded overhead had found a home in him.

"Whoa." He snatched the machine gun away from her. It was a good thing, because she didn't know how she'd have managed to tighten her hands around his neck otherwise. She pressed her lips to his throat just so she could feel the steady beat of his heart.

"Y'okay?" he whispered in her ear. And she allowed herself three glorious seconds to close her eyes and simply feel him against her. Then she pushed back to glare at him.

"Am *I* okay? I'm not the one who's been in the middle of another firefight and—" She stopped when she saw the blood spattered on his chest and the big, ugly stains on his shorts. "Holy shit, Bran!"

"It's not my blood."

Before Maddy could respond, Alex's voice, thickened by fear, sounded from behind her. "Mason?"

"Was fine when I left him to come down here," Bran assured her with a quick bob of his chin. "But I can't say the same for the Coast Guardsmen."

"Oh, thank goodness," Alex blew out a wheezing breath, doubling over from the relief. Then she straightened and winced. "I meant about Mason. I-I'm really sorry about the—" She shook her head. "Sorry."

"How many didn't make it?" Maddy asked, sending up a prayer for those lost. Simultaneously, she cursed those responsible straight to the bowels of hell.

"Can't say for sure," Bran told her, his jaw sawing. "I think all but two."

Before Maddy could fully digest the horror of that, the voice from above sounded again. "Madison Powers!"

"Who *is* that?" she whispered. And on the subject of bowels, hers threatened to loosen every time the man screamed her name.

"Hell if I know." Bran tossed the strap of her machine gun over his shoulder. "I only got a peek at him before coming down here. Thirty-five years old. Sorta slick-looking. He's holding an older man in a pearl-snap shirt and Wranglers hostage."

A pearl-snap shirt and Wranglers? Dread started at Maddy's toes and filled her until she was pretty sure she felt it leaking from her ears.

"Well, I reckon we better go find out what he wants, yeah?" she said, impressed with how steady her voice sounded.

Bran hesitated for a second, the look in his eye saying the last thing he wanted to do was to take her above deck. Then he puffed out a ragged breath and glanced over her shoulder at Alex and Rick. "You two stay here and guard the girls." *Great minds.* "This ain't over." *Gulp.*

"Be careful." Alex grabbed Maddy's arm again, giving it a squeeze. Her grip was strong, but her palm was clammy, her fingers shaking. "And if you see Mason, tell him to be careful too."

Maddy searched her eyes, seeing in them a whole host of familiar thoughts and feelings. "You got it," she assured Alex, giving her hand a squeeze before following Bran down the narrow hall and up the stairs to the bridge house.

The dread that had filled her was now something darker, a thick, murky foreboding. She wasn't going to like what she saw, *who* she saw, on that yacht. She knew it.

Bran stopped at the door to the bridge house when he heard the captain's voice. "Mayday! Mayday! Mayday! I have men down! I'm requesting assistance at the following coordinates and—"

Bran pushed open the door, and Maddy peeked around him to find the captain sitting on the floor, his back to the console, a satellite phone in one hand, a pistol in the other.

The pistol was aimed right at Bran's heart.

Maddy nearly fainted.

"Careful, Captain," Bran said easily, ducking into the room and dragging her down so their heads weren't visible in the windows.

"What the hell is happening?" Webber demanded. "Who the hell—"

"You know as much as we do," Bran said, cutting him off. "Now where's your other man? Mason is down on deck guarding this whole ship by himself, and I know he'd appreciate some backup."

"Backup?" the captain asked hysterically. His eyes were wide and unblinking. "All my men are *dead*."

"All of 'em?"

"See for yourself." The captain waved a hand at the bay of windows. "I count three on the yacht and two more on the deck below. My whole damned crew!"

From her spot crouched by the door, Maddy couldn't see the carnage he was talking about. And she was glad for it.

"*Fungule!*" Bran cursed, scooting over to the row of windows and tapping on the glass. He flashed a hand sign Maddy assumed was meant for Mason down below. The gist of the gesture, she reckoned, was something along the lines of *You're on your own*.

"Last chance, Madison Powers!" the man on the yacht called again, and his voice pierced her eardrums like an ice pick.

"Steady," Bran said when he saw her startle. He motioned for her to follow him across the bridge to the line of windows facing the yacht. "Stay on your knees and peek above the sill 'til you can see 'em."

I don't want to see them. I just want to crawl into a cabin down below and forget any of this ever happened.

But her daddy hadn't raised a coward. So with a firm chin and a quaking stomach, she did as instructed. At first sight of the men, she gasped, her vision tunneling as shock and confusion washed over her like a tidal wave.

"I take it you know 'em."

"Yes." She nodded, unable to believe her eyes. "The one with the gun is Tony Scott. And the man he's holdin' hostage is my uncle."

1:19 a.m....

"Uncle Gene!" Maddy called through the window Bran opened to allow himself a clean shot, should he need to take one. "A-are you okay?"

Her uncle tilted his head back and scanned the windows of the bridge house. Bran knew the instant the man spotted his niece because his eyes filled with tears and his handlebar mustache quivered around the duct tape pasted over his mouth. Bran wasn't convinced her uncle was nodding so much as trying to get away from the pistol pointed at his temple. But Maddy took the motion as an affirmative.

She made a little sound of relief and tightened her grip around the lip of the windowsill until her knuckles showed white through her skin. Bran longed to go to her, but his need to maintain his firing position stopped him.

"Give me a quick rundown on what the relationship is here," he commanded. Did he need to take out Mr. Slick, a.k.a Tony? Or should he hold his fire?

"Gene is my father's younger brother," she explained in a whisper. "He and Dad started Powers Petroleum together, but Gene's always been more an idea man than a businessman. He's real good at beginnin' things. Not so good at finishin' them. After a year, he got bored, cashed out, and used the proceeds to start up somethin' new. He's been doin' that for thirty years. Birthin' new companies and sellin' them off if they're profitable. Declarin' bankruptcy if they're not." Her lips twisted with disapproval at this last bit. Despite that, Bran could see her love for her uncle shining in her eyes.

"Three years ago he met Tony, who was workin' as a mid-level executive at BP." He assumed she meant British Petroleum. "The two of them concocted a scheme to use Tony's contacts in the business and Uncle Gene's family name to start an oil company specializin' in new and risky means of extracting oil from previously untapped sources like shale grounds, tar sands, and ultra-deep rigs."

"They're partners?" Bran asked, scrutinizing the two men.

Maddy nodded.

"So what's he doing holding your uncle hostage then?" Bran demanded.

"Let's find out," she muttered more to herself than to him. Raising her voice, she cried, "What do you want, Tony?" She pushed up slightly, trying to get a better view of the men.

A sense of warning crawled over the back of Bran's neck like a millipede. "Stay low," he commanded. "Low, Maddy." He scanned the interior cabin of the motor yacht through his scope. Or at least what he could *see* of it through the tinted windows. He didn't like anything about this situation. He didn't like that Mason was alone out there. He *certainly* didn't like that he had no idea if there were any mercs left.

"We tried asking nicely, Maddy!" Slick yelled. "But your father is a stubborn man!"

Bran could hear the dry sound Maddy's throat made when she swallowed. "What are you talkin' about, Tony? Why are you doin' this?"

Tony darted a quick look over his shoulder, and Bran narrowed his eyes. *Something isn't right.*

"We were fine until OPEC dropped the price of oil!" Tony cried, his face ruddy in the yacht's running lights. Bran bet if he looked through the scope of his rifle at Tony's eyes, he'd find them as bloodshot as LT's uncle's after he'd smoked some of the herb he grew out back of the Wayfarer Island house. *For my glaucoma*, the crusty old sailor always claimed, although Bran was pretty sure the man's eyesight was 20/20.

As for Gene's eyes? Bran couldn't see them. After the man's initial scan of the bridge house, he'd let his chin drop against his chest, his thinning gray hair falling over his brow and shadowing his face. He'd stopped struggling, stopped trying to pull away from Tony. Now, he stood there docilely, seemingly resigned to be a victim. It struck Bran as strange. From what Bran knew of Maddy's family, cowardice and surrender didn't run in the blood.

"Then the one venture we had up and running wasn't making enough to fund the expansion of the rest!" Tony continued. "OPEC knew this, knew all the businesses like ours that were finding new ways to extract oil couldn't bear bargain-basement prices for long. They don't *want* us losing our dependence on foreign oil!"

He certainly was Chatty Cathy all of a sudden. The more he talked, the more the mercury rose inside Bran's internal trouble thermometer.

Something isn't fuckin' right. He could feel it.

"They *want* us reliant on them for our fuel needs!" Tony kept on, talking so fast now that spittle arced from his mouth, catching the lights and glinting on its way overboard. "But we didn't give up! We just...we just needed a little help, a loan to tide us over until a few more of the new ventures were up and running! But your father refused! He's forced our hands! He's forced *my* hand! I *need* that money!"

So what? Bran thought, feeling like he was looking at one of those optical illusions that shifted shape just when you thought you were seeing it correctly. *He thought he'd hold Maddy and Gene Powers for ransom to get the funds from Maddy's dad?* How the hell did Tony think he'd get away with that? Surely a man didn't make it to the position of mid-level executive in a company like BP if he was an idiot.

Unless, he planned to kill 'em after he got the money, Bran thought. *Get rid of the witnesses and act like he received the funds from some other source. With Maddy and Gene dead, there'd be no way to prove otherwise.*

His finger tightened on the trigger, easily lining up a head shot. One pull and this could all be over. But there was something going on here. Something he felt sure he needed to understand. "Just keep him talking," he told Maddy.

She turned to him, her cheeks pale as winter's first snow. But her eyes were hot with determination.

"But what now, Tony?" she called. "What do you expect—"

Bran stopped listening because Gene Powers lifted his face then. Wet tracks glistened on his lined cheeks, but his eyes were as dry as a desert wind. Bran's antenna twanged. He recognized the look on Gene's face. It was one of crushing regret and…a scary sort of determination. Gene shook his head and did something weird with his shoulders. He sort of shrugged them and moved them around. Bran would've said he was trying get comfortable against his restraints, but there was something…*off* about the movement.

Gene lifted his eyes back to the bridge house windows, and if Bran wasn't mistaken, he smiled behind the duct tape. A curl of understanding unwound inside Bran. He sighted down the length of his barrel. Sure as shit, all at once Gene's hands were untied. They knocked Tony's pistol away from his temple. A split second later, Gene plowed his shoulder into the younger man and sent them both flying across the yacht's back deck.

"Uncle Gene!" Maddy screamed as the two men landed with a harsh-sounding *thud*, all the while fighting for supremacy and control of the pistol.

Bran cursed and tightened his finger on his trigger. But he didn't take a shot. Not yet. He didn't have a clear line of sight and—

Bang! Bang!

"Nooooo!" Maddy shrieked, jumping to her feet.

"Damnit!" Bran cursed, taking his eye away from his target just long enough to yank her back down.

They watched breathlessly as Gene kicked away Tony's body and staggered to a stand. Blood stained the front of his pearl-snap shirt, but it wasn't his. It was Tony's. Gene raised his face to the bridge house's windows again, his expression still one of regret and determination. Ripping off the duct tape, he flung it aside, and his throat sounded like it'd been scoured by steel wool when he yelled, "I'm so sorry, Maddy!"

"It's not your fault, Uncle Gene!" she called back.

"It's like they say," Gene said, his voice dropping to a more conversational level, making them strain to hear him. "When you choose the lesser of two evils, you're still choosin' evil. But I swear to you…" He raised his voice, pain and regret flowing like twin rivers through his words. "I swear it, Maddy! No one was supposed to get hurt!"

Maddy sucked in a wheezy breath, one that was filled with the horror of dawning understanding. "Are…are you tellin' me you—" she began, but Gene cut her off.

"Tony's guys were supposed to grab you and the girls and call in a ransom to Gerry!" Bran knew they were talking about Maddy's father, Gerald R. Powers. "Once the money was paid, they'd have set you free, no worse for wear! But then everything went wrong and Tony wouldn't stop! He wouldn't stop, Maddy!" Her uncle's voice broke on a hard edge.

"How *could* you?" The fear, the betrayal in Maddy's eyes cut into Bran's heart like a ragged piece of metal. "How could you *do* this to Daddy? To me?"

"It was for the greater good!" Gene swore. "Once we got the business up and runnin', all U.S. oil companies would profit, includin' Powers Petroleum. They'd stop havin' to sign foreign contracts. They'd stop havin' to kowtow to OPEC. He just didn't see and I couldn't make him!"

Maddy choked on a sob, and Bran wanted nothing more than to make this all go away. He'd barter his own sorry soul if he could somehow make this all go away.

Gene must've heard her, even through the narrow opening of the window, because he dropped his head, his shoulders shaking, and said something that didn't travel up to the bridge house. Bran could feel Maddy start to stand, and he reached out and grabbed her wrist, shaking his head. "Don't, Maddy. You can't go out there."

"But—"

"I wasn't a perfect man, Maddy," Gene said, lifting his head. Tears flowed freely down his lined face. "But before this night..." He looked around at the bodies splayed across the decks of both boats and shook his head, his shoulders sagging. "Before this I was a good man. I don't know how to live any other way. I *can't* live any other way. Tell Gerry I'm sorry."

Bran knew what Gene was up to a split second before he did it. "Don't do—"

But that was all he managed before Gene lifted the pistol and put a bullet through his right temple.

"No! No! *No!*" Maddy screamed, and Bran had to throw one arm around her shoulders to keep her from bolting.

He turned her away from the sight of her uncle collapsing onto the yacht's deck, head open like a melon, mouth wide in one last soundless scream. And then something on the horizon caught his eye and forced him to let her go so he could swing his scope in that direction. Moonlight caught the white water kicked up by the trawler beelining for them, making it glisten. Good thing, or Bran would have missed it in the dark.

"Get these engines running," he barked at Captain Webber. "Now!"

"What?" The captain glanced over at him, eyes wide with shock. "I can't leave without my men's bodies, and—"

"Normally, I would agree with you," Bran said. "But that fishing trawler you saw on the radar is coming our way fast. And I don't get the impression they're responding to your Mayday."

"What?" The captain peered over the console in the direction of the approaching boat.

"That's why Mr. Slick…uh…Tony was being so chatty. He was stalling. Buying time and waiting on backup."

I shoulda known. I shoulda—

"How can you be sure?" Webber asked.

Bran looked away from his sights to pin his stare on

the captain. "'Cause I got a sixth sense when it comes to this shit." He didn't have to say *Remember what happened the last time I got this feeling?* It was there in his eyes. And the evidence that his sixth sense was on the money was scattered all over the decks of the two ships or floating around them in the sea.

Captain Webber nodded. "Right."

Bran turned to find Maddy down on her knees, crying into her hands. He wanted to hold her more than anything else in the world, but there was still work to be done. He crouch-ran to the opposite wall of windows and threw open the nearest one. "Mason!" he yelled down. "Cut us loose while I cover you!"

He scrambled back across the bridge and scanned the deck of the yacht as Mason appeared below, knife in hand, ready to saw through the nylon cords tethering the two ships together.

"Captain!" he yelled. "We hafta get the hell outta—"

He didn't need to finish his sentence because the engines rumbled to life. He saw Mason cut through the last rope and hollered down, "Mason! Hold tight!" To the captain, he roared, "Punch it!"

The cutter was a fine piece of American-made machinery. It exploded away from the yacht, cutting across the tops of the waves and picking up speed with every second. Through his scope, Bran watched the trawler turn to give chase. His attention settled not on the man he could see on deck, but on the long shiny tube that caught the starlight above and glimmered.

As the incomparable Yogi Berra had once said, *It's déjà vu all over again*. The last time he'd faced down a rocket launcher was three month ago, when Maddy's father's yacht had been hijacked. He didn't hear the *thump* of the weapon discharging its load, but he saw the flash of fire and the explosion of smoke.

"Hard to starboard!" he yelled at the captain. "Now, now, *now!*"

The captain didn't hesitate, cutting the ship to the right. Bran grabbed onto the windowsill to steady himself, and looked up in time to see the rocket whiz by them, hit the ocean some twenty feet from the vessel, and send up an explosive plume of water on impact.

Lifting his weapon, he looked through his scope and was dismayed to see a second man appear beside the first one, another rocket launcher at the ready.

"Again!" he yelled when the second weapon belched up its projectile. "This time hard to port!"

The cutter sliced through the ocean like the war machine it was, easily parting the waves as its big engines roared with happiness. The second rocket missed by nearly twenty yards, and Bran steadied himself against the new list of the ship. He sighted through his scope, pleased to see the fishing boat was no match for the Coast Guard's ship.

When he assured himself they were outpacing their pursuers and the reach of their rocket launchers, he dropped his M4. The next instant, he pulled Maddy into his lap.

Chapter 26

"COFFEE?" MADDY GLANCED UP TO SEE A STYROFOAM CUP steaming in front of her face.

"Bless you," she told Rick, curling her frozen fingers around his offering. For some reason, she couldn't get warm. It was probably eighty degrees outside, but she was freezing. Feared maybe all the coldness was coming from her heart. From deep in her soul.

"I can't vouch for the quality," Rick warned. "But it's hot. And if the muddy color is any indication, it's strong as hell."

"I need strong as hell right now. I feel like I've been awake for a decade."

They were in the bowels of the Coast Guard station on Key West in some sort of utilitarian-looking conference room with no windows. So when she glanced at the clock loudly *tick-tocking* on the wall, she couldn't be sure if it was morning or night. She just knew she wanted sleep. *Days* of sleep. *Weeks* of sleep. As her grandma Bettie would've said, she was too pooped to pop.

Taking a sip of coffee, she closed her eyes and welcomed the burn. It made her feel something besides the cold of the AC units and the crushing despair of her uncle's last minutes. Rick was right; it was strong enough to raise a blood blister on a boot. *Just what I need*.

When she blinked her eyes open, she smiled her thanks and indicated the metal chair next to her.

"I think I'll just keep standing, if you don't mind." Rick blew across the top of his cup. "I was sitting in that chair in the interrogation room for so long I think I may have permanently flattened my ass."

"Do we still call it an interrogation room if we're not criminals?" Maddy asked, taking another sip. *Come on, caffeine. Keep workin' your magic*.

"I *felt* like I was being interrogated," Rick said.

When they'd arrived at the Coast Guard station, they'd been met by a swarm of FBI agents. Apparently, crimes in national parks and in U.S. territorial waters fell under the purview of the Federal Bureau of Investigation.

"I think I answered more questions this morning," Rick continued, "than I have in my whole life up to this point. How about you?"

"Mmm," she hummed noncommittally. The FBI questioning had been intense. No doubt. But the CIA's questioning after the hijacking of her father's yacht had been worse. Of course, she couldn't tell *Rick* that.

"Everybody else still being raked over the coals?" Rick asked, looking around the empty room.

"I don't know about Bran or Mason," she told him. "But according to Agent—" She blinked and shook her head. She'd spent hours in a little room with the FBI agent and she couldn't remember his name. Her brain was mush. Her heart was pretty much the same consistency. "I'm totally blankin' on the guy's name," she admitted. "Thomas or Thomson or Tomlinson. It's somethin' like that. Anyway, he told me they'd taken the girls to grab some food and make calls home to their parents. He's supposed to bring them here in a bit so we can board the private plane my father sent to take us h—"

Her throat caught. Thoughts of her father inevitably conjured up thoughts of her uncle. If she lived to be a thousand years old, she'd never forget the awful look on Gene's face right before he pulled the trigger.

"Hey." Rick slid out the chair beside her, plopping down and throwing an arm around her shoulders. The weight of it felt immense. *Everything* felt immense. All the violence. All the death. All the loss.

"And for what?" she whispered, searching Rick's youthful face for answers.

"What?" He blinked his confusion.

"This *night*," she said, setting her coffee on the table so she could wrap her arms around herself to try to keep the pieces of her heart from flying out of her chest. "All of it. All the awful things that happened were done for oil. *Oil*. Smelly, black sludge that spews out of the earth. It doesn't make sense."

Rick's lips twisted into a grimace. "Since the invention of the internal combustion engine, oil has been the altar that power, corruption, and greed pray at. So it makes perfect sense to me."

The noisy clock on the wall kept track of the half-dozen seconds she sat there looking at him, really *seeing* him. "You're pretty smart for someone so young, you know that?"

"I'm not *that* young," he insisted, and all she could do was smile. After tonight, she might agree. She felt like she'd aged ten years. No doubt he did too.

"It's all so ugly. So...*unnecessary*." She shook her head. "He was a good man," she insisted. "My uncle, he just..."

"Got himself into an untenable situation," Rick finished for her. "And then he couldn't live with the guilt of it, the shame of it."

She squeezed her eyes shut. "My father is wrecked." Her lips were quivering. "And the sounds he made when I called and told him what happened..." She shook her head.

"I'm so sorry." Rick gave her another squeeze. "I know those words don't count for much, but—"

"They count for a lot, actually." She blinked away the burning wetness threatening in her eyes. She wouldn't cry. Not in front of him. Not in front of the girls once they arrived. She still needed to be strong, project courage. Once she was home alone, then she'd let herself fall apart. *When the shakes come. When the nightmares come...*

She shivered at the inevitability of it all. Then convinced herself she'd beaten back the horror before, and she'd do it again. *With the help of Bran.*

Bran...

Could she really go on as if nothing had changed between them?

You promised you would, her conscience reminded her. *You made a deal with God. And He's not the kind of guy you renege on.*

"I haven't had the chance to say thank you for all you did tonight," she told Rick. "You were great."

Rick's answering grin made his dimples deepen. "Thanks. I'd say it was my pleasure, but..." He let the sentence dangle and widened his smile. That look was back on his face. *The* look.

Oh no. She opened her mouth to try to prevent him from saying anything. But before she could, he blurted, "You know, if you ever need anyone to talk to, I could give you my number and we could—"

"Rick," she said, cutting him off, "you are a sweet, adorable man." She almost said *kid*, but she reckoned maybe there was no more kid left in him. "Somewhere out there is a sweet, adorable woman who's goin' to give you everything you deserve."

His eyes dimmed. "But that sweet, adorable woman isn't you?"

"I've already given everything to someone else," she told him without prevarication.

"We're talking about Bran, right?" When she nodded, he sighed. "Well, I hope he deserves you." He flashed her his dimples again. "But if you ever decide he doesn't, you know where to find me."

Maddy hesitated a second before going with her gut and throwing her arms around his neck to hug him tight.

"Thank you," she whispered, closing her eyes. Then a sound in the doorway had her blinking.

There he was. The one. *Her* one.

Or at least he was for one wonderful, awful night...

9:52 a.m....

Red.

That was the color of Bran's world. The instant he saw Maddy in another man's arms, the monster inside him roared to life, and it always viewed things in shades of crimson. It urged him to run over, yank Maddy away, and flatten Rick the Prick with a haymaker to the mouth. Just *pow!* Then, once Rick was down and out, the monster wanted to stomp on his remains.

"Bran!" Maddy pushed out of Rick's arms. Through sheer force of will, Bran beat his dark side back and made sure his expression was blank as he watched Maddy scurry toward him. "Are they finished questionin' you? Did they tell you if they've found the fishin' trawler? Have they gone to secure the yacht and bring in…" She trailed off and gulped before finishing with, "the bodies?"

Bran didn't answer her immediately, instead glancing over at Rick. Something in his face must've revealed what he was feeling, because Rick cleared his throat and pushed up from the table.

"I need a warm-up," the young park ranger said, indicating his Styrofoam cup as he sidled by Bran. Bran waited until Rick disappeared down the hall before stepping fully into the room.

"They haven't located the trawler yet," he told Maddy, trying not to drown in the disappointment that filled her liquid-mercury eyes. "But they have planes in the air searching. And they've put the word out."

She blew out a breath. "Well, I guess…I guess that's somethin'."

Something. But not everything. They both knew this wouldn't be over until every last one of the men involved had been brought to justice.

And on the topic of the men involved…

"They ran the prints on the two bodies we brought

with us from Garden Key," he told her. "Both men were Army." *No surprise there.* "Both in the gun-for-hire business with their former CO, a guy named Rory Gellman. From what the suits told me, Rory and Tony went to school together."

"My daddy always says it's all about who you know," Maddy said with a disgusted twist of her lips that momentarily distracted Bran with the urge to kiss the expression away.

He had to look at the file cabinet standing in the corner to beat back the impulse. After a second, he managed, "Now, about the yacht…"

The tone of his voice must have told her the news he was poised to impart wasn't good, because she placed a hand on his forearm. Despite the fact that her fingers were icy cold, a hot streak of awareness shot through him. "What is it?" she asked.

And he wished he could save her from this final calamity, the last nightmare, but he respected her too much, *loved* her too much, to withhold the truth.

"It was burned, Maddy." She gasped. And when her lips trembled, he almost looked away again. But he forced himself to hold her horrified gaze. "All that's left are a few bits of charred debris. The Coasties are gonna try some recovery dives later this afternoon, but…" He shook his head, not needing to go on. Not needing to tell her they'd probably never find the remains of her uncle, and her family would be left with nothing and no one to bury.

Maddy nodded her understanding, fresh tears pooling in her eyes. Tears she blinked back and refused to let fall.

So damned brave. So strong. So…everything.

For a second there while he'd been giving his statement to the feds, he'd allowed himself to think that maybe he could make it work with Maddy. That maybe there was a chance for them. A chance for *him*. That maybe he wasn't so much like his father after all.

And then he'd walked into the room to see her with Rick…

You were wrong, Mom. You were so wrong when you said I only got the good in you both.

Maddy searched his face. "Bran, I—"

But before she could finish her thought, the girls filed into the room. They were followed by one of the agents. Maddy stepped away from Bran to give hugs and ask the girls how they were doing. When her hand slipped from his arm, it felt like a vital part of him went with it.

"The plane is fueled and ready to taxi," the agent said. "And I think these girls are as anxious to see their parents as their parents are anxious to see them. So whenever you're ready, Miss Powers."

Maddy turned back to Bran. "I…have to go."

"I know." If he gritted his jaw any harder, he'd likely break a bone. "Me too. I have a flight waiting to take me to Virginia."

Her brows formed a delicate vee. "What's in Virginia?"

"The family of one of the Coasties," he told her, sick to his stomach at what lay in store for him upon landing, nauseous too from the thought of walking away from Maddy for the last time. *It's for the best. You know it's for the best.* "I made a promise. Now I have to see it through."

"Oh, Bran," she said, not needing him to elaborate. She was a smart cookie. She could guess what his mission must be. "I wish I could go with you."

He didn't say anything to that. What could he say?

For a couple of seconds she searched his eyes, looking for something she obviously didn't find. Then she went up on tiptoe and wrapped her arms around his neck.

He tried to just stand there and take it. Tried to make himself give her a friendly pat on the back. But in the end, he couldn't manage it and crushed her to him, burying his nose near her temple.

"Thank you," she whispered. "Thank you for comin' for me. Thank you for savin' me. For savin' *all* of us."

He couldn't speak around the lump in his throat.

Maddy pushed out of his arms, and he had to fist his hands to keep from reaching for her and pulling her back. "So I guess…" She blew out a breath, watching him with wide, knowing eyes. "I guess I'll…email you then?"

When he nodded, a painful look of resignation tightened her features. If he'd still been armed, he would have capped his own ass for hurting her. For disappointing her.

"Okay then," she said and turned to the teens. "Let's go home, shall we, ladies?"

The agent led the girls from the room, but before Maddy could go, Bran found his voice and blurted, "Hey, Maddy?"

She glanced back at him. Even windblown and red-eyed and wearing grubby clothes, she was still so beautiful it hurt to look at her. "Yeah?"

"I'm sorry for…" *For your uncle. For all the bad shit you had to go through tonight. For not being the kinda man worthy of a woman like you.* He wanted to spit out the words but they stuck in his throat, choking him. So he simply ended with, "For everything."

She searched his eyes for what felt like an eternity. Then she nodded. "Yeah. I'm sorry too."

Chapter 27

Two weeks later…

"Any news on the trawler and the missing mercenaries?" Alex asked Bran as she grabbed a chair and scooted it next to his. "Have the feds found them?"

Bran was sitting at the rickety computer desk pushed into the corner of the ramshackle Wayfarer Island beach house. As usual, all the windows in the house were open to allow the sea breeze to trickle inside. Outside, the sound of voices was joined by the crooning twang of Jimmy Buffet drifting through the speakers of the old battery-powered boom box. Jimmy was singing about being a pirate two hundred years too late, and occasionally someone outside would join in with Jimmy's lament.

Ahhhh, home, Alex thought, crunching on a strawberry-flavored Pop-Tart.

"It's my turn at the laptop," Bran snarled, protectively hunching his shoulders toward the glowing screen.

She made a face. "I *know* it's your turn. But I saw you had the CNN website open, and I thought maybe there was something about—"

"They found the trawler scuttled off the coast of Mexico, but Rory Gellman is still missing," Bran said, scrolling up to the top of the article. The headline read: *Former Army Ranger at Large after Blundering Attempt to Ransom Oil Heiress*.

For the last two weeks, the details of what had happened on Garden Key had been the top news stories. Alex was grateful that Wayfarer Island was so remote or there likely would have been *more* reporters camped outside their door looking for exclusive interviews. As it was, after the initial story broke, a single ship had anchored beyond the reef. But every time the reporters tried to load up in a dinghy to reach the beach, one of the Deep Six crew motored into the lagoon, shotgun in hand, and informed them the island was private property and wasn't very welcoming to trespassers.

After seven days, the reporters had given up and sailed away.

"Gives me the willies knowing he's still out there," Alex said, shivering and taking another bite of Pop-Tart. A crumb fell to the floor. Meat, who'd learned to follow her around because she was usually eating and sometimes—*okay, more often than not*—made a mess of it, lunged at the morsel like his life depended on it. Lapping it up, he sat back on his haunches, panting and offering her a doggy grin.

"You're welcome," she told him, ruffling his ears and the fat row of wrinkles that made up his neck.

"Those things give him gas, you know," Bran said, looking at Meat askance like the Pop-Tart had already begun to ferment in the dog's belly.

"Everything gives him gas," she corrected, taking another healthy bite and continuing to scratch Meat until she found the spot. The one that made his back leg bicycle like crazy.

"True," Bran admitted, clearly unmoved by Meat's hilarious antics. *The man has become a total sourpuss.*

"So why don't you and Sir Stinks-a-Lot scram and let me finish what I was doing. I prefer my air to remain unfouled."

"I'm not sure that's a real word," she informed him while licking at the strawberry icing.

"If it's not, it should be," he insisted, shooting her a long-suffering look. "Now beat it. Both of you."

"So you can write a private email to Maddy?" She wiggled her eyebrows, trying to tease a smile out of him. She wasn't sure she'd seen one on his face since that awful night. And she missed it. "Do you guys have email sex? If so, how does that work exactly? Sort of like sexting, I assume, but—"

"Alex," he gritted between clenched teeth, "I'm warning you."

"Yeah, sure." She waved him off. "So what else is new?"

"What's *that* supposed to mean?" he demanded.

"That you've been stomping around here barking at everyone for the past two weeks."

"Have not."

"Yes, Benji," she assured him, "you have. So why don't you just admit you love her, you want her, and you're miserable without her? Why don't you go get her and make yourself happy, which, in turn, will make all our lives that much easier?"

He snorted. "That sounded so altruistic."

"Hey," she said in affront. "If I don't look out for number one, who will? And stop avoiding the subject." She skewered him with a hard look, refusing to let him get off track. *Yeah, I'm on to you.* "Why don't you go tell Maddy how you feel?"

"It's more complicated than that." Instead of the grin

she'd hoped to coax, he scowled so hard she was afraid his face might break.

"So you admit you love her!" She pointed a victorious finger at him.

His scowl deepened. She looked for a crack in his face. *Nope. Not yet.*

"Look," she said, "I know you have some sort of damage when it comes to your father."

He blinked and looked like he was ready to murder someone. The whole thing with him and his dad was a minefield. A tinderbox. An emotional Syria. But somebody needed to jump into the bloody fray and talk some sense into him. Never one to run from conflict, Alex figured that someone might as well be her. Besides, she'd grown to love Bran like a brother, and she hated that he was hurting.

"Don't worry," she was quick to tell him. "No one has been telling tales out of school. I don't know the specifics. And I don't *have* to know. Because I know *you*."

His jaw was sawing back and forth, but he didn't say anything.

Hanging out with Mason too much, obviously.

She sighed and pushed her glasses up the bridge of her nose. "You are a good and decent man, Brando Pallidino. Everything else, all that stuff in your past, it's just dirt in your eye. Blink it away."

"You're awfully young to have all the answers," he said, tapping his fingers impatiently on the desk.

"What can I say?" She spread her arms wide. Meat followed the movement of the Pop-Tart in her hand like a hawk follows a mouse in the grass. "I am the oracle. All knowledge starts and ends with me."

He harrumphed.

"And now you're starting to sound like Mason," she accused.

She knew her mistake the instant his dark eyes glinted. When he said, "On the subject of Mason," she groaned. "You still got the hots for him?"

The hots? Sure. If by hots he meant she couldn't stop thinking about Mason every hour of every day. Unfortunately, Mason had taken to treating her like the bubonic plague, running in the opposite direction every time she got near him. Which only encouraged her impish side, making her seize every opportunity to seek him out.

"Look," she said. "The man's got that whole I-paint-pictures-and-own-a-cute-flatulent-dog thing going for him. It's like girl porn."

Bran snorted.

"And on that note," she told him, "I'm out." She'd said what she wanted to say, planted the seeds. It was up to Bran to let them grow.

Pushing to a stand, she tossed the last bite of Pop-Tart to Meat. The dog caught it expertly and swallowed it without chewing. A familiar *squeak-squeak* sounded from the rusty hinges on the screen door when she opened it. But before stepping over the threshold, she turned back and imparted one final thought. "You know, in the end it's the love we withhold that we regret the most."

When he simply blinked at her, she stepped out onto the porch and let the screen door slam shut behind her.

Now, where is Mason?

It'd been a couple of hours since the last time she'd tortured him…

———

"She's right, you know."

Bran turned to find LT leaning against the doorway leading to the kitchen, bare-chested, beer in hand, freshly showered after a day spent doing search dives in an effort to locate more artifacts from the *Santa Cristina*. "Who?"

"Alex," LT said. "She's right about all of it. About your past bein' nothin' but grit in your eye. About the thing we regret bein' the love we withhold."

Bran felt a muscle in his cheek twitch. "Does no one on this island believe in privacy?" He pushed back in his chair and glowered at LT. "How long were you standing there listening to our conversation?"

"Long enough to hear you *not* deny lovin' Maddy."

What is that I'm feeling? Impatience? Exasperation? Anger? He couldn't tell for sure. The only one he could pinpoint with any certainty was heartbreak. The last two weeks had felt like two years.

Maddy had kept up her end of the bargain, going on like nothing had happened between them. Like nothing had *changed* between them. Her emails were just as funny and poignant and openhearted as ever. As alternately light and serious as they'd always been. Funny clips one day and mournful ruminations about her uncle the next. You know, just like always, she was being his...*friend*.

Except now it wasn't enough. Not when he knew what it was to have more. To have *everything*.

"So what if I love her?" he snarled. "It doesn't change who I am."

"And who is that?" LT casually took a sip of his beer. His calm only increased Bran's agitation.

"My father's son," he said. "You've seen me on the battlefield. You know what I'm like. You've seen the thing that lives inside me."

LT didn't say anything for a while, simply stood there drinking his damn beer. Then he finally spoke. "See, now, what confounds me is that you think you're the only one of us who has a dark, vicious side. That you're the only one of us who gets that look in his eyes when that side takes over. But we *all* have it, man. We all get it. Those dark, vicious sides of us are what kept us alive all those years. The difference between us and you is that we appreciate ours and you're afraid of yours."

"I'm not afraid—"

"*Yes*," LT stressed, "you are. That's why you always turn it off so quickly. Why, the instant the danger or whatever is over, you flip that switch inside yourself and start in with the jokes. You think you have to beat it back or it'll take over. But it won't, Bran. Don't you know by now you can handle it?"

It sounded so good. It sounded so easy. And he wanted to believe it. "My father couldn't handle it."

"Yeah, well, you may be your father's son. But you are *not* your father."

"You shoulda seen how jealous I was of that young stud park ranger every time he looked at Maddy," he snarled, remembering the red in his vision, the violence in his heart. Terrified of both. "When he touched her, I wanted to rip his arms off and beat him with 'em."

LT snorted. "Join the club, man. When Olivia and

I are in Key West and heads turn in her direction, I'm hard-pressed not to go on a murderin' spree. Feelin' possessive and protective and damn near nuclear about the woman you love is *natural*. Not actin' on all those feelings is what separates the men from the monsters. And you, my friend, are a *man*."

With his whole heart, Bran wanted to believe LT was right. Wanted to believe that what ran in his blood could be controlled by his brain. Wanted to believe that nurture had more to do with the making of him than nature.

Pa Ingalls…The name drifted into his mind from a long-ago memory.

Is it possible?

Possible to be as good a man, as decent a man as Pa Ingalls, the one who'd always made his mother smile? Asking the question, even to himself, opened up the prospect just a crack.

The joy that rushed in, the *yearning*, was almost more than he could bear.

"Now, I know you had some supremely bad shit happen in your past," LT continued. "But stop bein' a jackass and lettin' the past rule your present. You don't see yourself clearly, but the rest of us do. You're a *good* man, Bran Pallidino. An honorable man. And a *worthy* man. And we all think Madison Powers would be the luckiest lady on the planet to have you."

"I've said my piece," LT said, pushing away from the doorjamb and heading in Bran's direction. "So I'm goin' outside to make out with my beautiful fiancée behind a palm tree." He set his beer on the end table beside the sofa. "Don't drink my beer."

And with that parting shot, LT left. After the screen door slammed shut, Bran sat in stunned silence.

He felt like the bonds of the past, the *fear* of the past had unraveled in the last few minutes. Just a little bit. And what was left in the place of those lifelong threads was a glimmer of hope, a ray of dreamlike promise that he might have a chance for a future.

With Maddy.

Chapter 28

The next day…

MADDY'S MOUSE ICON HOVERED OVER THE SEND button in her email account. For the last five minutes she'd gone back and forth over whether or not she should click it.

"It's not like you're askin' to move in with him," she muttered to herself. "You're just askin' if he'd be okay with you comin' to visit. You *say* in the email you'll bring your sleepin' bag. So, no pressure. And *friends* visit each other, don't they?"

She sat back against her headboard and fisted her hands in her lap. She'd tried. Lordy, how she'd tried to go back to the way things were before. But things *weren't* the same as before. *She* wasn't the same as before and—

Ding-dong!

She jumped at the sound of the doorbell and glanced at the glowing red numbers on her alarm clock.

"What kind of person shows up at someone's house at seven-thirty in the mornin'?" she grumbled, setting her laptop aside and tossing back the covers. She threw on her favorite robe—it was green and tattered and totally comfy—before stopping to give her reflection in the mirror above her dresser a cursory glance.

Hair? Every which way.

Face? Smudged with the mascara she hadn't washed

off last night.

Breath? She blew into her hand. *Not daisy fresh*.

She padded to the bathroom to give her teeth a quick scrub and contemplated running a comb through her hair and a washcloth over her face. Then she figured, *Anyone comin' this early in the mornin' deserves what they get*.

Ding-dong!

"I'm comin'!" she yelled, running to the front door. She would bet her sweet bippy it was one of her big, dumb brothers. Either that, or another reporter looking for an exclusive. Either way, she was about to give someone an earful. She tossed open the door at the same time she opened her mouth. The latter snapped shut with a *click* of her teeth when she saw *Bran* standing on her front porch.

"God, woman," he said in lieu of hello, his deep voice swirling around in her ears and raising goose bumps over the back of her neck. "Would you *stop* getting more beautiful every day?"

Somehow, she managed to answer him around the heart that had jumped into her throat. "Har-har. Very funny. But let me tell you right now, bucko, if you show up at a woman's house before she's had her first cup of coffee, this is what you're in for." She did her best Vanna White impersonation and gestured dramatically at herself.

What in the devil-lovin' hell is he doin' here?

She could think of only one thing. A glimmer of hope ignited in the center of her chest. It grew to a small conflagration when he said, "Since you mention it, I haven't had *my* first cup of coffee either. You got enough to share?"

If her heart beat any faster, it was liable to hop right

out of her mouth and go bouncing across the foyer. Not wanting to see *that*, she kept her lips sealed and held the door wide. And bonus, she used the support to keep herself upright. Her knees had gone weak at first sight of him. *How cliché*. His words, and his possible intent, made them weaker still. *You really are a stereotype when it comes to him, you know?*

Yessirree, Bob. She knew.

When he brushed by her, she closed her eyes and breathed him in. Irish Spring soap and Tide laundry detergent and…Bran. The familiar smells tunneled up her nose and made her dizzy, like fine champagne. Like a roller-coaster ride. Like…*love*.

"And, Maddy?"

"Yeah?" She opened her eyes to discover he'd stopped beside her. She had to tilt her chin way back to look into his face, to see his dark eyes and the pirate smile that stretched his lips.

"I wasn't joking about you getting more beautiful every day."

Before she could answer that thoroughly devastating statement, he sauntered into her house. She watched his loose-hipped swagger the way you might watch lasagna after having been on a low-carb diet for a year. She was suddenly ravenous. Rabid for a taste. But not of pasta and sauce. *Oh, no*.

At the end of the entryway, he looked right and left. Without hesitation, he headed in the direction of her kitchen. Her house was built in the open-concept style, so navigating wasn't difficult, even for first-timers.

Her hands shook when she closed the front door. Her legs shook too when she turned and followed him into her kitchen. Dressed in jeans and a navy V-necked shirt, he looked very dark against her white cabinets and light-gray countertops. Dark and dangerous and totally delicious.

"Coffee cups?" he asked with a raised brow.

"Cupboard to the right of the stove." She grabbed one of the bar stools shoved beneath the center island and quickly hopped onboard. Number one, because her knees threatened to give out on her at any moment. And number two, because it took everything in her not to run to him. "The coffeemaker is on a timer so it should be ready. Help yourself."

Bran opened the cupboard and pulled out her *Lord of the Rings: The Fellowship of the Ring* collectors' mug. He glanced down at it, then looked back into her cupboard where all her collectors' mugs were arranged neatly on a shelf. She had one commemorating her favorite film of the year for each of the last twenty years.

Shaking his head, he blurted, "God, I love you."

She fell off the bar stool. Or at least she *would* have, had she not caught the edge of the island in a death grip. All the air left her lungs, and her head felt so light she was surprised it didn't float right off her shoulders.

He closed his eyes and shook his head. When he opened them again, he set the mug aside and walked to the opposite side of the gray marble countertop. He flattened his wide-palmed hands on the surface and leaned forward.

"It's true," he said, his eyes fierce. "I love you, Maddy. And I tried like hell not to. Tried to convince myself that you were better off without a man like me. Tried to tell myself that the risk wasn't worth the reward.

But it was like trying to walk to the horizon. No matter what, I just couldn't get there."

The words hung in the air between them like fat balloons. Maddy was afraid to move, afraid to *breathe*. She thought if she did, she might pop those balloons and then she'd be left to wonder if they were ever really real, really *there* to begin with.

She swallowed and licked her lips, racking her brain for something to say. *I love you too* was the obvious answer. But for some reason, maybe because of the anguished look on his face, she reckoned he wasn't ready to hear it. So she went with "You know, that's the problem with hearts."

He cocked his head, dark hair shining in the overhead lights.

"The damn things do what they want."

For a while neither of them spoke. They just stared at each other. Finally, Maddy couldn't stand it. He might not be ready to hear her tell him she loved him, but she was beyond ready to say it. "And in case you're wonderin', I love you too."

He sucked in a breath and his expression was so tortured she had to hook her feet around the legs of the bar stool to remain seated.

"I'm terrified," he admitted.

"Of w-what?" Her voice caught on the magnitude of her feelings.

"That I'll turn out like him," he gritted between his teeth. "Maddy, I love you so much, so completely, so *intensely*. Like she loved him. Like he loved her."

His mother. His father. Their poisonous relationship had tainted his whole life. But what he didn't understand was that they'd never poisoned *him*. He was bright and unblemished. Brave and strong and self-sacrificing. He was so much more than he gave himself credit for. She saw it. She was determined to make him see it too.

"I love you with all my twisted heart and all my broken soul," he croaked, and it broke her heart to see big Bran Pallidino on the verge of tears. "And what if that means I'll—"

Screw it! With a cry, she jumped up, rounded the island, and threw herself into his arms. He caught her close, buried his face in her neck, and trembled.

"You're nothin' like your father," she swore. "Nothing like your mother, either." She was so sad, so...*mad* that he'd spent his life trying to make up for something that wasn't his to make up for, scared of becoming something he would never become. But she was happy too. Happy because—

He loves me! He loves me! He loves me!

Her heart had been crying the refrain since the words first formed in his mouth.

"And we're goin' to prove it," she promised. "Month after month, year after year, you and me. We're goin' to prove that blood may be thicker than water, but it isn't thicker than love."

He made a strangled sound at the back of his throat. Then his lips were on hers. And just like always, once they started, they couldn't stop.

—◦◦◦—

"How goes the search for the *Santa Cristina*?" Maddy asked, feathering her fingers through his chest hair.

They'd spread her robe on the tiles of her kitchen floor and made love. Twice. The first time was fast and hard and desperate. The second time was soft and slow and delicious. Now they were both lazy and sated.

At least for the time being…

Bran knew it wouldn't take much to get him going again. Everything about Maddy turned him on. He ran his fingers down the supple arch of her back and blew out a breath. "Slowly," he admitted.

"What does that mean?" she asked, wiggling closer. Such a warm, wiggling, wonderful woman. *His* woman.

He was still trying to wrap his head around the idea. Still terrified that loving her so much would make him become the thing he hated most. But she was sure of him, sure of *them*. And her certainty was proving wonderfully contagious. He was beginning to believe. Beginning to consider the possibility that he could be more, be *better* than he'd ever hoped. And with that belief came a peace that ate away at his fear, little by little, bite by bite. One day, he prayed one day soon, it would be gone from him completely.

"It means we haven't found anything else that definitively points to the wreck," he admitted. "There have been some debris and a few pieces of iron that look like they might have been the ties on the ship. But nothing else."

She pushed up on her elbow and cupped her chin in her hand. Her eyes melted him when she asked, "Are you worried?"

"Nah," he assured her, dipping his fingers into one of the little dimples above her plump ass. "It's early yet. And the seabed shifts every day, not to mention what it's done over the past four hundred years. She's down there. She's just gonna make us work for it."

Maddy pursed her lips. When he saw the top one

plump, his dick flexed against his thigh. "The best ones always do." She winked.

"So I've been told." Round three of lovemaking was just around the corner, and this time he planned to bend her over the kitchen table. He'd love her and watch her flesh pinken in the morning light filtering in through the plantation-style shutters. "Doc thinks we should let Chrissy Szarek bring her customers out for treasure-hunting excursions. He thinks having more fins and tanks in the water will cut down on our search time."

"Chrissy Szarek?" Maddy lifted a brow.

"She's this leggy blond who runs a dive shop in Key West," Bran explained. "She and LT go way back. Their dads were friends or something. Anyway, she thinks people will pay a pretty penny for a chance to spend an afternoon diving for sunken treasure."

"Sounds like a good idea to me," Maddy mused. "More eyes in the water coverin' more ground. But I'm not likin' the sound of a *leggy blond* hangin' out with you every day."

She was jealous. And it was adorable. "I only have eyes for blonds with banging booties," he assured her, grabbing a substantial handful of her ass.

She narrowed her eyes. "You better make that *a* blond with *a* bangin' booty. *Singular*."

"That's a given." He grinned. He'd *been* grinning for so long now his face hurt. But he couldn't stop. He was…happy. In *love*. And it was amazing. And horny-making. That kitchen table seemed to be calling his name. "Anyway, LT isn't completely sold on the idea. He thinks the divers won't stick to the grid pattern needed to make sure every inch of the bottom gets searched. It's tedious work, and he's afraid they'll get bored. And then *Wolf* objects to the whole thing because he and Chrissy don't get along."

"Wolf doesn't get along with someone?" Both of her eyebrows reached for her hairline.

"I know," he agreed. "Weird, right? Wolf gets along with everyone." Bran had his suspicions about what the problem was, but he kept them to himself.

"Well, since you mention needing more hands on deck…" She let the sentence dangle. In the silence, every cell inside him seemed to strain in her direction, waiting impatiently, hoping beyond hope that he knew where she was going with this.

"Yeah?" Whoa. When had his voice turned into a croaking foghorn?

"I thought maybe I'd come to Wayfarer Island and stay for a bit. Help y'all out." It was exactly what he'd wanted to hear. Obviously, she couldn't see that joy had ballooned him to twice his usual size, because she continued to talk fast, as if she thought she might have to convince him. *Silly woman.* "With Mom and Dad gone, there's no one at work to approve more charity functions and I'm at loose ends."

Her parents had taken a trip to Europe, determined to get away from the press and the publicity, trying to put the awful events on Garden Key and in the Gulf of Mexico behind them. Maddy could have done the same. But her being her, all brave and stubborn and *wonderful*, she'd stayed to see it through. She'd given a couple of exclusives—he'd read and hung on every word—before shutting the door on the paparazzi who would have tried to sensationalize the story.

When he brushed his fingers through her short hair,

he was delighted by its softness, its silkiness. For that matter, *all* of her was soft and silky. That soft silkiness made him hard. The uncertainty in her eyes made him harder still. She was unsure just how fast to push him. How far. She didn't realize that he wanted pedal to the metal. Zero to sixty in five seconds. He wanted her. All of her. All the time. In every way.

"Babe"—he wrapped a hand around her neck and pulled her down until her lips hovered a hairsbreadth from his—"you don't need an excuse to come out to the island. You're welcome any time."

"Really?" She searched his eyes.

"Any time and all the time."

She smiled. And it was the loveliest thing he'd ever seen. "Well, how about we start with this vacation, and then I can fly in on weekends until..." She trailed off and bit her upper lip.

That's all it took. Her lip caught between her teeth and he was done. *Finito*. His cock was fully engorged.

"Until what?" he demanded, his hand drifting down her spine to lie atop her fabulous butt.

"Until I make you an offer you can't refuse," she said, quoting *The Godfather*.

"That was the worst Marlon Brando impersonation I ever heard," he told her, his heart so full he was amazed it didn't burst wide open. He pulled her down for a kiss that ended in them christening the room for the third time. Atop her kitchen table...

Epilogue

June 11, 1624...

SITTING IN THE CROW'S NEST HIS MEN HAD BUILT BETWEEN THE *two tallest palm trees near the beach, his spyglass raised to his eye, Captain Bartolome Vargas scanned the seas around him.*

Perched in additional improvised lookouts on opposite sides of the island, two more of his crew, the two with the best eyesight, helped him watch for passing ships. It was hot, monotonous work. But it was imperative. With the remainder of the sailors working on the reef and down in the sea at the wreck site—at least those who were still healthy enough to work—it was left to the three of them to ensure no pirates sailed around the corner and stumbled upon the others' efforts.

Lowering his spyglass, Bartolome blinked, giving his tired eyes a moment's respite. Then he raised the glass and continued his vigil.

The wind was a bare whisper, leaving the ocean around the island glassy. Nothing disturbed the surface except a pod of dolphins that frolicked beyond the reef. The sun was high. The tide was out. A number of large grouper had swum into the lagoon the evening before, making them easy to catch. He and his men had feasted and still had full bellies today.

A good day for lookout duty, *he decided*. And a good day for recovery work.

"How goes it?" he called down to Rosario when he noticed his midshipman stepping beneath the palm trees.

"Carlo says 'tis possible!" Rosario yelled. "Says the hold is cracked in half, but much of the treasure remains in clay vases and wooden crates!"

"Thank you, Madre Maria." Bartolome sent up a prayer, crossing himself.

"Carlo says 'twill take time!" Rosario continued. "Some of the deeper goods will have to wait 'til lowest tide, but—"

Hoorah! *The sound of cheering had Bartolome glancing toward the reef where a line of men hauled in rope. Two of Bartolome's best divers bobbed to the surface at the same time the crate on the end of the rope was pulled atop the reef.*

"We can do this, Captain!" Rosario grinned up at him. "Just look!"

It was too soon for Bartolome to celebrate. There was still much to do. "You know what to do with it, Rosario," he told his midshipman.

Rosario snapped him a salute, the smile still splitting his face. "Aye-aye, Captain! For King and Country!"

Author's Note

I tried to do justice to the beautiful setting, the rich history, and the magnificence of Fort Jefferson and Dry Tortugas National Park. I did change some minor details—like the ranger's station and the crack in the foundation—to better fit this story. Welcome to the wonderful world of fiction writing! That said, dear readers, if you ever get the chance to travel to remote Garden Key and Fort Jefferson, don't hesitate. *Do it.* It's a humbling and awe-inspiring place.

Acknowledgments

A big thanks to my husband. This past year certainly wasn't an easy one, was it, sweetheart? But through it all, you were there. Right beside me. Holding my hand. I couldn't ask for a better partner on this crazy journey of life.

I have to give a shout-out to Sean, Whitney, and Dan. In the name of research for this book, the three of you gamely hopped aboard an itty-bitty floatplane piloted by a bearded, barefoot, retired Coast Guardsman. You're all crazy. Which is probably why I love you.

Fist bumps to Deb, my editor, for making this book shine. Same goes to Nicole. This one was a doozy, wasn't it, ladies? Team effort all the way. A big thank-you to Dawn, my cover designer, for this amazing cover. And hugs to the whole Sourcebooks crew for always supporting me and my work.

About the Author

Julie Ann Walker is the *New York Times* and *USA Today* bestselling author of romantic suspense. She has won the Book Buyers Best Award, been nominated for the National Readers Choice Award, the Australian Romance Reader Awards, and the Romance Writers of America's prestigious RITA Award. Her latest release was listed as a Best Summer Read of 2015 by *Publishers Weekly*. Her novels have been described as "alpha, edgy, and downright hot." Most days you can find Julie on her bicycle along the lakeshore in Chicago or blasting away at her keyboard, trying to wrangle her capricious imagination into submission.

*Continue reading for an excerpt from the
first book in The Deep Six series*

HELL OR HIGH WATER

*Present day
10:52 p.m....*

"AND THE *SANTA CRISTINA* AND HER BRAVE CREW AND CAP-
tain were sucked down into Davy Jones's locker, lost to
the world. That is...until now..."

Leo "the Lion" Anderson, known to his friends as
LT—a nod to his former Naval rank—let his last words
hang in the air before glancing around at the four faces illu-
minated by the flickering beach bonfire. Rapt expressions
stared back at him. He fought the grin curving his lips.

Bingo, bango, bongo. His listeners had fallen under
a spell as deep and fathomless as the great oceans themselves. It happened anytime he recounted the legend of
the *Santa Cristina*. Not that he could blame his audience. The story of the ghost galleon, the holy grail of
sunken Spanish shipwrecks, had fascinated *him* ever
since he'd been old enough to understand the tale while
bouncing on his father's knee. And that lifelong fascina-
tion might account for why he was now determined to
do what so many before him—his dearly departed father

included—had been unable to do. Namely, locate and excavate the mother lode of the grand ol' ship.

Of course, he reckoned the romance and mystery of discovering her waterlogged remains were only *part* of the reason he'd spent the last two months and a huge portion of his savings—as well as huge portions of the savings of the others—refurbishing his father's decrepit, leaking salvage boat. The rest of the story as to why he was here now? Why they were *all* here now? Well, that didn't bear dwelling on.

At least not on a night like tonight. When a million glittering stars and a big half-moon reflected off the dark, rippling waters of the lagoon on the southeast side of the private speck of jungle, mangrove forest, and sand in the Florida Keys. When the sea air was soft and warm, caressing his skin and hair with gentle, salt-tinged fingers. When there was so much…*life* to enjoy.

That had been his vow—*their* vow—had it not? To grab life by the balls and really *live* it? To suck the marrow from its proverbial bones?

His eyes were automatically drawn to the skin on the inside of his left forearm where scrolling, tattooed lettering read *For RL*. He ran a thumb over the pitch-black ink.

This one's for you, you stubborn sonofagun, he pledged, flipping open the lid on the cooler sunk deep into the sand beside his lawn chair. Grabbing a bottle of Budweiser and twisting off the cap, he let his gaze run down the long dock to where his uncle's catamaran was moored. The clips on the sailboat's rigging lines clinked rhythmically against its metal mast, adding to the harmony of softly shushing waves, quietly crackling

fire, and the high-pitched *peesy, peesy, peesy* call of a
nearby black-and-white warbler.

Then he turned his eyes to the open ocean past the
underwater reef surrounding the side of Wayfarer Island,
where his father's old salvage ship bobbed lazily with
the tide. Up and down. Side to side. Her newly painted
hull and refurbished anchor chain gleamed dully in the
moonlight. Her name, *Wayfarer-I*, was clearly visible
thanks to the new, bright-white lettering.

He dragged in a deep breath, the smell of burning
driftwood and suntan lotion tunneled up his nose, and
he did his best to appreciate the calmness of the evening
and the comforting thought that the vessel looked, if not
necessarily sexy, then at least seaworthy. *Which is a hell
of an improvement.*

Hot damn, he was proud of all the work he and his
men had done on her, and—

His men…

He reminded himself for the one hundred zillionth time
that he wasn't supposed to think of them that way. Not
anymore. Not since those five crazy-assed SEALs waved
their farewells to the Navy in order to join him on his
quest for high-seas adventure and the discovery of untold
riches. Not since they were now, officially, *civilians*.

"But why you guys?" The blond who was parked
beneath Spiro "Romeo" Delgado's arm yanked Leo
from his thoughts. "What makes you different from all
those who've already tried and failed to find her?"

"Besides the obvious you mean, *mamacita*?" Romeo
winked, leaning back in his lawn chair to spread his arms
wide. His grin caused his teeth to flash white against his
neatly trimmed goatee, and Leo watched the blond sit

forward in her plastic deck chair to take in the wonder that was Romeo Delgado. After a good, long gander, she giggled and snuggled back against Romeo's side.

Leo rolled his eyes. Romeo's swarthy, Hispanic looks and his six-percent-body-fat physique made even the most prim-and-proper lady's panties drop fast enough to bust the floorboards. And this gal? Well, this gal might be prim and proper in her everyday life—hell, for all Leo knew she could be the leading expert on high etiquette at an all-girls school—but today, ever since Romeo picked her and her cute friend up in Schooner Wharf Bar on Key West with the eye-rolling line of *"Wanna come see my private island?"* she'd been playing the part of a good-time girl out having a little fun-in-the-sun fling. And it was the *fling* part that might—scratch that, rewind—*did* account for the lazy, self-satisfied smile spread across Romeo's face.

"I'm serious, though." Tracy or Stacy or Lacy, or whatever her name was—Leo had sort of tuned out on the introductions—wrinkled her sunburned nose. "How do you even know where to look?"

"Because of this." Leo lifted the silver piece of eight, a seventeenth-century Spanish dollar, from where it hung around his neck on a long, platinum chain. "My father discovered it ten years ago off the coast of the Marquesas Keys."

Tracy/Stacy/Lacy's furrowed brow telegraphed her skepticism. "One coin? I thought the Gulf and the Caribbean were littered with old doubloons."

"It wasn't just one piece of eight my father found." Leo winked. "It was a big, black conglomerate of ten pieces of eight, as well as—"

"Conglomerate?" asked the brunette with the Cupid's-bow lips. Tracy/Stacy/Lacy's friend had given Leo all the right signals the minute Romeo pulled the catamaran up to Wayfarer Island's creaky old dock and unloaded their guests. It'd been instant sloe-eyed looks and shy, encouraging smiles.

Okay, and confession time. Because for a fleeting moment when she—Sophie or Sophia? Holy Christ, Leo was seriously sucking with names tonight—sidled up next to him, he'd been tempted to take her up on all the things her nonverbal communications offered. Then an image of black hair, sapphire eyes, and a subtly crooked front tooth blazed through his brain. And just like that, the brunette lost her appeal.

Which is a good thing, he reminded himself. *You're gettin' too old to bang the Betties Romeo drags home from the bar.*

Enter Dalton "Doc" Simmons and his nearly six and a half feet of homespun, Midwestern charm. He'd been quick to insert himself between Leo and Sophie/Sophia. And now her gaze lingered on Doc's face when he said in that low, scratchy Kiefer Sutherland voice of his, "Unlike gold, which retains its luster after years on the bottom of the ocean, silver coins are affected by the seawater. They get fused together by corrosion or other maritime accretions. When that happens, it's called a conglomerate. They have to be electronically cleaned to remove the surface debris and come out looking like this." Grabbing the silver chain around his neck, Doc pulled a piece of eight from inside his T-shirt. It was identical to the one Leo wore.

"And like this," Romeo parroted, twirling the coin on the chain around *his* neck like a Two-Buck Chuck stripper whirling a boa.

Their first day on the island, Leo had gifted each of his men—*damnit!*...his *friends*—with one of the coins, telling them their matching tattoos were symbols of their shared past and their matching pieces of eight were symbols of their shared future.

Leo tipped the neck of his beer toward Doc. "Maritime accretions, huh? You sound like an honest-to-God salvor, my friend."

Doc smirked, which was as close to a smile as the dude ever really got. If Leo hadn't seen Doc rip into a steak on occasion, he wouldn't have been all that convinced the guy had teeth.

"But even a conglomerate of coins wouldn't be enough to guarantee the ship's location," Leo added, turning back to the blond. "My father *also* found a handful of bronze deck cannons. All of which were on the *Santa Cristina*'s manifest. So she's down there... *somewhere*." He just had to find her. All his friends were counting on that windfall for various reasons, and if he didn't—

"But, like you said, your dad tried to find this Christy boat for"—Leo winced. Okay, so the woman seemed sweet. But the only thing worse than mangling the name of the legendary vessel was referring to it as a *boat*—"like twenty-some-odd years, right?"

"And Mel Fisher searched for the *Atocha* for sixteen years before finally findin' her." He referred to the most famous treasure hunter and treasure galleon of all time. Well, most famous of all time until he and the guys made the history books, right? *Right.* "In shallow water, like that around the Florida Keys, the shiftin' sands are moved by wind and tide. They change the seabed daily, not to mention after nearly four centuries. But with a little hard work and perseverance, you better believe the impossible becomes possible. We're hot on her trail."

Hold Your Breath

Search & Rescue Book 1

by Katie Ruggle

―⌁―

In the remote wilderness of the Rocky Mountains, rescue groups—law enforcement, rescue divers, firefighters—are often the only hope for the lost, the sick, and the injured. But in a place this far off the map, trust is hard to come by and secrets can lead to murder.

That's why Callum, the surly and haunted leader of the close-knit Search and Rescue brotherhood, finds it so hard to let newcomer Louise "Lou" Sparks into his life. But when these rescue divers go face-to-face with a killer, Callum may find that more than his heart is on the line…

―⌁―

Look for the rest of the Search & Rescue series:

For more Katie Ruggle, visit:

www.sourcebooks.com

Fan the Flames

Search & Rescue

by Katie Ruggle

In the remote Rocky Mountains, lives depend on the Search and Rescue brotherhood. But in a place this far off the map, trust is hard to come by and secrets can be murder.

As a Motorcycle Club member and firefighter, Ian Walsh is used to riding the line between the good guys and the bad. He may owe the Club his life, but his heart rests with his fire station brothers…and with the girl he's loved since they were kids, Rory Sorenson. Ian would do anything for Rory. He'd die for her. Kill for her. Defend her to his last breath—and he may just have to.

Every con in the Rockies knows Rory is the go-to girl for less-than-legal firearms, and for the past few years, she's managed to keep the peace between dangerous factions by remaining strictly neutral. But when she defends herself against a brutal attack, Rory finds herself catapulted into the center of a Motorcycle Club war—with only Ian standing between her and a threat greater than either of them could have imagined.

Praise for *Hold Your Breath*:

"Sexy and suspenseful, I couldn't turn the pages fast enough." —Julie Ann Walker, *New York Times* and *USA Today* bestselling author

For more Katie Ruggle, visit:

www.sourcebooks.com

Gone Too Deep

Search & Rescue

by Katie Ruggle

———

In the remote Rocky Mountains, lives depend on the Search and Rescue brotherhood. But in a place this far off the map, trust is hard to come by and secrets can be murder.

George Holloway has spent his life alone, exploring the treacherous beauty of the Colorado Rockies. He's the best survival expert Search and Rescue has, which makes him the obvious choice to lead Ellie Price through deadly terrain to find her missing father. There's just one problem—Ellie's everything George isn't. She's a city girl, charming, gregarious, delicate, small. And when she looks up at him with those big, dark eyes, he swears he would tear the world apart to keep her safe.

With a killer on the loose, he may have no choice.

Ellie's determined to find her father no matter the cost. But as she and her gorgeous mountain of a guide fight their way through an unforgiving wilderness, they find themselves in the crosshairs of a dangerous man in search of revenge. And they are now his prey…

———

Praise for *Hold Your Breath*:

"Chills and thrills and a sexy, slow-burning romance from a terrific new voice." —D.D. Ayres, author of the K-9 Rescue series

For more Katie Ruggle, visit:
www.sourcebooks.com

Flash of Fire

Firehawks

by M.L. Buchman

———

The elite firefighters of Mount Hood Aviation fly into places even the CIA can't penetrate.

When former Army National Guard helicopter pilot Robin Harrow joins Mount Hood Aviation, she expects to fight fires for only one season. Instead, she finds herself getting deeply entrenched with one of the most elite firefighting teams in the world. And that's before they send her on a mission that's seriously top secret, with a flight partner who's seriously hot.

Mickey Hamilton loves flying, firefighting, and women, in that order. But when Robin Harrow roars across his radar, his priorities go out the window. On a critical mission deep in enemy territory, their past burns away and they must face each other. Their one shot at a future demands that they first survive the present—together.

———

Praise for *Pure Heat*:

"Will blow readers' minds and leave them awestruck." —*RT Book Reviews* Top Pick

"Meticulously researched, hard-hitting, and suspenseful… Buchman writes with beauty and simmering passion." —*Publishers Weekly* Starred Review

For more M.L. Buchman, visit:
www.sourcebooks.com